THE COOL PART OF HIS PILLOW

RODNEY ROSS

Dreamspinner Press

Published by
Dreamspinner Press
382 NE 191st Street #88329
Miami, FL 33179-3899, USA
http://www.dreamspinnerpress.com/

The Cool Part of His Pillow
Copyright © 2012 by Rodney Ross

Cover Art by Anne Cain   annecain.art@gmail.com
Cover Design by Mara McKennen

ISBN: 978-1-61372-504-7

Printed in the United States of America
First Edition
May 2012

eBook edition available
eBook ISBN: 978-1-61372-505-4

For GWC

Chapters

Prologue

"You Change."

LET me be very clear.

I'm not mocking the tiny cashier's fractured English.

As someone who is breezily called "ma'am" by pizza delivery dispatch, I don't dare.

I hesitate to even quote her. I was raised not to ridicule the accent or language barrier of another. Mickey Rooney's Mr. Yunioshi and his buck teeth in *Breakfast at Tiffany's* always disturbed me, and Jonathan Pryce's eyes taped back to look Asian as The Engineer in the original production of *Miss Saigon* was just wrong.

I could rephrase it more PC: "Here's your change." That would sound better. But I just handed this woman in Qiana with a bun a twenty-dollar bill, and it's what she said.

"You change."

My attention is elsewhere. I am lost, as friends have called it, in aesthetic astigmatism, my eyes twirling different directions in survey of my radius. It's what I do, what I *used* to do, edit your stuff, reduce clutter. I'm that precious someone who finds exposed electrical cords distasteful and wishes all lamps ran on batteries. I'm the dumbass who complains in the sports bar if an HD broadcast isn't set to the right aspect ratio. Little things, big things, they all count, and gift or curse, OCD Me is compelled to mentally reset this bodega, counter to shelf, beginning with the crowded checkout.

Yes, I know bodega is Spanish. This mart is Korean. But everyone in New York calls them that, and I am a Newer Yorker.

The first thing I'd do is find a new place for those small foreign-made American flags, since I stopped counting at fifty-two stars. Vials of ginseng energy drink provide companionship to Pilgrim salt-and-pepper shakers. A chalkboard tells me I can have a *$3 Sanwich!* For fifty cents more, can I get the D? Only in New York City is a cellophane-wrapped stale corn muffin an impulse purchase. And so many spools of twine. It takes a lot to lash your nerves together here, I guess.

This is the stuff that drives me bonkers.

A lot drives me bonkers.

Like that dairy case, which I want to squeegee. It looks like someone's been kissing it. I can barely see the Yoo-Hoo behind the glass.

She says it again, serenely.

"You change."

She could be congratulating me. It could be urgent instruction. The cash register says $18.03. It's a current model I would swap for something with period charm, before Hell's Kitchen became Midtown West, something she could really pound with those fists.

A male employee, trying to activate an edible color from the bottom of a soup kettle, stops stirring to stare at this wayward customer holding flowers.

"You change."

Here's an idea. Why don't *you* change? And how's that courtship working out for Eddie's father?

It has been said that most of the biggest moments in your life pass unnoticed or unremarked upon. That's funny. My last year has been accompanied by a John Williams score. I just did my damnedest to stay afloat. I can make order of your disorder, but for my own life, I'd need a considerably bigger feather duster.

This is not, you see, *not* where I thought I'd be on my forty-sixth birthday, buying two bunches of daisies in dripping, crinkled plastic for myself, ahead of another customer holding a plastic container of fake crab with the real stench.

No, this is not the life I thought I'd be living.

Chapter One

Blue Roses

WE ARE making our way downtown as others scurry home in the last gasp of Friday night rush hour in the last gasp of summer.

"The sunset is like the healing stages of a bruise," Andy observes.

"It reminds me of a church window lit from within," I suggest.

"Like you've been in church to know."

"Does the 'Church of the Poisoned Mind' count?"

The nightclub we're bound for *is* a temple of sorts—a sanctuary of hymns, sisters, at least one choirmaster—and there is sure to be ritualistic sipping. It is as close as we'll get to a place of worship on this, my birthday weekend.

At his request, Andy is at the wheel. I brake too much, he says. It makes him feel epileptic. We're in my 1971 Mercedes 280SL Pagoda convertible—Mercedes-Benz red 576 over a black leather interior. It's the same model and year my father once owned and always regretted selling. I called it Mercy B. The broad assumption was the car, purchased via auction, was the prickly heat of a midlife hot flash. A Caesar haircut would have been cheaper, friends mocked. They were correct. After my winning bid, the car was transported to the Mercedes-Benz Classic Center in Irvine, California, where it spent weeks—at $100 an hour—being rebuilt, restored, rechromed, repainted, replated. The wood in the car is show quality; even the upgraded armrests match the veneer. Mercy B. has only gotten better. Damn shame I haven't.

At first, Andy isn't taking one of the many alternate, and shorter, routes, and I decide this is fine. It gives us more time for what we do best: banter. He pushes my buttons until his finger cramps. I yank his chain until I need a heating pad. We pick each other's scabs like bored kids at summer camp.

"Did you realize we're the same age right now?" Andy asks. He turns forty-six at the end of October.

"Technically," I remind him, "I'm forty-four until September 16, tomorrow. Still and always younger than you."

Both of our fortieths were, by decree, private. Leaving our thirties was more tearshed than watershed. But after that, we figured, why not? We would intermittently arrange something special.

"So how shocked do I act when I walk in? Should I shit my pants?" I ask.

"And make that twice today?"

"I wouldn't pursue that. I do your laundry. I bought you new jockey shorts in camouflage."

This forty-fifth birthday party isn't a surprise. I hate surprises. That I surrendered the guest list to Andy's charge worries me enough. I requested that he not "mix it up a little," but I have to ask.

"I hope you didn't invite fillers to make the room look crowded."

"No meat-extender guests," Andy promises.

Good. I don't want to get drunk with the man who cleans our gutters. We've been to enough private parties populated by cardboard cutouts watching the lips of others, trying to figure out who's being toasted. What I like is anachronistic clash in the minutiae. Everyone will know, for example, that I commandeered party details when they encounter the concessionaire hot dog machine alongside ceviche. Andy is a banker for a reason; intended irony is not part of his astrological sign.

It's one of the many traits we don't share. Our longevity as a couple also doesn't extend to looking like one another or our pugs, Gertie and Noel, although I think we chose that breed knowing we'd also someday be low to the ground, wheeze a lot, and require that our facial creases be thoroughly washed. Many think Andy resembles Matthew McConaughey. I don't see it except during arguments, when his deep dimples smirk at me. Our physicality, though, is similar enough that we can literally give the other the shirt off our back. Not that I would want the Tommy Bahama shirt he's wearing tonight. It's too resort.

"Did Rick and Sarah get an invite?" They are new to our neighborhood.

Andy nods and says Sarah mentioned she'd never been in a gay bar. "I think she wet herself." Then he requests, "Find some tunes. Not the theme from *On Golden Pond*."

I shuffle through my iPod. "On the subject of loons, did you invite LezbyAnn?"

"She won't be there. She has a blind date. She's already making out a change-of-address card, I'm sure."

"Hers come with bubble gum by now," I observe. It will help her prospects if the blind date is also deaf. LezbyAnn has such a filthy mouth I'm surprised her face hasn't evicted it.

Andy warily watches my fiddling. Sometimes I invade his iPhone and add bizarre things, far worse than William Shatner singing. I wish I could see his face when he's on the elliptical and a lewd LaWanda Page comedy routine from her sixties stand-up act interrupts his Scissor Sisters playlist. Controlling music is a skirmish without end, one of many. The muffins don't have enough chocolate chips, our pool is too cold, why don't you ever shut off the hallway light? Then, when it's finally sorted, tastes change. Now the muffins are gooey, pool water's downright hot, I can't see where I'm going.

"Something other than show tunes, at least."

I think I hear a muffled cell phone ringtone. "You or me?" I ask.

Andy evenly notes, "Since it's not the Overture from *Gypsy*, it must be me."

"Better not be work," I warn.

"Like your employer never calls."

"I *am* the employer," I remind him archly.

"You know what I meant. We all answer."

He begins to counsel someone quietly. I won't have it. "What do they want?" I won't have him ignoring me, either. "Excuse me? What? Someone's debit card won't swipe at *Walmart*?"

Andy puts the phone to his shoulder. "Barry, I am talking a very wigged-out twenty-four-year-old IT programmer through a system workaround in Kentucky."

"It's my birthday."

"It's my job, you fucking brat."

"I hate your guts sometimes," I remind him.

People that many—and by people, I mean my mother—would call dodgy huddle outside an abandoned storefront and glare at Mercy B.

"Answer me this," I whisper, watching a toddler in a full diaper skip off a sagging porch. "Why are *our* bars always in terrifying neighborhoods? What about HUD housing attracts Nicki Minaj?"

The lowered caution arms, blinking red lights, and metallic clang at a train crossing represent nothing but a challenge to Andy. He maneuvers between, then around, the beams.

"Back up!" I direct.

"What is life but caution lights to be outrun, little butterfly? Nothing's coming. Really. Look."

I look. Of course something is. Suddenly, the train, with its warning blast, is zooming toward the crossing. We easily clear the tracks, but still I fume. "Everything's a damn dare with you!"

"And everything with you is sarcasm," Andy says.

As we turn west, we agree the sky looks like succotash.

IF YOU didn't know where the gay birthday party is, the rainbow arc of balloons flanking the entrance of Gyrate makes it very clear. They were not my idea. Nor is the *45 And Barely Alive* banner strung over the nearest thing to a VIP room: their Skybar on the second floor. It has the promised bar, but as for sky, one small oval window faces a vacant lot of trash and snakes. (And that window, it's cracked.) After only two months open, the sheer scrims and white divans are already dirty and stained, yet I chose Gyrate because I want the young owner, Joey, to succeed. He acquired the club, which had gone into default, as a lark, spending little on upgrades but expecting a lot of profit—another gay-owned enterprise overly ambitious and undercapitalized. I'm sure Joey's learning the hard way how employee theft has to be built into your budget like mixers and, from what I've heard, how important parking lot lighting and security is, which is why we stuck Mercy B. in a private pay lot a block away.

Friends drift in. I go into inventory mode. Ranking people like dry goods seems catty, but it's pretty accurate. Most of our life rack clangs with *caveat emptor*—damaged but sellable. Andy is my Display

Only *haute couture*, custom-designed, fit on me and altered as wear and gravity has dictated.

Dee is an exception. She would discontinue herself before ever being marked down. She was the Realtor representing the seller's interest when we bought our house. Despite being Ann Coulter's doppelganger, our rapport was immediate. We knew within minutes that she was divorcing for the second time and that she considered herself "Ground Zero for Erectile Dysfunction." After the sale closed, we—Andy was as smitten—delightedly called our immediate friendship Gift With Purchase. She is every gay man's idyll: the slave style confidante in the little microbeaded black dress. Dee appears effortlessly beautiful but works as hard at it as any listing. Girlfriend, balanced on Louboutin red-soled heels as thin as pencils, is right now talking creative financing with Vic and Neil. She's one of the state's highest producers, but she's been less successful in marriage—three husbands, so far. Her last, after a few too many, approached Andy and me in a bar and confided in us that "Miss Perfect has big moles on her ass, and some of them have faces, and those faces, even they scowl." We immediately called her to ask about those moles.

Stan, over there by the food, is our Sell-By. He's closer to seventy than sixty, a few years short of my mother's age. He sought a divorce and came out late in life after retirement from teaching English literature in public high school. Seeing him try to catch up is painful; he has what everyone assumes is a perm and his popped collar isn't so much hip as it is Elizabethan. His sons never speak to him, a cause of great pain, yet whenever we meet his newest underemployed twenty-four-year-old boyfriend, we do the math and shiver a little. We no longer bother learning the name of The Vapid he squires, since the arrangement usually lasts about as long as a rinse cycle. It's never quite May/December; it's usually closer to Bassinet/Dawn Of Man. I'd call the boys tricks but the word dates me, a throwback to when Fran Lebowitz actually finished a book. They're just a collective Protégé, invariably regifted. Tonight's Protégé is all bitchflip and clunky eyewear.

"Try this ceviche," I hear Stan urge Protégé.

"Fuck ceviche. I want a chili dog."

Kerrick, he's our Irregular with the ill-placed seam. His event company is called Planned With Kerr. He is all high concept and low execution and generally makes everyone uneasy. Local gay leaders were outraged at a charitable event when he crafted chocolate butt plugs for dessert. The crawfish boil in that FEMA trailer he got his hands on was especially heartless. He's pouting tonight. The only thing I let him supply for my birthday were two servers who, for no good reason, came dressed as Pee-wee Herman and Bettie Page.

Faith is tall and manages the human resources of a CPA firm I do business with; Suzi is squat, runs a preschool center, and isn't much larger than her charges. There's not much more to say except that they clearly came from Women's Separates.

Suzi implores, "So lay the Termination of The Week on us, Faith. Who got the Das Boot at ten 'til five and why?"

We often tell Faith she should alter her department's name to Humorless Resources, since they're well-known for overreacting and canning employees for arcane reasons.

Faith stiffens. "We *did* rightfully dismiss a financial analyst overheard telling a sexually divisive joke."

"What was the joke?" Tracy asks.

Tracy has hair somewhere between the color of Welch's Grape and red velvet cake. Cats are her obsession. She and her husband Matt have nine indoor cats, plus another three feral. She greets with a meow, not hello, and will excuse herself to the ladies' room by explaining she has to visit the litter pan. She oversaw the installation of voice-recognition telephone equipment at Andy's bank headquarters. It malfunctioned from day one and was eventually replaced; she wasn't. This makes Tracy a Consolation Gift. Matt is easygoing to the point of lethargy. I think of him as a Store Label: nice enough yet absent the finishing touches, bought for others but never yourself. We call him Doormatt (not to his face).

Faith crosses her arms. "What did the leper say to the prostitute?" The group waits. "Keep the tip."

"Divisive? Who felt singled out?" Andy laughs. "Do you employ the diseased whose genitals are falling off?"

As I pass, I wonder aloud, "People still tell leper jokes?"

Since they've been coupled, Greg and Greg have been commonly referred to as Gregsquared. They are Buy One, Get One Free. Like us, they have two dogs and saddled them with gay names: Abercrombie and Fitch. Unlike us, they dress alike: pink button-downs, khakis. Gregsquared circles the hot dog machine.

Emily, heavy with child, chugs San Pellegrino. She's been relocated to our Maternity Department. She stands with Miss Sondra.

I pat Emily's stomach. "Boy or girl, Em?"

"No clue," Emily says.

Miss Sondra drolly notes, "That's okay. Me neither."

Sandor Cornajo has been Miss Sondra Cornajo since we've known her. She is from Mix 'n Match. Her ultimate anatomical intentions remain unclear. We don't know if she's seen a real gender vendor, but she's had a tracheal shave to soften her Adam's apple and hormones diminished her penis to not an angry but a sheepish inch. "It's sorta like a piece of rotini pasta," she told us all one night, "without the spring-like appearance."

I compliment Miss Sondra's shawl. It is her dining-room table runner: "It went, so why not? If I didn't have such man hands, I was going to wear my new napkin rings for bracelets." *Who else at my party is in a textile*, I wonder.

Sarah Tanner pinches a centerpiece like it might say ouch. To her husband Rick, who's plucking a frankfurter from rollers, she says admiringly, "Wow. It's not silk." They are, obviously, New Arrivals.

When my gaudy birthday cake appears, ablaze, I close my eyes and pucker.

Vic casts his eyes heavenward. "Blow out your candles, Laura."

Sarah's eager to learn the lingo. "Laura? Is that what you go by on nights like this, Barry?"

Someone summarizes *The Glass Menagerie* for Sarah, or at least I think they are, because I hear Wingfield, not Petrie, Ingalls Wilder, or Brannigan. I hear someone else say pleurisy. Our best friend Potsy disbelievingly echoes, "...on nights like this."

I blow. All but one extinguishes. "See? I'm still forty-four."

Andy licks his thumb and index finger to snuff the stubborn candle.

Thank God everyone ignored his edict and tithed me. I flip around a playbill from the original flop—not the 2012 flop revival—*Carrie: The Musical* and announce, "Carrie. There's never been a musical like her."

Neil's justifiably proud. "See where the star signed it? Betty Buckle."

I laugh so hard I snort. "Buckley. With a Y!"

I walk among a shadowy subculture of theater queens who shoot shows through a small hole cut out of a Bloomingdale's bag, plagued with misdirected zooms and nervous blackouts if an usher is near. We also bid on glossy programs from shows cut short by awful reviews; we neurotically change passwords for the encoded websites where we barter a backer's demo CD for a bootleg of rare Ed Sullivan *Toast of the Town* kinescopes; I still scour used-book sites for the annual *Theatre World* volume I'm missing. We're all united in the so-far fruitless pursuit of the Holy Grail: a complete video of the original 1971 *Follies*. From the Boston tryout. At the Colonial Theatre. It's our secret handshake.

I wave a white cloth. "Look, Andy!"

"Surrendering to forty-five?" he gloats, to laughter.

"It's a hand towel Hugh Jackman wiped his sweat off with when he did *The Boy from Oz!*" I trill.

This is immediately passed around for obscene sniffing.

By the time our guests adjourn to the lower dance floor, the evening is no longer mine. I can barely make out my friends. Blanche du Bois designed the illumination here: ten thousand square feet, one night light. Sarah is jumping up and down with Rick. Faith pole dances. Emily presses her lower back to the music. Stan plays air bongos as Protégé undulates around him.

I find an Employees Only door and walk through it. I pace the tar periphery, past rooftop mechanicals. A starless cityscape surrounds me. A plane is passing over the dome of our state's capital building. Beyond blinks the spire of the tallest building, which houses the corporate staff of Andy's bank.

"How you durrin'?"

Potsy has trailed me to the rooftop. We've known Potsy, born Louis Van Bourgondien, almost the entire time we've been together. At Andy's first job, as an assistant bank branch manager, Potsy was the teller who made tsk-tsk sounds when a sheepish customer came in to settle bounced checks. He was verbally warned and sent to sensitivity training. Children only got the foul flavor Dum-Dums at his window because Potsy had taken the rest of the suckers. A note went into his personnel file. My favorite episode was when a carload of pranksters farted into a drive-through canister. Potsy opened it, gagged, tore out of the bank, caught the teenage boys at the exit, and caused about $1,000 in hood damage with his fists. Andy excused that one. But he could not excuse it when Potsy cruelly told a Depression-era customer who came in and worriedly checked their balance every day that "there's nothing left. Nothing." He became the first employee Andy ever fired. How his unemployment claim turned into a friendship is murky, but the next thing we knew, Potsy was in our new hot tub, announcing he'd just peed. This makes him hard to classify, but he's a little like the extra acquisition the cashier accidentally tossed in your bag at check-out. It's not to your liking but you keep it anyway. Occasionally, when he's a real asshole, we threaten him with Clearance.

We look down at the velvet rope and a doorman who thinks he's Vin Diesel. The deflating balloons arc has sprung partially loose, thumping the nightclub facade and, occasionally, Vin.

"That's me. I'm a sagging balloon." I point my finger at the fresh-faced boiz that Vin grants entry, then to whom he ignores: older gay men in ironed short-sleeves, too-white sneakers.

"We all line up for inevitable invisibility."

It's already started. One buzz-reducing moment was at a P'town Tea Dance four summers ago. I was playing a wood block someone had handed me and Andy impulsively leapt onto a cube. Someone near had catcalled, "Go, Gramps, go!"

A man with Sun-In hair—blond the goal, popsicle orange the result—is blocked by Vin.

"From pursued to pursuer." I tip some of my drink into Potsy's martini glass. "Here. No desire to be a morose old homo in his cups."

"Too late. Lose that long face, Judy. You own a mall."

I remind him that I am Laura tonight. "And it's not a mall. You can't buy a soft pretzel."

"But you can buy the imported mustard to put on it. You're a Williams-Sonoma in utero. Homes, plural. Here, Key West." He rubs his shorn head. "You still sport major hair, you son of a bitch." He lights a cigarette. "Plus a handsome husband since forever. That kind of monogamy pisses off the right-wingers *and* lets down your own whoring people."

I point to lightning outlining the clouds. "Even the sky has varicose veins in my honor."

"They said rain tonight, later," Potsy says.

"God's tears, to sanctify my forty-fifth year," I muse.

"The pearl-clutching move up here, boiz?" It's Dee, carrying her shoes and someone's hair. "Miss Sondra lost her clip-on bangs, and I can't find her." It's like a wide paintbrush minus a handle. "There's a Hispanic neuter loose covering her high forehead with a birthday napkin."

Potsy slaps his arms, neck. "Damn fruit-fly repellent didn't work again!"

"My fruit loop detector must be stronger," Dee hotly offers. "You don't treat LezbyAnn this way."

Potsy flicks ash toward her. "LezbyAnn isn't needy and bleedy."

"Seriously. I'm curious. What did I ever do to you?"

"I can't stomach women who act cool with gay men but secretly resent they can't change us."

"I couldn't even get a husband to stop washing his hair with a bar of Irish Spring, so I have no illusions that I can coax that dick out of your mouth, ass, or armpit." She gets in his face for this last part. "I'm not looking to convert anyone. Especially you."

"Maybe not," he admits, "but it's always like this. You're always *at* everybody."

Their Best Friend competition has always been intense and flattering. Potsy calls her The Thresher (this is when he's not calling her The Penis Flytrap). Dee has a brisk stride. Her arms chug, like opposing handshakes suddenly taken away. "Do you generate actual energy, like wind farms?" Potsy challenged her one night. "Enough to blow away the likes of you," she coolly assessed.

"Potsy, Potsy," she now purrs, then snaps, "always so superior. Just remember: everyone shits between two shoe heels."

"Not that gnarly ex of Paul McCartney." At the roof's edge, Potsy tilts the martini glass. "Not Totie Fields." A drop plinks the dome of

Vin, who looks up. Potsy steps back just enough. "And that shark-bit surfboarder chick they made the movie out of."

"That was an arm," Dee sighs. "Potsy, it must physically hurt, being so dumb." She wraps her arms around me. "Sweetheart, Andy's doing a cement-mixer-with-white-man-overbite." She demonstrates. "Stan is helplessly watching Pee-wee put the move on Protégé, who's trying to talk Andy into taking his blouse off."

"He hasn't worked out since Memorial Day!" I cry.

Potsy places his glass on his ribcage like a Madonna cone-bra. "Low-nip intervention!" He flicks off what's left of his cig. Balloons pop and a startled Vin screams in falsetto.

We all clomp back down into Gyrate. It is *so* time to go. I dance with—and try to dress—Mr. Potatochippendale, but he deftly pops his arm out of the sleeve I just got on him. At least I stop Andy from whipping Miss Sondra, who's shaking her padded ass, with his belt.

ANDY'S blotto, so I drive. The headlights sweep across the potted topiaries aligned with the heavy wood front doors I myself reseal every spring, across the signage of Great Rooms! in a typeface I chose not because it was retro but because it looked trustworthy.

I pull close and idle. This was formerly Packard Elementary, a large brick two-story school shuttered for lackluster performance. Dee represented me in negotiations with the city. I could never be impartial, but I'm always impressed. It's large and varied, now housing specialty shops and a culinary hub with everything from cooking lessons to knife servicing. Tomorrow, Saturday, is our weekly farmer's market in a rear parking lot carved out of a playground.

I had been with a collective of furniture stores as a visual design manager, the pay poor but the title, right out of college, impressive. I loved cultivating suppliers. I found colloquial inspiration in the tri-state area I was given. If there was a covered bridge festival, we built a bridge and, by God, we covered it. If mesmerized by the garish lighting of a Dario Argento horror film I stayed up too late watching the night before, I replicated it. Every store walk I had with upper management was lauded and rewarded with more locations and more work. I started hating the travel, walking through hotel lobbies bleary-eyed with damp hair and realizing every other guest smelled like the same cucumber and verbena shampoo/conditioner combo. And I missed Andy all the time. My ultimatum was addressed by creating an office-based position: VP, Creative Services. I came to find the Marketing golems cantankerous and quite content to steal promotional campaigns from other furniture chains. I remained, proofreading silk-screened signage for a series of never-ending sales, until Andy drove me past Packard and simply said, "Get out of your own way."

"I hate that phrase."

"Shit or get off the pot."

"Hate that one too."

Without the third option of a colostomy, I got out of my own way, then shat. I could claim I herded my background into a meticulous master plan, but mostly I relied on my under-capitalized instinct. At thirty-three, I had mortgaged real estate with significant asbestos-mitigation issues, in the kind of neighborhood you pray turns around so your customers feel safe enough to turn their back.

I figured many curious would come because they went to school here, so we kept the old chalkboards, desks, and globes. This wasn't just in tribute. I had a Visual budget of zero. (They've since diminished. Commerce trampled nostalgia.) We still use the hallway bells, now timed to signal the beginning and end of shopping hours. The PA system worked, so I still hop on occasionally, before store hours, and sing something from the score of *South Pacific*, which inarguably has no clinkers. The administrative space functions as the same; I took the principal's office. I kept the marble floors as they were, having hated industrial carpeting ever since my mother used her employee discount at the carpet warehouse she worked at to wall-to-wall our home in remaindered Celadon. We have no statement staircase, just two narrow flights to a second floor that still reverberate with those energized slap-slap-slaps toward recess. I reengineered the former cafeteria to display cookware. The gymnasium is seasonal: outdoor patio furnishings spring up like a migrant camp every March, and November brings pre-lit, pre-decorated Christmas trees so towering they'd only fit into a McMansion. The auditorium with its Depression-era murals had a serviceable stage, and I offered it for community rental or, if I liked the cause, gratis. Dipping into what little his late dad had left him, Andy bought four used delivery trucks. We washed them every weekend ourselves, knowing they were the moving sandwich boards representing Great Rooms! We went green and recycled, because I couldn't afford daily bulk trash pickup. Skids and shipping containers our woodworkers conjoined as storage sheds and kids' playhouses.

Still, I had vast and odd space to fill. I knew what Pottery Barn could do; what they couldn't, I made my niche. Ralph Lauren said somewhere that you can't be too hot or too cold. That sounded right to me. Flavor of the month is nice—we've had our share of tables made from things like orange safety cones—but comfort food is nicer. I began acquiring. The local newspaper admiringly called it synergism. I knew it better as sink-or-swim. I brought in a struggling upholstery firm and its four employees, and we encouraged clients to bring in what caught their eye from catalogs or online. I tracked down a steelworker whose gates I admired at a museum and asked about an alliance. He began turning out everything from kickplates to customized trellises and fencing; a daughter and son-in-law later started designing bracelets. Milliners made tapestries. Local artists got their own stalls for their hand-painted canvases. (As they began to make house calls and broadened into architectural detail painting, they timidly asked if they could call themselves Damn Hue. Just being able to okay a name like that, as the owner, made owning the gallery worth it.) The only thing I insisted upon was showroom presence during business hours; it was fine, actually better, for me if they kept their off-site workrooms. I didn't eschew heirlooms but I didn't want shelves of empty perfume bottles, either, so we contracted a husband/wife team to bid on estates that met their antiquity standards. Sourcing has become a huge part of what Great Rooms! is. I don't; others do. My days of bringing home a suitcase of filament bulbs when I travel are over.

Much to the chagrin of our customer service department, I started layaway, remembering how fanatically my parents paid weekly on a genuine arcade pinball machine for Olivia and me one Christmas. (It turned out to be more for them than us; we were more taken with Atari and bored quickly by the refurbished flippers and chrome balls.)

Dee goaded me into buying surrounding land when it became available. I gutted three old school buses, arranged them in a U-shape, repainted them a brighter yellow, and they became a specialty lighting depot. I added a freestanding custom home theater center, tracking down the same brick as that of Gentry Elementary. Even there I made my own imprimatur. I rejected pleas from sales for the typical sporting events as background visual for the bank of TVs; unless they're specifically demonstrating models, a video I had produced—interspersing commercials from the 1960s, digitized science-class filmstrips, and even snippets from some 8mm home movies of me and my sister Olivia—continually loops.

Mr. Albanese, a professional arborist nudged into retirement, then approached me. He and his wife overplanted a small wood behind us with seasonal produce and herbs that they sold under a side awning. Friends of his inquired, and it turned into a weekend farmer's market on what was the playground, where I placed picnic tables, swings, and a basketball court for families to make a day of it. He loosely manages it all with the hopeful but unenforceable rule that everything must have been grown or made within ten miles of here. All I ask is that the store name appear somewhere on all labeling. It's grown large, and Mr. Albanese wants to extend into winter with root vegetables and ice fishermen friends who want to sell their catch. He keeps telling me about two strange sisters who formulate artisanal ricotta from sheep they keep in their backyard.

No one was more shocked than I when *House Beautiful* accepted my invitation and portfolio to see some of our work firsthand; I had luckily stumbled into a new layer of regional editors. A six-page spread on a pharmaceutical CEO's Tara and the millwork I personally oversaw followed. When asked admiringly how I managed it all, I honestly told them it didn't occur to me that there was a different way to do it, and when they inquired about how I went about developing my business model, I just looked at them. More than anything, this article put us on the map, drawing customers from other states to what had been just another high-end backwater store. We became the destination others feed from and not the other way around. The quadrant transformed. A gourmet custard emporium, independent art cinema, Brazilian steakhouse, and a travel agent sprang up on the opposite side of the road. A long-dormant strip plaza was revitalized with a Greek deli, a watch repair shop, fondue restaurant, Apple store, and a one-hour photo center. And is any neighborhood metamorphosis complete until you can get your eyebrows threaded? That opens next month. I'm not thrilled about the new, small private airport and the potential noise a couple miles away, but I also know it's another testimonial to the area's rebirth.

It was all very heady, but it didn't happen as fast as it seems. I was, at times, impatient and irritable, discouraged, disgusted. We took a hit in that last bout of the country's economic woes, but our lack of snobbery sustained us. I lent, for a fee, underutilized sales associates to Dee as stagers, depersonalizing homes for sale. Other offices followed, and it became a significant revenue stream. I also didn't panic and depart from twice-yearly sales (and never on the same date). More, and you train your customer to adjust their cost expectation downward and wait.

Mostly, I'm still a little mystified and a lot gratified. It's a simplified summary of a complicated process, but it *was* simple in its hopefulness, and is still Mom-and-Pop enough that when Andy brings Gertie and Noel at the end of the workday, when they run wild and pee and no one can reprimand me, I still feel like I won something.

My biggest personal victory right this second is seeing how the variegated ivy Andy and I had planted over a decade ago—a daunting weekend project, hundreds of nursery cell packs—established a dense, seamless hedge on the exterior. The store looks like it's been here forever, a real business as rooted as the ivy.

"Who's the workaholic? Who? Who?" Andy is awake or, more aptly, has briefly regained consciousness.

I back out. "Only looking, just checking."

At the next stoplight, Andy slurs at a moody shop window of female mannequins in wedding gowns: "Here's a big howdy-do to Bethany's Bridal!"

"Shut up! Don't draw attention!" I warn. A DWI is one of those acronyms, like SARS or GOP, that you don't want associated with your name.

"Hey, Bethany, where are the boy brides?" he catcalls. Before I can clamp my hand over his mouth, he's taken my left hand off the steering wheel to massage my silver ring. "Would you marry me if we met now?"

"Driving here!" I go back to ten and two.

"I'm gonna do something to you," he growls huskily, trying for sexy but sounding like a state governor who's just denied a stay of execution. By the time we turn onto our neighborhood street, Dumbass has returned to mumbling out the window, now at an imposing Spanish stucco home. "Barry, order me two burritos and refried beans."

I lightly tap the brakes a dozen times to annoy him.

For once we don't have to repeatedly put Gertie and Noel down from the bed; we lure them away with a giant gift bow. As we thrash, they slash, all in flashes of lightning.

I AWAKE to canine asshole. "Noel, get your twinkler outta here!" I scream.

Andy's in his favorite cargo shorts with more pockets than anyone needs and his alma mater wife-beater. "But wouldn't mankind be better off if we all did the Presentation of the Anus? Summit meetings of world leaders should be preceded by a Presentation of the Anus."

"It would give new meaning to dirty politics," I say, still pushing Noel away.

"And would bring everyone down a notch, huh, Gertie? Right, Noel?"

We chose pugs because of their compactness—neither weighs more than thirteen pounds—their curly tails, lustrous eyes, and their overall jauntiness. Both are the common fawn color. Today is Andy's turn to take them for shampooing, something we let a groomer do because they've both caught colds when we did it. It's something else common to the breed: chronic breathing problems and allergies.

Noel jumps down alongside Andy and Gertie.

"Speaking of ass, someone's breath smells like butt." Andy waves his hand.

"Says more about you than me," I reply. "And don't think that counted as a fuck. That wasn't much more than a warm, soapy bowl." Warm, soapy bowl was our euphemism for let's-just-do-this sex. In 1940s wartime, a prostitute would carefully wash her john's penis in a warm, soapy bowl of water to ensure cleanliness and scope out visible disease. Excited, this often promptly brought the soldier boy off. This is another phrase we treasure: brought off. "And you didn't even finish," I also point out.

"'Toot my birthday horn' isn't exactly a reciprocal love call."

I wince. No one wants to be reminded of bossy shit said in the throes.

"It was all about you, baby boy," Andy says, laughing.

"Andy, take off their collars." The pugs are wearing their matching lavender collars, studded with cubic zirconium. "The groomer will forget and then it's a trip back."

"The puppets are glammin' for your birthday," he dismisses me. "I'll remember. The puppets have asked can they go in Mercy B."

I roll over. "Daddy says sure if they're on towels until their puppet nails get clipped." As Andy goes to get some from the master bathroom, I add, "Take the crappy ones!"

"They're all crappy. Great Rooms! sells such plush ones. Are we poor?" Andy asks like a timid housewife.

We kiss, all four of us. I see red soaring down our driveway. It's going to be a good day. I'm not even going to bathe, at least not yet. I put on the cast album of *I Had A Ball*, a 1962 musical vehicle for, go figure, Buddy Hackett. It's Karen Morrow, belting the title showstopper like it's a testicle she devoured, that I want to hear, my feel-good song. I put track number thirteen on repeat. I return to our bedroom and figure out a birthday suit that involves clothing. By the time I settle on a tee and pajama pants from the pine cupboard, the microwave coffee gone cold in a *Drowsy Chaperone* mug, it's 10:22.

The telephone rings.

"What's happenin', Hot Stuff?"

And so begins the yearly ritual, an unidentified, disguised caller among our friends. I'm not even convinced it's a male.

"That's pretty good. Was that a real gong I heard?"

I hear the sound effect again, then, "His name is Long Duck Dong."

"I don't know him," I reply.

"Fred, she's gotten her boobies. Oh, and they are so perky!"

"I don't know a single Fred, either," I reply, per the annual script.

"Fred, leave her alone. You'll make her tinkle."

"I've already peed and *Sixteen Candles* is not a handbook for life."

"I can't believe it. They fucking forgot my birthday," my well-wisher drawls.

"No one forgot. There's another call. Good-bye."

"Thanks for getting my undies back!" is the breathy coda.

The other call is my mother, Jeanine. (Some call her Jeanie, which makes it sound like she emerges from a lamp when it's rubbed.) Her telephone greeting is always the same: "It's just me."

"You always say that so apologetically. Do you have an inferiority complex, Mom?" I tease.

"Everything about me is complex," she announces. "I just know how busy you pretend to be. Get my card?"

I go out the back door. "Yesterday." My mother didn't embrace my homosexuality. She swallowed it whole. I never receive cards with barefoot boys in straw hats on toadstools. I get filthy limericks and monster dicks. "You like that particular card aisle too much."

I walk as far as a handmade teeter-totter, where I sit. This was Andy's wish. I was never the type of kid who was interested in a tire swing, but we have one of those, too, again at Andy's request. I right potted petunias with the late-summer legginess no amount of pinching will revive, like they're bungee-jumping out to self-seed. The small hedge of sedum has gone burgundy, another sign it's September. From here, all I see are landscaping missteps: massed coleus dwarfed by the feathery flowers of astilbe, bee balm invading the daylilies. Andy had given me Barbara Damrosch's *The Garden Primer*, an encyclopedic manual, paired with a nursery gift certificate, for my first birthday in this house. I didn't heed the admonitions that establishing any garden is a three-year process, hell no, I didn't. I dug every weekend until I spat soil out of my coffee mug, making no allowance for sprawl. It's too much and now it looks stomped by last night's storm.

"You had any rain there?" My mom is two states away and it's been a nationwide summer of drought, but, hell, it's conversation.

"Not a drop. You?"

"Poured throughout the night."

"Braggart! Watering right now. This is miserable. I hate a hot September. Don't start on global warming, Al. It was ninety-one the day you were born, and that was without A/C."

I know she's training the hose on her geraniums, dismembering them, probably in a hat that would make Aunt Pittypat envious. Mom is, in actuality, a little Anna Madrigal and a lot Violet Venable.

Distant emergency sirens intersect like an air raid.

I remove a Bradford pear tree branch from hostas that don't look so great, either. I make my way to our swimming pool. We've barely been in it this summer. In a climate that permits, at best, 120 days' use, it was an endless and losing battle with water chemistry. All we do is skim and test pH. I net out storm debris with the aluminum pole.

A mallard splashes down and defiantly paddles.

"Where's your buddy?" I ask.

"Who are you talking to?" Mom asks.

"A duck in the pool." I watch it do a figure eight. "There's usually two."

"Our pond has a whole flock. That's not counting the geese," my mother boasts.

Mom's lanai has become enough of a wildlife sanctuary that her condo board has expressed concern. Everything from birdfeeders with squirrel spoilers as big as garbage can lids to chopped lettuce on Melmac for rabbit colonies festoons her cement slab, plus a birdbath, windsock, chimes. Her grocery bill must be more suet and sunflower seed than actual food. When Andy drank a glass of what he assumed was cherry Kool-Aid from her refrigerator, she cried out, "That's the nectar for my hummers!" (This is what she calls hummingbirds.) He paled, she consoled: "It's just boiled sugar water and food coloring."

Mom wishes me happy birthday. I promise to call her later.

What appears to be a medical evacuation helicopter chop-chops dips overhead, then chop-chops out of sight over our house, which is larger than its roofline suggests.

I will not pretend that we want for much. We want for less. Five thousand square feet on three different levels has become too much to care for. Every weekend is devoured by patching things. We were attracted by the hilliest part of the city in a state generally known for its flatness. The price was good, too, since it was one of the older houses in a neighborhood overbuilt by new money. Given what I do, I should be appreciative of their contributions to the economy, all these houses tricked out with security cameras and steam rooms, but I'm mostly made queasy by the gluttony, where one man's potting shed is the next man's recording studio, where every water feature shames Niagara Falls.

After neighbors admired our rustic fire pit, one couple immediately commissioned a stonecutter for their own. We ooohed and ahhhed as we were led proudly back to Dante's Inferno. "I hear the damned screaming," Andy perspired at me. We heard the wife later speaking of how she had investigated manufacturing snow with several ski lodges during our last unseasonably warm Christmas because "it was all about the kids." She'd forgotten they have none.

Another childless couple built a tree house costing $175 grand (they let this figure slip twelve times). The few paths through our own sun and shade gardens and our lame teeter-totter were nothing when we saw the primitive bridge of rope, which swayed when we all crossed it. Andy asked if they charged a toll. No one laughed. They were all too dazzled by the moose heads and envying the hunting lodge chic which could provide shelter to the Swiss Family Robinson and the latest contestants of *Survivor*.

Then there was the couple who wanted to recreate Vizcaya, the fifty-acre Biscayne Bay estate they married at. The $7 million expenditure fell a few terrazzo and about forty-seven acres short, and then they wound up planting gallon saplings and arborvitae. The entirety of their landscaping fit in their car trunk. Nothing soars eight feet in one year, despite what the nursery promises.

The neighborhood still isn't gated, but a few of us have only barely averted a homeowner initiative to do so. From an outsider's perspective, our life is probably chic and social, but we still feel like outsiders ourselves. We live well, even without a private plane or a philanthropic endeavor named after us; the house in Key West is our big indulgence. We don't even have vanity license plates. But we're starting to feel like we're living in the shadow of Camelot, in the cul-de-sac's servant quarters, and I wonder when we here at Green Acres will be expelled as unwelcome.

It's 1:23 on the kitchen wall clock. I call Andy's cell. "This is me laughing how you're available to everyone but me." I hold the phone aloft. "Sorry. It's a silent laugh. So where you be? I went right to voice mail." I'm tracing among our kitschy refrigerator magnets for the groomer's card when the phone beeps. "Never mind. I bet this is you."

My world detonates when I look at Caller ID.

THIS is what I remember, in no particular order:

Grabbing Andy's Jeep keys from the back-door organizer.

"Mr. Barry Grooms? This is Saint Vitus Community Hospital. You're speaking with Ramona."

I'm not sure where St. Vitus is and I am in no mood for a fundraising appeal.

Ramona tells me, "Your registration was found in a car driven by Andrew Morgan. If you've got local news on, you'll hear that there's been a serious accident."

"I don't, but I will. I live with Andrew. What's going on?"

Shoving my bare feet into flip-flops on the garage floor.

Even in this chaos, I make a mental note to do something about those ever-bigger oily stains.

"I'm leaving right now. Let me ask, are our dogs, are they with him?"

Ramona doesn't know about any dogs. That, to me, is a comfort. If Andy left the puppets at the groomers to be picked up, they're accounted for.

I'm virtually airborne down the driveway.

My mind goes to Andy's insurance. If he's incapacitated, are they awaiting proof of coverage? Will they find the card on him? How does it work, who would I call?

I accelerate, crossing to the left, back to the right again, passing electrical substations and tire superstores, startling a mowing crew from prison, more focused on hatching an escape plan than in taming grasses gone to tall seed.

I turn on the radio to a local station.

This, I should not have done.

"—still coming in about a downtown construction site emergency. It's being reported that a crane and a portion of a twelve-story building have collapsed, with multiple passerby injuries and significant damage to nearby businesses."

Eighty miles per hour. I am passing multiple cars on the breakdown shoulder.

"For more, we go to Terry Chamberlain. Terry, what's going on?"

I speak aloud as if Terry is there.

"I don't want to hear this. This isn't happening."

"What we know now is that the ColonyScape condominium site—still in demolition phase—has been isolated due to safety concerns, so little is visible," Terry reports. "People have been tweeting from the scene but without verification we're reluctant to pass on those details, as specific as they are."

I activate the hazard lights.

Another unidentified voice, that of a woman, joins the reportage.

"One eyewitness now tells us—"

I take the volume up from the steering wheel to hear a breathless fragment: "…from the corner of my eye, I saw something yellow begin to fall. I started running."

A blurting police car intercedes in my race.

Exit signs jump by. I'm afraid I'll miss the one I was told to take but I don't slow for the pursuing pandemonium red, not when I hear "…another witness, a store owner in the vicinity, told me emergency equipment was brought in to rescue one victim from a parked luxury car as workers removed debris by hand."

That's not Andy. Please, God, have it not be Andy.

St. Vitus Community Hospital directional sign looms. I still don't defer to the police car, now parallel to the Jeep.

As preposterous as it seems, I think about the risk of disfigurement. Scarring is tricky. Dee could help on this. A competent plastic surgeon should be standing by ready to reset Andy's aquiline nose, to ensure his crooked mouth remains perfectly crooked.

Terry interrupts the female, whose name is Rachel. "Sadly, Rachel, it now appears that rescue was actually one of recovery. We have a report from St. Vitus Hospital now of one fatality, reportedly a male, attributed to the ColonyScape collapse."

I veer into the parking lot of a restaurant I'd never dine at.

It is you, isn't it, Andy?

I feel like I'm in a vacuum-sealed storage bag as all of the air slowly draws out.

"Stay with us. We'll continue to monitor this developing story, this mind-boggling tragedy, with updates."

Departing diners stop to watch as the police car slams to park inches from my Jeep and its HRC and *One Human Family* Key West bumper stickers. He strides toward my blinking hazard lights. I open the door.

"Sir? Sir? Hey, Mr. Human Rights sticker? What seems to be your problem?"

I have just enough gay umbrage to think, *Would it have to be a Cracker Barrel sign I'm staring at as I realize Andy is dead?*

I vomit so forcefully it sprays gravel on his boots.

Chapter Two

A Seismic Event

MY TRANSFORMATION into a beast begins, a creature with no restraint.

Some poor bastard from St. Vitus drew the short straw and had to drive the bereaved home, exactly retracing my path. From the front seat of his van, I see Andy's Jeep at Cracker Barrel, left when the cop drove me the rest of the way to the hospital.

"I can call anyone for you." He offers his cell phone. Mine is still in what's left of Mercy B., taking a charge. I've personally contacted everyone I could think of and told them Andy's been in an accident, turn on the TV or radio. If someone was unreachable, I left no message.

I try to reply to his offer and froth leaks out of my mouth. "Do you have a ready support system?" he persists.

Support system: a complicated series of straps, pulleys, and hand-cranks to keep Barry upright.

"My people are coming" is all I can muster.

The driver parks.

I'm rabid. My sticky hands clench and unfold.

The driver tells me, this wild animal loping out of the car, that I have an awesome house.

I cannot wait to destroy it.

If a crane can steal Andy and Gertie and Noel away from me, then I will be the wrecking ball that dismantles what is left.

Both garage remotes are AWOL. I can't remember the pass code, rarely used, anyway, since Andy's traditional workday brought him home first. I'm the one who comes in the back door, no keypad necessary, a drink waiting.

I go out to the pool. I scream at cicadas calling from the mature pines: "Shut up, everything, just stop!" They don't.

I'd begin with the concrete, I'd break it up if I could, but we don't have a sledgehammer. Or maybe we do. Tools were Andy's thing. He even installed a workbench in the basement, for what purpose I will never discover.

Instead, I throw everything I can into the water. I scoop stone from the fire pit and skim those across the water. I push the beverage cart down the three tiled steps. I tear a market umbrella from its base and swing it around and around. Spokes snap as I release it into the trees, where it snags on branches. Watch this! See the splash this urn makes! The soil swirls to the surface like an underwater smokestack. I pick up an outdoor speaker and catapult it. It floats and roils before sinking.

I swing the ragged jump rope Gertie and Noel would endlessly tug between them like a lariat, and it joins the umbrella in the tree.

I am bound for the diving board with Venus de Milo over my head when hands restrain me. The voices of people I know, my people, coax me down. The support system is wobbly but quickly grows. Hands stroke me. Other hands steer me into the house and away from more destruction. Still, I manage to chuck an obelisk into the pool before they can stop me.

THE beast is tamed, my destructive acts righted. I am a little embarrassed I threw what is commonly called a fit, that someone had to fish it all out. Not knowing where everything went, they stacked it. If I scale the pile, lie down, and ask nicely for a light, maybe someone will set the pyre ablaze; I don't think I have self-immolation in me.

From my bedroom Recamier, I look at the steam rising off the sapphire-blue pool. Is it so bad that it crosses my mind to turn the pool heater off? We won't be in it for naughty midnight dips again, so why run up the bill?

The phone rings. It's quickly answered. I had proposed canceling our landline one day, saying we're archaic, no one has one. My God, how would the hospital have contacted me?

I hear the doorbell. Friends are making their way, their vehicles lining the driveway and street, consoling one another, carrying bags with banana bread and ranch dressing. We've toted the same into the homes of others.

My turn.

I watch the single mallard restlessly pace the pool decking. "How do you know omens are omens?"

"What omen?" Kerrick asks.

"One duck."

Faith comes to look out the window. "Omen for what?"

"That I could have delayed Andy," I reason. "I should have argued more about the puppets' collars. Or less. I'm not even sure why he was where he was. It's nowhere near the groomers."

All I know is that, even though Noel and Gertie loved the detachable hardtop off, it was on. It wasn't when we collapsed in bed last night. Which tells me Andy put it on, because he either had many intended stops or a prolonged one. Neither of us would leave the Mercy B. open to bird crap or a jealous lit cigarette.

Dee is trying to kick the *45 And Barely Alive* banner under the bed. I hear the grommets clicking. I snatch it from under her sandal and hold it up.

"Talk about prophetic. God made a fucking sash." The plastic still smells of Gertie and Noel's slobber, where their dog teeth scalloped the edges. "And it was for Andy, not for me."

Another fit is stirring. Faith and Kerrick sense it. They hurriedly take the uncomfortable Italian slipper chairs. I bought them for their outline; they were never intended to seat anyone. Potsy and Dee remain standing. All of them watch me. I watch them. I remember my camera, passed around to document my birthday night. "Hand me that." I direct Potsy to it on the nightstand. I press through the photos and carefully inspect.

"Should you be looking at those?" That's Dee asking.

Many were taken when I was on the rooftop, time I should have spent with Andy. But I find no suspicious shadows, no wispy figures waiting to pounce and guide Andy toward the light, no Grim Reaper unless I count Stan, desperate to keep up with Protégé. The final photograph is my shirtless man in motion, unembarrassed, about to be hauled away by his embarrassed boyfriend, about to die.

"Were there any issues at the hospital?" Faith asks.

"They were very helpful and cooperative."

"Who told his fucked-up Catholic brood?" Potsy asks.

"I called his twin brother Alexander first. Then Dolores, then Yvonne."

"Remind us what we're up against," Potsy says. "Don't they all live within a couple miles of each other yet barely speak?"

Andy's mom was a large woman who grew larger, and diabetic, with twins. Labor brought a massive stroke. Alexander, and then Andrew, were taken via C-section. She died in the emergency room without ever holding her twin boys. Dad reacted like a real gem by blaming the babies for bringing on her death and handing them to Dolores and Yvonne to raise as he drank more than ever. "They just wanted to stay out of his way. He was every bit as rough on them. Worse," Andy told me. I never wanted to know what *worse* implied. In Andy's sophomore year in college, before we'd met, his father died of cirrhosis. I tell them all of this.

"Did the boys resemble Mom or Dad?" Faith asks.

"Mom, from the couple of photos he had."

Andy had exactly one of his dad: a studio sitting. The rustic portrait is nearly satire: a lower middle-class family, minus the maternal grounding, grazing against baled hay. His father, unbelievably, had a visible toothpick. Andy said the lady assisting the photographer recognized Yvonne's blouse from her garage sale. She went on about how good it looked as Yvonne flushed and probably wanted to leap into the lifelike well behind them.

He rarely spoke of his father. When he did it was consistent: "I never knew the man." At my nagging, he recalled one sadistic story for me. When the boys were eleven, the father drunkenly ordered everyone into the car. They headed toward stagnant water surrounded by pea gravel, which he called a beach. It was a two-hour, hellishly hot drive, all farmland. Midway, Andy noticed the gray pavement changing color, to pale green… and moving, rippling. It was zillions of little caterpillars, crossing the road, from one field to the next. He began yelling at his Dad: "Stop the car so they can cross!" Andy described to me how they arched their backs, if they have backs, patiently propelling themselves forward a millimeter at a time. His dad slowed down, turned off the radio, belched, and told his four children to listen to the pop pop… popopoppopopopopopp of them being squashed. "It's their world too! They'll become butterflies!" Andy protested. "It sounds like a bubble pack," Alexander said, his head protruding from the window. Dolores read her paperback. Yvonne spit on her fingers and rubbed at various skin discolorations. His dad said pesticides would otherwise get them. Andy was bawling. "They're traveling together, they're looking out for each other!" The road was carpeted by caterpillars, and they were slicing through the thickest pockets of them. Andy said he had visions of them writhing on the hot tailpipe, frying, screaming, if caterpillars scream, and their offal splattering up into the trunk, into their cooler, in their potato salad. "Back up over them," Alex pleaded. Their father, still laughing, put the car into reverse for over a mile to hit all he had missed.

And I thought I had it bad when our Impala lost its muffler one morning when my dad dropped me at school.

Kerrick carefully asks me, "Where is Andy now?"

"I'm having him taken to Frey Funeral Home."

"*Having* him? Where is he?" Dee asks.

"The county coroner. They weren't done."

Something glacial settles over the bedroom as the implication of "they weren't done" sinks in.

Morgues, large drawers, dissection. TV is cluttered enough with fictional procedurals that I don't want my own factual one. Seeing one of those Bodies exhibits was enough. I refuse to see the pathology report. I have no need to know what Andy's spleen weighed. I do not want to know if Andy suffered massive head trauma, internal injuries, suffocated beneath the collapse, or hemorrhaged slowly. I asked that his death certificate, multiples of which I'll require to sate the death industry, be sealed in envelopes so I don't have to even touch it. Excessive detail is unnecessary. In the guise of helpfulness, hospital administrators suggested I could meet with those who first responded to ColonyScape and extracted Andy. To offer a thanks or a gratuity? I declined. I already know that everything I could count on drew its last breath when Andy did.

"Had you guys ever made arrangements?" Faith asks.

I nod. "In general. He'd want no formal service, no doves released, no priest, just a meet-and-greet."

"What about a Life Celebration right here at the house? People reflect in a room of his stuff you picked out," Kerrick explains.

"Like a shrine? His first abacus and a pair of ice skates?" I shake my head. "Andy would hate an interactive death."

"Will you scatter his ashes here or maybe off a pier down in Key West?" Faith asks.

"He won't be cremated," I declare. "Andy always said 'I have never smoked'—"

Dee completes this. "—'and in my casket is no place to start'."

I open a nightstand drawer. "I need to write stuff down while I'm thinking about it. Like any donations should go to the Matthew Shepard Foundation."

Faith waves a notepad. "I have been. Have you thought about an obituary and a picture of Andy to go with it?"

Oh, God. We've all seen the unfortunate photographs family think best represent the deceased. Over PowerBars, Andy and I would critique the twice-weekly Great Rooms! display ad, bitch about lousy placement, and scowl about what competitors were touting. Then we'd turn to the back and share a yuk over the Obituaries grid, more entertaining than any political cartoon. A man holding an accordion in lederhosen. A grandma wearing a corsage as large as a head of lettuce. A lifelong librarian with frosted hair reminiscent of a sideways swan's ass. A man with a strange beard Hula-Hooping. A hard woman cleaning a fish dockside. A Shriner in a fez, smoking—jarring then to read that donations be directed to the American Lung Association. There were also the heartbreaking photos: a bald child in a gown proudly holding a solved Rubik's cube, a husband and wife in their sixty-first year of marriage who died seventeen minutes apart. We would chuckle over the ethnic names or those full of hyphens and the quote marks drawing special attention to nicknames like "Bad Boy," "Polywog," and "Sherlock"—this an obvious detective novel buff who, in the accompanying photo, holds a magnifying glass to an eye milky with a cataract. What were her loved ones thinking when they publicly identified their Grandmother as "Jugs" in her last press clipping? We'd only skim the paid death notices, which usually paired pious testimony that rivaled the Bible for heft and a feathered-edge photograph we'd search for stigmata.

I remember my own father's. Mom chose the last one taken of him: ashen, haggard after a quadruple bypass at sixty-three, in a tie too wide, trying to stare down death, which came two years after the sitting.

In the end, I'll settle on a professional photograph from the annual report of Andy's bank. No one will be able to ridicule it. It's bad enough that his obituary will be regarded with "Whoa! Wrong place, wrong time!" the freaky reminder that free will is superseded by fate.

"Let's talk about what *you* want to be in it," Faith moves on. "I see *special friend* a lot."

Potsy sneers. "Sounds like he's on a porch swing with a banjo."

"Companion, then," Faith supposes.

"Sounds like a Protégé."

"Partner."

I jump in. "That sounds like we own a paving company together."

"Domestic partner," Kerrick modifies.

"That sounds like I shacked up with the help." I walk to the bathroom for Advil. "Let's try soul mate."

"Like they'd allow that!"

"What's wrong with *soul mate*?"

"I thought you said *hole mate*."

I never find the aspirin. Inside the medicine cabinet, I find a *Happy Birfday!* envelope propped on a shelf. I lower to the toilet seat. "Guys, come in here, please." As they do, I ask them to "Read me this."

Faces darken in horror. Potsy opens the card. "Buy yourself a Coke or something. With Pugs & Kisses, Andrew." He holds up two crisp one-dollar bills. "That Andy. Always extravagant."

I take them. "Our first shithole was a double. Something was seriously wrong with the slab it sat on. It wasn't settling, it was sinking.

Lay a ball down, it rolled to the other side of the room. We rotated our dinner plate so the gravy wouldn't run off." Not wanting to, I cry. "An old lady lived on the other side. We'd take out her trash, and every now and then we'd pick her up a six-pack. Eighty-two, and she still dearly loved her Pabst Blue Ribbon. She found out my birthday and she taped a card to our door. In it were two one-dollar bills, and she wrote *Buy yourself a Coke or something.*"

Dee cannot stifle her sob. Faith weeps too.

"The randomness of the phrase stuck with us," I continue. "So Andy always puts two ones in my card and writes that. *Buy yourself a Coke or something.* Kicker is, I only drink Pepsi."

I just broke relationship code, relinquishing one of our little insider jokes. But if I don't, they die with Andy.

There's a knock. Even in great sadness, Faith behaves like it's her office and barks, "Busy!"

Stan, outside the door, whispers, "Barry's mom just got here."

As if to underscore his update, which has the same dire urgency as "the SWAT team has this place surrounded," I hear a wail downstairs.

"Where is he? Where's my boy?"

I take tissue. "The dressy sweats, imposter cologne, and Tootsie glasses have arrived. Call the exorcist," I beg my friends.

"YOU'VE got a floodlight out over there."

This is the first full sentence my mother says to me, in our small white gazebo, after she's asked that we go outside to be alone.

"Not being critical," Mom adds hastily.

Like me, my mother is a stickler. What's wrong needs righting. Too bad my life can't be stood back on its feet.

"Remind me to get pictures this trip," Mom says. "I'm always bragging how it's like Kensington Palace." I can almost hear the clucking of her friends. She chides herself aloud. "God, that sounded awful, like I'm sightseeing."

She then waits for me to break the seal. I do.

"I'm not so foolish to think that things like this don't happen to people like me. Someone goes first and never the way you'd like. But now?"

"No one can answer that."

"He was only forty-five!"

"Linger, like your father? Going to our lockbox for living wills, withholding life-sustaining measures, comfort care only, that's better?"

I toss my wadded Kleenex into a planter. "Apples and oranges."

She nods. "Dad was sick. We could prepare. But then you finally enact that cardiopulmonary clause, the Do Not Resuscitate, DNR, and everyone assures you he's in a vegetative state, it's the right thing to do, it will be over in a day, maybe a couple. Two weeks pass. You can't exactly say, 'Never mind, this isn't working, let's try to make him better again.' That apple, it's still death. And the orange is still—"

"—death. Forget prepare. I don't even get to *see* Andy, Mom." I rock, holding my kneecaps, then shoving my hands under my arms. "He was so ripped apart they can't even make him presentable. Their exact words were 'Reconstruction constitutes a challenge'."

"It's the body he used."

"It's the body I knew! I didn't touch his aura, I touched the shell it inhabited every day! Now he's not recognizable as human! And they outright disposed of Noel and Gertie. *Disposed*!" I take the hand she offers me, squeezing her fingers. The dry skin around her many rings easily shifts. I'm beginning to lose it. "What happened in that car in those few seconds? Did he throw himself on Gertie and Noel or did they pile on to protect him—"

"—they were together. That's what counts."

I lose it. "Or was it just noise and darkness and death?"

She brings her hands up against my eyes. "Don't dwell."

"Keep those there forever, Mom. I don't want to see life without Andy and my beautiful puppets."

"You'll see them all, honey. Just not on this shore."

"I don't swim so well."

"For them, you will. You were a good team. I loved watching you two wash and dry dishes, stepping over your dogs underfoot."

I cry for awhile under her blindfold until she releases her hands to offer, "Your duck is still here."

We watch the mallard fold into repose nearby.

She asks of the jumbled pool area, "Did you do all that?"

"Sure did."

Mom plucks my tissue from the planter. "Times like this, I go back to something your Grandma Lola harped on. At any given time, she warned me and your aunt, 'Girls, hell is never more than a half mile away.'"

"Which meant?"

"Which meant holocaust is just around the corner. Sunbathers can get caught up in a tornado. A semi loses a wheel as a kid with a new driver's license goes to pass it. Go out looking for the end of a rainbow and there might only be a Port-A-Let. 'Good people and bad people, they all look the same', she'd tell us."

"Not the affirming homilies one typically hears at a mother's knee." I shudder. It's one of those sound bites that provide a glimmer into what my mom's miserable upbringing was like.

"Just be careful of the what-ifs," she warns. "They'll tumble in your head like laundry that won't dry. You'll pummel yourself about the long work hours when you could've been with him. The office parties of his you refused to go to. The things that were too much trouble will now seem no trouble at all. And then there are the things you shouldn't have done. Do not go down that path."

"I'll put regret on my To-Do list for later," I assure her.

"Now this is your Mom talking, but I resent your special day is forever tainted."

"Forever ruined, Mom. I guess it could be worse. He could've been killed on Christmas Day." I realize what I've said, but like a bad discard in gin rummy, it's too late to reel it back in. At seventy-nine, my grandmother, Lola, had nightwalked sometime between the twenty-fourth and twenty-fifth of December. Frantic employees at her assisted living facility, which specialized in memory care—ironic, since they'd forgotten to lock her door from the outside—discovered her missing. On Christmas afternoon, she was found curled and frozen in a ravine.

"You forget about Grandma?" Mom asks immediately. I admit

yes and I put my head on her shoulder to demonstrate how sorry I am. I touch her synthetic hair, which feels like a blend of lint and rubber bands.

"Why the wig?"

She pulls away. "Leave it to you. It look phony?"

I pretend tucking something behind her neck. "Not after I hide the care tag."

"Funny boy. I didn't have time for the salon. I had a one-hour $1,500 flight to catch."

"That's outrageous!"

"The airlines suck. Olivia and Teddy's were worse yet."

My sister Olivia is two years my senior. She reminds me of the actress Sandy Dennis, because she's windblown on the calmest days and does not, can *not* think in a linear way. She's also a little Stevie Nicks. With the layered lace, shawls, and cameos, it takes Olivia an eternity to get ready and present herself. Godot will show up faster. Her marriage to Ted, about the sturdiest man I have ever known, put a splint on a lot of Olivia's insecurities, but when flustered, she's like Billy Bibbitt. I leave it for you to guess who plays Nurse Ratched.

"I'll reimburse you all and I don't want any argument," I promise.

My mother has never even slightly let me help, not that she needs it. When I decided to add flooring and carpeting to the gallery, I offered her a consulting fee. She said no to even that. "Always replace tacking strips and give your installers periodic drug tests. There. No charge." Even the occasional luxury I have forced upon her, like a mink shrug, embarrassed her. So it's not a surprise that she boxes my ears.

"Pipe down. I put theirs on my Visa. I told them to leave 9A Nosepierce behind to catch up on miso soup and pregnancy scares."

She is sighing, which she often does, about Olivia's daughter Nina, which is pronounced like the numeral nine with an ugh. The hard "I" and the "ugh" infuriated Mom. "Livvie, kids will call her Nine-ugh Vagina!" They did. She embraced it and now defiantly signs everything "9A." "My only grandchild, the suite," Mom grouses. Nina is anti-everything, including herself, probably in response to her mother's otherworldliness. I watched my niece mature by the holiday, mostly secluded in a bedroom, phoning friends, very typical. I tried to be the uncle I wished mine had been: mindful of what that closed door meant, generous with fifty-dollar bills. Nina, now twenty-six, is still at home, in her fourth year of a fourteen-month data entry curriculum at a vocational school. Olivia has herself been office temping for years and has the same commitment aversion.

"How long does it take to earn a degree as a Malcontent? Is Nina mastering keyboard skills one row at a time?" Mom demanded of my sister.

"She enjoys learning," Olivia replied.

"Almost as much as delaying responsibility. Nina's never even had a W-2" was Mom's parting shot.

Now she tells me, "They're due in at ten-something and I said you could line up somebody to pick them up."

"For sure."

She slips her arm through mine. "Good. Let's head in."

FRIENDS with swollen eyes are gathered at the granite counter. Many hold drinks. I can't help but check if they're using coasters. When they see Mom and me, some join hands like they might serenade us. I'm not real sure who is facedown, inconsolably weeping, except that she used hot rollers. Miss Sondra slides Costco mini-pizzas into the oven, then wipes her nose with a strawberry print mitt. Dazed as I am, I still know it is not mine. People came with their own oven mitts. *That's* friendship. On the kitchen island cooktop, a buttered skillet holds sizzling bacon, proving everything, even an untimely death, is better with bacon.

Most everyone is staring at the flat-panel TV tuned to a newscast. A male news anchor is saying, "One man in a parked car was killed and four others seriously injured today when equipment failure at a downtown demolition set off a deadly chain reaction."

A remote is quickly aloft, aimed at the TV.

"Don't you dare. Turn it up," I request.

A solemn reporter is in front of an artist's rendering of a proposed building. "Killed at the ColonyScape Luxury Townhomes project was local banking executive Andrew Morgan, along with his three dogs."

"Two dogs," I rebut.

"If it were fucking sweeps, by tomorrow, it'd be four pitbulls, a sack of unmarked bills, and a clown doll in a car seat," Potsy yells.

Alarmed footfalls rumble toward the kitchen, coming to warn. "Jesus Christ, whatever you do, keep Barry off Channel 12!" Sue sees me and stops.

"This is no good," my mother agrees. "You don't need this right now."

I shush them all.

"My first thought, honestly, was terrorists," a paint store clerk is breathlessly saying.

"Tarantella Demolition Contractors is pursuing answers."

A harried spokesman says, "We've even reached out to the National Earthquake Information Center regarding a possible seismic event."

Sue's incredulous. "An earthquake? Keep dancing, boys! It only registered on the Richter scale of negligence!"

Dee adds, "Those Tarantella creeps are notorious for low-balling bids. This will lead back to them."

An Occupational Safety and Health Administration logo replaces the spokesman's face.

"A call from WWOH-TV to OSHA has revealed three citations of conditions called 'serious infractions' since work began after Memorial Day."

"This isn't ColonyScape's first brush with controversy, is it, Adam?"

A condensation of time-stamped city council sessions where dissenters speak rushes by in digital page turns. I remembered some of this, but why would I have paid attention?

"To be sure, Lynn. This project was beset with complaints from historical groups who monitor the revitalized downtown. Then came legal challenges from business owners on sewer concerns and inadequate parking."

Here comes the best part.

"Astoundingly, a production company shooting a TV commercial was there when the accident occurred—

"—what an amazing age we live in, satellite imaging, TMZ, Google maps, surveillance tapes," her co-anchor marvels.

"—and this remarkable footage was shared exclusively with WWOH-TV."

"Some prick sold it to the news?" Potsy yells.

"We must warn you: what you're about to see, while not graphic, may be upsetting to some viewers."

Heads swivel. Lips part to implore. I raise my hand to halt them all. "I'm a big boy."

It's like deadly dominoes falling. First, a grinding of unknown origin. A massive yellow crane crumples onto suspension bridges. These break loose, sparking as they bounce against utility wires; the pole snaps in two. Bystander screams intermingle with the exclamations of those watching this in my kitchen. The hollow building visibly quivers. An exterior wall caves inward, forcing another wall outward. The crane's counterweight surrenders with a boom. Concrete dust obliterates it all. Mostly all. Except for the shaky camera zoom to Mercy B. as it's flattened in a metallic crunch.

As it goes into immediate replay, this time enlarged, with animated circles highlighting the red car's burial, I remember closing my eyes to the horror of it all.

I may have even said something predictable like "Oh. My. God."

And then this big boy was unconscious. I'm told Mom hurriedly placed a damp tea towel on my forehead while Kerr checked my tongue and Miss Sondra, who didn't see me on the kitchen floor, offered pepperoni or veggie.

Puking, now passing out. I'm pregnant.

IT IS 11:33 when I awake, or come to, in my bed, still wearing flip-flops.

I slip into the hallway. I must be quiet. The dogs will give me away.

No, they won't.

How in the hell do we know so many people? It's a real crowd downstairs. They all love Andy and they also apparently love cold cuts and they are all discussing me. What's going to become of him, they worry, like I'm a foundling, cradled and passed around. I'm an intruder in my own home.

A man's voice says, "This is a minefield of shit for Barry to handle. And the first piñata says lawsuit."

I haven't even thought of legal action, but I realize it's inescapable, no matter who initiates it.

Newcomers are being greeted: Lynn Dutro, who we nicknamed En Utero, and Joyce Hadge, who we call Moist Vag.

My friends blaze a curious distraction from grief, forming a salon to talk about the deaths of others. More specifically: bizarre, public deaths. If stories like this distance them from the awfulness, maybe it will work for me. I crouch beside an armoire, not like a grown man but like some gargoyle who didn't like the cathedral ledge and moved indoors. I hear about the electrocution of someone installing yard lights in the shape of pineapples. Then it's all about a tarantula that had burrowed into a nursery cactus and struck down a dad in front of his children. I rethink buying succulents. I really could have done without the details of the newborn, a hospital's laundry chute, and a horrific mix-up. My guests begin to talk about other things that have broken loose and collided with people, as though Andy's death was competing for a red ribbon. There's the elderly couple on a tandem bicycle who were halved by a pallet that fell from a truck. That woman who leapt off the interior balcony of an office building and landed on a man getting a shoeshine, killing them both. I don't at first recognize the husky woman's voice that offers, "A neighbor's daughter's husband was hit by lightning during their outdoor wedding. He might still have been her fiancée. I don't know if he got out 'I do'." This is followed by her unfortunate guffaw. I now know it's Leni doing the telling. She's always the one to ask for a half-drink more, then has eighteen of them.

Someone speaks of five years ago. A spring day when storms pop up out of nowhere, the woman in her ninth month of pregnancy, the bowling accident. It seems her husband insisted the mother-to-be participate in the final round of their supermarket league tournament.

She rolled her turquoise ball underhanded down the lane a few times before claiming pain. He had too much to drink, witnesses agreed. He mockingly poured beer onto his crotch and whimpered that his water broke. She fled to the car. The sky was green and warm wind was blowing things around.

I hear Emily's sudden protest: "I refuse to listen to this." Everyone falls silent in deference, remembering her belly.

I know the rest. Both Andy and I often passed the bowling alley on the way to a SuperTarget. A twenty-five-foot bowling pin, part of the monolithic sign on a raised platform, was the tallest thing in the area. That is, before it creaked on its axle and fell down, the bulbous tip smashing the window of a station wagon, the base striking down and crushing the pregnant woman and her unborn child.

I remember our county fair, when a single car from the Crazy Dipper ride broke free and landed on the roof of a grocery almost a block away. The two brothers and a sister in it were killed. We were there that night, but earlier. Olivia and I had cherry snow cones with extra cherry, strolling livestock barns with our father until the manure overwhelmed us. The Crazy Dipper was judged "too big people" by Mom, so Olivia and I and our string bracelets made do with boring attractions like the Tilt-A-Whirl as many times as we wanted. Those children had a Mom less fretful. Up it shot, then dipped, then lived up to its name and went crazy. Calliope music disguised any sound of the lug nuts releasing. Their car alone was set free. It doesn't seem aerodynamically feasible that it completely left the midway, but it did, with their parents transfixed beneath them. The car skimmed over the treetops, ticka-ticka-ticka. Those kids looked down chimneys and pigeons stared back up at them. Suddenly, there was the tar supermarket rooftop. The little one in the middle begins to cry as they drop, flipping over a power line. They hit.

We were kept from the subsequent coverage, but I heard my father rehash it at a block party. All Olivia and I cared about was that the county denied an amusement ride operator a permit for four years afterward.

I give Dee a fright as she emerges from a guest bedroom. From my perch I hiss, "Make everyone leave."

"I'm trying. Your sister and her husband arrived, and everyone's catching up."

Dee sits down. "So your mom, she says to me, 'Barry's always telling me how you're a real go-getter.' As I puff all up, she says then, 'So get me a lime for my G&T.' She *is* a stitch."

"More like receiving about twenty of them, without anesthetic. Her feistiness isn't always funny. She's a small doser. Mom is relentless. She'll pursue something, back it into a corner, pummel it, and then ask for a hug. Dad called it long ago. He said, 'Give her an inch and she'll take your smile'." I stand. "What were you up here ransacking for?"

Her admission: "After the card, I thought there might be a gift hidden too."

"So what'd the scavenger hunt turn up?

"I didn't find anything."

Someone has started the vacuum. Dee and I look at each other, knowing who. The house is full of unspeakable grief, but Mom has decided the carpet nap must be perky.

Dee dims the hallway. "Go lay back down."

I hand her the two dollars in my pocket. "Buy yourself a Coke or something."

Chapter Three

Flock

THE star of a funeral is the departed. Their performance, however, will be understandably low-key and in pantomime. It's left to another character to anchor the action.

That will be me. And it's the archetypal actor's nightmare: I don't know all of my lines.

I've come out of wardrobe dressed for the part. I study myself in the enormous ornate mirror I'd rescued from a beautiful downtown supper club. A large triangle of frame broke off when I pried it from the plaster wall. Rather than patch it, I dabbed the jagged corner in red paint, like an appendage had been brutally hacked off in a gold leaf ambush. Placement on the stairway landing wall was intentional, the final pause for Andy and me to check our look. The reflection back connected the dots of our life in this house—when Andy learned home highlighting was a bad idea, that suspenders made me look like Mork, that the male equivalent of cameltoe was moose knuckles.

Was it only three nights ago that Andy linked his arm through my own? "We look like American Gothic," he'd grinned. "And yes, you're the wife. At what point do we frost this looking glass?"

These are the kinds of things we would suppose, staring into a proscenium that would gradually transport us from Calvin Klein to cardigan to caftan.

Now I see a black suit. Maybe I'm someone's consigliore, or a maître d', a member of a jazz band, but not someone bound for a funeral home. I also see the beginnings of a fever blister. Tragic widower, tragic herpetic.

I go to find some Abreva and peer out the window. Parked in our circular driveway is a gunmetal-gray van with Imagenation on both sides. "Videography, Post-Production, Multi-Media," its doors tell me. I hear the doorbell. Mom and Olivia duel in stereo: "I've got it!"

"Keep doing what you're doing."

"I'm closer."

Then there's Potsy: "Your fiery mother/daughter dynamics are entertaining, but someone please answer the door."

I hear fragments of an exchange between Mom, Olivia, and an unknown person:

"You're off your rocker!"

That was Mom.

"Your timing leaves a little to be desired." Olivia is all tact after Mother's belligerence.

"It's beyond ghoulish that you would even show up here! So inappropriate! Like he wants to relive that again and again? Shoo!" Mom yells.

I come down the stairs. "Ladies, what was that about? Really, Mom? Shoo?"

At least half of Olivia's white linen blouse is unbuttoned, its tail untucked into an ankle-length prairie dress. Despite a dozen people telling her, it will remain that way all day. One shoe is also untied. She looks to Mom, who answers.

"One of your neighbors with a nose problem. They saw the people and the commotion. It's called a phone."

"That's not what it sounded like."

Mom wedges something into her purse and changes the subject. "Your Aunt Sarajane called. She isn't coming but sent a planter. At least Hayley won't have to go to the kennel." To Potsy: "Hayley's my little Ewok. She's a Pomeranian."

Potsy's face alights. He might not be able to stop a sniggering reference to the urban legend of old ladies coaxing oral sex from their Pomeranians. Before he can go there, I ask, "How's S.J.'s balance problem?"

"What's a balance problem?" Potsy asks.

I struggle with a black onyx cufflink. "Our aunt claims she has to walk backwards or otherwise she collapses like a marionette whose strings have been cut."

"Sounds like inner ear," Potsy supposes.

"They've tried physical therapy, tubes; just like a child, but nothing helps," Mom says.

"Try inner child." Olivia turns to Potsy. "Aunt Sarajane has always been competitive with illness. If you had a heart attack, she's had two. Poison ivy? She's got shingles. She permanently lost her sense of smell when someone at Rotary had bronchitis."

"Anosmia! It's called anosmia, and it's the real deal!" Mom interjects.

"After a neighbor broke a hip, Sarajane developed this 'con-deeee-shun', as she pronounces it," I explain.

"If she had a good backbeat, she'd be moonwalking," Olivia adds.

"Don't you make fun, Livvie! My only grandchild sounds like a seedy room somewhere!" Mom wags her head. "I myself have stopped S.J. from pitching forward. She's very self-conscious."

My aunt is a pill, which my father also fondly called my mother, which makes the two sisters medications, likely something to do with mucous or phlegm. Sarajane drove a city sanitation truck for years, the only female in the department, after her alcoholic husband abandoned her and their daughter Clementine. At fifty-eight, she got Bo Derek-inspired cornrows. About two years ago, she was arrested on a utility pole helping herself to her neighbor's cable television, something she called "sharing." This was, of course, before she went into irreversible reverse.

Potsy sits on a step. "I'm confused."

Mom kicks his calf. "Well, silly, everyone is. We can't even tell if she's coming or going until she says hi or bye." She hands off her purse with "Take this to my room, Livvie." Olivia excuses herself.

"Her, on an escalator, that would be wild," Potsy muses.

Mom takes the tie from me. "Give me that." She loops it around my neck. "What a great pattern this has."

"It's Andy's," I tell her.

Potsy yells from the kitchen, "I would give Sarajane a hundred bucks to shoot a lay-up."

Mom kisses my cheek. "Go do something with that lip."

WE TAKE our lost episode of *Mama's Family* on the road. I insist on driving Andy's Jeep. Olivia and her husband Ted are in back, with Mom between them. Potsy is in front.

The octagonal corner signage of Frey Funeral Home looms. The brass U in FUNERAL is gone.

Potsy is looking at it too. "Who steals one letter?"

"Fraternity hazing," Ted theorizes. "They'll sneak back one night for an F."

"Maybe it's subliminal advertising. *The only thing missing from F-NERAL is U! Join the party!*" I say tightly.

People are already walking through the parking lot, joining the party before the host.

"It's possible I can't do this," I announce.

Mom grips my shoulder. "Honey, do you feel faint?"

"No, that's not it."

Potsy checks his seat belt. "That's good, since you're at the wheel."

"Keep going if you can't." Mom squeezes my shoulder again.

"I'll go once around the block."

My mother nods. "As slow as you want."

"This sums you up, Mom," Olivia protests. "It's why neither of us finish what we start."

Mom leans back. "God, Livvie, I love you more than my new partial, but this isn't about you not able to work this morning's Sugoki."

"Sudoku," I correct Mom. Then I mutter lamely to my sister, "Olivia, I finish lots of things."

"Just like you never approved of our friends," Olivia announces.

"Where does this come from? *Please* tell me this isn't about that filthy little Taylor girl you dragged home. She had bites and sores all over her legs."

"Their house had fleas. That didn't make them bad people."

"That house was the Gulag with latticework, always dark and closed up. God knows what went on in there." Mom shivers. "The entire family should've been put on a flatbed truck and run through a car wash."

"Bites and sores," Potsy repeats between laughs.

This is how it has worked for years. To Olivia, every perceived slight is a branding iron; Mom vigorously acquits her harsh parenting skills like Judge Judy without the lace collar.

"There's a playground near here," I suggest. "Maybe you two could just throw sand in each other's eyes."

Tense rapidspeak, now. The topic is Mrs. Taylor. "The mother had a face like a pan of slugs."

Olivia ignores this. "Of course you have to go in, Barry."

"Livvie, he doesn't have to do squat! It's barbaric! I wish you'd sit up straight. You're going to end up with a hunch."

"I've got a hunch, lady, that's for sure."

Trying to referee, Ted says both of their names, pausing meaningfully between each. Ted often speaks like this, like he's reading an eye chart, never wanting to be misconstrued.

Potsy tries to reignite the skirmish. "What does a pan of slugs look like?"

I just want to get out of this Jeep and get inside. In comparison, the funeral home will be my day spa. The five of us walk in measured steps until we all see the WWOH-TV van, idling not far.

"I'm hoping that TV truck isn't about Andy," I mutter.

"Isn't that the station you went all Nate Berkus on?" Potsy asks.

I nod. I worked, very briefly, as a correspondent for a local network affiliate after I was named a Rising Star Finalist by The Fashion Group International, Inc. A young producer wanted to try something highbrow. I would be their Cultural Enthusiast, reporting on design and art trends, what motivated them globally, what they meant locally. I debuted with a segment on the semantic difference between a keeping room and a family room. We watched from the sofa. I began shrieking as my jazz hands played Dixie and silk purses tumbled from my mouth. "Was that just a sssssssssibilant S with a lithp chaser?"

Andy roared. "You're speaking in two gay tongues!" I quit the next morning.

I still have Nate's same calculatedly sloppy forelock. Plus Nate Berkus and I now share one other common element: horrendous loss.

Mom stops. "A private funeral is newsworthy how?"

"The incident was in USA Today," Ted says, which I didn't know. "You're a big city now. You've had a crane collapse."

Potsy reluctantly adds, "Stay off YouTube."

Mom asks what that is; Ted describes it for her as Potsy says that "some morbid fuck—sorry, Jeanine—uploaded it."

"Didn't Nina show us that riot on there?" Olivia asks Ted, who nods. "And a tornado tearing up a farm, those poor cows running for their lives?"

Mom can't help a parenting jab. "It's good to know when Nina's head isn't in the clouds she's gloating over the misfortune of others. What's that word?" She takes several swipes at pronouncing schadenfreude.

I laugh. "You mangle the English language so bad it's homicide, Mom."

"Someone please tell me how this is legal?" she demands, outraged. "Can't you get a restraining order against YouToo?"

"YouTube, Mom." I try to be practical. "Internet 101: once it's out there, it can't be taken back."

DUTIFULLY somber employees greet visitation arrivals. Olivia takes her place at Guest Registry; Ted stands with her. Mr. Frey talks to me with his fingertips, like he's playing Itsy-Bitsy-Spider. He thanks me as though I sacrificed Andy to scratch his back for steering business to Great Rooms! when we opened floral. His peculiar wording suggests he might next offer me a loyalty punch card.

I move into the main parlor. I pause at a beautiful epergne of Meyer lemons. I find no card. Maybe the sender thought it statement enough on my life now: make lemonade.

The air becomes heady with tuberose. These, massively bunched, are from the Great Rooms! staff. People's clothing will still bear the scent when they return home, it's that thick.

Potsy dances past me. "Eerie, creaky joint." He touches the flocked wallpaper. "The walls don't have ears, they have whiskers."

A woman of tremendous girth lumbers past, barely nodding at me. Potsy lunges before I can identify her. "Who's the total babe with the stomachs in her legs? Those calves look directly fed."

"Dolores. Andy and Alex's oldest sister."

"She wore a polka dot sundress to a funeral home?"

Kerrick is almost apologetic for her. "In fairness, the dots *are* black."

"One word: sleeves," Potsy offers. "Her arms remind me of those long lumpy bags of popcorn you got at the ten-cent store."

"That's Yvonne, the other sister," I point without pointing.

"Yvonne loves her hush puppies too," Potsy snarls.

She's as big as Dolores, even more imbalanced by a sugar-spun coiffure. She eyes clustered cock's comb with suspicion. Dipped carnations are more her style. She'll happen upon those soon enough, the eighty-five dollar FTD arrangements holding seven dollars' worth of flora.

"She puts the *air* in hair," Potsy trills. "And wearing a harlequin blouse! They know this isn't a Punch n' Judy revival, right?"

Yvonne doesn't hide her disgust for me. She actually bares her teeth, which are very small, like baby's teeth, with lavender gums encroaching upon them.

"She has a likeness of the Pope textured into her living room ceiling," I tell him.

"This cracks my shit up," Potsy whoops.

Dee joins us. "Funerals equal fun."

"Even without the U," I remark.

Ted's right behind Dee. "So is it Potsy like in *Happy Days*?"

"It's Potsy like in stoner," Dee says with disgust. "Look at his glassy eyes. This'll be the first time you see a pallbearer do a one-hitter on the walk to the gravesite."

His breath is usually a heady halitosis of marijuana and the mints he sucks to blunt the smell. At work, though, he is professorial, with his shaved head and round, silver Lennon specs.

Olivia, somehow wronged again, comes huffing. "So why is Ted not a pallbearer?"

I sigh. "No one is. Dee's being facetious."

"In fairness, our city magazine named Potsy Finest Concierge in their annual recap," Kerrick offers.

"Because he knows all the best dealers and pimps," says Dee.

"And listening to you, Dee, is like slow-stirring risotto." Hearing everything is part of Potsy's concierge prowess. He anticipates what hotel guests want from their private lobby conversations before they ask.

"Barry was chosen Best Store in the same issue," Dee continues.

Potsy cuts off Dee before she can add she was listed Top Realtor. "Barry, Alexander's coming in."

Dee's sharp intake of breath probably sucked some flock off the wall. "I forgot how much they looked alike."

"Even with his carbface," Potsy observes.

He is Andy's double with a considerable paunch. His lazy gait is that arrogant John Wayne walk certain men develop. Sun-loving blonde wife Melinda holds his arm.

"Terracotta Donatella there, she's the wife?" Potsy asks.

"Melinda… Mindy. She runs a tanning salon."

"Or eats a shitload of carrots. Or dove into Georgia clay on the way here." Potsy stares.

"Dolores and Yvonne hate her too. She's too bronze, I'm too pink."

Potsy's voice softens. "Maybe it's just me, but Alexander pings a little."

"*Everyone* pings to you, Pots. Your head must sound like an arcade."

His voice remains sultry. "Well, I've always had this twin brother fantasy. Andy ever say if they fooled around, all horned-up-teenaged-boy-stuff?"

"We are in a funeral home without the U," I state, then I relent. "Once they laid side by side and jacked each other off."

Potsy is wordless. It is better than he expected.

I prep myself for a confrontation. "I need to be proactive about the obituary. The paper misprinted that Andy was survived by a *bother*, not *brother*. He'll say I meant to."

Potsy awakes from reverie. "Wait a sec! Did Andy say if they had identical dicks too?"

"One appetizer is all you get."

I go over. Alexander waits for me to speak. I don't. I did the heavy lifting and made the approach. Finally, he manages, "This was bad news."

His identical twin had perished and that was it, as though the Dow had unexpectedly tumbled.

"The worst," I reply.

Mindy tries. "We appreciated not hearing it secondhand."

Alexander swivels his neck awkwardly in a white shirt that's tight and worn. I can see the mushroom pattern of his chest hair through it, just like Andy's. "I suppose you've had the calls," he says.

"Such like?"

"Ambulance   chasers,   then   that   construction   company headquarters. We figured you'd already sicced some hotshot on everyone, but we gave them your number, being legally entitled." Then, the jab. "As Andy's notarized, hand-couriered envelopes to all of us made very clear years ago."

He wants to spar, I'll spar.

"With almost no rights, we count on our paperwork, Alex."

We'd spent thousands with our attorney Raoul, anticipating situations like this, thousands more to have our living wills scrutinized anew during the Terri Schiavo debacle. Complacency meant being barred from hospital visitation, house locks being changed by moralizing family members. Any ambiguity was completely rewritten to be very explicit about our estate(s). We even considered one of us adopting the other to legally share a last name.

"No eulogy. Nothing faith-based," Alexander notes.

"Andy's wishes."

He snorts. "That's right. He considered religion a 'narcotic'. Well, God helps me sleep, that's all I know."

I turn to Mindy. "Where are the boys?"

Alexander flips a hand toward Miss Sondra. "They're not coming. We didn't know what to expect."

Mindy takes his arm in reproach. "Lexie, don't point at him."

"You mean shim," he snorts.

"It's herm," I offer.

Suzi edges in. "Barry? I think your mom's being sick in the Ladies Room." I follow her. Suzi blurts over her shoulder, "Actually, she prefers *fellady*."

I find Mom. She's wan. I grab a bottled water from the many on every table. Apparently, this is the new tissue of mourning. I don't get it. When my eyes, cheeks, and nose are damp, the last thing I care to introduce is something else wet.

"It's just all in my gut," she says between sips. "No parent wants to see their child in this kind of pain."

I find an adjunct room for us to get our bearings. This could be dangerous. A wrong door and it's Mason jars of formaldehyde, a glowering embalmer, and someone's naked great grandfather on a metal table. The one I choose opens to a very pink graveyard. It's like a Container Store. No casket is larger than thirty-six inches long. We have larger ice chests in our garage rafters.

Mom stands alongside one of the elevated vaults. "They brought Dad and me to a showroom like this when Daisy left us. They called it Babyland."

Mom rarely spoke of Daisy, the dead sister who preceded Olivia and me. She had drowned in her own fluids in Mom's arms after a brief respiratory issue. We were never privy to the mind-numbing terror our parents felt as medical intervention failed and prayers in the hospital chapel went unanswered for the little broken doll handed to my devastated mother. Shattered, they didn't try for another child for five years. When Olivia came, Daisy's crib, toy box, even a mobile made of daisies, they all sensibly became the new baby girl's. Those Daisy petals left behind, more than anything, informed my sister's young sense of self, that she was the replacement. It goes without saying Olivia was endlessly ill, on so many antibiotics her sweat could open up sewer lines. Most children put up lemonade stands; my sister talked of opening a pharmacy. Her fixation on sickness turned into one for food, so she grew very fat and then, by her Sweet Sixteen party, very thin, a raging bulimic stockpiling laxatives.

With no visual representation available to us, Daisy was a cipher. When we asked about the origin of Daisy, we were told about F. Scott Fitzgerald and Gatsby, but after a Sunday afternoon of musicals on a local TV station, we knew it might have more to do with Dogpatch and Li'l Abner. Olivia asked who she was named after, and she was told the actress, de Havilland. Mine was after a boyish actor/dancer. I looked it up. That was Ken Berry, with an E, I protested. Mom shrugged. "That would be a stupid way to spell a boy's name." We were mostly relieved Mom had gotten botanical names out of her system. Olivia's life would have been harder if christened Peony, and I can't wrap my head around Basil, even though I love pesto.

My mother pets every small casket, tamping down lace trim on a tiny satin pillow. She frowns at one, painted and accessorized to look like a racecar, and seems to ready to speak. I wait for her to elaborate. Daisy's death cast a lifelong shadow. Mom would extinguish news reports about children starving in third-world countries, and she and Dad contributed mightily to St. Jude Children Research Hospital, any and every annual tax refund. But I'm not to learn more on this day.

"The faces change, but the script remains the same," she finally says. "Full Crock-Pots, empty words. 'Oh, Jeanine, he's at peace.' Malarkey! And watch for people's agendas! You and Olivia were no better with your jabbering. 'Make no changes for one year. Stay in the house! Keep the boat, we'll go skiing!' *That* was rich!"

I remember. "I guess we were know-it-alls."

"Don't let anyone tell you how to grieve." Then she stage-manages the pathos. "You don't owe anyone out there tears, my dear." What she means is remain dry-eyed in public, period. She didn't cry at Dad's funeral. "Just treat it like an assembly line, honey." She walks me through the door. "Do the work, then clock out."

This is so my mother. Set your face and keep it that way. The advice is unnecessary. I want no more cracks to show, especially not after my poolside antics. Mom is, of course, right. I keep my emotions in check, not to assuage my mother or be a tough guy for Alexander, but as a tribute to Andy. He grew up dodging his father's tirades and his sisters' rosary-wringing and would have hated my scene at the pool.

Not that it's easy, with the hot breath on my neck that leaves behind this sad dew of consolation, with the handshakes that smell like someone's steering wheel. Whether I'm on a conveyor belt or a Lazy Susan, I can't decide. The former implies one efficient pass at condolences whereas the latter, with several visitors coming back for a second helping of grief, is more accurate. One woman returns to grab at my chest. I'm startled until I see the small angel pin she intends to affix.

"I almost forgot this. I wore one of these the entire time Brandon was in Iraq."

I thank her. Knowing that he had died there, however, gives me little confidence in its restorative power.

Someone sneezing and hacking hurtles toward me. I feel helpless. One violent cough blows the card out of a spray of gladioli. It would be poor form to take out the travel-sized Purell from my left inner jacket pocket.

One man signs "I'm sorry." He worked in the bank's proofing department. He once shared with Andy that the one sound he longed to hear was himself peeing. Haltingly, I gesture back.

Someone follows him with a white cane. He wears no dark glasses and his unfocused eyes are weird. I don't know anyone blind. Maybe Andy did. It could be a Great Rooms! customer. Or someone neither of us knew, a "Looky Lou," as Dee disparages those Sunday open-house arrivals who have no intention of buying. Well, he can't see. Good luck with the Looky.

His sightless eyes find me.

I feel like I'm in a horror film.

Which I am.

Kerrick has an alert: "In walked The Totem Pole."

That's what we always called the other VPs from Andy's bank, three-piece suits and low heels. Some I like, others were his frenemies, a few I don't recognize, probably transplants from governmental seizures and mergers Andy always survived.

"They're here to revoke my free checking," I predict.

LezbyAnn punches the air, ready to fight. "This has fucked me up ferocious, and I'm no pussy. I threw shit at my goddamn TV and it's not even paid off. 'Bite my left tit!' I told that newswhore."

Yvonne and Alexander's eyes meet and roll at her man's tux shirt.

"All the useless spooge mules in this universe who deserve to die, Andrew Morgan gets took? The Lord truly fucking blows."

"LezbyAnn," I say, nodding, "you took the words right out of my... sewer."

"You can always count on the cunning lingo of LezbyAnn." Potsy smirks, mussing my hair like I'm a child.

Dee takes LezbyAnn's arm and drops her voice to congratulate me. "That no-minister thing? Good call."

Absently shaking hands, I watch and listen, fearful of LezbyAnn's fearlessness.

"Find me an ashtray, dude," she's saying to Dee.

"You can't light up in here."

"Fuck me with a table leg! Who doesn't need a cigarette to work through this shit?"

Potsy shakes his head. "This gets more *Sordid Lives* by the minute."

I glance at my open palm at a business card. "Whoever handed me this was good, like a pickpocket. I didn't even know it."

Potsy takes it and reads: "*G.R.P.L.* Grieving Person's League. Some support group."

Kerrick offers me a piece of chewing gum.

They keep coming.

Potsy whispers, "It's The CoDepends."

A Liberace pompadour and Dame Edna's eyewear shuffle toward me. Lou and Herb are old queens we met at gay tennis. They sat on benches and provided hilarious commentary on whose balls were out. They are both wearing something at the throat not quite ascot, not quite tie.

"Did you know that your Andrew helped straighten out our retirement?" Herb says, his smile kind.

Lou leaps in. "And thank God! We'd have been destitute! Tell Barry how you got into day-trading on margin, Herb!"

Herb yanks him away. "This isn't the place, Lou!"

Gregsquared offer their thoughts. This is when I begin to notice everything is in past tense.

"I hope you know how you two were admired," Greg Number One says. "You were role models, even."

In almost any other circumstance, it would be pleasurable to be told that Andy and I were not envied for our creature comforts but for our individualism. Today it just makes me realize I didn't know what we had.

"Well, the thought of being role models, like adulterous pro golfers and larcenous ministers, is kinda ick-producing," I tell them.

"He means you never became shorthand, like us," Greg Number Two adds.

"I'm sure we did," I smile. "Bardy, Brandy, Andry, whatever."

Greg Number Two shakes his head. "No, you didn't."

"Well, you're both named Greg," I point out. "Gregsquared makes sense."

Greg Number Two says, "It's gotten damned old."

Greg Number One looks stunned. They retreat. I hope they don't break up right here. They just can't. This is *my* day.

Potsy is at my side, pointing to Gregsquared: "Before." Then, to Herb and Lou: "After."

Andy and I will never be an After.

An ugly confrontation, inaudible at first, flares between Potsy and Andy's sister Dolores. I quickly make sense of it.

"You intentionally stomped my foot," Potsy accuses.

Dolores hunches her formidable shoulders. "If you weren't flitting around so much...."

"Say you're sorry."

"Wear a masculine shoe." She turns away.

He grabs one of her many elbows. "Lend me yours, you fat bitch."

Alexander intervenes. "What did you call my sister?"

"Aka America's Largest Domino?" Potsy snaps.

Kerrick and Ted, even LezbyAnn, intercede.

When a tall man with long auburn hair and a longer beard in loose linen and sandals, Andy's massage therapist, enters, Dee says softly, "Our Lord is here." His stride has quiet dignity but his aura is only an essential oil.

I scan the room. What I see is a tranny who refers to her penis as a vagina with a neck, the morbidly obese, the luridly thin, a lesbian in a cummerbund, a hopping gay man, a Mohawk, the deaf, blind, and halt, octogenarians, a woman the color of butternut squash, several blacks, and one Hispanic. With the exception of Jesus, it looks like a recruitment ad for Equal Opportunity Employment with the state.

I do not let my eyes drift to the conveyance. That's what Mr. Frey called it. To me, a conveyance was Mercy B., which I have renamed Merciless Bitch; all that money and effort, and my luxury car was the machine that delivered Andy to his death. I'm glad Merciless Bitch wound up in a salvage yard, just as I want nothing to do with the stainless-steel vault. To acknowledge it will acknowledge that I know that Andy isn't just detained by a train he this time waited out; it will make a lie of the amnesia scenario I conjured in bed last night. I had declined to provide something personal to be placed inside, but were I to, in a moment of shrieking madness, fling open the lid, would I see that Mr. Frey had barely bothered stitching the wounds? Was Andy's hair repositioned properly after the autopsy scalping? Or had I been told the awful truth: that his body was human carpaccio, unfit to look upon?

I can't even kiss him good-bye, much less back to life. I'm going to pretend the casket is our refrigerator, on its side, without the icemaker, that just happens to have a framed photograph on it of Andy in a baseball cap, crouched in front of Gertie and Noel.

That's what I'm going to do.

Chapter Four

Aftershocks

GATEKEEPERS insulate me from the inquisitive, the intrusive, the interlopers. Dee takes messages. Kerrick opens mail. Potsy lies a lot. Others, like LezbyAnn, try to busy me with excursions. She invites me to a grocery dumpster to help catch fresh rats for her new python. As appealing as rabies sounds, I still say no. Tracy and Matt invite me over for game night. I don't feel real lucky these days; I beg off. I finally leave the house when Stan takes me to the southern part of the state to shop for gourds and pumpkins and walk among the fall color. A recent chemical peel has left his face vaguely feminized, almost like he's wearing a rubber mask. He has brought a new Protégé. Fade describes both the boy's haircut and the way he finishes most sentences. "Indian corn's funny…." I lean in, ready to hear why, but that's it. The day trip ends badly when I see someone walking a pug. I have a come-apart at the base of a great oak. Stan, in $300 ripped jeans belted too high, herds me back into the Prius and gives me a chamois from under the seat to blow my nose. The Protégé gazes out the window. "When I cried this one time…."

But many of them have demanding jobs or just spider plants to water, and slowly, they get back to it. I send each off with their own, personalized condolence relish tray. My hope is to never see a cornichon again.

Olivia and Ted left five days ago. When Mom burst into their bedroom without a knock to announce it was time to go brassiere shopping because "a decent fit is critical, and you're looking swayback," I'm surprised my sister didn't snatch Mom bald-headed.

Mom is the last sentinel. She departs today. I'm retrieving from the dry cleaner what she calls her good dress.

Gwen latches the good dress and my black suit onto a hook and plucks off a stapled baggy. "This here is stuff what was in your pocket." In the baggy are the angel pin and the GRPL business card. Gwen glances at the register. "My machine tells me your better half's also got a shirt here going back to September 17."

She goes off to part whooshing plastic.

So one of that Saturday's stops was here, to leave the shirt that he couldn't keep on. I'm flummoxed by both this and that she doesn't know. How could she not? Andy's face had been everywhere for several days. But the kidnap of a convenience store clerk, and her discovery barely alive in her own car trunk and left in a parking garage to die, bumped Andy from the front page. The details of this young mother of three's brutalization—two thugs, still at large, had apparently used a vegetable peeler up and down her arms and back—were so chilling Andy's death couldn't compare nor would he, competitive though he was, have wanted it to. The newspaper updates on the ColonyScape Luxury Townhomes crane collapse became smaller, then pictureless; Andy went from banking veep to a local male, easy for Gwen to miss.

She returns with Andy's Tommy Bahama shirt.

"Tell Andy we cracked every button," she teases. "And you tell him Gwen said hey."

I back out, saying. "You know I will."

Why didn't I just carefully tell her? "I lost him, Gwen."

What if she, eternally sunny, sassed back, "How do you mislay a 185-pound man?"

Then I'd have to say, "No, Gwen. Really."

I BRING the day's mail in. Most bills and correspondence are joint. I open what's addressed to Andy. There have been no soap-opera bombshells—a secret child, Swiss account—just mostly invitations to resubscribe to something. My sympathy cards I divide into two stacks: those who didn't visit the funeral home and want to explain why, and those mourners who did but are following up, double-dipping like it was a job interview and they want to reiterate their resume's strengths.

Some sweetly acknowledge Noel and Gertie by signing their cards with their pets' names.

Mom is tidying the kitchen in her pink clam-diggers, choice leisurewear from a Blair catalog that she calls "my clams." In them, she looks ready to stomp grapes. She studies our coffeemaker as though it has athlete's foot. "I should run vinegar through this. Andy probably took care of things like that."

"The same way Andy would wipe his butt with Kleenex before he'd replace an empty roll. And, if he did, the cardboard tube just bumped around on the floor, never making it to a trash can. Yeah, Mom, let me tell you what Andy took care of."

Perceiving this as the precursor to an irrational fit, Mom announces, "I do believe I'll change my ticket for four thousand bucks and hang around a little longer."

"It's been two weeks. You're worn out."

She is. Her wig looks like a flat beanie and her face is the color of my wrist. It's also worn *me* out.

"I'm just not used to all these stairs." She runs hot water. "Some woman brought three boxes by from the bank. She'd been crying. They're by your office bookcase."

How awful that Andy's assistant was given this unenviable cleanup before being tossed back into the secretarial pool. She secretly loved Andy. She would stay as late as he, unasked. I'm sure the packing peanuts inside are still damp with her tears.

Mom scoops up the matching silver dog bowls that say Gertrude and Noel.

"Leave those, please."

"Just going to wipe them out, honey."

I hand her a paw-shaped card I'd opened. "Everyone from the dog groomers signed it."

She sets aside her soapy cloth. "Sweet."

Then I offer the window envelope that was in the same stack of mail. "Here's the bill they sent separately."

She polishes Gertrude. "Remember when I took up dog grooming? When I became Werewolf Mom?"

I was in middle school when Mom, antsy, decided she could shear the dogs of friends and neighbors in our house at discount pricing. *How hard can it be*, she rationalized to our skeptical dad. She had a sign made with just her name: *Jeanine Grooms*. "How perfect-o is that?" she declared, dreaming of a franchise. But many of the dogs were skittish. She'd isolate them in a downstairs half-bath wearing her grooming uniform of acid-washed overalls. Olivia and I would often arrive home to be greeted by a growling standard poodle and Mom's neck and arms looking like they had been seasoned. She had a literal five o'clock shadow. Werewolf Mom. When that shingle came down, she went to work for a carpet outlet, where she remained until my father's first heart attack. Then life became about a home defibrillator, Dad's slide into pneumonia, endless intensive-care stays, and fatal ventricular complications at sixty-five.

She casually hands me Gertrude. "I wish you'd call that big-shot doctor friend of yours I met."

"Steve Chaney? For what? Dr. Steve is an HIV specialist."

"He can write a scrip for venlafaxine, can't he?"

"Are we at a spelling bee?"

"Livvie told me it's the biggie for depression and anxiety."

First Mom insults my cleanliness. Now, in cahoots with my sister, she goes after my stability.

"What are you talking about?"

"I'm not big on tranquilizers. You know how our mother sedated us girls with Miles Nervine." Miles Nervine was a tablet dispensed liberally and often by my grandmother to her "high-strung" daughters, the way copious amounts of Robitussin can calm a child's "recurring cough" today.

"Olivia was on Ritalin, then Prozac."

"A professional diagnosis that got her through a rough patch," she bristles. "Like you, now."

"Mom, I don't need dolls. Sparkle! Nudies! Boobies!" I try to joke.

She's scrubbing Noel. "I introduced you to Jacqueline Susann."

"Actually, I lifted *Valley of the Dolls* from your naughty stash when I was ten." I had devoured them. I didn't then know about Jackie's autistic son Guy or her obsession-and-maybe-an-affair with Ethel Merman. I just craved glamour and its downside.

"Camp doesn't become you. You seem edgy, that's all."

"I have vodka."

"I saw. People now send liquor in lieu of flowers. Here, smartass." She hands me the second bowl. "It's that smartassedness, your sense of humor, that will get you through this."

"I'm now the fun subtractor, the living Post-it that *Shit Happens*."

"That's in your head. I've seen you work a room. You will again."

I reposition the empty bowls on the tile floor. "There's not a big enough lampshade to make the party guests forget."

She's done scrubbing so she busies herself by taking credit.

"You're hardwired like me. You can go from bitchy to breezy so fast pictures go crooked on the wall. Your charm came from your mom, not from your dad. Where your sister got her outlook, who knows? The collected works of Edgar Allan Poe, maybe."

I load the Jeep with her luggage. When I go to find Mom, she's walking the grounds, as she said she would, taking pictures with a disposable camera. "I'm going to show these off Thursday at my Bright Spotters potluck."

Mom and women with names like Ella and Bev, who equate boredom with community service, designated themselves the Bright Spotters and share a mission: to reinvigorate my hometown. The downtown's blight, raped like so many by a Walmart Supercenter, had crept into virtually every neighborhood, and blocks of glorious Victorian and Tudor homes, once historic, became transient boarding houses, a DIRECTV dish the only thing holding roof shingles on. Every month, the Bright Spotters trolled for nice homes, essentially pitting neighbors against one another in an upkeep competition they knew nothing about. If a house didn't have a barking dog tied to a metal pipe wearing a dusty doughnut into the front yard, it qualified. The reward was a large sign placed in their grass: THIS IS A TOWN BRIGHT SPOT! Mom proudly carries a laminated proclamation from the mayor, a high school classmate of mine who everyone knew set small animals afire. The only thing I ever thought he'd proclaim was "paper or plastic?"

"How are Our Ladies of the Fluorescent Rash?" This is my own name for her caucus.

"Shut up."

She dons these weird wraparound sunglasses. I change my mind about the grape stomping. Mom is clearly going to spot-weld.

She's thoughtful as we drive to the airport. "Your sister held up well."

"Olivia's coping mechanisms were not uppermost," I say, trying not to sound tight.

"You were close once."

"We're not *not* close."

"She says you rarely talk on the phone."

"That doesn't mean we're estranged. She could call."

"You have to take the initiative. You know how she can drift."

"She just exists on a different plane. Olivia's existential."

Mom corrects me. "She doesn't meditate or chant. She just stops thinking. She lapses into a faraway gaze if you ask her the time. Give a girl credit, though… it can't be easy, ceasing all thought. You can look at her and practically guess her PIN number." She glances furtively behind, as though Olivia hides in the backseat. "Your sister, she was on to something that day, in the car. Her disadvantage was being born after Daisy. We never made her finish, we enforced nothing. Feel clumsy in ballet, drop out, choose what you wear to school, your bedroom's a wreck, fine by me, fall off horseback riding and we won't make you get back on. We set the bar too low for her."

"You should be saying all that to Olivia."

Whatever culpability is within Mom's reach retracts. "So she can second-guess every life choice and stick her finger down her throat all over again? No sirree. She is a triumph of therapy and Ted." Mom rifles through her paisley carry-on. "Very early we knew you'd exceed all expectations. You didn't come from much, but look how you turned out."

I negotiate the confusing lanes that funnel us toward the departure terminal. "Oh, come on, you and Dad were fine people. You make yourself sound like the Joads."

"No one ever gave us awards or interviewed us or put us on TV. "

"Publicity is about the gallery, not me."

"The gallery *is* you. It's your footprint. Dad was so proud. I'm glad he lived to see your swimming pool. He thought a person had it made when they could put in their own swimming pool."

Mom trades out her Crocs for an open-toed sandal that cries to be closed. Her feet look like baking potatoes with five eyes. "You need a Ped Egg! Pronto!"

"Concentrate on the road."

A jet takes flight over a St. Vitus Community Hospital and Wellness Center billboard and folds into the overcast sky.

"What will get me through this, Mom?"

She takes my hand. "Find joy whenever you can. Something as piddly as a baby smiling at you in the mall."

"Will I ever be happy again?"

"Do we even know we're happy when we're happy?"

"This is my question, not yours."

"We all ask variations of it. Just please. Stay off that TubeYouth."

"YouTube, Mom."

"Promise me you will."

"I promise you I will."

NO WAY smartass can keep this promise.

Great Rooms! general manager, Isaac, has sent checks that require my signature. I can tend to these checks anywhere in the house, but I choose my office. I want to maximize temptation. I find Isaac's offer to Skype me into staff meetings. I'm not ready to face them, wrapped fisheye around the long table so they can all be seen, all unwarranted bursts of applause, then, after "see you soon!" and the conference room camera is determined to be safely inactive, they will concur that my voice was shaky and I looked really down.

I sign everything. I jot *you're good 2 go w/o me* on the bottom of Isaac's note. I put the ledger in the old galvanized metal milk box on our front stoop for pickup.

I return to my office. I look down at the boxes couriered from Andy's corporate office. I lie to the corrugated cartons by promising aloud to tend them later. I have no intention of going into his office upstairs, maybe ever.

I disable my pug screen saver. I left-click the mouse. YouTube digests my typed keywords, words like crane, the city, the date.

I have at least a dozen options. All are about forty-six seconds. I scroll. Unbelievably, I find more.

Still more.

Some people have channels uniquely dedicated to the documentation of death, a horrible party line tapping into a 24-7 world of snuff films, once so vilified by anti-porn crusaders, now readily accessible and totally unregulated. Hit after hit after hit. The beheading of Daniel Pearl. That Nyda video from Iran. The NASCAR driver in Las Vegas. Stage rigging collapsing at an outdoor venue. Unflinching slaughterhouse footage grabbed by animal-rights infiltrators.

Of the three thumbnails YouTube typically provides the uploader to select from their video, some chose a still frame where nothing has yet happened; others, a burst of debris and dust, the blurry hint of what's to come; a few went for full apocalypse. It's all about marketing. I suppose, if pressed to select one, I would opt for the second, the first being boring, the third too obscured.

I will not faint this time.

If I do, at least I'm in a chair.

I click on a high-res version from *BoomCrunch11*.

Some of the very beginning is indecipherable, phrases like "... get more B-roll," something muffled, then "no, no tripod, we'll get it handheld," more conversation with holes in it.

I see Merciless Bitch, no movement within. Then the crane crumples.

Crashes. Screams. It's easy to convince yourself it's CGI. It looks almost staged, with *Blair Witch*-y camerawork as its operator runs toward the site for a zoom-in money shot of Merciless Bitch being slowly buried.

It freezes.

I watch it again.

Not being a civil engineer, it is hard to understand what I see. As precarious as it appeared, why still did nothing hold? It is not hard to understand why no one could survive it. The pelting brick is like shrapnel.

I watch it again.

I see other things. A jogging man in a rugby shirt comes into the furthest corner of the frame. His head jerks up. He was one of those bloodied and injured, I assume.

I watch it again.

I see a bird take flight from a pole seconds before. It knew.

I click on another. This version appears to have been shot off a TV screen with a video camera; I can see the reflection of an ottoman in the lower left corner.

I'm filled with rage by the juvenile, pointless viewer comments beneath:

Dyam that's intense!

awesome $100k car

boring you can't see a body or anything

faked... looks professionally shot

been kewler if the car fuel caused xplosion 2

Hawt! Post more like this

How phucked. Do these short attention-span necrophiles keep hand lotion on their mouse pad for the juiciest stuff? It's a safe bet these are the same folks who circulate fake celebrity death stories.

Another artsy uploader has made it a very contrasty black and white. Why? Did they think Windows Moviemaker would pump up its appeal?

I understand a certain addictiveness. Hell, I myself tingled when I got positive eBay feedback. But this discomfiting viral access *is* new. I'm bewildered. What are my rights? My loss may legally be public domain. Can I stop this from turning up in a *Faces of Death* compilation? During 9/11, I pitied those families who recognized the face of a jumper on TV, who wondered what coworker was holding hands with their son on the way down. Now, that's me. Even if some cease-and-desist miraculously managed to strike Andy's video from every search engine, it's still too late. It only takes one ghoul to capture it as his Clip of the Week, and it's resyndicated seconds after the posting was removed. Because it's all about that. Don't fact-check, don't be fair-minded, just be first. Andy's accident will forever be an .flv or .avi or .mp4, compressed, coded, embedded in hundreds of social and networking sites. He's a URL link. To what end? This was unavoidable, unlike the teenager who swallowed a handful of pills on his webcam as people passively watched his suicide and did nothing but LOL. It's not like Andy pulled a thread and made a sweater unravel. The car was inside the lines. If his parking had actually been more careless, at a slight angle, he might have been severely injured, but alive.

Nothing can be learned from what happened to him, not like those others. Don't be a journalist in a war-torn country. Don't be president. Don't race professionally. Don't go to concerts at state fairs. Don't eat meat.

I click on the next. It stops to buffer repeatedly. I grow restless. Let's get on with the show. How shameful.

I return to *BoomCrunch11*. His at least disallowed viewer comments.

I watch the forty-six seconds many times, pretending I have a touch-sensitive overlay that allows me to manipulate what happened.

I brush the screen. If I move the crane twenty yards to the left.... I could parallel park the Mercedes on the opposite street. I'll brace the left quadrant. If that doesn't work, I can cup the rain of mortar. Mostly, I blot the dust with moistened fingertip, trying to find Andy and Noel and Gertie.

This is how I spend my next few days, playing this haunting videogame.

I GO to where Andy rests, to sprinkle grass seed on the cracked mound. Necessity had forced my hand; of all the things we'd preplanned, interment was not one of them. The plot overlooks nothing special. I saw no reason to pay a premium fee for a sunrise view. Unless this is a George Romero film, what's to appreciate?

A groundsman on a riding lawnmower is slowly chugging through wrought-iron portals when I flag him down.

"What's the deal with the watering system?" I want to know.

He diminishes the mower. "The summer help, they're kids, they ain't careful mowing and they break the sprinkler heads. I'll look into it."

I tell him I'd appreciate that.

He adds, "So late in the season, though, seed probably won't take."

"I hate it so bare. I like things filled in."

The groundsman points to the mower. I'm just mouthing words.

I blow away what seed has collected in the laser-etched name—Andrew Wayne Morgan—on the flat, rectangular plaque with an optional icon, that of a pug dog, and my own name, Barry Tyler Grooms, and my birthdate. This doesn't make me feel vulnerable. It somehow makes it easier to accept the perverse symmetry that he left when I came. I am recalling his loving vow, after a huge fight: "I promise to spend the rest of my life with you." The unvarnished truth of it is haunting.

"You got no choice now," I tell his gravesite marker.

I GO to where Andy died. It constitutes about three retail blocks: a bank—not Andy's—a Coach outlet, boutiques named Tantrum, Tweenies, and Blend. Some still show damage. I feel sorry for them bearing the brunt, when any downtown business is in itself a struggle. I look into Chien Chaud et Froid Chat, a pet store. A window sign indicates that kittens and puppies are "Locally-Bred or Shelter ONLY!" What appears to be an authentic Mexican restaurant is unscathed but nearly empty of diners. Few want an order of guacamole and a window view of the unimaginable.

A small canal is very near, with a paved walkway. Maybe Andy diverted here for a last-minute walk with Noel and Gertie, something picturesque, a place to think quietly before slaying the day's dragons.

The smell is still acrid. I approach the foggy tableau of the worksite. Not even its skeleton remains, all flesh sheared and disemboweled. It seems to smolder, as though burning within, not plumes of smoke, more a fine mist. I realize it's the pulverized dust of stone fanned by a late afternoon October wind. Cordoned off by a mishmash of safety deterrents—chain link and wood panels wired together—a restraining order restricts access to preserve any evidence. What a joke. Anyone with a boost could be over the barricade and have unfettered access to the wreckage. I study the massive pile of infrastructure, instinctively sifting for remnants that would be of interest to the gallery. Demolitions can be a goldmine of deco exit signs, banisters, and finials.

"I'd get away if I was you."

I acknowledge the stocky worker in garden clogs sipping ice water on a stoop by the Mexican restaurant by stepping back. My mother would have called him Pedro, but she calls everyone in a Mexican restaurant that, even if their badge clearly reads Charlie.

"Shit's still falling," he warns me. "We hear stuff moving in there. Rats, maybe."

"Were you working the day it happened?"

Clearly, he's answered the question before and basks in it. "I was starring in a commercial. They filmed me holding a skillet in the window. Then boom! Things started hitting the roof. I thought it was a freak hailstorm."

What I want to know is if he noticed three souls ascending toward heaven and if he could see a Welcome Wagon of others, killed by machinery, taking the crook of Andy's arm, petting my dogs.

I cross the street, to bent parking meters.

I touch dents in the asphalt. I see a jagged streak of red. It is not blood. If rain hadn't washed it away, a company whose job it is to scour away unpleasant things from crime and accident scenes would have. I once saw a van outside the apartment of a notorious local murder/suicide: Trauma Restoration Associates. They come in with Lysol and scour someone's shotgunned sinuses off ceiling fan blades. Guts R Us. What this is, is paint from Merciless Bitch, her blood.

I kick through rock and retrieve a piece of tire, like a black orange peel. I trace the tread.

Then, on a curb ground into sand, I find a section of lavender dog collar. It sheds a rhinestone into my palm.

MOM, others, had predicted sleep would not come easily, but I find waking the worst. It would be nice to not immediately be aware that something is missing, but the realization always comes, the sorrow firing on all cylinders, not even lollygagging between yawns. I manage to float above the horror at night. A college roommate, deep into his Psychology major, had taught me how to control my time asleep. All very pre-*Inception*, he called it "dreamweaving." Think of the act of rest as a loom. Fix a specific image, moment, situation. Explore it while you're dozing and it will sauce your dreamstate. If that doesn't work, become your own bouncer. If something in the scenario turns violent, locate yourself and snap your finger. It will stop you, for example, from falling. It requires a certain level of consciousness, but it works. I've barred Andy from showing up.

Until tonight. I have my first nightmare. It's a doozy.

It is a dusty junkyard I find myself in. Pickaxes collide with stone far away. I have been equipped with no tools, just a lantern. Its downturned beam dances across this sandstorm.

I kneel.

"Hello up there? Can you hear me?"

It is Andy.

I lay the lantern down so I can better illuminate the brick, cabling, and glass.

"It's becoming so hard for us to breathe."

He is buried alive, like an ancient Egyptian with his beloved pets, calculating how much air remained, wondering if shallow gulps were more prudent than deep intakes.

"Whoever it is, please don't give up," Andy begs.

My fingers bloody as I dig, as I push metal and stone.

I press my ear to the debris.

The faint barking of our dogs.

And Andy, confident and comforting: "It's okay, guys. Someone's up there. They're going to get us out of here."

I wake myself, hoarsely assuring him, "I'm trying! Andy, it's me, Barry!"

I push away the toss pillows plumped horizontally under the duvet to approximate a body alongside my own. Of course, Andy always said I would spoon with a vending machine if it found its way into our California King.

I will never again hear him whisper into my ear. "Sleepy time now."

I will never again cop the feel of the heartbeat in his chest when he wakes from his own nightmares, yelling for a mom he never knew, holding onto a spindle of our headboard.

I will never ever again kidnap the cool part of his pillow. It was just one push/pull in our twenty-three years on the push/pull continuum. When my own was airless and warm, I would reach out, pat, find that unoccupied part, the cool part of his pillow. I would slowly pull the pillow toward me until his bare shoulders grazed my breastbone, nestle my head behind his, look into his hair, and go to sleep. Of course it didn't stay cool for long, and I'd restlessly return to my own, or he'd awake enough to take it back with a grouchy harrumph, but two, three times a night, minimum, my right hand, like a divining rod jerking toward a source of water, would go wandering for fresh, for safe, for cool. It was like winning a prize. I will miss those two big heads full of alpha male dreams sharing one pillow. Now it's all mine. I can have as much cool as I want, can dominate every bit, which is very different.

I hear barking, actual barking, somewhere outdoors. I look down at the Burberry palettes, the eternal impression of my dogs' form on each.

I hate the foam memory of this mattress. I wish we'd kept our very first lumpy, concave mattress. Andy's dent would still be in it. I could sink into it, let it swallow me up.

Chapter Five

Pronounced Like Grapple

THE seasons change. My underwear doesn't.

That's not true.

I don't bother with underwear, nor anything with a neck or pocket. Some days, I just wear my post-shower towel.

When I shower.

Having withdrawn from the store, whether it's Tuesday or Saturday is no longer of consequence. We've had a power outage, but it's days before I notice, a week before I care. The stove annoys me. Why does it have a clock? It's not due anywhere. I need to know my oven's ready to bake, not that I'm late for dinner at the Gundersons'. I let the PF flash. Power failure. Maybe it's taking my temperature. When darkness ends and when it begins doesn't matter. The sun and the moon tell me whether to open or close my shutters.

If the house seemed too large before, now it's like I've been tossed into a well, a Chilean miner surrounded by Oriental rugs. Since its sole occupant isn't moving enough to stir up dust, I release Phylidia, our housekeeper, on her answering machine during working hours when I knew she wouldn't be there. Neither of us could ever say her name without giggling. Phylidia was stirrups and female problems. I wish Phylidia well, without giggling, and expound that I'll probably call her in remorseful panic in a month. I know I won't. I mail her a big check. I send Gracie, our dogsitter, one too. She wasn't redundant, like Phylidia; she'd been retired.

I stare at the pad of checks afterward. It's a household account with two names. Something else I need to change.

THE landscapers are making short order of the season's final mow and blow. Neither of us has been home to see it for years. We just paid the bill, stuck in our door. Neither is handsome or young, not like my first boycrush, at ten, on two enterprising high school seniors with a lawn-care business. How obvious I must have been, trotting out Popsicles, dragging a box fan and an extension cord and oscillating it myself as they stood still on the patio. Most mortifying, I offered one suffocating day to hose them down, citing something about dehydration. I don't remember snickers but what must they have thought, as I soaked them again and again, or for that matter, the amused neighbors? By late summer, they were replaced by a man riding his mower in a straw hat, plaid shorts, dark socks, and a hard shoe. I had assumed that, school back in session, their days were no longer free.

Much later, Olivia told me that Dad sacked their asses. He came home for lunch and through the screen overheard those boys say, "It's time to take a break and give Fairybarry his baby boner."

My poor Dad, hearing his son maligned by fact.

After that, I always hated the word boner.

I SPENT yesterday sorting and identifying keys, both Andy's and my own: house, house in Key West, store, warehouse, bike locks, storage shed, Mom, Potsy, Dee. Those unidentifiable I threw away, but I still have as many as LezbyAnn. They somehow look better on her dungaree belt loop than they will on mine. Maybe I should buy a key ring like hers, the size of a Hula Hoop.

THERE'S my cell phone. I have been alternating between answering and not. This time I will not, so it will be like a musical whose curtain never rises as a portion of the *Gypsy* overture plays.

At first, I was stupid about it. Dee hung up every time I didn't answer and Potsy would yell that the only acceptable excuse for ignoring his call is if "you're getting a colonic, cupped, or they're sticking leeches on you, whatever it is people do to decompress and cleanse." People were being kind and I was being kind of a dick. Soon, words like intervention and electroshock would be bandied about. So now I occasionally answer, reassure, pass on plus-one invitations, decline casseroles, pretend to have another incoming call by saying, "Hear that? I need to switch over." Stan has called to ask if I want to volunteer as an SAT test monitor. I tell him I'm not ready to double-date with him yet. He seemed to appreciate the joke.

I want to ask my carrier about additional, customized voice prompts.

"If you're worried I might kill myself, press 3 and wait for the sound of the gunshot."

"A little blue yourself? Press 6 for our special *Misery Loves Company* operator."

The one phone call I do not get daily is my mother's. This is a surprise. They're so infrequent I occasionally ring her to offer assurance I'm okay, that I'm hanging on. It often sounds as though I woke her. Just as much, she's not at home at all. She's probably out Bright Spotting, indulging her innate nosiness and making others feel good while making herself feel better.

The landline is different. It's way too accessible, too dangerous. I leave it off the hook. The legal machinery is churning, tucking into the messy feast formerly known as ColonyScape Luxury Townhomes. I remain aloof from even my own attorney, Raoul, and the wrongful death lawsuit filed on behalf of Andrew Morgan's estate, nor am I willing to join nor even meet with those who survived the accident. The feeding frenzy is not limited to law firms, so many it seems the entire American Bar Association is somehow involved. It's also a chance for politicos up for reelection to pile on. The district attorney is treating this as criminal negligence. The county prosecutor's office works their own reckless homicide case. Once a preliminary investigation was made public, the mayor tried to score firebrand points by denouncing sloppy and too rapid urban redevelopment. Although not yet a formal conclusion since Tarantella Demolition's fine hasn't been determined, OSHA has concluded that the collapse was a perfect storm of:

1) Tarantella's poor safety and health records on other job sites, which included numerous citations for insufficient training, improper inspections, and noncompliance fines dating back six years;

2) Soil compacted by heavy overnight rains on 16 September;

3) Key support beams and at least one load-bearing wall prematurely dismantled, resulting in a kind of osteoporosis bone loss;

4) Malfunctioning Caterpillar Ultra-High reach equipment, modified without manufacturer consent and now the focus of a separate lawsuit between the crane rental company and Tarantella.

Everyone wants a piece of the action. Even the land owner charges that the market value is irreparably stigmatized and worthless. They too have filed suit.

Again my phone rings. It is apparently not lost on worried friends that today would have been Andy's forty-sixth birthday. I have tried to put it from my mind. The day didn't belong to me, it belonged to Andy. And, of course, Alexander. I wonder if he celebrated or told Mindy to skip the cupcakes.

Now it's the doorbell. I dash up the kitchen stairs to the second floor and stand carefully to one side of the shutters. I am the subject of a stakeout.

"He won't answer." Kerrick returns to the front and snaps his cell phone shut. "It's hard to tell when, but the pool's been closed and the furniture's put away."

Potsy begins to ring rhythmically, achieving some annoying melody in his head as he puffs reefer. He begins to talk as though I'm there, which I guess I am. "Goddamn it, Barry, how long is this going to go on?"

Put on your big boy pants, Barry. Pick yourself up, dust yourself off, you smell like Lemon Pledge most of the time, anyway.

"You want to end up like that behemoth shut-in dude who fell off the crapper and died trapped between the tank and the wall?"

I read about him too. I'm pretty sure I won't check out with my PJs around my ankles, kissing porcelain.

"Time to come out! Unless you're in that shorty robe!"

That was actually Andy's robe.

Next he tries teary. "Barry, today we all cry for Andy." He kicks a rolled newspaper. "Effie, we all got pain. There's something you can understand." He picks up the newspaper. "Fine, then! Wallow! Watch me take your Sunday ads."

Take them. I looked through yesterday's. No one had clarity on sale.

Kerrick thrusts his hands into his pockets. "It's going down into the twenties tonight. Barry should cover plants he wants to protect."

"Look around. This place is usually lousy with mums. Barry changed out nothing." Potsy races like a child through leaves I have no intention of raking as he finishes his joint. "Fall is so over, Kerr."

"Then let's go. I'm getting my teeth brushed." He's not referring to personal orthodontia. Kerr and I first met when he made an appointment to discuss a "quirky" light fixture idea he had for his lobby. Quirky meant Mondo Cane. Kerrick asked if we could custom manufacture a Chihuly-like composition of dentures, upper and lower. He had a box in his trunk, discards from one of these teeth-in-one-day manufacturers, plus a pouch of loose bicuspids he thought might work as dangling prisms. I gulped and called in our lighting guy, Morris, who told Kerrick he was no better than Jeffrey Dahmer. Kerrick ultimately persuaded him and they became quite collaborative on what became their denturelier. Lit from within, the gums are incredibly beautiful. I'm not sure who comes to clean it for him. Perhaps a really fucked-up dentist.

"First, tell Barry about the fundraiser at the Kubelik Art Center," Potsy goads. Kerrick refuses, so Potsy continues. "Kerrick had the tables set with paper plates and finger paints and told arrivals to illustrate their ideal meal. By the time actual food arrived, over half the party had left, starved and stained."

I continue to peer out.

Potsy places the plastic sheath from the newspaper on his head like an old lady expecting rain. "Kerr, drop me off at the hotel first. It's brunch, and some tool probably needs directions to the Belgian waffles."

"Barry?" Kerrick is unsure where to look. "If you can hear me, Emily had her baby on October 16. It's a little girl. They're both fine."

"And Em drank part of the placenta in a smoothie and is dehydrating the rest!" Potsy yells.

"Science says it helps post-partum depression and aids lactation," Kerrick tells him.

"Redefining self-absorption. Now you can eat *yourself.* I'm not kissing her on the mouth when I see her next, that's all I know."

Kerrick almost manages to lock into my eyes. "The baby's middle name is Morgan. After Andy. Emily figured you'd like that."

DOING it on his birthday would have been untoward, so I wait a day to renew Project Expunge Andy. I rid the shelves of the ionic blow dryer he paid too much for and stubbornly used, despite it making his hair too big. I throw out the preventive Rogaine that assured his hair would remain big. His night retainer in its case. Almost two rows of expired palliatives, lined up like spices, in case he had the same illness again. Some ancient colognes. All of it goes into the trash can. I proceed to the master bedroom closet. I gave Olivia's husband, Ted, Andy's golf clubs and shoes, since I don't play. Andy was very choosy about his business persona, eschewing the Brooks Brothers sack suits of his colleagues for European lapels set high, the natural shoulders. But too bad: I don't care that the French-cuffed shirts and slacks with a cuff that breaks just right could be donated to our male friends. No way can I handle seeing Andy's $2700 Gucci tux with Potsy's head superimposed on it. Missing, of course, is his biggest extravagance: a tailored Armani suit acquired on our last East Coast trip, which is what I sent to Frey for a body unfit to be seen. I fold everything into piles on the floor.

Except the Tommy Bahama shirt. This, I keep.

I slide out sweater boxes and take out the cashmere V-necks he loved. Those too constitute a pile. In the bottom of one box, nestled in cedar chips, I find a three-inch ponytail, held intact by an elastic band, a relic of our annual I-want-to-try-something-different. Mine usually involved facial hair or tinted contact lenses sworn off as irritating within a week. His was long hair slicked back in deference to the stodgy at the bank, culminating in this brown tassel. He vowed to save it as I snipped it off for him. Any scent of his pomade had long ago been surrendered to storage.

I find Andy's shorty robe on a hook. It too goes into the trashcan.

This takes all day. It's dusk by the time I've stacked the last box in a charitable wall curbside for Goodwill.

Nightfall activates landscape lighting. Children in goblin costumes dash by.

Keep running, kids. I don't have any candy in the house if you come to the door. Plus, I'm way scarier than you.

I AWAKE every morning to sheets saturated like a Handi Wipe. I may drown from crying. Maybe this GRPL card, which I found on my bureau, which I now tap the steering wheel with, is my life jacket.

Gentry Road Community Center is quite close to Great Rooms! I cut a paranoid swath to avoid being seen by any employees, yet I pass Isaac in his Lexus. I'm sure he saw me and assumed I was doing some gutless drive-by. Beyond providing hot meals to the indigent, hosting senior citizen sock hops and providing space to assorted groups, the cinderblock center is also a floodwater retreat and a bomb shelter. I wouldn't chance it saving my life, but I've decided to let it try and save my sanity. Just please let this not be a free-for-all series of confessionals. I endorse teamwork, but I will not share a snot-rag.

I was here before. It was how I earned a bleeding ulcer. A group of homeowners in the working class neighborhood that no longer worked hated my snotty store in their midst, so they had rallied in NIMBY pushback of a Great Rooms! expansion. In their outrage, they had forgotten that, shucks, we already *were* in their backyard. Oh, and BTW: your backyard is mostly dirty diapers and Mountain Dew cans. We began the acrimonious meeting by pointing out that our success was theirs.

"Elitist bunk! Don't treat us like we're on skid row!" I heard a man yell.

This rankled me. The expansion was clean, yet the room of dissent made me feel dirty. I wasn't some predator circling foreclosures. No one was being displaced. They had conveniently ignored the alleyway cleanups we'd organized to make the area more inviting than a shooting location for *Slumdog Millionaire*. Andy's bank had underwritten some public art, and we had already lobbied for, and contributed to, city dollars for a pocket park. I was to be flagellated for being a stabilizing presence? We asked that they consider the many benefits of our growth: rising property value, more traffic lights, employment opportunities. Their leader maintained that recent appraisals had sent their taxes soaring, more traffic lights only meant more traffic violations, and could I actually name one person we'd hired from that township? A woman testified she couldn't sit on her front porch anymore, truck emissions were so prevalent, which she coupled with some fake wheezing. The man behind her proposed limitations be placed on incoming and outgoing deliveries because "our kids aren't safe on their bikes." I actually expected someone to pull a Norma Rae and hop up on a table. I assumed a mental crash position and began to worry about blocked entrances, harassed employees, and general sabotage.

But Great Rooms! prevailed. The backlash quieted. Still, to feel resented was unpleasant. ColonyScape encountered similar unrest in their downtown bid and their legal team countered with a similar dossier of statistics. They just hadn't made allowance for human life. I want to believe I had.

I push the handicap-accessible button to open the center door and follow arrows. It smells like today's lunch and feels like tomorrow's misgiving. I pass a boisterous chorus of "for he's a jolly good fellow." Behind that closed door, cake is being sliced and something extra has been snuck into the punchbowl despite a premises ban on alcohol. I want to go in there. They're having fun. I'm sure GRPL won't, but I hope this coming-together isn't accompanied by dirges. I'm just grateful, when I come upon the room, that it's not the assembly hall that held the Great Rooms! debate.

An empty hand must be offensive, because a mug of coffee is promptly encased in my hand by a sparrow-like woman who reminds me of Joyce Carol Oates. This is Adele, founder and facilitator, whose smile is so exaggerated that the corners of her mouth meet the corners of her eyes.

"It's pronounced grapple," she clarifies. "It says what we do: come to grips with what happened."

Actually, it sounds like we might wrestle. Or maybe it will be like *Scared Straight!* Adele will turn profane and browbeat us weaklings with tough love.

She gives me the long story short of her own tragedy. Her entire immediate family, wedding-bound, was killed in a plane crash; she had stayed home with the flu, and the survivor guilt plagued her until she started GRPL, pronounced grapple. She tells me all of this while twirling and biting a pen. I'm pretty sure she stirred my coffee with it. Adele is prone, I will discover, to looking down her tinted glasses and shouting out encouraging and clichéd things. I am then shown where bottled water is kept. I'm starting to believe tissue has been quietly banned.

Everyone stands. I'm momentarily convinced we are going to say the Pledge of Allegiance. They're just politely acknowledging me. Everyone is dressed up. GRPL-pronounced-grapple is their evening out. Now I can smell Salisbury steak *and* newly extruded polyester. I tell everyone to please sit. A black man, Oscar, brought *US* magazine for the lulls between reflection and sips. All-taupe Janet—face, hair, jewelry, purse—mostly hums. Roxanne holds husband Paul's hand. Barb holds her purse on her thighs as though she might leave at any minute. Sally's in a beret and has lips the color of circus peanuts. Others say nothing and don't participate, like they're auditing a class. When people do become engaged, everyone overlaps, and it's like a 1970s Robert Altman film to stay abreast.

"Try being alone *and* ancient. Numb feet yet restless legs, my bladder's overactive yet my bowels underachieve. Everything on me is at odds with each other."

This comes from an elfin man whose feet just touch the floor when he sits. He is also the one who, when I first walked in, kept excitedly saluting me, like his arm was stuck doing it.

"Barry, meet Shorty Iverson. He lost Mrs. Iverson going on two years."

Shorty salutes me again.

Roxanne hesitantly says, "By the way: I sure can't afford much in it, but I love your store."

I thank her for the compliment, even if it was drowned out by the rattle of her tin cup.

Sally adds, "I saw those pictures in that home magazine. Sure was something. You know those Fabulous Beekman Boys?"

"Nope. I don't know David Bromstad, Christopher Lowell, Cindy Crawford, or Ty Pennington, either."

Roxanne offers that "you must see décor flaws everywhere."

Andy had always noted that we weren't invited to private homes as much as you'd suppose for fear I'd arrive in enormous white gloves, swipe the tops of bookcases, then decide if we'd stay, try to sell them something, or rearrange things when no one was looking. The host's upfront pre-apologies were mostly annoying.

Barb's rejoinder is astute. "He probably also gets asked for hints, like Heloise, like tax preparers and doctors."

I smile at her. "Turning it off can be hard." I know how much you paid for your new vase and if it was discontinued; I know how your sofa will fare after cranberry juice is spilled on it; I know which tile grout separates. I know it all. Gift/curse.

"The boss giving himself as much bereavement as he wants," Oscar tells me, "is not a good thing."

No one is ruffled but me when Adele suddenly barks, "Get back to your store! Lose yourself in work."

I'm already lost, I think, picking at the paper cloth on a table of pitch-in food.

"Busy hands, busy mind," Sally announces.

I want to ask if masturbating counts, but I don't since I haven't. Of course I know I belong at the store. Christmas merchandise has arrived, judging from the reconciled packing slips appearing in the milk box. The great cones have appeared on our pine trees, their own holiday harbinger.

"One door closes, another opens!" Adele announces for no good reason.

That's not living, I think. *That's a funhouse.*

"You have to own the damage!" she continues, still without pom-poms.

As though I had the option of surrendering a deposit and reclaiming the life I had before. Maybe I should start a blog, submit it to The Huffington Post. But how do you document a void? Mine would be series of zeroes, one long ooooooooooooooo.

Adele tries one more time: "The person you are is not the person you will be! Follow the road to your identity!"

"I have one," I finally speak. "What I don't have is Andy."

Sally seems pleased with herself as she observes, "He completed you."

I thought that sentiment had been rightfully put into exile.

Janet brings a cross out of her blouse. "You a churchgoer, Mr. Grooms?"

Someone repeats "church."

Adele refills her coffee. I smell conflict as surely as I smell that beef hash. "Janet, you know that our charter acknowledges religious teachings have their place. Just not here."

"Even Dr. Elizabeth Kubler-Ross came to the Lord's truth," an undaunted Janet points out. She reminds me of Joyce Meyer, without the lesbian hairdo.

Even Mom had brought up that "other shore" hereafter business like she was some spiritual Diana Nyad, but we were never churchgoers. As Andy's were Cafeteria Catholics, picking and choosing dogma and observation and always leaving room for after-dinner sin, our family were more Automat Agnostics, a little afraid not to buy into something but stopping by only when our spiritual budget was low, a Christmas Eve service, Easter morning.

Adele frowns. "Our focus is on life after death *for the living*."

"God helps us accept that everything is on loan to us." Clearly, Janet is recruiting, a woman who uses her old boobs to gain leverage, then brings out the Bible.

"Why was my balance called in all at once? My partner plus my dogs?" I ask tersely.

"Do you believe in ghosts?" Sally wants to know. "The reason I ask is after my man passed, for about a month, I'd pull in the drive and up the garage door would go. I didn't touch a thing."

"The remote opener has a short," Shorty offers.

She gives him a fragile look. "It was comforting, yet frightening. Ghosts, angels, maybe they're one and the same."

I want to tell her I heard someone on the roof last week.

Well, some *thing*.

This is not the first time. "Up there," I heard Andy's spooked whisper as I woke to his push. Our investigation yielded a large mother raccoon watching approvingly as her three babies played peekaboo. Once our presence was felt, they obediently followed her down our chimney. We had them humanely trapped and released, or so we were told, since, unable to watch, we both left. Maybe the raccoons were back, but I hope it was Andy. I don't quite know where he went, but if it wasn't to a cloud, why not our shingles at 3:18 a.m.?

"What would you say if he suddenly materialized?" Sally asks.

"I'd maybe ask him if he can still see me. Or can the dogs talk."

This irritates Janet. "That's not how Scripture says it works."

Barb follows up with, "And you'd say…?"

I hope you finally met your mom. I hope your dad still isn't drunk. I hope it's like *Lovely Bones*. None of those would mean anything without elaboration, and I'm not ready to do that. So I say, "I will never love anyone like you again." I don't expect high-fives, but GRPL-pronounced-grapple has clearly said and heard it all before. All I get is a woman popping a Cert into her mouth and a man turning another page of his *US*.

Adele's next question has all of the subtlety of an alien's body cavity probe: "Ever wish you were with Andy and your animals?"

She laughs when I reply, "If I say yes, do I have to leave? Is there a Suicidal Persons League, pronounced supple, down the hall?" I try to include everyone in my look around. "I don't want to die. I didn't want to exist, not at first, but I never wanted, or want, to die."

Roxanne squeezes Phil's knee expectantly. The mini-kick he gives grants permission. "You a card player, Barry?"

I tell her a little.

"We're always on the lookout for people who appreciate a good hand of euchre," she offers.

"See? Now, just like that, you've got us," Sally chirps.

Roxanne eagerly wants to know, "Do you do friends and family discounts?"

Uh-oh.

SLEEP was miserable. I'm running a slight but palpable temperature. I'm bloated, sore, and I have lower back pain, right side. It's not a flare-up of my ulcer. This sensation is different. I'm also light-headed, and I'm not the type who dazes easily.

But I was also never prone to fainting.

I review the symptoms of a heart attack. That's not this. Andy had an app, iTriage, that claimed to diagnose illness, but I never downloaded it. Maybe this has come from inertia. It has become my new pastime. I'm trying not to nap as much. My sleep creases are turning into origami. So I've been sitting a lot in my favorite leather chair, the one constructed of vintage bomber jackets. (Yes, I have a chair.)

I grab my side. It's like I've swallowed a lit candle. I watch a lot of The Food Network. This could be secondhand indigestion. I check every day to see if Paula Deen's hair is white, silver or blue, or if Giada has finally taken a tit completely out. Maybe GRPL constipated me. I have not had a bowel movement in four days. Not by nature a person covetous of what others have, this morning I'm jealous of anyone who has pinched a loaf. I need milk, ice cream, something to coat my stomach. I'd buy Activia but I'd get my hand slapped, since it seems to be manufactured just for women, like some deodorants. Men must shit and stink more.

I wait to go to the supermarket until well past midnight. I doubt I'll chance upon anyone I know; I've never understood why anyone would grocery shop at this hour, unless they have absolutely no time-management skills or a really troubled complexion. Rarely did I come alone. Andy and I together treated it as a found meal, snacking on the samples, critiquing what was most nasty, the food or the person spooning it out. We might part down separate aisles if time was short, but we'd combine our baskets into one cart, whereupon I'd add one extra this, a larger size of that. I always pantry and prepare too much food. Andy called this wasteful, but it was a throwback to my prudent mother, who would appallingly run out as hungry guests extended a hopeful plate for seconds. Maybe she wasn't trying to stretch a budget as much as she was trying to shrink my sister, but she bought and cooked just enough.

I pause at dog food. That was one aisle Andy and I visited together, lingering over label ingredients as though we personally consumed it, wondering what a Snausage actually tasted like. We were so obsessed with Gertie and Noel we wanted to take a heartworm pill too.

Two aisles over, I toss Prilosec into the cart. Maybe it will help. Nothing else has. If I chew any more Tums I'll be able to nurse.

I pass a male custodian buffing the floor. He smiles. Is this his primary job or a second, part-time shift? I decide primary. I'd kept my own late nights to prepare for three-day holiday weekend sales, but I wonder what it's like to initiate your shift when most are in a REM state, to have such an upside-down life.

Pushing my cart from one pool of parking lot light to another, I realize I am inhabiting it—the shameful wide-awake sleepwalker whose register receipt says 2:06 a.m.

MY OWN family practitioner cannot see me for almost three weeks. My stomach will be cheesecloth by then. I call Dr. Steve Chaney. He was friendlier with Andy than me; they had partnered one summer at gay tennis when I bowed out of the competition when a broken pipe flooded part of the gallery. Dr. Steve finds time for me the next morning, before his office opens. By then, I'm so tender I can't even fasten my seat belt for the drive there.

Dr. Steve sits at a curved Lucite desk with neither legs nor drawers. I remember this desk. It was a Great Rooms! special order. We gave it to him at cost. That's why he came in early. He opens his Mac to construct a makeshift file for me of past illness and known allergies. This is what doctors mostly do now: type, and badly. I concede I've been lax about exams, especially the kind involving a finger cot, so he stops and addresses it. I have a healthy rectum, he tells me. I ask, before I pull my pants back up, if he wants to hear it cough. He doesn't even smile. He just hunts and pecks.

We proceed to symptoms. I explain, as though a physician

wouldn't know this, that emotional upheaval manifests itself as physical ailment. Maybe I earned this, maybe I deserve it for not bawling and convulsing at Andy's calling, pain as a metaphor for pain, maybe it's psychosomatic. "My mother thinks I need a mood elevator."

"No, you don't."

"How do you know?"

"Caving to emotion didn't build your business. Take the compliment and lay down."

I do so with effort on the padded table.

"Unbutton your shirt."

I touch my abdomen. "It hurts the most here."

"Sit back up for me."

As he wraps my arm to take my blood pressure, he asks that I stop swinging my legs like a child, which I didn't know I was doing and don't know why. My doctor office memories hardly burst with merriment: stitches beneath my chin when I fell off the curly slide at a town park, a sprained ankle.

"What have you been eating? Any extra fat in your diet lately?"

"Haven't you heard? I had extreme gastric bypass; I recently lost about 180 pounds."

"Barry, that's rather glib."

"Barry Glib. It works," I retort too loud. "I can do it in falsetto, if you want."

"You don't have to pass a laugh test with me."

What I thought was dark humor was just distasteful. My voice falters. "It's just so raw." Then I crack. Tears find their way even into my ears.

He crosses the room. "I'm just tired of flippancy. The barebacking little shits that come in here don't know a single person who died of AIDS, they've never read *And The Band Played On*, they pop a Viread when they remember to, and when they turn up poz, they just think they're the new diabetic. News flash: controlling diabetes doesn't give you a buffalo humpback or facial wasting. People our age aren't much better. Lot of complacency out there. 'I heard there was a cure. What about that guy with the stem cells in Berlin?' We're back to believing safe sex is not getting your teeth knocked out afterward." He hits his desk. "I want to knock most of them out of the building with an air hammer."

I sit up. His head is going to blow off.

"Don't worry." Dr. Steve smiles. "I have a standing weekly appointment with an anger management coach. You just don't have the perspective yet of being on the flip side of this."

My tear ducts must think of my eyes as a dirty windshield, because they automatically fill up again. "What will I find there?" I choke out.

"Sorrow replaced by fury." He hops up on the exam table beside me as I dab my eyes. "Andy was beautiful inside and out. I even told him so when he was here."

When he was here?

I know nothing about this but pretend to. "Those silly bank-mandated physicals."

Dr. Steve gives me an odd look. "He thought he'd torn his rotator cuff in a doubles match. In June."

I remember him whining how the pacing of the clay court had been unfamiliar to him, alternating ice and heat on his right, no, his left shoulder, but nothing about a consultation with the state's preeminent HIV doctor.

I point to an OraQuick twenty-minute oral swab placard on the wall. "Was Andy hiding something from me?"

"This violates my confidentiality oath, disclosure laws, some state statutes, and the HIPAA Act." Dr. Steve grips my knee. "Andy wasn't hiding anything from you."

He at least hid a visit to this office.

Dr. Steve taps on his keyboard. "I'm ordering imaging right away." He scribbles on an Atripla pad. "CAT scan, ultrasound. It's your gallbladder. Stones is my guess. It was probably percolating before what happened to Andy, and you chalked it up to indigestion or a pulled muscle."

"Can't I try something homeopathic? Like drink a lot of olive oil to dislodge them?"

"That would be like using a garden hose on Stonehenge. Sometimes an organ just gives up."

The street name on the medical order he hands me is unfamiliar. "It's two streets over." Suddenly, he says, "You have an eye. Tell me what you think." He brings up a watercolor, nicely matted and framed, that is propped against the side of his desk. "A patient painted it for me. I need to hang it somewhere."

It is both oceanic and celestial, with what looks like crude Xs heaped on sand dunes. A dusky-skinned man in a grass skirt is holding an outsized X up.

"I was told it's from a parable," he explains. "Starfish wash up on the beach. This villager, walking along, stoops to throw them back into the ocean one at a time. Someone asks him, why are you doing this? There are so many. He could never save enough to make a difference. He looks at a starfish he is ready to toss. 'It makes a difference to this one.'"

It should go on the wall behind his desk, I tell him.

On my way out, I recognize the man who captains many of Kerrick's events. My friendly smile is met with a chilly glare. Have I somehow violated his privacy? Andy was in this lobby, and it was just for his arm. Maybe the poor guy's just embarrassed that, last time I saw him, he was dressed like something out of an H.P. Lovecraft anthology.

My inflamed gallbladder, opines the lab technician, shows dramatic indication of rupture. Things happen fast. I'm immediately prepped for an outpatient laparoscopic procedure. Tiny incisions, it is explained, will permit miniature video to guide a low-impact extraction. I have no reason to seek a second opinion, and now that I know the diagnosis, I'm in agony. If it goes well, I will be able to leave by the end of the day, the surgeon assures me. I want to tell him to take my broken heart, sliver by sliver, while he's at it.

The IV is started. A cap is placed over my hair. Right about now I might ask for a deep-conditioner to kill two birds, but it's the wrong demo. My gurney and I are parked in an empty hallway to wait for the anesthesiologist, who's finishing another procedure. I feel like I'm in M*A*S*H.

I obviously dozed. I now wear hospital-issue footies, probably put on at the same time they clasped the plastic band on that identifies me, and I am at a nursing station. Surgeons and doctors on-call and RNs congregate. I listen to water cooler chatter. They discuss the lancing of frightful goiters that medical school barely touched upon. Someone talks about the obese woman's complaint of a burning, foaming discharge, who, it turns out, had misplaced a full bar of soap deep in her vagina. A gastroenterologist mentions a patient who has been farting for eight months. He just keeps cutting them, no end in sight. Food allergy tests, blood work, stool samples have yielded nothing. Beyond the obvious personal torment of uncontrollable flatulence, it's causing worry at his job, where he's being excused and excluded from meetings.

"He's hit a gas ceiling," his gastroenterologist jokes.

They make sport of this chronically gassy patient. One doctor suggests he vent his butthole out a window, like a dryer. His gastroenterologist adds that the smell lasts forever, like it has feelers. It's become a physical bother, too, this farting: chafing, waking him and making a full night's sleep impossible. They're even exploring the psychological; he's been sent to analysis to discuss his potty training.

I'm still laughing as I count backward from ten.

IN POST-OP, I awake mid-fart. The joke is on me. They inflated my abdomen with gas for more work room, and now I'm being deflated by my nurse in Recovery.

I cough and stare directly up at Melyssa, who's pressing my gut.

"Do you have anyone to drive you home?" Melyssa asks as she inspects my rearranged mid-section. I begin to shiver violently.

She hurriedly unfolds a blanket over me from a warming bin. "Are you cold?"

Someone just walked on your grave, my grandmother would have direly intoned, which never made sense; I didn't have a grave.

Now I do, a grave prepared just for me that can be trod upon. What makes me cold is that I never considered my exit strategy. This is one of the things you take for granted when you become one of two. I'd even put down Andy's name on the surgery form as my principal contact. Who else? Next of kin would be Mother. The 193 hours, 47 minutes, and 16 seconds I endured eight weeks ago is more face time than I need annually. Plus she'd somehow blame me for alienating my own gallbladder.

My first surgery. An organ that just gave up. Something I survived without him. I don't have a timeline, no age of innocence, that wasn't push-pinned with Andy.

The obstacles in building a business, my father's lingering illness, first time overseas, first puppy, first remote control chewed down to the battery, second puppy, another remote control, including the battery, but being dispatched to the widowed legions—this, I never saw coming. I didn't fall in love for a ready caregiver in the same way no new parent thinks of their gurgling progeny as a future safety net. But if this had been chest pains in the center of night, my neighbors in sleepwear watching the lonely man being loaded into the ambulance he called himself, then what?

I think how Olivia and I, the jabbering know-it-alls, blithely supposed that widowhood came prepackaged. Mom could go all madcap with this sudden predilection for adventure, or maybe she'd write a slew of bestselling mystery thrillers, be the next Mary Higgins Clark. And really, she was just alone.

Of course I have someone, I tell Melyssa. I dress myself, studying a dietary sheet I am given.

"Don't overdo the turkey stuffing," Melyssa jokes, acknowledging a Thanksgiving that I won't.

She points me to my belongings, in a sealed bag. In it, my cell phone contains the number of a car service we use for vendors. This is who I call.

After the hospital apothecary fills my prescriptions, I'm taken to the lobby in a wheelchair. I have never been in one but it seems sturdier than the one I pushed Dad around in for those brief hospice excursions to clear his lungs, his barrel chest pummeled by recurrent ailment into a permanent patient feebly hoping for one more good day. I will never forget his awful, plaintive bargain: "Roll me on home, why don't you, son?"

I see Miss Sondra in a short suede skirt. She's loping bowlegged, like a cowboy. Or maybe she's a cowgirl. Could it be she just had her new vagina dilated? Normally, this would warrant a series of castration texts and calls, but then, why are you at the hospital, Barry? Exhaustion? We all know what that means. There's a psychiatric wing. I can hear it now.

I roll behind a ficus tree and bite my bracelet off.

I CAREFULLY shower. The small abdominal incisions look indecisive, like a chef pricked me to see if I was done; only my red navel, as big as a satellite dish, betrays interference.

The Vicodin does little to alleviate the soreness. It just makes me jittery, not at all the Valley of Mary Tyrone I'd thought I'd rock climb into. I'll save them as a stocking stuffer for Potsy. The antibiotics make my scalp itch. Or maybe I'm already starting to dry up, like a spinster, from the top down.

For such a minor surgery, I cannot pull up my socks. They straddle my ankles with the same forlorn grip as my Grandma Lola's hose did when she tried to dress herself with full-scale dementia. She had someone to help her, though.

At least I have an unimpeachable excuse to skip my crunches.

And one more blessed delay in returning to work.

Chapter Six

Lesson/Plan

LOW clouds over the parking lot of Great Rooms! form an impenetrable canopy, full of the precipitation predicted for tonight. It's like looking up into the folds of a gray parachute. Too little snow will be an annoyance, too much a hindrance, just enough will jumpstart December sales. Twinkling white lights have been snaked through the topiaries, along with berries, but those are too bright, like red hots, and I wonder where they came from. Cold wind whips our American flag, cracking as it unfurls.

Employees pull in. Over time, most have upgraded to better cars, some now have car seats, one has a handbrake and a handicapped-access permit. I know every name, every backstory. Georgia's been with me since the start, she and her three-quarter-length sleeves. Joy collects butterflies. Vince talks too loud but he's such a gentle soul he'd be devastated to be told so. Brooke ends almost every sentence with a little laugh, like underwater bubbles. Darren's on his sixth marriage. And on and on.

I had taught them what I'd learned. Touch people, but not too much. Use "sir" and "ma'am" even to those your junior. I mandated that there would be no disapproval, no patronizing. I stressed community visibility. We had no qualms about compromising. That was the biggest lesson: you have to have a strong ego in an industry that will endlessly require you to surrender it. We fondled B'nai B'rith, swapped spit with YWCA, faced Mecca with the Muslim Women's League, and tongue-bathed every Junior Leaguer countywide to build brand awareness. When a female employee balked about a craft show sponsored by Right-To-Life, I stressed that she didn't have to sell her womb, just a handcrafted crib from Great Rooms! I was shameless, closing my own eyes to pretty much rim a Promise Keeper's chapter. I even made a display table with muskets for legs and displayed it at an NRA expo.

I outwait them all to walk in alone.

Holiday décor engulfs my store, as it should. I'm glad to see our accessories still transcend the typical cherubs and Department 56. I smell the mulling spices at our new complimentary beverage kiosk. The batch is brewed too heavily with clove, but today is not the day to micromanage apple cider.

Of course I recognize the store music, since I chose the times of day when what music should be played. It's a hissy album of choral Christmas by The Caroleers, Andy's favorite album as a kid.

Even my store is no safe haven. He is everywhere.

I get no further than Jonathan Adler dishware when Trish Babcock and Evelyn Overton approach me. They are two of the prominent names you can find on, respectively, a local symphony hall and a sports stadium—the graffiti of the affluent.

"The man who has been dreadfully missed," Evelyn purrs, or maybe it was her fox jacket.

"So much." Trish can't really smile but she does her best. She's never met an injectable she didn't invite back.

"Many subscribers expressed condolences on our blog," Evelyn says. She is referring to their collaboration, a daily online spoon of self-congratulations. People don't subscribe. People are scared to unsubscribe. Women like Evelyn and Trish blithely toss out a phrase like "anyone who's anyone...," and they mean it. One or usually both in tweed, they are embedded in the society section of the newspaper, where the shallow run deep—two photo-driven pages as reliably funny as the obituaries (which, by the way, I no longer find funny). That they adopted us from our humble get-go, in retrospect, shouldn't be surprising. They like the feeling of personally nurturing success as much as they like destroying it. In their embrace of Great Rooms! they kicked another fawning shop owner to the curb.

"Those were a comfort to read," I lie. I always immediately delete her daily e-blast. "And how nice that you're my welcome committee."

And how these un-old women know committees! And boards and

advisories, covens, cauldrons, cults. Their rich husbands' souls are just as ugly, but at least they stay away.

Trish can't really frown but does her best. "When the cat's away, though," she says.

A small winter split appears in her obese, orange lower lip. I watch closely to see if a gluelike substance oozes out.

"Some of your people don't maintain the same level of community involvement you do," she adds.

I turn my hands up. "Which people?"

Isaac has sensed danger over his latte and walks toward us.

Evelyn bats her hollow, jack-o'-lantern eyes nervously and clears her throat, but Trish plunges forward.

"Owners want to be told, Evie. Barry needs to know that Pat in floral let us down."

Isaac speaks before I can. "How so, Mrs. Babcock?"

"Our banquet centerpiece was too tall to see over, and the petals were obviously freezer-burnt. Never ever ever would our Barry send it out like that," she announces.

I'm suddenly very, very, very tired of kissing the nonexistent asses of—deconstructing Sondheim—the ladies who skip lunch. I feel like their obsequious servant and I hate the courtliness of it.

"Mrs. Babcock, what's my last name?" She, Evelyn, and Isaac gape at me as though I've just had an aneurysm. I don't give anyone time to respond. "I know yours. It's hard not to when you come in after a tea with a badge on." I gaze at hers. "Mrs. Frank Babcock. Did you toss out your last name *and* first when you married well?"

Isaac rubs my shoulders. "Barry here's stressed."

I twist away. "I have zip stress. No one to hide the last piece of KFC from. No more arguments about who picks up dog crap—"

Evelyn interjects, "Barry, if our board—"

"No. *I'm* bored, Mrs. Jerome Overton."

I offer my back.

Isaac, aghast, trails me past a virtual room where staff and customers do space planning. He keeps saying my name. We round the corridor into the small executive suite. I walk into my office without turning, and he follows.

"Do we have a revised business forecast I need to know about?" he asks. "Is that what you've been working on as you ignored us for the last two months? A plan to have zero customers by year's end?"

"Actually, Isaac, I dreaded coming back to empty people who would remind me how empty my life has become," I say, not facing him.

"So what if they don't know your last name? Those two spend a lot and refer a lot, and we comp the occasional dais arrangement. You taught us that's how it's done. You bored us with stories about women we'd never know: Brooke Astor, Pat Buckley, Nan Whatever."

"Kempner."

"Well, we fed those monsters."

He makes me feel like a mad scientist whose creation mutated when he left the lab to pee. Except these Brides of Frankenstein don't eat. It's me who has the vinegary aftertaste of their entitlement. These doyennes resent their dependence on you, and you hate loving their richness.

"I rue the day I drank the poison and became their William Haines," I say.

"I don't know who the hell that is, either," Isaac retorts.

"Nothing," I decree, "gives them the right to lay my staff to filth because of an oversight."

A bullpen of accounting personnel stare. I close the door.

"*You* picked that fight! Maybe Pat *did* fuck up," Isaac counters.

From my window, I see pumpkins left to decay in the distant gardening space.

"So much for Mr. Albanese's twelve-month market," I snort. "That brown mush out there looks like brains."

"Mr. Albanese sliced a tendon in his left hand cutting things back. I hope it was okay that he took a few days off to regain its use," Isaac explains sarcastically. "You iron your own dress shirts now?"

"Why would you ask that?"

"Because you obviously couldn't be bothered with the back or the cuffs," Isaac coolly deduces. "Warehouse Lester looks nicer today."

"I'm in a dispute with my dry cleaners," I reason. I haven't been back. I can't now, so belatedly, acknowledge to Gwen that Andy was killed, and, if she has since heard, I don't want teary apologies or condolences.

"Your dispute is with yourself. Are you seeing someone?"

I haven't grappled with that semicircle of shrunken heads, chattering their sewn lips open, since that one time, but I reply defensively, "I go to a group." Then I turn so he can't count the wrinkles on my unstarched shirt's back.

"Why haven't you returned my calls?"

"About that reporter? The store has no comment on Andy. Isn't that self-evident?"

Isaac's voice darkens with disgust. "What's self-evident is you sent my last message to New Delhi! No one calls about Andy anymore. It was about the fire. I winged it."

"Fire? What fire?"

"A fire broke out, Barry, across from the men's room, two Mondays ago. It was small—paper towel, a solvent—and mostly smoke damage. We discovered afterward a mantle clock missing."

"Not the 1950 marble art-deco one," I groan.

"Yes, the French pink and cream. The cops called it a diversionary fire… arson to shift attention from another criminal act."

"So Great Rooms! got struck by a pyromaniac kleptomaniac. Or the other way around." I roll my fingers on my desk. "What else?"

"The Salvation Army asked again if we'd allow them at our entrance."

"Ask them again about their philosophy on homosexuality."

"Sometimes we put service above self."

"My service comes with strings," I snap.

"They do good, too."

"So does the United Way, yet we don't shame our people into promising a percentage of their paycheck. Anything else?"

"Moberley's across the street says our coffee bar has hurt sales."

Time was I'd stroll over and make amends by offering them an annex in Great Rooms! Now, "I don't give a shit."

Isaac's tone is shaky. "There are still people here who *do* give a shit. People who need this job, who come to work because it gives them great joy, all on the same long limb wondering what you're going to do."

Me too, Isaac. But saying that is unlikely to dispel his insecurity. The staff didn't deserve someone second-guessing them who's no longer fluent in Decisive or Helpful. "Iz, I should start by firing-with-a-capital-F my wretched, insufferable self." I grab chalk and slash a massive F on one of the chalkboards that line my office walls.

"A wretched boss wouldn't have given me Purim off."

I take a wooden paddle, leftover from the former principality, from the wall. "Here. Have a go."

"First I'd put a rusty nail in it," Iz says.

"At least make me bang erasers." I grab two.

"Worse. I'll make you bang a chick."

"Does everyone think I've had a breakdown?"

"A few." From my door, he offers, "I'm sorry the day started this way. I should go smooth this over with the ladies, somehow."

"Just don't let Pat send flowers," I suggest.

Iz hurries out. This time I lock the door.

I append to the F an INISHED because I am. I stand there a long time looking at it, rigid, like a coat tree in the corner of my office. I consider standing there until the noon lunch bell—yes, it rings too—my self-inflicted punishment for being a boor. When I turn, I see what's on the blackboard facing me.

Fernie spent 15 Bucks.

It's in Georgia's hand. She has dotted the I in Fernie with a small heart, as she always does when she leaves me notes. From this, I know Fernie has been in and, as always, was frugal in what she chose. Fernie was hard to miss and could be easily mistaken for a character in a life-sized Dickensian display. The temptation to romanticize this first sighting eight years ago, to make her the sweet grandma I never had, a character thumbnail from some short story, is great, but the fact is many shopkeepers would have kept a suspicious eye on her speckled hands holding the merchandise. She held each item at least thirty seconds as if, with this laying on, she absorbed their essence, even pressing some against her cheek. Then she addressed them. From where I stood, I heard her tell a snowman he ought to be "proud of that big carrot nose." And she complimented a trio of bisque carolers as "look at you, singin' ladies!"

"Fernie turns up every day to look at what she calls the pretties." Georgia sidled up beside me. We watched Fernie stroke the stiff robe of a papier-mâché angel. "Stays about an hour. I've talked to her some. She doesn't have a tree, so this is her Christmas."

When I asked if Fernie had family, Georgia gestured that I "come out and shoot the shit with me and my best friend," which was a cigarette. Between frosty hacks, Georgia said that "when Fernie's husband passed, she was left with nothing. Lost her house, car, and no kids to help out." Georgia ground one butt into the crunchy snow and lit another "smoky treat" (her folksy names for carcinogenic agents were endless). She told me where Fernie lived, a boarding house at a frightening address almost five blocks south. I told Georgia, "She can have whatever she wants." As Georgia's eyes reddened, I hurried away. "Just wait until I'm in my office."

That was when I formally instituted The Fernie Endowment. Georgia's subsequent note indicated Fernie chose something for $4.95, literally the least expensive item in the gallery. Of course, she inquired about this gesture from a stranger. A few days after that, a small envelope made it to the store despite the indecipherable handwriting. In it was a carefully folded piece of lined, yellow tablet paper that said, *Bless you. Fernie Timmons.*

It was not until I was making stew that next fall on a Sunday, or maybe it was when I noticed the kids at school bus stops go from sweatshirts to thick jackets, that her face inexplicably popped into my head. Each year, I reminded Georgia, who didn't need reminding, and she encouraged Fernie to choose something new. Even given inflation and the gallery's upscale uptick, she always chose the cheapest thing we shelved. Each year, I got Fernie Timmons's thanks and blessing.

Year six, I learned she was felled by a bad influenza and probably wouldn't make it in at all. I suggested Georgia select something Fernie had admired. She knew my take on brick-and-mortar religion when she apologetically pointed to a Mary and child.

"I'll run it by to her after work. Unless you'd want to?"

My immediate "No" startled Georgia, and we both spoke at once about everyone's flu.

Why did I not want to meet the stranger I was indulging? What if she cried? What if I cried? What if one of us was so disappointed in the reality of the other that we had nothing to say? Was it that to witness firsthand her life would make empty my own seasonal gesture? The woman might have gone hungry in April or needed her winter heat bill paid, and all I did was grandly underwrite a reindeer made of pine cones. Not knowing her circumstances freed me to create a less painful reality for Fernie. Perhaps there were good reasons she was alone. Maybe she was a hateful drunk or just made one stupid decision after another. But at what age are you forgiven your trespasses?

In challenging my motives, why I was content to be semi-anonymous, I decided it was from observation. My father himself was paying it forward before Haley Joel Osment ever knew what hit him. He and his family spent his Texas childhood picking up what cotton the machines missed and never forgot what poverty looked like. Dad was not without flaw. He hated Greek people or, as he called them on his most intolerant days, "bearded women and fetabreaths." But he genuinely believed that "those who can, do... those who can't, you help." He would even go so far as to help someone maintain their façade of leisure. I remember the woman in a steakhouse Dad favored: her fake knotted pearls, either really bad rosacea or textured rouge, Lovee Howell in decay. I stood next to her at the salad bar as she put soupy coleslaw on her plate. "Nova Chambers can't afford to eat here," I heard Dad tell Mom on the way back to our booth. "She's on a fixed." This was shorthand for fixed income. He requested Nova's check with our own, asking that the waitress "please not tell her who took care of this, just that it's been paid." Mom pinched his earlobe and called him "my Good Samaritan."

I have never yet formally met Fernie, who spent fifteen dollars this year. Another year will pass without me thinking once of her. I also know the December will come that I will get an uncomfortable look, that "oh, shit" look, when I casually ask of Georgia what Fernie chose.

It will be the same look I gave dry cleaner Gwen. Uh-oh. Barry hasn't heard.

Thankfully, this is not that year. No, this year I *am* Fernie, lingering in corners, looking at what others have and I don't.

I go to my other window. I see that the basketball net will definitely need to be replaced by spring. As I make a note to also have someone check on the well-being of the two basketballs, now in storage, our receptionist timidly calls to ask if I'm available to Mr. Raoul McCollum, my attorney.

I am, in fact. What a coincidence. I want to talk to him too.

IF THE GRPL collective appliquéd sweaters and Santa caps isn't Charlie Brownish enough with its misshapen dwarf tree, it's downright Mary Tyler Mooresian with a cheese ball that looks rolled in mulch and a Jonestown of mushy shrimp felled around rivulets of cocktail sauce.

Once Adele opens the floor to any announcements, I make mine. This will represent a good dry run for the disbelief from friends and colleagues.

"I've put together a proposal to sell Great Rooms!" I tell the room.

When my attorney called to triumphantly talk about a settlement, I let him go first. Tarantella's insurers had prevailed upon his team, pointing out I didn't join legal forces with anyone else. This, to them, demonstrated a willingness to negotiate out of court, without a seated jury, for-hire experts, and reconstruction specialists. I'm not so altruistic. There is no forgiveness. I'm just unwilling to publicly exhume those details in what could turn out to be a miniseries, replete with sidebars of Tarantella's many good civic works, the workers they employ, and those families they support.

"They're as anxious to put this behind them as I'm sure you are," Raoul smoothly noted. Apparently I've played Merry Widower long enough. I'm on everyone's nerves.

Any capitulation will be reviled by the survivors, peeved by my cash grab while they brandish torches and seek justice, Raoul warned. Well, I don't want to lead a lynch mob. Their lives, shattered as they are, are still theirs to live. Andy's isn't.

Raoul's known our general finances since my first Great Rooms! expansion. I'm acutely aware of the envy in his summary of the money involved, that "this many zeroes don't fit on the allotted line." What he's thinking is that this is a sum that gives a person the footfall to outrun sorrow. I can put it all behind me. Raoul then read me a carefully parsed press statement drafted by Tarantella that also emphasized Andy's estate has waived any future action. He asked if I wanted to insert my own remarks.

I didn't want.

What I wanted to do, I began, was figure out an easy way for employees to buy a majority of my interest of the store, a no-cash outlay stock swap. Vendors had long made me aware that other stores have quietly shopped us, trying to turn what they see into a starter kit for something similar elsewhere. The occasional and outright acquisition feelers—one even put out by my own former employer—I always treated gently but firmly, like a centipede: it's nothing to cruelly squash, but you also don't want it on the dining room table. All of the arduous gestation was not to sell out and suckle at a corporate teat, to lie about delivery dates and sell what a former boss called "content." I admire those gay titans of our industry, Mitchell Gold + Bob Williams, but I never want to be them.

Raoul roughed out some transaction details as we talked. I suggested elements to make the agreement clean with no hidden clauses to burn anyone, yet a measure should also be constructed to prevent an outside takeover. Capitulation to any former suitor who perceives weakness in my departure cannot be an option, nor can a quorum of employees resell Great Rooms!

I have him activate his phone recorder to take just one verbatim codicil: "Isaac might leave our employ, Georgia could retire, but Fernie is never to be turned away. She is always to be allowed her choice of Christmas item, cost irrelevant." Raoul wasn't even curious why. He just asked her last name.

His corporate specialist would assemble this into an immediate presentation prospectus. Still, he pressed me: Are you sure about this?

My mourning is a trail of bread crumbs that clearly needs to dead-end here and now, so I brightly repeat his own words. "I want to put it all behind me."

"Good for you!" Raoul congratulated me.

I hear the GRPL tongues clicking, the sound I used to make to wake my hamster.

"Honestly, I've stopped going to High Point and the Merchandise Mart. I only went to New York market so we could write off Broadway tickets. It'll be the same managers, designers doing the bids, workroom folks. Minus Barry."

"We caution about no life-altering decisions for one year," Adele says.

"What brought this on?" Sally asks.

I tell them about my run-in with Cruella deVil and Candy Spelling.

Adele shakes her head. "You were awfully tough on those gals."

"I regret it." Not as much as I should, but I do, about as much as Adele should regret wearing all red with that white Russian-style fur hat. She looks like a bottle of ketchup.

"Barry forgets that his situation is unique," Janet adds.

"I know it was incredibly public."

"What I meant is some don't know what to say about your friend," Janet clarifies.

"Not friend, not roommate. Husband, Janet. I lost my family. That's not unique."

"We tend to think of pets as kids." Janet focuses on everyone else, one face at a time. "It's not, however, procreation."

"At least look at me when you condescend, Janet." I'm trying to remain calm. "Barb told us about the frustration and sadness that she and her husband couldn't have kids. Should they have divorced?" She knows my argument has no logical answer and knows better than to put forward an illogical one in Barb's presence. I press on. "And same-sex couples *do* have children. Haven't you ever seen *Modern Family*?" I wait out the murmurs of familiarity. "That we opted out of strollers, Janet, didn't make our dogs a substitute anything."

"Someone brought us his anger," Adele decides.

"I had the impression this was the environment to heal all that in."

"If we make it into your Blackberry," Barb says, smarting because I cited her deformed cervix.

"We haven't seen you for three weeks," Adele says.

"I didn't realize there was a mandatory roll call," I reply stiffly. I'm not going to say anything about my surgery or the downtime, because a member will invariably cast their arms wide and implore, "Why didn't you reach out?"

Sally's smile is treacly. "There's comfort in consistency."

Marnie tries to interpret this as informational. "Besides, it helps us *all* understand."

"Understand what? Your gay panic?" I hear myself demanding.

"I adore a niece who's very mannish," Marnie points out.

"I'm not here to educate any of you. I'm tired of seeking approval. Trying to gain my own, then a half-assed endorsement from the rest of the world. Have you known the degradation of being turned down for a loan because of who you are?"

I was dredging up when I stupidly refused to exercise Andy's clout and went to a local bank to underwrite another gallery expansion. A homophobic loan officer with hair on a hinge snickered at the numbers I'd compiled, suggested I was a "flighty risk," and declined my application.

Oscar closes his newspaper to look at me. "Actually, yes."

Adele seems to revel in this from the punch bowl. "Everyone feels disenfranchised. When you didn't come back, we thought we'd wronged you, so we hashed out some tolerance issues."

The chastened silence now is just as infuriating. "My disbelief is official." I bracket the air. "Thanks for *tolerating* me."

"Poor wording on my part." Adele takes a deep breath. "Barry, listen."

I clap my hands. "Actually, no, *you* listen! Me and Andy had managed to cultivate an idyllic zone where we were insulated from snickers. Then *bam*! Cranes and beams fall on my life, and I'm back to being 'hashed out'?"

"Valid, but off topic," Barb decides.

"Off topic?" I yell. "We know every excruciating detail about Roxanne and Phil assembling a trampoline for their granddaughter."

"That's unwarranted," Roxanne whispers.

"Get off the kid's back!" Shorty says.

From some flashcard she's committed to memory, Adele recites that "grief is a process, like composting."

The kid stands. "Both smell like shit. I hoped this would help me move on, not move in. For example, you, Sally. Your daughter was killed in that gas explosion how many years ago?"

Sally looks down at her salt-stained boots. "Seven."

"Seven years ago. How can you help me bury my dead when you can't bury your own?" I boom.

Gulps of indignation.

"I don't even know how I ended up with a Grapple card."

Adele's face turns as red as a tomato, which, given her outfit, is appropriate. "We do outreach!"

"You cruise funerals!"

More gasps.

I thrust my arms into my coat. "I never respected people who identified themselves as victims. That was before I was victimized. I didn't know where to go. I don't trust whoever took over for Dear Abby and Ann Landers. Miss Cleo was a phony, Dr. Phil's a horse's ass. I looked in the Yellow Pages. There's The Pozibilites, Red Hankies—whoever they are—I could even whine about my circumcision in a Foreskin Restoration Group. I ended up here."

Adele is distraught. "Please sit down, Barry!"

"No, I won't sit down. Grapple, crapple! I was better off at home rereading my sympathy cards."

I stomp down the hallway, then outside. The flurries when I arrived are now snowfall that is sticking. I run into one of those spiral trees that looks good from a great distance but is, in fact, a fiber-optic corkscrew when you get close. In my Jeep, I wipe away tears. I feel foolish. I acted like Fred Phelps and his ilk were advancing toward me. I just couldn't help it. Dr. Steve was right. Fury has replaced sorrow.

Someone is beating on my window, obviously dispatched to check on my well-being or to see what other words I can rhyme with grapple. Snow collapses inward as I roll the window down. I compose myself for contrition.

A GRPL male in antlers whispers, "Hey, what more do you know about that foreskin get-together?"

I drive under colored lights strung over intersections, mostly the same red and amber and green of the stoplight itself, like it has reproduced. Christmas in grotesque derivation is everywhere. A car with a wreath wired to its bumper honks several times at me. I don't know anyone who wires a wreath to their bumper. Well, yes, I do. My mother.

Friends have tried to involve me in the holidays. Kerrick called with an idea. We'll sup in a stable on the backs of real live reindeer. Elderly midgets will be employed as elf food-runners, permitted to speak to us only after they've sucked from a canister of helium. Won't that be fun? I think he's kidding, or exaggerating, at least about the elf bit. I say no. Then we'll exchange, Dee announces, even though it was decided years ago to stop. They need nothing and I need less, unless someone has access to a time machine that can take me back five years backward or forward five years, any time where my life is bearable again. I say no. No. No. No. My mouth forming the words must look like a rodent's butthole.

I select on the tuner an all-Christmas-all-the-time station, the kind sought when Andy and I would fill a Thermos with Bailey's and just enough decaf and jump in the car to taunt holiday excess. For every tasteful row of white shrubbery that glowed within, there was the juxtaposition of Frosty the Snowman holding a flashing Star of Bethlehem above that ol' silk hat those kids found. Our windows would steam with cheers and jeers. We loved the display where the proud homeowner had repainted weathered nativity scene figurines with a heavy hand and did a little customization with putty along the way too. Mary was more Magdalene in what seemed to be lip liner and a French manicure. The Baby Jesus had been reconstructed from a meltdown and was now a child of Thalidomide, limbs stunted, little fingers fused, and his redrawn eyes too far apart. The Wise Men had some pretty serious vitiligo.

Our second favorite was when somebody decked the halls and took their inside dispute outside by hurling the family tree lights, ornaments and all, onto the front lawn. How bad had it gotten in that house? It's really hard to retract that kind of gesture. Still, in a very environment-hostile way, it was sweet to see starlings fly in and out with tinsel that would provide them disco nesting.

Then we stopped doing all that. When was that, when it became too much a hassle to go look at Christmas lights? Was it after we took Noel and Gertie with us and they puked all over their cranberry sweaters, then the seats, then into a heat vent? It's exactly what happened to our weekly date night, when it became our weekly crash-on-sofa night. It wasn't remarked upon. We were just too tired to share lettuce wraps at PF Chang's.

So here they are, those time-release misgivings Mom predicted, home for the holidays. They've come to piss in the snow. Andy might have died on my birthday, but he also died on Christmas, he died on the Fourth of July, he died on every holiday I will spend without him.

I flip the warm air toward me. I could have tolerated Roger Whittaker, the Ray Conniff Singers, even Enya while hoping for The Ronettes, but no, it has to be "Merry Christmas, Darling" which comes into rotation. The lyric a little too applicable, I turn off Karen Carpenter's mournful voice.

Stupidly, I think about what Sally said. A child might be a comfort right now, might carry me over the threshold. It could also be a burden, someone else to ignore, and the neglect of a child also in mourning is unpardonable. This is why Andy and I dismissed it. With our fourteen-hour workdays, our latchkey offspring would have been eating Cool Whip for dinner. And we weren't prepared to forego three weeks in Europe during what would be the school year, and we were smart enough to know it, which is why I stop thinking about what Sally said, damn her.

It is snowing horizontally. An enormous possum waddles across the drifting road. One wind gust is so hard it feels like it lifts the back end of the Jeep. If I had a legitimate accident, no one would believe it. They'd say, there you go, Barry was sadder then he let on, look how he crawled out and froze just like his grandma, blue-lipped at the base of a yard inflatable, same as that agoraphobic fattie wedged up next to his toilet brush.

I slow to take a good gander at this year's merry monstrosity as I enter our neighborhood: a replication of The Polar Express at what I guess is about 50 percent of actual size. The conductor is a passable

Tom Hanks mannequin and kids with dead eyes are carefully positioned in the train windows. The owners are childless. The insanity escalates.

My driveway is iffy. The snow on it appears shin-high. The neighborhood kids in their private school uniforms were too privileged for manual labor and the professionals who reliably plowed the gallery lot weren't as reliable with residential accounts. Somewhere in the garage is a snow blower, but Andy took care of that. Its operation is as foreign to me as steaming new drapery was to him. A blizzard is not the time to peel the instruction manual pages apart.

I rock for momentum. Yelling always helps. "Act like a fucking Jeep!" I lose the battle. The Jeep makes a sharp left into the front yard. Swirling white pelts me as I get out into snow that is actually knee-deep. Maybe it's the chip on my shoulder that is making me walk so lopsided.

Jesus, I just tripped on a bowling shoe. A navy blue dot on the back says "Size 4."

Okay, it's really just a bit of branch brought down by the weight of wet snow.

Through bursts of my own breath, I see something else.

Him.

There he is.

No, really.

It's Andy, in the cargo shorts and tank worn the day he died. He, Gertie, and Noel are coming toward me from around the towering gingko.

Andy doesn't look cold, yet he's frozen in time. He will always look the same. I won't.

Andy sets our pugs free. "There he is! Go see Daddy!"

A squall erases the scene.

I stumble over the milk box, already buried, as I come in the reclaimed oak front door of my dark house.

I even refused friends' entreaties to help decorate, and so my Christmas tree has no lights. I brought out every plastic tote, but I got no further than the red skirt.

I look down. Slush from my shoes puddles on the velvet.

If Andy were living, I would have untangled and tested lights; we would have unwrapped tissue from the dated ornaments we commemorated every year together with; we would have then reminisced about those brought back as souvenirs. What a joyless travelogue these ornaments represent, a chronology that abruptly ended. We went everywhere but now he's not here. I reach into a bin. This one holds the M's. Mount Rushmore. Machu Picchu (he climbed, I shopped). Mykonos. I pull out Maui Christmas. Andy would always tell a story, a true one, to whomever had joined us to trim the tree and drink. Usually, I'd leave the room, but I still hear his words.

"I was walking around downtown Maui. It's called Lahaina. Maybe you knew that. Barry was napping. I saw this big barn. What had to be hundreds of the most gorgeous parrots—African Grey, macaws, budgies, cockatoos and cockatiels—were hanging from the ceiling on wood perches, like trapezes, staggered at different lengths. Price tags hung on the rods: $1,000. $2,000. One was $5,000. Not one of them was tethered. The owner ambled over. I asked him, 'This is a lot of money in here and not one of them's secured. What keeps them from flying away?'

"He said, 'They're like humans. They don't know they can leave'."

He loved to tell that story, commenting on it himself if he had to: "That's pretty deep, right? Right?"

I see how someone could fling their decorated tree out onto the lawn. They couldn't bear to look at the goddamn thing anymore. I don't, however, think I can get it through the doorframe. I withdraw a tropical snow globe from another tote and shake it so that the sand flies around a palm tree. Once it settles, I activate the cell phone I had turned off at GRPL request.

I text Isaac that he will be feeding and watering the staff at our holiday party. I add that I will be busy eating a humble pie of shit.

I don't have a wishing tree or anything like that to retreat to. Key West will do. I call Delta to book a flight. I head into our bathroom when Reservations puts me on hold. I begin decanting toiletries into TSA-friendly bottles. I stop. I have product down there.

Which also means I will again have Andy's to throw out.

Andy and I each carried a kindergarten school photo of the other in our wallets, behind our driver's license, a reminder of who we were before we knew the other existed. His is all ears that eventually settled close to his head, or so he liked to believe. I wonder if it was Yvonne who combed the slick part in his hair, if Dolores chose the tan turtleneck and burgundy cardigan. The photo was trimmed with pinking shears, surely by a sister. The pall over their household, twin baby boys bathed in a sink by sisters robbed of their mother and their adolescence, makes me cry so hard and for so long my ribcage is wet.

Mine must still be in his wallet, salvaged from his bloody pocket and returned to me, only to be dispatched immediately to a fireproof chest in the basement.

I move my license to a monogrammed travel billfold Andy gave me years ago. It will hold an itinerary, boarding pass, cash for tips. Then I slide in his photo, my talisman.

Chapter Seven

Above the Fold

SURPRISE COLONYSCAPE DEATH SETTLEMENT REACHED

The estate of the man who died in the mid-September crane collapse at ColonyScape Luxury Townhomes will receive an undisclosed settlement, it was revealed today by those familiar with the out-of-court agreement.

Insiders indicate that the compensation could exceed $20 million.

Four separate insurance companies, none locally based, are involved.

News of the swift settlement will not bring a close to many of the lingering legal issues surrounding the most infamous industrial accident to ever occur in the city.

On September 16, the boom extension of a stationary crane used in demolition at 1621 Wooster Avenue suddenly gave way, initiating a chain reaction collapse of the empty ten-story building.

A parked car, occupied by local banking VP Andrew Morgan, 45, and several house pets, was crushed and buried.

Autopsy results concluded Morgan perished instantly of blunt force trauma.

In addition, one male and two females in the vicinity were struck and severely injured by falling debris.

Litigation continues with the three survivors, who require various extensive surgeries and long-term rehabilitation.

Without confirming the agreement, Beaumont Shelby of Tarantella Demolition Contractors issued a statement, saying, "Any action will reaffirm industry safety standards and avoid long-term legal costs associated with pursuing a jury trial."

Local attorney Raoul McCullom called it "the saddest case I have ever witnessed" in his legal career.

"While avoiding adversarial litigation is always preferable, there are no winners here as we close this chapter. Our hope is that any settlement will be a tribute to the man who died," McCullom noted, "and provide an opportunity to share information on crane safety and demonstrate real commitment to a safer work environment."

The executor of the Morgan estate had no comment.

Chapter Eight

Tropical Depression

HOW naive, to think the front page safe again. Not so, not after Raoul's media statement, which reasserted Andy's worthiness with chronology coverage, engulfed with file photos of him, the site, the other survivors. Even dry cleaner Gwen must have put two and two together by now.

A parked car, occupied by local banking VP Andrew Morgan, 45, and several house pets, was crushed and buried.

Two is not several. Stop making it worse.

Autopsy results concluded Morgan perished instantly of blunt force trauma.

The medical coda I didn't want to know.

The executor of the Morgan estate had no comment.

What vindication for Janet. It's the money shot, and I am not even a friend or a roommate. I go unacknowledged in any way, which is what I thought I wanted, and maybe I'm being touchy, but now it saddens me. If I hadn't put my name into the obituary, I wouldn't have existed in a public forum. I'm just the executor, which sounds like I'm masked and waiting with my axe at a chopping block.

THE airlines do suck, as Mom prosaically determined.

During holiday travel, they also use their teeth.

What used to be a pleasant jaunt south is grueling, exacerbated by college students heading home for break, families shamed into opening gifts in Ft. Myers with their retired parents, and one bossy woman who claims she has always been permitted to bring a jug of wine aboard.

I watch everyone avoiding checked baggage fees by hoisting into overheard bins and cramming under seats. Deplaning will take longer than the flight itself. When the word Christmas was replaced by Holiday, they also banished merriment and replaced it with misery. Air rage is not limited to the ticket holder. One attendant, probably disheartened by the corporate box cutters taken to wage and benefits, claps loudly to "better get a move-on if you want to leave on time" at a woman struggling in thick leg braces.

My seatmate is a giantess who loudly demands two seat-belt extensions as though she's Constitutionally guaranteed. It is big enough to bundle utility poles. She unwraps an overstuffed sandwich from wax paper she has toted aboard. A tangle of sauerkraut drops onto her blouse from the soggy Reuben and there it remains, like a membership brooch in The Girth Club. A businessman in front of me reclines and crunches my kneecaps. I wish I'd brought that Vicodin.

To make my tight connection, I sprint through the Hartsfield-Jackson Atlanta International Airport, which is larger than my hometown. We cattle are whisked to the next holding pen via monorail. At the gate, I determine that most people lack a decent hem in their slacks and that people in general are getting shorter. At exactly six feet, I seem to tower over others. Or maybe travel just beats everyone down. Maybe this is the reason it is called a terminal.

The adjoining seat is empty, which gladdens me. No one will ask me to switch because they prefer the window or they want to sit next to their spouse. I try to be accommodating, especially if a child is involved, unless it means I'm transplanted near the bathroom. Someone's in there a beat too long, that door flies open, and you pray flight nerves haven't given the occupant explosive bowels, or they at least flushed and flushed throughout.

We're already past Miami. I can see the archipelago of keys that terminate at Key West.

It was all about early retirement, Andy more than me. Did he somehow intuit he wouldn't survive to his sixties? We were making great money and responsible with it, but we wanted investment opportunities that weren't just pieces of paper, so we decided to explore winter getaways that would also fit long-term goals. Dee found a Palm Springs Realtor. We canvassed the California desert first with Gorham, an imp who had unwisely used what must've been a high school yearbook photograph in his ads, making what stood before us seem like a fixer upper. He was dressed in madras for, or from, golf. His eyelids looked like scrotums. Every time he opened a door of a prospective ranch house, he hopped a strange little hop: "This is it! I feel it!" After Gorham's seventh rumba, Andy grabbed my arm. "The lawns feel fake, and I can't live in a home that looks like a clay incense burner."

Sensing he was losing us—Andy, up front, actually went through the glove compartment in boredom—Gorham suggested, stealing some listing sheet's hyperbole, that we tour a community "for fifty-five and better."

"Better than what? Better than a stroke? No thanks," Andy declined, so sure of many healthy and hearty years ahead.

Houses aside—many also involved restrictive land leases we didn't understand—the downtown was seedy and based around a sprawling casino, and we couldn't figure out where Palm Springs ended and the next town began. We were troubled that major avenues were named after dead celebrities like Mary Pickford, George Montgomery, and Gene Autry and even questionable celebrities that were still alive, like Monty Hall.

"Somebody obviously made a deal," Andy scoffed.

"How long can a town dine out on the fact it was a 1930s playground for Hollywood stars?" I wondered. "Can't they at least designate a street after Barry Manilow? Or if they want real edge, Robert Downey Jr.?"

"Who in the hell is Buddy Rogers?" Andy asked.

We thanked Gorham and took the Chino Canyon tram, where Andy got a nosebleed. We endured an overpriced theatrical extravaganza of senior showgirls that we renamed *A Chorus Cane*. We ate at a restaurant on the gay street Arenas (quickly renamed Our Anus), where the AARP logo so dominated the door we actually thought its name *was* AARP. Neck bones popped like breakfast cereal as we walked in. That spaceship at the end of *Cocoon*, this was where it detoured. We were frightened by this flash-forward. Everyone was either as snowcapped as the mountains, which the desert sun slid behind by four thirty, halting any practical activity outdoors, or was a Tom Bianchi clone. It was hard to ignore the WeHo exiles, the rough trade hustlers and the people who didn't belong together beyond the economics, harder yet not to notice the many wellness clinics and twenty-four-hour pharmacies, how handicapped spaces engulfed Ralphs' parking lot and were always occupied, and how we never saw a jungle gym. When I commented on the vast number of carpet outlets in Coachella Valley and how Mom would be impressed, Andy retorted, "That's because *das eldergay* shit and spit up and stain the wall-to-wall."

When we saw our sixth home delivery of oxygen, I repeated what I'd always heard: "People really do come to the desert to die."

As if to underscore this, Andy turned left on Fred Waring Road. "Any tourism-driven community who built their town around Bob Hope has none," he decided, swerving to avoid a waxy woman on a walker as she inched into a hat shop.

We flew out of the Sonny Bono Concourse. Point made.

Before we'd commit to another house-hunting trip, we asked around about Florida. People we knew in Lauderdale griped about traffic congestion. People we knew in Miami griped about hip-hop, which we knew was code for other things. We zeroed in on Key West. We'd been once, enjoyed the parasailing, ate a lot of stone crab claws. When Dee decreed, after endless virtual 360-degree walk-throughs, that you can't make a decision based on a cursor, we went down.

When Hayward DeMott spoke, his mouth didn't seem comfortable with whatever dentistry he'd had. He took us to the eyebrow house we'd found viable and affordable. The exterior was the color of Pepto-Bismol. Built in 1912, it was smothered under unchecked, thorny bougainvillea. The rotting shutters were more decorative than protective. The tin roof was a colander and, judging from the piles of sawdust, the front door was a termite Pop-Tart. We liked its survival instincts.

"Minnie Pearl slept here many times," Hayward told us, making a sucking sound like an ice cube had pressed on a filling. "Her relatives owned this in the sixties." I began looking for oversized price tags.

We walked its square footage and discussed necessary enhancements. We got our first taste of the we-iz-po-don't-got-nuffin' moroseness some Key Westers seemed to carry piggyback.

"Now, boys, boys, don't go over-improving," Hayward cautioned, chewing his tongue. "We here in Key West don't need much."

"Do you need to wash your clothes?" Andy asked, searching in vain for laundry facilities.

"And do you then need to hang up those clothes?" I had crawled onto the floorboards of the only upstairs closet, three feet high, with three staggered dowel roads. Hayward had to help me out.

"It's a workable space," he said with a little whistle, like he'd bitten into aluminum foil.

I brushed more sawdust from my hands. "If you wear nothing but onesies."

To round his negative sales technique, our Realtor wanted us to know that "the Lower Keys means low-key. You might find South Beach more happening."

"We already happened, thanks," Andy dismissed our naysayer. "We've been hip. We're looking for somewhere to break one."

Andy's favorite American poet from college was Wallace Stevens, who wrote the dense *The Idea of Order at Key West*, about a stranger enchanted by a woman singing somewhere along a Key West seashore. I don't know what Andy admired more, Stevens's Modernist art or that he sensibly accomplished most of it while running an insurance agency, but he took the poet and his poem as a sign we belonged here.

He was good with signs.

Clearly, I am not.

Andy hurried us off to a bookstore where he collected a pile of self-published volumes about Key West by authors you'll never again hear of. Everything was fascinating research to him, and he kept laying trivia at my feet. Like how it's never dipped below freezing in Key West. Why each key lime tree is unique. How you could do about 22,312 things with a mango. By the time we'd walked back to our inn, he'd read me a history of the nineteen-acre town cemetery, how it was above ground due to the impenetrable coral but, more importantly, also at the island's highest elevation in Solares Hill. Established in 1847, this was the second attempt at a cemetery. Its former location, near the ocean, was disinterred after a hurricane. Ocean surge and wind flung human remains out of graves and into the trees, nature's prankish way of toilet papering: Mamaw's skeleton cross-legged in a royal poinciana, most of your uncle lounging in the canopy of a lignum vitae.

And did you know, he recited as he flopped on the bed, that a Cat 5 hurricane forced the evolution of Henry Flagler's railroad into the Overseas Highway and that the highway, now known as US 1, opened in 1938?

"Why don't you go to work for The History Channel?" I advised.

"Why don't you go to work on my scholarly cock?" he said, spreading his legs.

He powered his iPad to get the basics of taxes and windstorm insurance, then gathered more minutiae from newspaper archives and blogs. Local legends like house hauntings, prayer grottos, secret underground smuggling tunnels, where part-time resident Divine used to eat Cuban press sandwiches. He summarized the whole Conch (not like *lunch* but *honk*) thing—how the locals named themselves that after a bottom-feeding mollusk. He affected some incomprehensible scalawag brogue as he told me all about the island's violent piracy beginnings.

"You're kinda crusty, too, come to think of it," I noted.

"Suck my peg leg," he growled.

On Hulu, he even found a 1995 episode from a lame and short-lived FOX sitcom called *Key West*. After Fisher Stevens wins a lottery, he flees to Key West. There, he befriends Jennifer Tilly, playing a high-class hooker, which Key West has exactly none of; they are all skanky, dumpy, and in flip-flops, probably like the one Kelly McGillis's ex-husband was arrested soliciting. (This was before she admitted to the world what locals knew.)

Our second inspection was perfunctory. We already knew we were going to buy. We'd even christened it Pinkie. And so we did, at asking price, and after months of wayward city permits and wastrel contractors, the upgrade of Pinkie was complete.

We are low enough now that I see a grouping of loggerhead sea turtles in a perfect diamond, submerging when a boat comes near them on the Atlantic's turquoise waters. I wonder if Andy now can, if he so chooses, swim with them.

We'd make the two-day drive to Key West if our stay was longer than a week. We always brought Gertie and Noel. The goal for Day One: make it to Florida. You know you've made it to Gainesville, especially grim, when you see shirtless people stomping along the road in what you assume is a retreat from vehicular distress, but then you never see the vehicle. Day Two: the slow slog through South Florida. We would have at least one argument about whose responsibility it had been to have replenished our SunPass online. Hold your appetite and water; the Florida turnpike has the worst rest stops in America. And watch your speed. After the final toll on Card Sound Road, a series of speed traps are another revenue resource in a state with no personal income tax. We might stop at Baiha Honda Park and let the puppets dodge the waves, but we were usually in a rush to get to Pinkie.

We descend near the Seven Mile Bridge. The attendant asks us to gather our discards from the seat back pocket. Considering the price of a plane ticket—plus fuel surcharge and overweight luggage assessment—I refuse. I wish I'd brought extra trash aboard to cram in: rancid foods, cigar butts.

The runway of Key West International Airport is abbreviated, due to zealous protection of surrounding wetlands, which means touchdown is like being tossed off a high-rise.

Music begins playing somewhere to set the mood for the new arrivals, still staggering from our abrupt landing. Luggage retrieved, I call Mom.

"I'll spend a few days with you when I return." I look beyond the parking lot of the Key West International Airport and the South Roosevelt seawall. "You understand, don't you, Mom? I wanted to be elsewhere. Everyone will be aching to know how I made out in the settlement. It was in this morning's paper. Not the exact amount, just speculation."

"No one with any decency would ask," she chides, then she asks indecently, "How much, honey?"

"MYOB," I reply.

"We didn't sue about Grandma."

She disapproves, her tone says. Of course you didn't sue, Mom. In life, Grandma was already stiff and cold. The nursing staff did you and S.J. a favor. You were remarkably calm when you said, within hours of the body's recovery, "At least I kept the receipts," meaning the unwrapped gifts we'd intended to take over Christmas night.

I end our conversation by asking if, while I'm in Key West, she'd maybe like something from Lilly Pulitzer. No, Mom says. Just more shells, please. She scatters them around her garden, piles of them. She must tell neighbors they mystically washed up there.

I get into a van to be told we're going to "wait for a coupla more folks". Ultimately, it's a clown car, so tightly grouped we are virtually fucking. Our driver drives along the ocean and pontificates on the fecal run-off that's contaminated and closed some beachfronts, so "too bad about you." I know his type. *Welcome, folks, to your shitty vacation, since I can't afford to go on one.* Andy and I had quickly found that second-home buyers were suspect, every Northerner was a carpetbagger, cruise ships were decimating the coral reef, and tourists were a reviled necessity. We liked that Key West didn't have a lot of class—no one acts like they're a catwalk model unless their catwalk happens to be Sears—but we quickly discerned a class distinction. From groceries to fast food to gasoline, Key West has never been a cheap place to live, always a delicate matrix of economics where poverty and prosperity could coexist. Now, they clash.

Our driver continues to gives us the lowdown on what he calls "the world's largest open-air asylum." He urges us to bypass the high-wire walking cats at the "pre-fab" sunset gathering at Mallory Square. "Front Street always floods when it rains. The Israeli Army launders money through most of the T-shirt shops, so stay out. Every other parking meter is out of order, but they'll still tow your ass if you're at one."

I can't help but chime in. "That's what I come here for. The continuity."

Another brave soul suggests maybe city government needs to be overhauled. Good goddamn luck, he sputters, since the whole town is manipulated by three or four families whose names end in *ez*. "And you don't vote here unless you're dead." I know this is true. At least one-eighth of the voting bloc in the last, discredited city commission election, according to an investigation, lived in the cemetery. Rod Blagojevich had nothing on the literal skullduggery of Key West politics. Monroe County is largely ignored by the rest of the state.

Every deal is cut in a back room, eclipsing the ideal of Florida's Sunshine Law. Graft and theft are the two prevalent vocations. We rather liked the rampant cronyism and the blatant nepotism, Andy especially. It was such a departure from banking regulations. We could be pretend renegades in a town full of the real deal.

Our driver is not done ripping up these folks' postcards home. Don't count on running into Jimmy Buffett: "He got all uppity and moved to West Palm."

I want to interject that we've got author Judy Blume, but I guess she isn't the same kind of crowd-pleaser, unless you're a censorious school board.

We drop off at hotels and inns. With my Old Town address, I am last.

The deadbolt lock sticks from the salt air. Pinkie smells like a stale sink sponge. Unrented and unoccupied throughout storm evacuations and my own lack of aggression, our commissionless management company obviously pink-slipped the caretakers. All of my plug-ins are empty, diffuser sticks are dry. Andy used to question my reliance on artificial scent by pointing out jasmine doesn't grow from outlets and there was nothing offensive about a house smelling like what's been cooked. But after being entertained by others and wondering what had died behind their drywall, he came to grudgingly appreciate my Glade spray holster.

Over the next few days, I do the upkeep chores we always divided. I WD-40 the lock. I replenish the wall plug-ins and bask in gardenia. I power wash the oily coral dust from the house. I soak dormant orchids, strapped to trees with pieces of pantyhose, with Bloom Booster. I toss magnesium pellets under the palm trees. I inspect shutter hinges. I cut down a chenille plant that looks diseased.

Then I tackle my biggest worry: the massive green coconuts dangling from our front tree. Just one could split a person's head open. This was always Andy's assignment. I put on his Tommy Bahama shirt and extract what I can. My right shoulder immediately bothers me. That I will need Icy Hot after something so basic as shaping a tree bothers me more. If I pick up the right tube. I've misplaced all three pairs of my reading glasses and might end rubbing toothpaste on my shoulder.

"I saw the lights on the other night, but I thought it was holiday renters!"

Without looking I know that it's Testosterina (full name: Testosterina Estrogina Jorgenson), a local drag queen at the Duval Street show club Barrage. Although caulked and powdered from sternum to hairline, he's in boy clothing. We were both fond of Teste, the male-ish name we coined and he adopted, since he detested his given name of Leonard and those who gave it to him. In turn, he called us Papa Bear and Andy Panda.

"I do the meanest tuck since *Silence Of The Lambs*, but I like my ding-dong and I know to use it when I get the chance," he would boast. "Like this Sloppy Joe's bouncer," he lamented after his country/western show, *There's a Ho Down*, one night, "telling me how beautiful I was, stuffing ten-dollar bills between and under my cutlets. Then his club chub went all soft and gooey in the bedroom." Actually, Reba McEntire was lamenting this to us, and that was the problem: striking the balance between drag and fag that suitors inevitably insisted upon. It's hard to butch it up as you massage the welts left by a waistnipper with French tips.

"Ack! Ya nevah call, ya nevah write!" Testosterina is swinging his hand like a windmill, very Bette Davis or, rather, very Charles Pierce as Bette Davis.

We double-kiss the air.

"Maybe, Testosterina, because your phone is always being disconnected and you move every three weeks."

"We can't all be land baronesses, Papa Bear. But surprise, surprise, I *am* moving again." Testosterina fidgets with his bracelet. "Me and my drag Mom—you know ShastaFantaFaygo and Sofonda Cox, our drag daughter—we're desperate to find something together."

"I don't remember Sofonda."

"Formerly known as Tarry Stool. We made her change it. Had no class."

I touch his contoured jawline. "Why the deadly daytime drag?"

"Some fat black bitch diva with a booger wigline is down from Miami and took over our dressing room for New Year's. I did my basecoat realness at home because I'm hosting today." We often lingered after Texas Hold'em tournaments for the Early Bird Karaoke he was referring to. "Last week, this old piece of shit I called on was full of mojitos or was featuring a blood clot, I don't know which. He thought the mike was an electric razor and started to shave with it. Fuck it, I let him. I just had the DJ play a low-level hum for a coupla minutes." Before I can say anything, he continues. "Did you hear about the Reverend Antoine Warren? No, of course not, not up north. He's a local black minister, always chastising the deviant lifestyles. They found him in a lap dance stall, bottle of poppers in one hand, pious penis all hard with rigor mortis in the other. Stripper just left him there. Tried to hush it up, but even the village idiot knows."

This death gossip is the ripcord. I know what comes next.

"You guys drive?"

I plummet into the biohazard site without a parachute.

"Flew."

"You and Andy Panda didn't bring the puppets?"

Here it is again. I didn't know about Reverend Warren up North, no one down South knows about Andy, and I've been fibbing. When I talked to David, the host and owner of Sarabeth's, an *our* tripped me up. David asked where Andy was, and I told him he was dieting. Vi at Flamingos Café gave me a curious look when I took a stool at the counter. I said Andy wasn't a breakfast person. At Camille's, Denise steered me to a two-top.

"I saw Andrew did The Smart Ride again," Denise observed.

The Smart Ride, usually staged in early December, was an annual 165-mile bike trip from Miami to Key West, an AIDS/HIV fundraiser. Andy had participated twice.

"No, he didn't," I said. *He couldn't*, I wanted to say.

She frowned. "I was there when most of them arrived. It looked just like him."

My immediate thought: Alex did it as an unannounced tribute to his brother. I just as immediately dismissed this. On weekends, Alex got off the sofa only to get into bed.

Denise remained unconvinced. "I could swear it was Andrew. But of course you'd know."

Yes, I'd know.

I took the two menus from her. After three cups of coffee and pretending to watch the door, I said the little shit had apparently stood me up. Denise smiled. I ordered.

Three months, and I still have no preamble into articulating his death. I learned my lesson about snappy comebacks in Dr. Steve's office.

I lay aside the trimmer and pat that Testosterina join me on a step.

"No! I won't sit!" He shakes his fist toward the sky. "You two broke up! I know that look!"

You don't know this look.

I fix my eyes on the Fleming Street signage. It takes less than one minute to tell him. A bereft Testosterina falls into my arms. His sobs are so great he can't catch his breath. I feel bad that he will have to repaint.

SANTA'S reindeer do not wake me Christmas morning. A rooster does, strutting down the bike lane of Fleming Street announcing the approach of dawn. If it hadn't been cock, it would have been pussy; territorial catfights are commonplace under deck planks.

First light breaks through cumulus clouds that look like Marshmallow Fluff. I debate if the family-owned grocery where I fetch my café con leche—a small allotment of coffee and scalded milk in a big cup that makes you feel a little cheated until that first bold swig—will be open. Turns out they are. Maybe Cubans don't celebrate Christmas.

Andy would have known, of course.

I finish the second of the two books left me by a nameless, literary-minded benefactor the night of Andy's burial. One was nonfiction, the other a slim novel. The first, *The Year of Magical Thinking* by Joan Didion, I was familiar with. Maybe it would resonate. It did not. The text was soulless and clinical. I understood the ordinary instant stuff. Look away at your own risk, because when you turn your head back, you're widowed and life has changed forever. Hell is never more than a half mile away. Got it. Finishing it in the shade of an Australian pine at Fort Zachary Taylor beach (nicknamed by my people as Liz Taylor beach), I felt even more removed. Joan Didion and John Gregory Dunne had written a Barbra Streisand movie. He was old and had prior health complaints. She weighs about eighteen pounds. They named their daughter Quintana Roo, way worse than Daisy.

Andy and I were none of those things.

I left the book on a picnic table. A Carnival ship came in, passengers waving at every level, thrilled to momentarily escape their all-inclusive hell and waddle into town.

If Didion alienated me, the book I'm working on now in our pool angers me. It is *A Single Man*, by Christopher Isherwood. An inscription inside implored me not to see the movie. *It's boring... all extreme close-ups and grainy film stock... Tom Ford naked for two hours would've been better. Please read this.* Written in 1964 and hailed as a forerunner of gay fiction, it concerns George, a middle-aged California college professor, over twenty-four hours. His lover Jim has been dead for several months. He was killed in a car accident. Their dog was in the car. All closeted George does is mope. I'd rather be Sally Bowles, one of Isherwood's other creations. My benefactor must think of me as this English-born protagonist, the ex-pat outsider. Isherwood lazily doesn't even give George a surname and ultimately leaves him drunk and probably dead. Any Cliffs Notes for this would be printed on jaundice-colored paper.

I flip myself off my mat, watching the book pulp up with water, momentarily float, then sink under my green mat that's blue mate is still coiled in a docking rack.

Everything here is in twos.

That was the point.

Two chaise loungers. Matching pool noodles. Dual towel rack. Our two scooters, chained to a fence. Too two. Everythingsquared. Even the lizards scampering up the fan palm are partnered; he keeps mounting her, and she wriggles away. Or he. Shame on me, assuming it's a she in a town where mayoral candidates don full drag to win the LGBT community's vote.

I press my crotch up against the pool jets, the mechanical equivalent of a warm, soapy bowl. It might as well be a blowtorch. Nothing, not even the stirrings of an erection. Everything about me has flatlined.

WE'VE been here when it's been gusty and rainy, in a town where virtually no one has a furnace to abate the chill, but tonight promises to be magnificent. If I didn't know it was New Year's Eve, the tourists on Fleming directing shrill noisemakers at one another and the residual thump-thump-thump of Duval Street would have told me.

A Barrage doorman collects New Year's Eve tickets. Courtesy of Testoterina, I have one. The doorman hands me a safe-sex package. I'm approached about raffle tickets for something. Key West is a caring community, protective of its own, in constant fundraiser mode, and when snowbird money returns, they really accelerate. Broken hip, broken heel, broken spirit, someone is ready with a deviled egg and a pledge card. I buy six for twenty dollars.

The owners of Barrage spot me and shift their heads to locate The Missing One. My smile betrays nothing. Lovers, they are dressed as a bearded Father Time and an infant with a pacifier in a fat diaper made of white pillows. Their names always escaped us, but we noddingly knew them from when they opened the club. They kicked things off by trucking in sand to cover the floor for a four-day beach party. Patrons lost sandals and fell. It was a convenient ashtray. I saw a sunburned couple vomit into the sand. By Sunday night it had clumps in it from stray cats who wandered in to use the world's biggest litter pan. A few more misadventures, like the S/M night, when a participant lost consciousness during a flogging, and their enthusiasm gave way to cynicism. They learned the variables of what constituted season (mid-February to April's end), mini-season (Thanksgiving through the New Year), and Sister Season (when locals, with scant tourists to choose from, fucked each other from the Fourth of July until Halloween). Teste had told me their most recent manager had fled back to Czechoslovakia with the contents of the safe, and good riddance. It seems that, fucked-up and operating the stage lights, the Czech threw Teste into darkness during the final notes of Celine's "My Heart Will Go On." Theft is forgivable. Stepping on a drag queen's chestbang is not.

New Year's Eve, at least, is easy. No drink specials, and the blenders are unplugged. I hover near the reserved tables with bottle service facing the stage; I recognize Keith Strickland, of the B-52s, who lives here, at one of them. I see more tuxes than I'd counted on. The bar is too slammed to get near; they've even enlisted Pauline, a semiretired bartender in her late sixties, to help out. She's what the local paper would call a Key West Karakter, with long hair puddling on her shoulders that no woman after forty should have. She sees me and screams, hurrying out to hug my waist as her veiny breasts nearly jump out like incredibly affectionate alien facehuggers. She kisses every inch of my face before asking about Andy. At least I'm getting used to people looking past me for him, wondering if he's coming later. I guess we were AndyandBarry, after all. I toss my hand clockwise, like he's circulating. I ask about Fred, the man she raised three daughters with yet never wed. Toying with the bejeweled pins that fasten her wiry hair, she says she just keeps the old so-and-so around for sex but he's become too tolerant of Cialis and "the pill mill needs to figure out something fast before I start straddling the southernmost buoy." Pauline nearly sends me tumbling with a hip-check, rasping, "I love you boys!" then dashes back to her post.

Testosterina, a convincing Lady Gaga, taps my back in passing. "You okay with standing room?"

"Thanks for getting me in, Teste," I offer.

"Thank me when your knees lock."

We pause for the raffle drawing. I check my tickets. I can't read them in the haze from a fog machine, but it doesn't matter; as usual, the announcement of the winners is inaudible. Then I offer, "Looks to be quite a show tonight."

"That dressing room is like *Showgirls* without the judo. If I have to touch up, I'm walking down to the Holiday Inn. See my eyelashes?" To me, they look like dead cellar spiders. "They're real sable. Someone from PETA will probably try to blind me with red paint."

"I have a proposal for you, Teste."

"Well, you're something old, I'm the something new, I can borrow someone I blew."

"Don't pick your nosegay yet," I reply. "Call me tomorrow."

"You know it, Papa Bear. Look for me onstage at midnight if her big fat ass doesn't upend it."

It's a big girl, all right, who takes the microphone as a backing track commences. Her dress is a series of overlapping straps, like an extra-wide drive-through car wash. At least she's singing, and well. The song is one of those rousing inner-strength ballads redone every few years for a new generation.

Midnight approaches. I sneak out to Duval to find a place to stand.

We'd spent every countdown in Key West since buying Pinkie, sipping cheap champagne from plastic cups we'd walk downtown with. Our first had been 2001. Ridiculous Y2K panic governed Andy's corporate office, yet he ignored the no-vacation embargo and assured the other dyspeptic VPs he'd stay in constant touch, which he did. That New Year's Eve day, bolstered by a passion fruit martini lunch at Louie's Backyard, we set our speed limit at fifty-five. Once we reached that age, we'd retire—no excuses, no more goal setting. We had already achieved more than we set out to. Every New Year's Eve, we reiterated it. Last year, we even recited together, "Just ten more years." It never occurred to either of us that one would forfeit life less than twelve months later. How silly to entertain such a morbid thought. We would have as many New Years as we wanted in our charmed life.

Every New Year in Key West is essentially interchangeable. Local police are placed to manage the unmanageable. Very young children, some asleep, will rock on the shoulders of very young parents unwilling to stay home. I don't clearly remember a New Year's Eve until my teens but here, a pacifier is interchangeable with a noisemaker. Popguns will detonate confetti from rooftops, and a drag queen will be hand-cranked down in a supersized red pump as a prematurely gray CNN correspondent leads the countdown from Times Square cut-ins.

All of the above happens as described, except I have no one to kiss. I look up at fireworks in the sky, from both ends of the island. It is officially a new year.

Among the drunk and disorderly and those desperate to be one or the other, I recognize a Harry Reems porn mustache. It's Captain Reg, owner of The Naughty-Call boat. I stop him before he can ask. A strand of beads hits me in the forehead as I tell him. After a hug that picks me off the pavement, he insists I join his sunset cruise the day after tomorrow. I manage to promise nothing. He squeezes me a dozen more times.

I leave Duval, past barricades erected to divert vehicles away, to, then around, The Green Parrot. Pods of celebrants are falling like wooden soldiers onto Whitehead and Southard. I want to be far from this. I keep walking.

A free-range descendent of a Hemingway cat on its enormous polydactyl feet saunters by. I follow it to Olivia Street, where it takes off after something in the ferns. A small Bahamian church is *Open For Prayer and Meditation*, its main door propped wide. I admire how they would unwaveringly push salvation on a night when the entire town is holding a bottle or can. I consider going inside. I like the image of penitence it will present to passersby, a lonely queen trying to find redemption to the far-off loudspeaker music of Kool & the Gang. I walk a few more steps and see that Eleanor Rigby has already claimed my pew, with a yellow boa she borrowed from Father MacKenzie bunched around her shoulders.

I walk without purpose, cutting through blocks, taking dark lanes. A sudden slice of air, the kind only felt in Key West, makes tree foliage rustle like the brooms of innkeepers cleaning their stoops. Like a truffle-seeking pig, I follow the briny scent to the walkway approaching the White Street Pier. Key West was an early epicenter of HIV/AIDS, and here is the only official AIDS Memorial in the United States, The Quilt notwithstanding. The names are inscribed on flat black granite faceplates, flecked with the crap of sea birds. The moon, as bright as a flashlight, shows me a few names I recognize. Richard A. Heyman was the first openly gay mayor of Key West in 1983, and here is Cal Culver who, as pornstar Casey Donovan, owned an all-male guesthouse. So many, victims of the notoriously debauched 1980s, when Tennessee Williams was writing unplayable plays in his meltdown era and cocaine was a party pollen piled high on tables that people flitted to and from— what many considered the best era of Key West. Not for these men, who didn't survive long enough to benefit from lifesaving antiretrovirals.

I walk to the very end of the pier. The starry sky looks exactly like that drag queen's backing curtain, white lights punched through the holes of indigo blue fabric. The water seems sinister, like it always does at night. To my surprise, no one is here making out or making a resolution. The resolutions I could make would outnumber the celebrants on Duval, but with no one to tell them to, it's pointless. Just as I'm convinced that a diary's keeper really wants their innermost to be infiltrated and read, a resolution only counts when it's said aloud, so the someone who heard it can bust your chops when you break it.

Returning toward town, I pass at least seven houses the color of a nectarine. Peach must be the new pink. I also pass several front doors completely open to anyone who might lurch in. It looks friendly in a careless way, but I could never do it.

Something rustles, scampers. It might be an iguana, the newest Keys pest. The first one we ever saw came with fanfare: Noel and Gertie, tough guys when they'd corner a scorpion, yelped, scampered away, and hid from the Jurrasic-y thing lunching on a hibiscus flower and staring in the patio windows. At first I thought it was the neighbor's dachshund, whom they often costumed as a Harlequin or in a tutu, this time wearing a Komodo dragon mask. We called various wildlife specialists. Humane eradication, the local animal control insisted, consisted of trapping it then placing it into the freezer, which lulls them to death. Just what we wanted: a frostbit reptile next to the Ben & Jerry's. Instead, we watched it sun a tail as long as its body poolside, shit in the water, and amble away. But they're not nocturnal, I think Andy told me, so it's probably a foraging palm rat I hear.

I go to shortcut through the cemetery, but the gates are locked for the night. I wish now that he were in one of the glowing, white-washed vaults.

At Pinkie, my answering machine is blinking. I listen to Mom.

"It's just me. We're on some gambling boat called The Lamplighter. S.J.'s backing into the ladies' room right now so I thought I'd try you before we get ourselves in trouble. Woo-hoo! Happy New Year, sweetheart."

I wash off the glitter that dusts my face in the small downstairs bathroom. This was the scene of a huge quarrel with Andy. Its size doesn't begin to accommodate two adult males, a stepladder, and a pail of solvent, so we should've known better than to remove the wallpaper together. The ensuing frustration—giraffe-print paper coming off in thin, fibrous strips—generated nibble-sized insults. When Andy belched up his calzone, all onions and garlic, it turned into a mauling, accusations about the division of domestic tasks, wastefulness, inconsiderate gas. The beady-eyed standoff cast a shadow over the rest of our twelve days there. I finished the bathroom myself. The pact wasn't verbal, but we never undertook any home renovation project working too closely again. I even incorporated this lesson into the Great Rooms! course on wall coverings. If you want to preserve your relationship, either DIY or do it on an empty stomach.

If only I'd known. I would have been the first to apologize, not just then, but every time we battled. Early in our relationship, my suitcase had been packed by me and, a couple of times, *for* me, once being told, "Go home to mother!" I scurried for the front door, screaming, "At least I have one!" This made him cry. Over time, the luggage got nicer and the arguments remained petty, but we were careful they left no permanent nicks.

I splash some water in my mouth, but it isn't cold enough to satisfy, no matter how long it's run. Andy explained it was the way it makes its way from Miami to the Lower Keys.

I need to stop this. Andy didn't know everything. It just seems like it.

I head for the owner's closet we'd built to lock personal stuff away from tenants. I find a photo album and a bottle of premium vodka we hid from renters. I open both. Here we are in Bermuda. I cook with their onions, wear their shorts. Maybe I should move there. Loved Rio de Janeiro, but I was always uneasily waiting for that Christ The Redeemer statue to creak into stop-motion life like some Ray Harryhausen epic. Vieques was too small, although I hear they have a great W hotel. Monterey: can't surf, don't hike. Hated Canada and their television fare. I like Chicago. No, scratch that. The blood vessels on my cheeks burst one sub-zero night during a miscalculated walk home from the Merchandise Mart. Paris. Can read French but can't speak it. I love London, but shuttling between The Dorchester and The Savoy and having dinner nightly at The Ivy isn't exactly realistic. (Or maybe it is, once Raoul tells me the check cleared.)

I get to the New York section. Here we are, at the World Trade Center. Nervous, in a subway station for the first time. In shirts with improbably full sleeves. Outside an Urban Outfitters.

I walk our house, drinking from the bottle.

I refamiliarize myself with the cast listings on Broadway posters: *Passion*, *Sunset Blvd.*, *Spring Awakening*, *The Color Purple*, *The Mystery of Edwin Drood*, *The Light in the Piazza*.

I rifle a stupid collection of matchbooks and swizzle sticks from New York restaurants long-gone: McHale's, Blue Chili, Bobo's, Sam's.

They don't seem so stupid now.

I stare out the French doors. It's past 3:00 a.m. Cuban tree frogs chant, emitting a guttural sound like a wino's throat being cleared. A neighbor once found a live one in their toilet, and power outages are often traced to a frog that has crawled into a transformer box. They're not to be touched, I recall Andy telling me; at around six inches long, they are nonpoisonous, but their skin's coating can be an irritant.

I stumble on the rattan mat where we kept hackabout shoes. I bring Andy's close to my face. They're still ripe with Dr. Scholl inserts.

Fuck Joan Didion. Andy's not coming back.

I throw his Topsiders in the pool.

Then I empty another medicine cabinet.

It seems I will be weeding Andy out of the nooks and crannies forever.

I try to sleep, but the balmy breeze through open windows has turned belligerent. The netting I fitted our pine canopy bed with comes to strangle me, as Andy predicted it would. That was another fight, when he mocked "we aren't in or out of Africa" and had no indoor mosquito problem. Wide awake, I am able to avoid becoming Isadora Duncan. I save myself from dying alone, like George with no last name.

Again, I close my eyes. This time, and I don't know why, I keep going back to those Maui cockatoos who didn't know they had freedom.

I FOLLOW through on Captain Reg's invite to watch the western sky aboard his twenty-six-foot-wide Naughty-Call. On the Harbor Walk, I try to remember where in the seaport's maze the commercial boats are segregated as I pass the docked private ones that make the fire pits and outdoor cinemas of our neighborhood seem feeble. Unoccupied for months, these boats are nevertheless impeccably kept, mahogany bows so buffed you could check your lipstick in them. Andy and I often speculated the owners must have done something nefarious, like traded arms overseas or took out a hit on the rich grandpa clinging to life. It's funny. With my windfall wealth, I could probably afford one, and the upkeep crew, now. People could speculate I'd bumped off Andy.

Twilight catches in a face craggy before its time as Captain Reg smiles. He's genuinely surprised I'm here. "Look who's all dressed up," he observes of my linen pants and light sweater.

I'd packed everything else for my return flight tomorrow. "And look who's dressed" is what I reply.

"I didn't want Wessie to catch a cold in the night air."

Wessie is his dick. We've met. The time Andy and I first saw Captain Reg, he was naked, shaking the hands of passengers after we'd boarded. This was during Fantasy Fest, the island's Halloween-week costume bacchanal. Our captain had what Potsy called "a two-liter peter." It was uncircumcised and rubbery, and Andy whispered it looked like something brought up from the ocean floor, slick, exhausted from thrashing, its one eye probably half-blind. Dejectedly, he added, "My penis looks like the seedling from which his grew." We both tried not to stare as he found our names on the reservation list. "His foreskin just brushed my pocket," I said. "Do you think the head has a tan line?" We couldn't help but envy how he so breezily scratched his balls, as casually as he might check his watch, during the cruise. A couple men doing shots of Sambuca immediately stripped. Once we were well past Sunset Key, a private island, he sat with us. His was such a story we nearly forgot that his dick lay on his thigh like a baguette with a vein (I admit I wanted to pull on it a little, just because it was there). He'd been a Versace model and like so many wound up stranded in an eroding South Beach sandcastle of coke. Migrating further south, he stripped with a group called Local Motion under the name Kickstand for bachelorette parties. In the Lower Keys, a private party grew crude, and the coarse wife of a fisherman broke a two-inch acrylic fingernail off in his anus. This resulted in an abscess and his departure from Local Motion. When he moved here, his ginormous penis became local legend and was admiringly named, as in the Loch Ness Monster, the Key West Monster, and then, like Nessie, just Wessie.

Not long after we depart from the bight, the boat slows to gently rock on teal water. Captain Reg eases down on a striped cushion alongside me near the back.

"Someone's power-thinking."

"About what comes next," I answer truthfully. "I don't want to be the one tennis shoe you always see on the highway shoulder."

"I'm down with that. What *does* come next?"

I don't tell him that today, after my sleepless New Year's, I made some calls. Unlike those New Yorkers who monitor ambulance runs for a livable square footage at a decent price, it wasn't difficult for me. I found a manufacturer's rep who had taken a new job upstate, in Syracuse. I knew, from previous lunch conversations, a sizable family trust afforded him a midtown co-op most salespeople hawking Arts and Crafts spittoons couldn't afford. It was vacant. After my call, it wasn't.

What I tell Captain Reg is that "I leased out my house today."

He makes a noise. "This rock's jumping with grifters. I hope you were careful who."

Me too. I've rented Pinkie to Teste, ShastaFantaFaygo and Sofonda. They spent most of the afternoon at the house, divvying up closet space, having a group gay grand mal when they determine I already have illuminated magnifying mirrors mounted in both bathrooms, turning doorknobs like this was a live-action Mystery Date board game and a gent waits with roses and a $100 tip.

I listed caveats: "No wigs in the dishwasher, Teste."

"My lacefronts? As if!"

ShastaFantaFaygo rummaged in the plastic Hello Kitty purse I have never seen her without and put a plastic gardenia that she must carry for moments like this behind my left ear.

"You're our Mrs. Roper!" Sofonda spat out. "Thank yeeeewwww! Thank yeeeewwww!"

"The lease is limited to the people standing before me. The three of you is like twelve of anyone else," I told them sternly. "And eat anything I've left behind." Sofonda began to plow through a bag of blue tortilla chips.

"What I want is something Minnie Pearl left behind even if I have to strain the insulation," Teste announced on the front porch. "I'll build a character around it: Minnie Pearl Necklace. I can already envision the shocking neckline I'll sew!" He hugged me. "Thank you so much for this, Papa Bear."

I made one final request.

"Please don't *Bedazzle* the scooters."

To Captain Reg, I don't identify my new tenants beyond, "It was to three sisters."

"I hope you mean retired nuns. Shit, down here, even *them*."

The Coast Guard clips swiftly past, maybe off to help a sunburned boater in self-created peril or turn back Cuban refugees afloat on a dozen car tires.

"So when did you know you needed a change?" I ask.

"When I had a fake fingernail stuck up my asshole. Stripping's dangerous."

I drain my beer. "You really let a woman finger you?"

"She tipped extra for assplay. Those Marathon bitches, they're rough. Was it worth the lancing and the Cipro? No." He whistles. "I couldn't sit on a chair without a pillow for months. But I got clean. I learned the water. I financed a boat and a new septum. Charters are where it's at. I can still get naked and I have final say-so on my butt." He casually replaces my empty Rolling Rock with a new one. "So Key West lost its luster?"

"This was our soft landing."

"Meaning?"

"Transition into the rest of our life." I make a visor of my hand. This sunset is not a bruise, it's not succotash, it's a melting strawberry parfait. "A joy-seeking missile blitzed my life, and now, Key West is just another unrealized dream. I need a new horizon to wish on, Captain Reg."

"Look again and tell me that. You ain't going to find that up north, up there it's all fluorocarbons… you're dreaming on deodorant."

The sky quickly ebbs from sienna to mandarin.

"Gypsy it awhile," he suggests.

"I'm not a backpack and Thermos guy."

"I didn't mean campground, bitch."

I like how "bitch" comes as naturally to him as an ocean breeze in his pubic hair. "I need a base of operations," I tell him. "Where, I don't know. I need to recalibrate, hit the reset button."

"Piss on reset. Wherever you land, when you get there, man, hit *play*," Captain Reg laconically drawls. Suddenly, he bellows, "Guys, slow it down!" Dolphins hopscotch across the water. The Naughty-Call comes to a standstill in deference. "Not like you'd ever consider this old seadog," he continues, "but give me a shout whenever you get back down this way." He hastily adds, "Don't tense up. You're stressed-out enough about being a Nike on a road. It wouldn't be a date. Maybe you'll want to get sucked off or want a butt buddy, NSA. Or we could go fake bowl."

My wee-wee or Wii, it's all the same to Captain Reg. I like his sensible promiscuity. He doesn't expect seconds in a tourism-driven community.

The dozen or so other male passengers cheer the final disc of sun with the first mate as it sinks into the Gulf. I hadn't intended the cruise as metaphor, but it works.

Chapter Nine

Apples

THE Mother/Son scene Thornton Wilder and I collaborated on went something like this:

ME

My intent is to move to New York

City one week from today, but I can't

without your blessing. And I'll need a

photo of you in that beautiful apron.

MOTHER

Oh, honey, it will be rather like a

halfway house toward rehabilitating

your life! New faces, new routine.

Finish your fresh-squeezed OJ while

I get you a slice of cheddar for your

apple pie, then we'll hug.

Had I forgotten my mother keeps David Mamet on retainer as script doctor? The woman never holds back a sneeze; I should have anticipated the soaking spray of her invective.

MOTHER

At twenty-two, it's a post-collegiate cliché. At

forty-five, it's grasping. I'm glad you think

this country's secure. New York will

always be a very big bull's eye. They're

still finding bones.

She pushes away the last gift opened, a jumbo bag of seashells, like a baker who needs more of the round table to properly pound out my news.

MOTHER

Any other announcements? Maybe you

can sew on Miss Sondra's spare parts and

join a sideshow.

Breakfast is finished in the glass porch enclosure off my mother's kitchen and so, apparently, is Christmas joviality.

"Who's this Miss Sondra?" Sarajane asks, stacking our dishes. "What was removed?"

"This friend of Barry's who's undergoing the world's longest sex change. Evolution might accomplish it faster." Mom shakes her head like there's a buzzing noise. "Let me think on this for a minute. I want to get it right."

"Do not," I say, heading her off, "start with your Columbo routine. I hate it."

Mom disingenuously pretends to seek clarity in confusion. Someone can enter a room and she'll chirp, "Were your ears burning?"

You have been discussed, it probably wasn't flattering, and suddenly you're apologizing for transgressions yet to be determined. When that doesn't work, she'll act befuddled. The result is the same: defensive hackles raised.

I remind her of her own words, "to do what's right for me."

"I meant within reason," she reminds back.

"You meant without risk."

"If life lacks excitement, get a motorcycle."

"Heck, even I'd try *that*!" Sarajane exclaims.

"Then you two should become the Knievel Sisters."

"Evie in Building D got all inked up at seventy-nine," Sarajane adds.

"Ladies, I don't want a tattoo, a gold tooth, or a personal trainer and if I want a tag-team makeover, I'll choose better aestheticians."

Mom slowly hands pieces of her half-eaten omelet to Hayley. "You've never been impulsive." Her tone is earnest. "It's abrupt."

"It's spontaneous. In a way it's a tribute, me moving there, to Andy." I rearrange my sleigh-shaped placemat. "I would have lived life so regimented. Andy didn't allow it. He pushed me to not underestimate myself. I've come to realize how much he was my liberator. He's why I started my own business at thirty-one." I do my best James Earl Jones. "Why work for Da Man, Barry? Be Da Man."

"Ethnic humor has never become you." She waves. "Consider yourself lucky you had someone who didn't hold you back."

"And look how the gallery held *him* back. All the bank promotions he wouldn't take if it meant relocating."

"There's a Chinese proverb that goes 'When two ride a horse, one must ride behind'," Sarajane says.

"Try another fortune cookie, Confucius," Mom demands of my aunt. Then, to me: "Andy did nothing he didn't want to. You can be very hard on yourself sometimes."

"I'll leave the other times to you."

My mother curtsies.

"But giving away your business to your subordinates," Sarajane tsk-tsk-tsks. Or kst-kst-skst, were this done backward too.

"It's not free. Their buy-out is a plateaued percentage based on...." I stop. This is all too GRPL pronounced grapple. "They aren't subordinates. Indians deserve to become chiefs. It's handled, S.J."

Mom claps at Sarajane, who is letting Hayley lick a plate. "S.J., don't give Hayley maple syrup!"

"But bell peppers and Bac-O bits, those were okay?" Sarajane turns to me. Or on me. "You've been to Florida, you're laughing some, you seem to be coming right along."

"The path of least resistance is actually quite exhausting."

Her hands fly up. "I don't get that at all. Do you, Jeanie?"

Mom is listening to a large ivory shell. "Barry often says stuff for the sake of saying it."

Sarajane scoops up cutlery noisily. "Things could be worse."

"Remind me about human suffering, S.J. Let's relive Haiti."

"I meant you don't have to worry about making ends meet."

"There is that," I say evenly. She's not done and I know it.

"So do they meet, double back around, and meet again?" Sarajane probes.

"S.J.!" Mom chides.

"Then just answer this: how do they go about taxing settlements?"

"Vigorously and mercilessly," I reply.

"S.J., stop!" Mom says, louder.

"Beware the idle rich. Lot of Pinot Grigio," Sarajane warns. "Getting loaded, staying loaded, life turns into an endless Happy Hour."

Mom spins it. "Barry's not a drunk and he's never happy for an hour." She checks her African violets, planted in teacups, on a baker's rack for equal sun. "Under these circumstances, what would Andy do, I wonder?"

"Why stop there? What would Jesus do? For starters, he could raise the dead, so Andy'd be sitting here, but that's not an option."

"Indulge me," Sarajane begins. "You could come back here, be closer to your mother, do charity work."

A *Hi, I'm Mrs. Frank Babcock* name badge boomerangs from one temple to the other. My God, she's proposing I move back to Peyton Place minus the New England scenery.

Sarajane tries to make her eyes childlike, but she just looks insane. "A home-cooked meal sounds awfully nice."

Mom plucks yellowed fuzzy leaves into her cupped palm. "Barry cooks way better than me or you."

"I wasn't talking about our slop!" Sarajane says wearily. "He'd cook for *us*!"

I'm absolutely stricken by the thought of me, dressed like little Edie Beale, ladling up cat food pâté. "Not. Going. To. Happen," I state.

"Live long enough and you learn never say never," Sarajane says tartly. "What's Plan B if New York fizzles?"

"I don't have a Plan B. I'd never commit to Plan A. You have a fallback, all you do is fall back."

Sarajane tries to replace a saucepan on a suspended grid.

"Speaking of fall back, be careful, S.J.!" Mom cautions.

"I wouldn't talk. Tell Barry how *you* fell."

"Mom!" I exclaim, concerned.

"Tell him about that knot on your noggin."

Mom's angry look is sisterly shorthand for STFU. "I tripped. No biggie." She shares sudden private words with Sarajane, who doesn't take it well. Mother walks off mid-sentence. Sarajane's hands are on her hips. She retreats slowly, like she might head-butt. Her walking backward, while surreal, generally also means she's backtracking to have the final word.

But she just sighs. "I don't like where you hung this pot rack, Barry."

Hayley barks at the inevitable crash.

"What can I say? Some of us face forward, S.J."

She whistles. "Yet still see nothing."

"Maybe you should have your head flipped," I suggest.

"Maybe you should have yours examined," Sarajane retorts, staring at the swaying pan.

Mom explores a new angle. "You're getting up there to develop a whole new circle. Making friends gets harder. Old people become cliquey. Someone has to move or die around here before you can take her place. You'd better file down that sharp tongue of yours."

"You never filed down your fangs and you did okay," I reply.

Sarajane returns to refill. "You're also an oddball."

Oddball is S.J.-speak for gay, not such a bad word when compared to others.

"Thanks for topping off my coffee and my confidence." I stir in enough sugar to make it drinkable. "I intend to get some sort of job. I'll meet people that way."

"This I gotta see. Mr. Entrepreneur becomes Mr. Time Card," Mom poo-poos derisively.

"Worst case, I'll get a roommate," I assure her.

"Nothing screams success like a boarder." Mom rubs Hayley's ears. "You'll end up living in Tome Village."

"Very funny."

"Is Tome Village an especially bad area of New York?" Sarajane asks.

Mom bursts out with "Ha!"

I cross the kitchen. "Tome Village is in a state of my mind."

"When you were what, ten?" Mom elaborates. "Barry drew this little town on the basement walls: huts, citizens, very detailed."

I unwind paper towels from a dispenser and gesture expansively. "Not on the wall, Mom. It was on oyster craft paper, the kind our butcher wrapped pork chops in. And I used Magic Markers, crayons, I sewed, glued, layered."

"That's called mixed media these days, S.J.," Mom interjects.

Sarajane brandishes a whisk. "I've been to a crafts store, sister."

"I named it Tome Village because the townspeople grew nothing but books," I explain.

"T-O-M-E," Mom clarifies, "is another word for book, S.J."

Sarajane advances with the whisk. "I also own a dictionary."

"They would plant seeds and sell their literature to buy sunscreen."

"Why this emphasis on sunscreen?" Sarajane is all over it now that it's health-related.

I simulate circles with my hands. "The town had four suns. Even the children pitched in; their little gardens produced coloring books and comics. I was mayor, a good one. I'd chat up my constituents by name."

"I would hope. You named them. And also exposed them to melanomas with all of those suns you drew," Sarajane observes. "Oddball."

My aunt who sifted garbage doesn't understand, and therefore suspects, creativity. She's not in touch with any side of her brain or she'd walk normally. She would never consider herself an oddball. To understand Tome Village is to inhabit the isolation of growing up an oddball. It sounds vaguely Roald Dahl, but I didn't know who he was for several more years and even then it was just Willy Wonka. Maybe I'd read, or read about, *Fahrenheit 451*. Just a few years later, after Jacqueline Susann and my own discovery of John Rechy, it would have been a very different hamlet, sweaty sailors and Puccified pillheads.

Mom brought this up yet now she gets all protective. "Barry had a very rich inner life."

Because I had no outer life. Tome Village represented more than a precursor of things to come, how I'd define and fill spaces. It was a created colony I could retreat to, where everyone had to be my friend.

Demonstration done, I scrunch up the paper towel. Sarajane makes a backward rush toward me.

"Don't be wasteful!" Sarajane winds the paper toweling back onto its mount. "Not everyone can afford to buy the Bounty factory, my fine sir!"

Another reason to go, windfall zingers like that one. This is how it will be if I stay. I scratched off three cranes and hit the lottery and now *he has more money than he knows what to do with*. It's the same awe I heard from Raoul. It will be the concealed joy buzzer in every handshake: sparks, my palm smoking, *zap*! I can't wait for the whoopee cushion when I actually sit down. "Dinner and drinks are on Barry! Forever!" *Pfffft*!

I wipe condensation from the windowpane. A large daisy suncatcher is adhered to it. Mom joins me to look through the colored glass at the snowy grounds.

"I like your hair short," I say admiringly. "It's spiky."

"I hate yours long. It's stringy," she replies. It's not been cut since Andy's death, and after my lame attempt at ironing a business shirt, I'm not going to trim my own bangs. "It just drags your face further down, if that's possible. You also have an eighteen-inch eyebrow hair, the left one. Find a barber. Tell him to try a part somewhere, for starters." Suddenly, she decides, "Let's go feed my deer."

It seems she recently spotted a deer and its offspring in a wood behind her house and now worries about their winter feeding options. She buys little green apples and hurls them in the deer's general vicinity.

Sarajane taps a pill on the counter. "Before that, take this."

Mom swallows it without water. Before I ask, she tells me it's a baby aspirin. I hear her whisper to my aunt, "You are not my keeper yet."

I'm told to go retrieve my coat and the bag, heavy with apples, Mom keeps in the closet. I notice the mashed pillows and a blanket on the living room sofa.

"Since when do you sleep on the sofa, Mom?" I call back toward the kitchen.

"That's me," Sarajane yells back. "If we watch something on Jeanie's show machine"—this is what S.J. calls a DVD player—"I curl up here."

Back in the kitchen, Mom puts on the biggest down coat I have ever seen. She explains how "the deer might get spooked if they smell a human," so we don Playtex gloves. Carrying the sack of apples, I follow her puffy body with her small porcupine head. She tries to right a windsock snagged on a downspout. I try too, but it's frozen solid.

She indicates where we should take our places. "I just throw the apples as far as I can." She extends a bicep. "Feel that muscle!"

I hand her a green apple. To the little stem, it looks like the wax ones she once piled in white ceramic crockery centered on the dining room table. We aim, we let go, and I'm humbled. She really *can* throw farther. She easily wins Bambi Shot-Putt. I think I hear distant running, snorting, deer watching and waiting for us to leave. I'd like that: a herd cautiously coming forward to bite into and carry away what we project with our yellow latex hands into the leafless trees backing her community.

But what I mostly hear is thump-thump-thump—our apples hitting, bouncing, leaving knock-outs in the snow.

Chapter Ten

Crossover Scenes

IN THEATRICAL terms, a crossover scene disguises a set change or other stage alteration by parading actor(s) in front of a curtain. They'd sing something stale that recaps but doesn't advance the plot, crack wise about a supporting character not present, maybe some soft-shoe. Computer mechanization has relegated them to purist revivals.

I have no one to shove out front.

The curtain stays up.

Here I am, impersonating myself, on a heavily raked stage with my flat feet, pushing my own scenery.

WITH Mom handled—she'd bristle that she was a chore to be gotten out of the way, but it's a relief—I compress everything else into one exhausting week.

The blood money comes next. I want nothing to do with it, which sounds cavalier. It's a lot: Andy's life insurance (we were both overinsured so that any survivor's lifestyle wouldn't deviate too much), his own investments and 401(k). Plus the settlement. I inform Grover, my CPA, to shop Jumbo Certificates of Deposit of ten years' duration, give me a monthly income stream from the interest, then forget about it. I need no more monthly statements than I already have, no Maria Bartiromo fixations. Grover is comfortable enough to call me a pussy. If Faith knew one of her employees dared say this to a client, she would hand him a letter of reference that only confirmed what floor he had worked on.

He says something about diversification, about assembling a robust portfolio of growth stocks.

I interrupt to tell him the word robust makes him sound like a wine snob. "I'm not interested in the upside as long as there is no downside. Just make my money so safe it's neuter."

"You might as well bury it in your backyard."

"Fine," I impatiently come back with. "I'll give it its own headstone, while I'm at it, so I can remember how I earned it."

That shut him down.

Then I deal with Kerrick. He has brainstormed a party. He extols how it will be divided into four distinct sections with a common thread: the Muses of Manhattan!

"Okay, first you're Anne Welles, fleeing dreary Lawrenceville for the Valley of the Dolls. We'll run a real toy train around the dining room, rain down multicolored Tic-Tacs."

I foresee at least one person falling, but I play along. "And maybe play old Dionne Warwick before nicotine got the better of her."

He screams, "Yes! Then, cut to: Ann Marie, *That Girl*, same train, soaring toward Donald Hollinger. Everyone has to wear a center part, like she did in the final season. Morph into Rhoda Morganstern. Headscarves for everyone. Right into *Looking for Mr. Goodbar*... disco music, strobe lights, I'll hire some rough trade to do push-ups in a jockstrap."

I wondered when it would go macabre.

"And then stab me repeatedly?"

"That part we skip. Finally, it's cosmos and Miss Carrie Bradshaw. You'll wear a pink tutu. Very briefly, okay? We'll flick water on you. Then we'll have an after-hours breakfast. SJP always insisted the characters eat breakfast as a good example."

Before he can tell me that, for the grand finale, he will fire me from a cannon facing east, I pass. It's all very thoughtful even if it's more about his ingenuity than my departure. And, not that I'm the superstitious type, but the last party in my honor ended on a rather sour note.

Word that I demurred any bon voyage gets around quickly.

"When we lost Andy, we apparently lost you. And when I say that, I'm speaking for many of us," Miss Sondra's message begins. She literally *is* speaking for everyone, as her voice races the scales from press-on to five o'clock shadow, proving that, yes, she still has her balls. "I used to be in such awe of your self-control, how self-aware you were. Turns out you were just self-absorbed." Before slamming the phone down, she lets loose a string of Spanish epithets. From the "madre," I think she just called me a motherfucker.

Stan actually *reads* something on my voice mail.

"'It is a splendid desert, a domed and steepled solitude, where the stranger is lonely in the midst of a million of his race. A man walks his tedious miles through the same interminable street every day, elbowing his way through a buzzing multitude of men, yet never seeing a familiar face, and never seeing a strange one the second time.'" He pauses. It sounds like he's moisturizing something, maybe his elbows. "That's from Mark Twain, about New York, written in 1867."

Gosh, thanks for stepping outside the pages of *Death in Venice*, Stan. Best wishes on that Big Brother program.

POTSY doesn't know what to do with the roll of tape. He tangles strip after strip. "I always just throw shit in Hefty bags!"

Not even. The last time Andy and I helped Potsy move, we carried staggeringly heavy bureau drawers and had to stare down at his underwear.

I hold up a flapped box reading *THIS SIDE UP*. "This is how people who vote and pay taxes do it."

"I don't understand why I can't go. I can put in for a corporate transfer and be miserable anywhere."

"You're a concierge. You don't know Manhattan," I remind him.

"I can learn."

"Why should you have to?"

"You won't know a soul."

"Why does everyone think I can't make friends? They're not unicorns."

"You wouldn't go to Benihana's if our group wasn't big enough because they might sit you with strangers."

"I sublet from a manufacturer's rep. He comes into the city a bunch. So there's him. Plus I know plenty of vendors. They're built-in friends."

"When you're holding a purchase order." Potsy seals a box of dishes. "So, so alone."

"I'll be okay."

"*Me*." He looks away. "What a dumbass I've been, building my day-to-day around a couple. Now both are gone."

"Understand that I need to do this on my own."

Potsy leans into me. This is closing in on awkward. I don't think he's infatuated with me; he might be infatuated with starting over too. I'm spared whatever he's about to say because Dee comes into the room bearing documents.

"Your lease, signed and dated. You officially live vertically. Oh: plus photos. Pre-war building, one exposed brick wall, washer and dryer, nice windows with natural light."

Potsy intercepts them. "Faxes don't hold up in court if he has a landlord dispute."

"Actually, they do, Potsy," Dee replies. "You know almost nothing about virtually everything." She faces me. "You have access to a shared rooftop terrace. It's the best feature."

"Barry shouldn't have to share," Potsy announces.

"Pots," I swiftly correct him, "I'm very willing to share a rooftop terrace, and I'm still moving."

He runs his finger along the pied-a-terre verbiage. "Nine hundred square feet! That's smaller than your bedroom! This is a Hummel's starter studio." He inspects each page again. "How much does this deeee-luxe apartment in the sky go for?"

Dee's eyebrow arches. "One month's rent is more than what you paid for Andy's Jeep."

"Barry, tell her I offered more!"

From the window, Dee asks in alarm, "Why are Alexander and the boys heading up your walk?"

I motion for her and Potsy to stay out of it. I hurry to the front door. Despite my own extended hand, Alexander's remain jammed in his coat pockets.

"Mindy said you called about Luke and Duncan picking out something of Andy's."

I try to be casual. "I sure did. Dump your jackets on that chair, guys."

Alexander tells them, "We won't be that long."

In comical slow motion, Duncan takes his zipper back up to his collar.

"If you men want to head back to the library, we'll take it from there." They look at their father and hesitate. "Oh! It's been awhile since you were here. The library is to your right, down the short stairway."

"Come on, Dunc." Luke hitches his head.

"I'm sorry about Uncle Andy," Duncan says, very serious.

"Thank you, Duncan." I smile. Duncan trots behind Luke.

I look, really look, at Alex. His face is fuller than Andy's, especially his cheeks, like he has gills. I wonder if he has the same pointy tip at the base of his spine, the same beginnings of a tail I would tease Andy about. Or if Alex pinches Mindy's calf with his toes when he's too tired to say goodnight. I don't even know for sure what this man does for a living. It has something to do with excess rubber, trimming it off flyswatters, maybe.

"I assumed Luke would drive," I say to him.

"Dad's here to make sure they choose something user-friendly," Alexander makes clear.

I reach down into an open carton and hand him a photograph of Andy in a square-cut bathing suit on a Key West beach. "What I don't get is how can two guys who looked so alike be so unalike?"

Alexander studies it. "You think this is easy?"

"I think it must be doubly awful," I respond, "like gazing into a mirror your whole life and suddenly someone stealing the reflection."

"There was a time we were inseparable."

"You mean before the love that dare not speak its name?"

"Spare me your poetry."

Defiantly, I continue. "That's what creeps you out. I had sex with your carbon copy and that indirectly makes it seem like we had sex too?"

"Spare me your psychiatry."

We both realize the futility. I indicate the photograph. "I want you to have that." He lowers to a bench with it.

I round a corner past Potsy and Dee, eavesdropping.

Luke and Duncan have grown up. When? Oh, that's right, when Andy and I were deliberately avoided. Cursive writing was Duncan's struggle last time I saw him. Now, it's a general clumsiness from the knees down. Luke doesn't in the slightest resemble his father or uncle. He's shorter, his shoulders broader, biceps developed by free-weight curls. If reincarnation proves more than wishful thinking, I will get a gym membership in my next life at age six.

Duncan has selected a compact, fully functional Las Vegas slot machine. It wasn't even Andy's, but he doesn't need to know that. Luke demonstrates how to feed the quarter in, guiding Duncan's hand onto the arm to pull it. They watch winless symbols align.

"Will it fit in our trunk?" Duncan frets.

It clanks as Luke jostles it. "Hear the money in it?"

Duncan wonders, "If it's real, will Barry let us keep it?"

Duncan's shirt looks snug. Luke's sneakers are filthy. I hope their household isn't one of deprivation.

I announce myself with, "It's real, and it's yours."

Duncan squeals, hugs me, and runs off to tell his dad about the inevitable payout.

"Mom and Dad head to Vegas three or four times a year," Luke says.

These are the people who made Rita Rudner Comedian of the Year.

"It's at least one way of seeing Rome, Egypt, Paris, and Italy without ever leaving The Strip," I tell him.

"The Strip's too snooty, they say. Last trip, they stayed a couple miles away at this place where they share a bathroom in the hall. They couldn't stop talking about Carrot Top," Luke remembers.

They just keep coming.

"Have you picked out something yet?"

"This is beyond wrong. Andy's stuff is yours."

"I'm taking very little," I assure him. "It'll mildew in the basement or melt in the attic."

"Know what I want?"

"What?"

"To be you when I grow up," Luke blurts out.

"I was thinking I want to be you in my next life," I say with a smile.

He's fumbling for words. I know what they are, but they're for him to say.

"Me, you, Uncle Andy, we have some things in common."

There. He sort of said it.

"We kinda sensed that, Luke."

He is shocked. "When?"

"Before we were shut out. When you were Dunc's age, we felt protective of you. Just in observing you, without even talking, me and your uncle both checked the GIFY box in our heads."

"Gify?"

"Gay. In. Five. Years."

His eyes nervously flick to the doorway. His caution—it's been a long time since I have felt it, but I understand.

"It's all good. We could be talking about anything. Do you have someone in your life?"

"I'm seventeen. This isn't *High School Musical*. Shit gets back to your parents."

"What about a friend you really trust? Girls are usually better."

He goes to a framed photo of Dee in a director's chair. It's from several years ago, not of the mall variety but close, a blend of professionalism and eroticism, blazer and camisole. Meet your Realtor, who negotiates with dirty talk. "What were you shot through, a neglected aquarium?" we roared when showed proofs. "Was he Lucy's cinematographer on *Mame*?" We demanded one for display. She could never live it down. To her chagrin, we moved it to a new, prominent location when she came over.

Luke sighs. "You have Size 3 Dee, but I'd wind up with some totally infatuated fattie in, like, *3-D*, cutting herself over me. That's even more dangerous."

"You sound like someone I know." I laugh, wondering if Potsy has whispered in his ear.

"I wish Andy had been my dad," he says.

"Don't. Because then you wouldn't have a living father. And living is better," I say seriously. "You can still work on your stuff. I had that chance with my own dad. It doesn't have to be denial and despair."

"Even if you get disowned?"

"I came out at twenty. I even announced Andy gave me crabs."

"Seriously?"

"My mom replied 'big deal'. Dad said 'small comb'."

"Did they suspect, before that?"

"They knew." I don't want to overwhelm the kid, so I don't mention the boys mowing, the teacher, Tome Village, or Mom offering to take me to see *Making Love* when I was still in high school. "I regret we haven't had much of a relationship." I pause. That sounded stiff. I want to give the kid my credit card, or a bunch of cash, but in practicality, all I can really promise him is access. "We can now. How's about I give you all the ways you can reach me?"

I grab an Atripla pad I swiped from Dr. Steve. That won't do. I tell him I don't have a new cell number yet, but will soon. Does he have my current one? He doesn't.

"I had Uncle Andy's."

"Ever call him?" I'm curious. I thought not, but maybe Andy kept it to himself, like seeing Dr. Steve about his sore arm and maybe lots of other things.

"I wanted to. Almost. Never did." Luke looks at the library walls filled with theatrical keepsakes, then at the address I've written. "Wow. You really *are* gonna be on Broadway."

"And 55th. Yes."

Luke carefully folds what I've written into a postage stamp and slides it under the tongue of his left shoe. "You don't know my mom and dad." In this one precautionary move, I see the slyness of Andy.

I PROMISED to attend the Great Rooms! unveiling, scheduled around me, so I arrange for the car service to take me to the airport on the penultimate afternoon.

My house grows small, then smaller, and once we're to Andy's Taco Bell, the Charleston's Spanish stucco, I can't see it anymore.

I am not happy when Fernie toddles up to the group. She's dressed too warmly for this moderate January day in a plaid down coat and mittens. Both could have been a grade schooler's, and might have been. Her snow boots anticipate a sudden blizzard that might pounce from behind the cold sun. My immediate look to Georgia accuses. She mouths, "I said nothing to her."

She, Isaac, Mr. and Mrs. Albanese, everyone, plus Dee and Potsy, applaud as a temporary facing falls away.

I absorb the new signage, in their own chosen typeface: Rooms Great & Small. I agreed to the name change even if I didn't agree with it, not from ego but from economy. Letterhead, store tags, stickers, everything will need to be altered, and it won't be realized back in revenue. It's not the thriftiest way to kick off new ownership, but they want to be independent of me.

The celebration moves inside. Champagne flutes raise in salute. Fernie, who has followed, passes on the one offered to her. She studies our group, probably wondering how to approach the man who anonymously pitches the green apple at her every year.

Many more of these metaphors, and I'm going to turn into a fable.

I duck out among backslaps. I hear Warehouse Lester call after me, "Don't be a stranger!"

Lester, I couldn't feel any stranger.

Inside the car, I feel trapped, like Tippi Hedren's alarmed café window poses in *The Birds*.

Potsy pounds the hood. The driver fixes a warning stare at me. "At least cancel this car. We'll drive you to the airport," Potsy roars.

Between blubbers, Dee manages a cell phone photo.

I tell the driver to go now.

Potsy offers me the finger.

I'VE unpacked very little except a coffeemaker, our bed pillows and a framed photo of Andy between Gertie and Noel. I'm watching a small television. I haven't seen one this tiny since my college dorm room. New York City is now in the grasp of a furious snowfall.

It started during load-in of my possessions, but the moving company began encountering whiteouts in Pennsylvania, so they were spent when they arrived and actually saw my twenty-six-story building. I'd been confidently assured they were experienced in Manhattan relocations. Their estimate declared that *Nothing Phases Us!* not even correct spelling. They'd even pointed out the "pain in the ass surcharge" in the itemization. I was in a hurry, but I should have called their supplied references, because, as angry honks and epithets surrounded them, they looked quite phased. Trying to secure parking proved impossible, and we had just about decided they'd probably have to circle and toss out more of my stuff at each pass when the building manager, Saul, intervened and identified something reasonably close.

At least the freight elevator worked.

Until it didn't.

As the exhausted two-man crew crammed and stacked what they could into the small main elevator in several trips, I investigated my surroundings. The minimalist lobby of brown Sarancolin marble and bottle-green windows had no doorman but seemed secure. I scouted out emergency exits and fire extinguishers. The hallways were larger than those in a Vegas hotel; every corner I rounded I expected to see pale twin girls holding hands. I ran into Saul briefly again, who told me that a reviled Broadway choreographer, a supermodel no longer super but still modeling, an admired politico with a fondness for drink, and a disinherited bin Laden all lived here.

The mover with the Danish accent and impressive forearms was awaiting my return. "Your measurements are bad."

My King Stickley headboard and bed frame barely fit wall to wall. Leaving it behind had not been, however, an option; I mean, I brought our old pillows.

There was also no room for the footboard, leaning against the end of the mattress. I apologize for my miscalculation.

"I guess that will have to stay there," I said, gulping. "It'll be kind of a handicapped access ramp in and out of my bed."

"I guess." Dane Forearms took a wary step back, like I sleep with Jerry's Kids. If that was flirting, I needed a hoopskirt or a tutor, and quick.

I saw that there was also absolutely no room for the Mission nightstand, much less its mate. The window wells were deep. I could keep rolled socks in them. Maybe I can put up a camping tent and sleep in the hallway.

So I am moved in but I can't move. I'd carefully edited yet it was still too much. I'm sitting on a stack of annual PLAYBILL Yearbooks—something else I shouldn't haven't brought. The living room wainscoting looks as though it were done by someone in the final throes of Parkinson's, hopscotching over the oatmeal walls. The ceilings are high, which is good. Maybe I'll hang a porch swing since there's not room for my three-cushion sofa. What my landlord called a charming parlor is a scatter rug. It wasn't among the pictorial Dee presented to me because it's too small to stand in and photograph. The lithographs left behind are of sad-eyed children. This was a vendor I badgered for state exclusivity?

I return my attention to the female broadcaster, talking of accumulation: "... and Central Park could receive twelve inches of fresh snow by daybreak, folks, on top of the six already measured there. So let's talk about morning, Sam...."

A gust of snow slaps the windowpane. It's not yet 11:00 p.m. Midtown is barren, except for city plows, and somewhere, a saxophone is being defiantly played outdoors. A man walks down Broadway's center; his two dogs plunge into drifts, curving into commas. I close my eyes.

When I open them, they're still out there. This time, they're real.

I REACH to shut off an alarm that is across the room, not on the nightstand that isn't there. My fingertips meet the wall. When I roll to jump out, I kick the facing wall. I take the ramp.

As I toast a muffin, I open kitchen cupboards. One shelf is sprinkled with what I first believe to be chocolate chips from a broken Nestle bag. Then I realize what they are. I make a note about D-con. I want to tell my landlord, when he phones to ask how I'm settling in, that a red sink stopper shaped like a cherry does not constitute a renovated kitchen.

The claw-foot tub looks a little lame in one paw. Water from the showerhead is the color of apple cider until drawn for three minutes. The bathroom light fixture is encircled by a scorch mark of recent vintage. I remind myself where the fire exit is. The toilet has the slowest flush I have ever seen.

I force silver hoops through ear holes nearly healed, pierced on my fortieth birthday at Andy's urging: "I can't, working where I do, but you should." That was his general axiom: get away with it if you can. It was an infection, or maybe I lost an earring, I don't remember, but I had stopped wearing them.

Layered for my walk to midtown, I don't expect to meet a bin Laden this first morning, but I come close. A male resident, head tilted down, boards on the fourteenth floor.

"G'morning," I say.

He doesn't return my greeting but raises his head. A toothbrush protrudes from his mouth. He brushes loudly for the next thirteen floors and then he spits into a lobby fountain.

I'd seen enough breast-beating on The Weather Channel about South Florida hurricanes to shrug off Al Roker's hyperbole, and sure enough, the final snow accumulation wasn't close to the record they predicted. Nothing is hobbled. A new snow in New York City is actually pretty. For one hour. This is that hour. White clings to storefronts. I hopscotch owners and employees tossing salt and shoveling paths en route to a Times Square newsstand, which smells of incense. I take a newspaper from under a stone.

A man alongside me lowers his Starbucks with a grin. "It's you! You're the one!"

"One what?" I back away.

"The one who buys the one newspaper we *all* count on."

I'm wary. "I'm glad I can make everyone's day."

His playful condensed breath inches closer. "You just moved here. I can tell. It's like a pen. Never pay for one. Just steal the one you're handed when you have to sign something somewhere." He chuckles. "No one buys the dailies. A section on a subway, another part in McDonald's, the whole city kinda takes turns piecemeal with the same one."

"So following around people who litter makes me savvy?" I snarl.

Squashed by my retort, he joins the Times Square herd, but not before saying, "Well, you make *me* feel like a complete and total asshole. Thanks, dick!"

A woman next to me in chartreuse boots winces through her matching chartreuse muffler. "Kiddo, you gotta have thick skin to survive in this town, but not that thick."

I really need that flirt tutor.

My eyes shift to a small girl of undetermined ethnicity on stacked magazines inside the structure. She crouches beneath the tobacco products, under an oversized WE CARD! Sign. Poking out from under her buttoned coat are the feet of pajamas. Cultural customs aside, everyone's feet get cold, and she should have on extra socks. Better still, she should be at home.

"Hey, you!" I gently say. "I bet you don't have school today."

Eyes big and dark meet mine.

The male newsstand worker slides open a Plexiglass panel to accept cash. Through it, he tells me, "No school."

He must be her father. They share a unibrow on the same broad forehead that is the color of perfect toast.

I say to the girl, "No school is always good. What's your name?"

She says something like Hella Pelme. I lean in.

"Halum pe."

That's what it sounds like, this time. Whatever she's eaten, heavy with unidentifiable spices, warms my face.

"That's pretty. That's like Hayley. My mom's best friend in the whole world is named Hayley."

This seems to delight her. A bubble of spit forms on her lips.

"You have a really good no-school day," I offer.

The girl dances an Ariel figurine from *The Little Mermaid* on a peeling ledge. That's when I notice that her left leg is tethered by a black strap to a post.

I walk, looking down the numbered streets, up at Broadway marquees. For someone who used to know the most minute cast replacements, I don't recognize much of what's playing. I'm out of the loop. I live here now. I'll see all the shows.

I settle with the Classifieds in The Paramount, within Dean and Deluca. Andy and I always liked it here: smartly staffed and pricey enough to keep out the riff-raff. I quickly determine that a manager is being sought for an unspecified Broadway district store of sheet lyrics, CDs and DVDs, calendars, newly published plays, and librettos, a lot of authorized crap. It's early, but I call.

A woman's voice, a gargle of Eileen Heckart and Colleen Dewhurst, immediately challenges my non-Manhattan area code: "Where the hell are you?"

I tell her where the hell I am.

"My Gawd, you're practically up my ass."

I choke a little on my coffee but recover to give my name and briefly detail my background. I hear her type, then address whatever her pecking produced.

"Mmmmmm, interesting."

She tells me the name of the store, Theatrilicious. It's a short walk from here, not quite up her ass unless her ass is Shubert Alley. We are to meet in thirty minutes, before store opening.

I know the store well. Lots of theater district shops stock basic souvenirs; Theatrilicious was different. The demise of like-minded Midtown emporiums, like Applause Books, Footlight Records, and Coliseum Books, or their diminution—One Shubert Alley has shrunk to the size of a fast-food take-out window with a limited menu, and Colony Records is like a messy garage sale whose reluctant proprietor has priced everything too high—left Theatrilicious either the stupid holdout or uniquely positioned and far larger than its biggest international competitor, Dress Circle in London. The store is overstuffed with one-of-a-kind rarities that no corporate ownership would tolerate. Andy and I had first been in 1992 in fruitless pursuit of

Volume 17 to complete my *Theatre World* collection. We'd even made fun of its name. It sounds like an energy drink marketed to the dramaturg.

I recognize Marjorie Lewis-Kohl from Broadway.com opening night photo galleries. I'd put her at sixty-two, sixty-three. She is wearing a crocheted cape in wheat, and from the self-impressed way she moves in it, you can tell it is her trademark, like a monocle. All that's missing is a small, shivering dog.

She traces along the job application's small lines I have been humbled into reducing education, employment, and three professional references onto.

"You're a teensy-weensy bit overqualified," she says, squeezing her thumb and index finger together.

I'm comfortable enough with how our discussion has progressed to squeeze my two same fingers together.

"Maybe a smidge. But I already feel like I own this place."

She rubs those two fingers roughly together like she's trying to spark a fire. "Don't. I own. You would manage."

That was uncomfortable. "I meant I've shopped here for years as a collector." I've also probably stumbled on her cape as she bustled around.

"I know. You're in our database. I had you vetted by Artie before I got here. He's our webmaster. Still, I'm apprehensive. Number one: you did your own thing and you did it very well."

I thank her, waiting for her to bump this from pro to con.

Which she does. "That kind of success gives you a head rush of power and that belongs to *me*. Which takes me to number two. This feels very rebound, and we know what happens with rebounds."

"All I can say is that this was not a rash decision."

Her arms emerge from silk lining toward the store interior. "Beyond retail and Internet, we also work with a slew of producers and management. Opening night gifts, premiums for showcases. I have powerful connections. I sit on the Board of Trustees of the New School. Mike Nichols takes my call."

I think, *Sure, even before Diane Sawyer's.*

"He's always been appreciative that my late husband Gunnar and I were one of the original investors in *Annie*," she proudly adds.

"Right. He directed *Annie*."

"With more staying power than *Billy Elliot* ever demonstrated!"

She gestures that I walk with her.

In my surface assessment, I can see nothing much gets changed except price tags. Theatrilicious is as much a wreck as its owner. Shelves bow under dusty goods. Sweatshirts aren't folded, they're bunched. Cast recordings aren't alphabetized, and a placard actually calls them "soundtracks," a big no-no. Everything from the mundane to the essential needs to be done, and I'll need a time machine to do it four years ago.

Marjorie ushers me into a small office that we will share, "but I'm rarely here and I rarely sit." A small sofa is slip-covered by what is surely a cape she grew tired of. The desk is the Audrey II of office furniture; white corners of paper protrude from its closed roll top, like it's not quite finished digesting the monthly payables. I notice a Krispy Kreme on a credenza that I think might be like one of those "fooled ya!" spilled cans of Coke, but gag items usually aren't manufactured with pocked spoilage this detailed.

She buttons her collar. "The pay's insulting."

"This will be my walking-around money."

"Take the steps of a geisha, then."

She demands I always be reachable and that I must wear a beeper, which I assume means a pager. Are there Simba plush toy emergencies? I haven't worn a pager since my first job at twenty-three.

I stare at her. "That will be fine."

"I hope you also don't mind submitting to a drug test."

Not if you don't mind conducting it yourself so I can eat a big plate of asparagus the night before.

"No problem." It's almost too easy—a job my very first day. I'm working for Da Man again, but I hope Andy can see how spur-of-the-moment I've become, ramifications be damned.

"What I am *not* looking for is some wise guy to blow me shit about how I operate my business, Terry."

"Barry Grooms is not looking to blow you any." Notice how I worked my full name in to politely correct her.

Marjorie extends her hand for a done-deal shake. In it is a Motorola unit held together by electrical tape. Stuck in the black tape is one of Marjorie's long gray hairs, as strong as twine, like a personalized carrying cord.

It will become more my leash.

Chapter Eleven

Cape Fear

I COME to regret that pager.

That I corrected my name.

That I supplied a Social Security number.

My first week I have worked, conservatively, ninety hours. I woke yesterday holding a roll of thermal credit card machine paper in my hand. I am not sure how it got there or why I brought it home.

Marjorie has stayed away, but her pages are incessant. She was up all night worrying, she yawns in my ear, if we'll ever unload those 400-plus teddy bears wearing a *Phantom* half-mask. I am more worried about the carton of Twin Tower toast holders I happened upon in a drop-down storage area. I wonder who approved a prototype that holds just one bread slice and what morbid spinster would buy it.

From another page, I decline her offer to circulate an e-press release about my hire. She does it anyway, quoting herself extensively, listing her citations and her affiliation with *Annie*. She also misspells manager. I am the new *manger*. It is reprinted verbatim in several industry publications. I now know how Alexander felt, being called a bother.

She paged me to inquire if the employees are accepting direction from an interloper.

"They'll close ranks on you," she warned.

Actually, the staff, who alternately call the store The Lish or T-Lish, seemed grateful that the pressure's off. Many were quick to blab how Marjorie first offered each of them my position and sneered what ingrates they were when everyone immediately refused it. I take it as a good sign when someone scatters my desk chair with straw after the whole manger debacle.

I am trying to, but cannot, remember all of the employee names. There are so many more than Great Rooms! Some work as little as five hours weekly; few get more than a total of twenty-five hours. Marjorie imposed these insanely small shifts. She occasionally, after posting schedules, changes up everyone's hours so "no one gets comfortable," which means we have too many employees, yet not enough, since they've all had to take second and third jobs. They've also been screwed out of paid time off, promised free tickets that never materialized, you name it, so a bunker mentality permeates—more accurately, a bunkbed mentality, when I realize how little they're paid. She's worked very hard to earn this disrespect, and it will be just as hard to salvage any esprit de corps from such a dispirited bunch. The store should be renamed Theatrivicious. My last two decades are so steeped in drag queen reveals that I keep waiting for her armadillo shawl to split like a chrysalis and a pleasant Marjorie to emerge.

This doesn't happen.

Actual Marjorie sightings are not dissimilar to those of a UFO: vivid yet fleeting, verified by witnesses left scorched or violated. When our mothership lands, calling other occupants of interplanetary craft, the pyrotechnics are at first awe-inspiring, but closer inspection reveals it's just an electrical malfunction and the sheen is silver primer slapped over rust. Her hyperactive arrival anywhere else would be followed by an immediate "ma'am, I'm calling Security."

Most of the rude nicknames cooked up for Marjorie and her signature capes have been passed from one generation of disgruntled employee to the next. Some are obvious, like Psycho Nanny; some are pretty good, like Sylvia Miles o' Fabric; some, like Cape Cod, are borderline offensive, even if it came from a female; some are obscure, like The Other MLK, which are her initials.

"To her, every day is MLK day," Artie explains. "Well, I have a goddamn dream too, that I'll get one off as a paid holiday."

"I'm not even convinced Large-orie has a body. She's just a head connected to some support system housed in a pickle barrel," Carla says.

"Wait until you see Marginal's roach-brown pleather cape," Karen adds. "It looks like she stormed out of a beauty salon."

"The royal blue is the best," David Paul adds. "She's a roof tarp."

Not long ago, a curious Midwesterner mistook Marjorie's cape for the costume of a street performer and asked, "Does that lady have a magic act?"

Elaine drily responded, "Yeah. She made our cashier disappear about an hour ago."

"The woman is a serial drapist," Artie sums up.

When she arrives one evening in a black cape with a pointy collar, Artie dashes the length of the shop, warning coworkers, "It's Dracula's daughter! Cover your necks!"

When I tell Mom all of this, she states, "Marjorie's a bully. Hit back."

I have dealt with overcompensating women who conveniently became frail and cry when a superior overrules her decision; I beat back the pasty middle managers who issued endless CYA memos and went through office waste cans late at night, conniving for an edge; I have handled the Machiavellian stunts pursued in the name of a promotion. I can handle Marjorie.

I don't hit back.

When conversations turn confrontational, I hum "Away in a Manger." When that doesn't work, I ignore her number on the pager. She's often forgotten what she wanted by the time I call back, anyway. This is all useful but not foolproof. I reach for my last weapon. I decide to hold up a mirror and see how she likes it. She can't page me if I tie up her line with a steady flow of ideas, inquiries, decisions "only an owner should make," I defer cheerfully. When I receive an annual invoice from a Secaucus warehouse, with no idea what is housed there, I grill her. She hates supplying answers to reasonable questions.

I invite her to a sales philosophy meeting for all Theatrilicious employees. It will be at 8:00 a.m., before the store opens, and they will be paid for the ninety minutes I ask for. You would think I've convened something really awful, like a Zig Ziegler event. The only excuse out is class or proof of a work shift elsewhere. I even insist Cecile, who works off-site combing statewide estate sales for the bounty of some dead show buff, attend.

"Most of you are theater students," I tell them. "Most of you sound like you're auditioning for a fibromyalgia commercial. This is your stage. Act. Use what you've studied."

I know their general disinterest isn't personal, it's just common showroom malaise, but still, it's deadly. I remind them that customers can buy a knock-off tee of the musical they saw anywhere. So dish about which actress needs to start playing her own age. Send them to another show you think they might like. Push the opera glasses if you know a play has nudity. No fingers need be pricked in a lifelong friendship pact, just be engaging and bring your uniqueness, I conclude.

Marjorie, in a gray burlap hooded cape, lurks with a thimble of espresso. "I like staff meetings."

"Which is why we haven't had one since the Mark Hellinger was still a theater," Elaine says, snickering into her *Annie* mug. Everyone else also snickers into their *Annie* mug, one of the treasures from the Secaucus warehouse.

"Barry, have you assigned the Weissler's cast gifts to anyone?" Marjorie suddenly asks.

"I stayed last night."

"You framed thirty-two show cards yourself?"

"I was in a twenty-four-year relationship. I know a lot about dry-mounting."

This gets more laughs. A little self-deprecation goes a long way in establishing rapport and currying favor.

"Just make sure they're at Tavern on the Green no later than four tomorrow." When Marjorie pops up her fur-lined hood, the pelt suggests mutton chop sideburns—a little like Abe Lincoln, minus the honesty.

IT WOULD come as no surprise to anyone who has ever met me that I syncopate immediately with the working rhythm of New York. New routines emerge. Morning begins by seeing if Sam Champion is wearing a vest, checking how bald Matt Lauer looks, and reconfirming that Pat Kiernan on NY1 still gets on my nerves something bad. Then I make lunch from leftovers. Andy and I used to alternate days packing vintage lunchboxes for one another. Cute, but it was at least twenty years ago, when I'd frugally add water to the jug of laundry detergent to get one more load of wash, when Andy hoarded extra ketchup packets from McDonald's, those lean years that seem so rich now. I've been too tired to cook. Carry-out is one thing Manhattan does well: ferrying hot foods to you when you don't want to get dressed, and in about twelve minutes. It's Harrod's Food Hall, without the intimidation. Where I'm from, home delivery involved a sullen college-age driver and a soggy bun. Here, I've had pumpkin dumplings, osso bucco empanadas, pappardelle Bolognese, lamb sausage over wilted mustard greens, batter-fried eggplant, a dozen Long Island oysters with a ginger mignonette, and an amazing green papaya salad. Then I had them again. I need to tell Mom this. She'll routinely get two meals out of a sole almondine, so she'd be pleased that I am doing the same. Lunch today: Vietnamese pho, a beef and noodle soup.

Coffee in one hand, brown bag in the other, I await the elevator. Mr. Floor 14 joins the ride down. Oblivious to his environs and those who populate it, if he could drag a toilet into the elevator, he'd insert a suppository and get on it. His grooming rituals have become a fascination and are a better barometer of my day ahead than any horoscope.

When he licked marmalade off his sleeve one day, I remembered to get pastries for our store's breakfast meeting.

As he held egg-like cups to give himself an eyewash, I interpreted this to mean I should watch the store closely. I caught a shoplifter before lunch.

I watched him trim his fingernails with clippers and, as I flicked a thumbnail off my peacoat, I told myself to order more *Wicked* lapel pins.

After he buffed both shoes with what appeared to be an old pair of his jockey shorts, I stepped in fresh dog shit. Twice.

When he unwound floss from his finger, then used it, I remembered we were almost out of picture hanger wire in the workroom.

When he joins today's ride, I neither expect nor hear hello. I hear humming. He has inserted a cylindrical hair trimmer into his nostril. What could this portend? I touch my own nose. Marjorie's probably going to put it out of joint.

At my daily newsstand stop, the little girl is diving Ariel with mittened hands onto a stack of magazines. They're explicitly adult. I try to distract her.

"Do you know how to swim like Ariel?"

"Helopymell."

Jumbled syllables or new vowels are all she seems capable of. I just return her smile.

She's still secured to the post, worn pajama leg grimier and bunched around the knot. The binding frustrates her as she glides Ariel around her small world. I can tell the worn figurine is what another child dropped or discarded from its one eye and a fin that looks teethed upon. I'd bring her a replacement, but Disney guards authorized memorabilia zealously and shuts stores like ours out.

"School closed again?" I ask of her father, who slips new magazines into a pocket.

"Vacation."

DREAD flickers in Elaine's eyes.

"Welcome to Pandemonia Gardens," she moans. "Hello, Doily!"

Marjorie approaches me, like an armless Caligula in a winter white poncho. She is not, unfortunately, larynxless.

"As soon as Artie gets here, I want the website modified pronto to promote *My Bad Luck* on the home page. Free shipping, big, everywhere! Switch out this counter case: I want it all *My Bad Luck* until further notice," she commands.

Calling a show about twenty-four hours in the life of a manic-depressive loser *My Bad Luck* assures disaster. Disparaging reviews had been quick to lampoon the title. One memorable headline was *Good Luck with Your Bad Show*.

"*My Bad Luck* is running at 31 percent."

"Exactly. My best friend Paulette is a producer, and she diverted her grandchildren's college trusts into it."

By now, I have shimmied up a ladder to clear the highest shelf for *The Suzanne Somers Stage Study Guide*. Marjorie had met the actress and found her enchanting enough—yet only refers to her as Crissy—to order a carton of her book. I push as many as I can hold next to the *Kaye Ballard Does Fanny Brice* CDs Marjorie also thought people would fight over.

She circles the collected plays of J.T. Godwin on a round table. The noises she makes are either indigestion or indignance. "I also want you to cancel Godwin's book-signing."

I do not come down. "Why?"

"That pig was gushing and supportive of our mayor on NPR this morning, and you know how I despise that son of a bitch," she rails.

"The event is tomorrow afternoon. That's not even twenty-four hours—"

"You, of all people, should know one of the few pleasures of having your name on the door is eighty-sixing whatever displeases you."

I must've missed that carved inlay of BITCH on the door. I'd drop Crissy's study guide on her head but it's too slender to do permanent damage.

"J. T. Godwin won a Pulitzer Prize for Best Dramatic Play three years ago. We fliered, sent press releases, took out ads in *Time/Out* and *Backstage*."

"Call. His. Agent."

Chapter Twelve

The Widder Douglas

I NEED a drink.

Not because today is Valentine's Day, our anniversary. It has come without dread, malleable as it was. We never quite decided if we should mark it when we first dined somewhere with a tablecloth; when we first had oral sex; when we first had anal sex; or when we decided to move in together off campus. February 14 was the most practical day to cultivate.

I need a drink to cancel out today, fraught for other reasons.

The week began easily. I made a couple hires: Sophie, who goes by Soapsuds, due to her frothy platinum hair, and Desliles, who goes by Desliles. Soapsuds has recently been a bottle hooker at a downtown club, selling $30 bottles of vodka for $1,200 to professional athletes, and Desliles can give up moonlighting as a living Statue of Liberty for tourist photo ops (which explained the verdigris-stained palms he tried to hide during our interview). I promise them the same weekly schedule and a review after a probationary period—policies previously unheard of.

Tuesday brought an e-mail flash from the Times Square Alliance that a suspicious cooler had been isolated. All pedestrians were cleared. This has become commonplace since the Pathfinder incident on 45th. The benefit is evacuees retreat to nearby stores to wait it out and, anxious to be consumers, consume. A pre-matinee tour bus of thick women from Buffalo invaded like red fire ants, acting like they're in Filene's Basement except the spoils here are XXL *Jersey Boys* satin jackets. Once I reported law enforcement had given an all-clear, they stampeded down Shubert Alley. I heard one of them screech they'd spotted Regis Philbin.

Today, in a hydrangea-and-Boston-fern tapestry that looked like a chair slipcover had stood up, Marjorie questioned our credit card transaction fees. She wants to permit them for web sales but decline them in the store. Cash or traveler's checks only, she was *thisclose* to implementing. Appalled, I reasoned with her. After the predictable standing ovation, tourists want to immediately recapture the wonder, or at least the logo, of the show they've seen. A spontaneous purchase is emotional, but it won't be plentiful if we rely on the content of their wallet.

Then came the messenger.

The letter, addressed to her current management, required a signature. Our rent will be almost doubling, I immediately gleaned. I had been led to believe Marjorie owned the building outright. From italicized legalese, it seems Marjorie has steadfastly dodged four previous registered letters. Most disturbingly, this increase is due to several late remittances and, at least once, a check returned due to insufficient funds.

I call the leasing office on the letterhead and ask for the man named. He's apologetic but firm. Marjorie's tardiness triggered the clause.

"Her imperious attitude sure doesn't help her case," he adds.

I am a smart, reasonable man who should have known better. Things never come this easy. Internet research I should have undertaken before I accepted the job swiftly pieces itself together.

Marjorie lost a considerable, unrecoverable amount via Uncle Bernie Madoff.

She surrendered a home in Palm Beach not far from The Breakers and was essentially left only with her Upper Westside townhome and Theatrilicious.

She is no longer flush. Her last influx of real cash had been the TV version of *Annie*. She is basically supping on royalties from high school productions.

Her resilient bravado in the face of it dazzles. All of her bluster is actually the air being let out of her securities. The Empress has no clothes. Or cape.

Once I've processed all of this, I feel a little like Annie myself right now. My eyes are white zeroes.

I really need that drink.

I join some of gay Manhattan in a new bar in an old space. Its windows blaze red like a whorehouse. I see this isn't a celebration with mundane heart-on/hard-on and VD plays on words.

Chin Up! Tits Out! No Queer Tears In Your Beer!

That's the callout. Earn a free top-shelf drink by bringing a photo of yourself and your former lover and vindictively tearing it up. Here's a bar that knows how anxious its self-pitying clientele is to display survival moxie.

The ferocity with which they halve photos, some being yanked out of frames, tells me that violent crimes of passion potentially lurk behind every door. Encouragement is shouted. One guy uses his teeth to chew up the face of whoever wronged him. He spits the pulp on the wall.

I wonder if heteros are also rushing in to their bars tonight to decapitate that ex-special someone. Dee would. It was on this very day she stormed out on, and later divorced, her second husband on the grounds of hurried penmanship. He had signed her card *I Love You, Sweatheart.*

I admit to the doorman, who's in a suit and tie and is informing everyone he's costumed as a divorce lawyer so they won't mistake him for respectable, that I don't have the required photograph. I won't get that complimentary drink, he informs me, then points toward a bowl of red water pistols. I can have one filled with the liquor of my choice for a fiver. Otherwise, I can hold it under a water tap and take aim for the amateur soaked-and-stripped contest if I stick around until midnight, which means it will begin at 1:00 a.m.

"We're looking for volunteer fluffers," the divorce doorman adds.

Exactly how I wanted to spend Valentine's Day: benevolently fellating a stranger.

My eyes adjust. Except for counter-level light for staff to see by, all bulbs have been replaced with red. In the crimson light, everyone looks sunburned or livid. I find a wall to stand against. It is faux-painted mauve and it was a bad idea when it was done in 1991. The red light transforms the glazed splotches into a gory miasma—a wall stripped of the shackles but where torture, or at least fatal paintball, might have taken place.

WWAD? He'd be sensible. *Get your back off the prison camp wall, Barry,* he'd command. *Sitting doesn't have to mean slouching,* he'd add, and he'd sit on the tail of his shirt to keep it from bunching up.

I do just that when a barstool becomes available. Staff are in Valentine's Day drag: devils with pitchforks, Lorelei temptresses. My bartender, in a red bustier and matching thong, swipes glasses half-heartedly through a sink of lukewarm water and then acknowledges me. I order a vodka tonic, which tastes of detergent. I forgot the rule of a busy bar; always ask for a plastic cup. It's four—I give him five, keep the rest. He fiddles around and never makes it to the drawer. He's a thief. He's either keeping a tab of what he never rings up and sneaking the overage out before a safe drop or implementing his own elastic pricing to let customers show their gratitude.

My hand, looking for a napkin I didn't get across the sticky bar, hits a stash of small stubby pencils, the kind you only see at a miniature golf course, and stacked, unevenly cut paper squares. I play with the pencils. I am good with props. I consider sticking two up my nose, or in my mouth, like tusks. Now *that* would get me noticed. I don't need to be the *most* popular, I don't need to be the one picked, but sure, I'd like to be noticed.

Who am I kidding? I don't think I'd recognize a come-hither look unless it was holding lube.

I could take notes, look smart, impress people. *He must be a roving bar critic for some gay travel guide,* they'd say. It might also look intimidating. *Crap, is he writing about me, am I nuance for a withering expose? Is the guy scribbling raptly from the ABC, closing in on the drug transactions on the premises?*

There's nothing much to write. Women are scarce. What few there are all look like Rachel Maddow. To my left is a man with dark sideburns that gradually taper to the corners of his mouth. The bisected effect suggests his cheekbones are supported by felt braces. He looks like Rachel Maddow too. I see a cross-dresser who resembles Don Knotts in his daughter's prom dress. Surely he can't miss the whispered-behind hands as customers cross the room to avoid him. I think of Miss Sondra and the derision she has endured. One guy is obviously a fan of Flock of Seagulls. He somehow manages to have both of their hair on one head. Worse is the tinted hair that came out cordovan on the prissy queen with the sweater tied around his neck.

I want to scream at the codger in the age-inappropriate hoodie, "Wake up, Obi-Wan!" I want to scream at season-inappropriate attire, "Your shorts are making make *me* cold. Your biceps are stunning but it's winter!" I want to scream at the dandy in the beret that this ain't France.

Obviously, I need to do some screaming.

Despite the antiromance thematic, a few are there to flaunt their relationship. These couples don't know that, in doing so, they are already breaking up. Possessiveness flares. There is so much pissing on territory I wish I had catheters to sell. I too have known Cupid's arrow, but I feel resentful. These people don't know what lost love really is. I am angry because I am alone with no one to deride this crowd with. I am not just Andy-less, I am posse-less. I didn't ever really have or need one, but there was always a familiar face in a pub, or a customer who wanted me to join their table. Not now.

My own Inevitable Invisibility came faster than I'd ever suspected. Maybe people my age become alcoholics just waiting for someone to talk to them in a bar. Their hopeful expressions collapse when bypassed by the young and the taut, and they order another drink. So I order another drink. The same vodka tonic is three dollars this time. Red Thong keeps the rest without asking or ringing it up. Even he doesn't talk to me. That's all, really, I want. Someone to talk to me.

I will be more specific next time I make a wish, because I suddenly see Artie playing a game of darts against himself. He's the closest of the Theatrilicious staff to my age, and I don't care to be humanized this much, but before I can hide, he's on me with a smirk.

"This red light suits you, boss."

"Because it hides my embarrassment at being caught here?" I mutter.

"It hides your gin blossoms," he says. "I was ready to watch some world premiere Lifetime movie where Joan Van Ark was all fertile, as if, and I thought, hell, go hang with the hopeless and loveless."

"I'm neither," I huff.

"Fuck it. I am." Artie sits without being asked. "Bars, they're like

Pick-Up Stix. Remember how you grab what you can from the floor?" He grabs a slip of paper. "I wonder whose prep duty this is? Quarter limes... ice beer... chop up paper into three and a half by four."

"Have you ever tried speed dating?"

"Don't! Rejection in three minutes or less just gives you more time to be depressed. My feelings have been hurt enough. I stick with the Internet."

"Where you can have an emoticon that looks like feelings," I counter.

He thinks about this. "Yeah." He points to a small platform of monitors where men are waiting to surf. "That's The Toolbar. It's a cybercenter where you can hang out in chatrooms, Adam4Adam, XTube. The Internet is like a Barrel of Monkeys. Remember playing that too? Except you don't have to dump them out. You can contain them in the barrel, and the Internet, that's the barrel. You can just hook right onto the Rhesus whose ass isn't completely inside-out yet."

"What do monkeys eat, besides the eyes, nose, and hands of someone who displeases them?" I ask, imagining my new plastic arm entwined with the plastic arm of another monkey.

"You're forty-five, right?"

I say yes.

"You can get away with forty."

It smarts a little that he didn't say thirty-five, but I won't let him know it. "I've always thought that kind of lying was backasswards. Maybe I'll try truth in advertising. I'm forty-five years *young*."

"The hell you will!" Artie wails. "You're too young to settle for faggot commentary from your perch at Townhouse Bar. If you don't know where that is, follow the smell of Polygrip to East 58th."

I know he's right. I've borne witness to the swift and brutal descent from the flattering "Wow, you don't look your age" to the flattening "Well, it's only a number." Ageism is our community's third rail. Just ask Bob Bergeron.

"And I bet your Facebook has permanent Bell's palsy."

"MySpace, actually."

"That's worse than dial-up!"

"Farmville steals IQ, and all that status update stuff is narcissistic."

"And all of it necessary! Where else can you amass over a hundred Happy Birthdays?"

"I don't need reminded about my birthday."

"So does MySpace still say you're in a relationship?"

I just look at Artie.

"Does it mention you're in Manhattan?"

I don't answer him.

"It seems you've carefully constructed a series of impenetrable firewalls into your life."

"Whoa, You're-So-Nellie!" I try to restore the delicate balance of superior versus employee. "You're all fisty-hipped about my erotic cyberlife because you got our site issues resolved?"

"You may inform The French Lieutenant's Woman that the PayPal stinky link be fixed." He zeroes in on my silver band reproachfully. "And there's *that*."

"There's a lid for every pot. I had my lid."

"I have a pot without a lid and I use a round cookie sheet to cover it in a pinch. Not every lid has to be a perfect seal." He pauses. "You know, it's possible Act II might surpass the first."

"Name me one musical or drama or comedy where Act II is better."

He can't. "Don't let your Intermission go on too long."

"I prefer Interval."

"You're pretentious." Artie leans back. "Do you know the Rudnick play *Jeffrey*?"

"So we're back to my life as a theatrical piece? Yes, Artie, I do. This isn't about fear of commitment, yenta." I lift my glass. The sodden heart coaster comes with it. "This is the wrong day to discuss this."

"Check your e-mail when you get home. I'll forward my Favorite Places. Well, some of them. Get subscribed to the GayLetter e-zine. It lists can't-miss events. I'll attach this week's. Please get yourself an avatar that isn't Whistler's Mother."

We finish our drinks in silence.

"One final thing." He politely waits for an old queen with a wedge haircut, stripped and ready for the contest, to pass. His ass is eating his big girl underpants. He does a special dance just for us, like he's on hot coals. "Everyone at The Lish thanks God for you every day." Artie's face is almost kindly. "You've made life bearable again." His sincerity so mortifies himself he flees without a good-bye.

Should I tell him that today's paycheck could already be an IOU if he didn't bank it and, if it didn't bounce, it's a collectible?

I lose and regain my footing in the entryway of the bar, by now the French Revolution of glossy paper. I check my shoe sole for a head.

When I return home, since I do some of my best thinking when immersed in the mundane, I run the vacuum cleaner. Probably there's something to all this. My wingman, Fagmaylion, would know. Artie was born and got bitter here. But that schoolmarm/rube lesson made me feel that if I go much beyond my expiration date, I'll cause salmonella.

Sitting at my bright laptop compounds my shame, an adulterer without dignity skulking in the darkness. My wrist is limp enough. Am I ready to risk carpal tunnel syndrome to snag a dinner date? Would I go out with me if I wasn't me? How did, all of a sudden, my middling desire to spend quality time in another's company become overwhelming? So much for grandly wanting to start sentences with I. I'm already looking for We.

I sift many of the sites Artie suggested. If I encounter a pop-up porn clip or a cam site invite to watch ugly guys ass-fuck, I click off. I won't pay, nor do I want a free twenty-four-hour trial pass that still somehow involves a credit card. On my own, I find Daddyhunt.com. The name gives me pause, but the site touts itself as *the* resource for the over-forty gay male looking for a partner his own age. I click on a few profiles, read some stats, cringe, X out. This is the equivalent of adolescent stalking—calling your crush and hanging up. I register elsewhere. Some require real introspection. Am I a big bore? I'm not wild but I'm sure as hell not going to check mild. What *are* my interests? Broadway, not so much. Theatrilicious has been a real appetite-suppressant. I'd rather take hot liquid from cupped palms than from one more logo cup. I check Travel, Museums, and Home Improvement and ignore Fetish sub-categories like Urethral Play. I don't pretend to enjoy opera; why should I pretend I'll insert a sounding wand into the tip of my penis? I state in all uppercase NO PNP. Andy and I never messed with drugs. Why start now? Celebrex and Plavix loom as it is.

I tick through the few photographs I have of myself. The angle's too low and crappy, creating a gelatinous second chin, like a fanny pack, or I'm doing a Zoolander. I omit a photo, since it takes just one snark you know to stumble upon it and cc: it. Besides, the blank silhouette it defaults to sums me up, although I would have made my shoulders bigger.

I will allot this experiment—no, project, because when effort and application are required, that's what it is, a project—three weeks.

When I can't remove my relationship band, I cram my finger into my mouth and it eases off. Now, perhaps, I can find someone who will help me pull up my socks.

Chapter Thirteen

The Drilled and the Notched

I POPULATED the final generation of twelve-inch records, Spencer Gifts, and condomless sex. Once I discovered movie soundtracks and Broadway cast albums, I would make a beeline for the record store in any mall. Eight-tracks had succumbed, and I was glad. I had never warmed to them, objecting to how a song's intensity was interrupted by kerchunk! They also seemed to be favored by bullies. (A local artist made and sold very cool media centers from them at Great Rooms!)

I smuggled into the house the *Last Tango In Paris* soundtrack. I remember how the composer's sultry name, Gato Barbieri, fit the score, which I was completely uninterested in. I was more enthralled by the jacket photo of Marlon Brando and Maria Schneider having sex. If that's what they were doing. From the way their bodies were intertwined, I still cannot figure out what their heads were both thrown back in ecstasy about. The only merit of the audio recording of *Oh! Calcutta!* was strictly visual too. I was titillated by glimpses of pubic hair in the back cover cast photos.

Three quarters stacked on the turntable arm sufficed in eliminating the worst skipping, but a single sinker from Dad's fishing gear worked even better. It was the perfect weight. His heart must have soared with gladness when he found me rummaging for one; I always grumbled about fishing weekends with Dad and his brother Wally while Mom and Olivia dined on sliced peaches and cottage cheese in department store tearooms. Finally, I'd come around. We shared something. He could stop apologizing to buddies about his son's apathy toward team sports and untoward interest in his older sister's Rona Barrett gossip magazines. Then I explained I was trying to eliminate an abrupt jump in my *Rainy Days and Mondays* forty-five. My gentle and patient dad helped me balance, then tape the sinker, to the turntable arm. He was still sharing something with me. It just wasn't bait.

As compact discs supplanted records, indifferent store placement and ninety-nine-cent stickers weren't enough. Distributors would also drill a hole or slice a corner off the cover to underscore that this was no longer desirable. The damage inflicted was minor but intentional. Cutouts weren't loss leaders. They were usually playable but had fallen out of favor and the rear of the store was the end of their road.

This is what I will go out with.

The Drilled and The Notched.

SOME responses in my inbox are neither Drilled nor Notched. Inferior pressings are promptly melted, sent to the scrap heap. Many never advance beyond an online minuet. I call this lifting the needle: we haven't met, but you stepped on my feet, so you're blocked. It's more polite than sneaking out of a bar, I figure.

Until it's done to me. Then I think it's awful. One pleasant exchange ends so abruptly I wonder if part of Manhattan is in a blackout. Guess what, Artie. Feelings *can* get hurt.

Many are battle-scarred, as cautious as I, men rejected so often they've fashioned nom de plumes. Tone is hard to discern. Nothing and everything seems rhetorical. I am dumbfounded by the dumb I find. I try to not be Strunk & White about punctuation, but I'm not going out with you if you greet me with "Hey their!" Several are from failed heterosexual marriages, still staunchly maintaining that they don't feel gay. They're exploring. They just want a gay feel. Those who say they're discreet are probably still married. The worst is the unreformed reformed gay. If he can't keep track of what he likes, how can I? Homunculi tiptoe out of the attic, lair, or cave to reply with their TMI. Oversharing is rampant. People would never dare verbalize the things they type or send to a stranger. I have earned an online diploma in felching, edging, docking, and snowballing, they've been elaborated upon so often. I just learned what tossing a salad means. After accessing the man's photo, I'd use tongs.

I send to the recycle bin anyone who thinks the offer of "Can Host" will win my heart, as though I squat at Port Authority.

I avoid anyone who considers himself a foodie. They will be fussy.

Without knowing my situation, someone freely reports that he lost his partner of eight years in the Freedom Tower. I don't want to compare notes. I do not respond.

One man thinks it's important to tell me that "I bruise like a really old person." I suggest iron pills and sign off.

A Toby Keith enthusiast who describes himself as a "big 'un'" wants to know if I own shitkickers. He sends me to his Flickr account, where he has posted over fifty photos of himself line-dancing in dungarees with the thickest rolled cuffs I have ever seen. Doesn't he know the soundtrack to most gay bashings is country music?

I delete anyone who begins with "Into…?"

No, we cannot meet outside the Church of Scientology. The word "audit" makes me nervous. I sweat enough. Pre-surgery blood work did not show me to be niacin deficient.

Ezra's weekend hobby is beekeeping. He makes honey for his Long Island neighbors. He sends me a photo of himself fearlessly sporting a bee beard, which is exactly what you think it is.

BRYCE is an actor, and, because he doesn't own a bee hive or consider rearranging his Netflix queue a hobby, I meet with him. Should all else fail, we can talk theater.

He tells me he has a callback for *The Fantasticks*, which half the world has seen and the other half has been in. He is wearing multiple shirts, something buttoned over something collared over something T-shirtish. He either chills easily or he's hedged his bets and underdressed, in Broadway parlance, for the next scene, which may or may not include me.

"I love this time of afternoon," I tell him, wasting eloquence. "Lavender glazes everything. The violet hour. That's what playwright Richard Greenberg called it in his play."

"Who?"

"Richard Greenberg. He wrote *The Violet Hour*."

If his look were any more blank, he'd have no features.

"He also wrote *Take Me Out*… the baseball play with the onstage showers and naked men."

"Yeah, yeah," he says, nodding. "I thought it was called *Take It Out*."

"It should've been."

The more we talk, the more meager I discover his knowledge of theater, his chosen profession, to be. He has a corrupt database.

"I worship the score of *Evita*," he tells me.

I nod. "I love Patti LuPone too."

He screws up his face. "Who's Patti LuPone?"

I wouldn't expect my plumber to be able to give me a verbal tour of Manhattan's sewer system, but he'd better know who Josephine was. I patiently explain that her star-making role, equally iconic Mamma Rose aside, was as Eva Peron.

"Madonna wasn't first?"

This is feeling like a blackout skit in which I black out.

"Just in the film," I say.

"What else has Patti LuPone done?" he asks.

I degrade myself and Patti by telling him the TV show with the retarded kid. Bryce demonstrates his disinterest by taking Ecstasy.

OLAF identifies himself as a performance artist. When we meet, I discover that Olaf actually aspires to be a sideshow artist. Big difference. He longs to master sword-swallowing, despite childhood throat infections that left his gag reflex unpredictable.

"I'm also available for party tricks."

"Party tricks?"

"I extinguish cigarettes on my tongue. Or lit things in general. Like a sparkler."

I remember the cautious pail of dunking water for the aluminum rods Olivia and I waved around in our backyard, and how Mom saw the red embers as hazards to any bared flesh. Olaf sees them and says "ahhhhh."

"So what's the highest-paying party trick out there?"

"Probably the lady who can pop her eyes all the way out onto her cheeks."

"She must spend a ton on Visine." I think about how she spends her evenings with her Pez eyeballs bobbing on raw skeins.

"She can afford it. She earns a shitload," Olaf recounts admiringly.

I wonder how many guests flee when a woman who can offer mixed nuts from her vacated sockets joins their group.

I wonder if I should get her contact information for Kerrick.

Olaf lives with others of a like mind, a bustling commune of people driving shish-kebab skewers into their own cheeks. When he mentions that one sleeps in an Iron Maiden, I've heard enough.

As we part, the best I can offer is, "Call me if you ever need some old capes for your act."

CAM and I meet at a fake Irish pub on St. Patrick's Day because it's close to Theatrilicious. As the crowd clamors for pints, I honestly present my own backstory.

"Let me tell you about tragic." Cam's voice is thick and haunted. "My sister killed my parents and a visiting aunt when I was eight. I hid in a hamper but ended up in horrible foster homes, so maybe I should have let her saw me up."

I look down toward the Empire State Building, uniquely alit just for this evening. I wonder if I am the same shade of emerald green.

HUGO ITTADINI works on Wall Street. He evades my follow-up request for more specifics, which tells me it probably has something to do with a pushcart. He does offer that he's furry. Is that something I'm interested in pursuing? His stats claim he's six foot two and 190 pounds. I've always considered a Bear a homo who lost his battle with weight and depilatories. From a "Bears Come Out Of Hibernation" weekend Potsy wrangled Andy and me into attending, all I remembered was a strange Mr. French look-alike competition. But I let the God of Hirsutism take a whack at me by telling Hugo furry is fine. After a few more aimless e-mails, we agree drinks are in order.

Hugo doesn't even have facial hair. The swarthiness must be under wraps. We talk about what I did pre-Manhattan. He instantly begins calling me Mr. Homestore. I can forgive that. Everyone likes a good nickname. He tells me he works for J.P.Morgan.

"How is she? I loved her on *The Gong Show*."

"What does that mean?"

Never make sport, no matter how lighthearted, of someone's vocation.

Hugo lets drop that he lives at Palazzo Chupi, Julian Schnabel's West Village building. A cultish fascination surrounds this off-pink building, where a duplex rents for upward of $50,000 monthly. Richard Gere owned there, or did.

"Maybe we should move our conversation there," he says with a smile. "You won't be disappointed, Mr. Homestore."

That I said an immediate yes sounds shallow, but please consider the person who used his address as bait.

Hugo insists on paying. He plops his arm on the tab when it comes, shielding it from me during signature like a fourth grader during a test. Maybe he doesn't want me to see his credit card, like I'll memorize his number. Knowing how poorly the wealthy tip, I leave an extra twenty on the table, and we make the short walk to what he calls "The Chupster."

I follow Hugo through a floor-to-ceiling steel mesh curtain in his foyer. The overwrought apartment is like walking into a series of Faberge eggs laid end to end, albeit with nineteen-foot silver tea-paper ceilings. If that's not enough, he owns a framed original William Eggleston photograph. It takes a certain élan to decide there is artistic worth in a desaturated color photo of a pack of opened AA batteries. He name-drops that Anna Wintour tried to outbid him for it. He also owns a late-period Picasso, but it's been loaned to a museum.

Hugo takes my trench coat. It is a bad idea, in general, to surrender your coat without discerning where it is bound. Andy and I would retain our coats at obligatory winter parties or hang them on a chair so we could make a quick getaway. I acquiesce. He goes off with it.

Coming in from the balcony, which is epic, I am given a Campari and soda with a twist, unasked, which is what he's been drinking, not me. I move to a barstool.

"Boyohboyohboyohboy." He fans himself. "Looks like Mr. Homestore smudged my wall."

"Did I?"

I glance down. The mark is no bigger than a quarter. I'm not convinced I did it. It might even be a shadow.

"It must've been my foot," I apologize.

"It will need repainting."

I stand. "If you run a rag under some warm water, I'll blot it off."

"Where it's worn from rubbing will show."

"Not if I feather it. I know what I'm doing."

The inky veins on his temples fill. "You of all people should value the nice things of others, Mr. Homestore."

"If you'd let me—"

"Just drop it, foxy."

Foxy? I haven't heard that term since people were dancing the Achy Breaky.

Hugo says something I don't quite pick up about Sherwood Forest. I make a joke that I'm a merry man.

He abruptly excuses himself.

I look through a Cecil Beaton coffee table book.

When Hugo comes back, he is wearing Cousin Itt's slippers.

Did he slip something into my Campari and soda? Maybe this is how he cleans his floors. Am I really seeing hooves on a human being? Is this some lightning-fast evolution into a character from some Sid and Marty Krofft Saturday morning show?

Silently, he sits, crosses his legs, awaits my response. One Sasquatch foot taps. I concentrate very hard so I won't giggle. This has all the underpinnings of a hidden camera show, their take on the farcical perils of Internet dating.

Hugo isn't furry, Hugo *is* a Furry.

I know little about the Furry subculture, except that devotees dress as small woodland creatures, then frolic and have sexual congress with each other. I never got the whole reenactment thing in general—Renaissance era, the Civil War—and certainly not with bushy tails. What do they define as the height of sensuality? Combing out each other's pelt?

When he finally speaks, I am grateful he doesn't gnash his teeth like a woodchuck.

"I'd estimate you'll fit a size medium, Foxy."

Hugo invited me over to be a real fox. Which is, I guess, better than a skunk. "We can fuck in it." He explains how it has front and back-door panels, like a little child's pajamas.

Still looking at his feet in disbelief, I'm reminded of the hairy boots favored by 1960s rock-and-rollers. They were usually paired with a coordinated vest.

Hugo exits again. He is undoubtedly going to return with the paws of a sheepdog or pointy, rust-colored ears for me, and I frantically try to recall how we came in and if I can get the hell out of here the same way. Can I leave the building unescorted?

Turns out yes, I can, and I do, with the hope that my trench coat will be very happy at Palazzo Chupi.

LATE one night, especially frustrated, I initiate an AOL M4M chatroom game. *Use one word to describe your best feature.* Not one man refers to anything above the pelvis. I get words like meaty and girthy or, my favorite, cheesy. During this, I receive my first dick pic. I primly respond that I prefer a face pic. I get a second dick pic, with a face drawn on it. The lips were especially upsetting.

ARTIE advised me to gang bang—double-dip, or schedule dates back to back. Tonight, I triple-dipped dipshits.

At 6:25 p.m., at a sushi bar, on 51st, I was told by DeWayne, who wore a strange military jacket, that "I wrote you a song in the cab on the way here." It was based, he says, on our online chats. He extrapolated words and phrases. When he rhymed "Levi's kinda guy" with "this eagle's gotta fly," I looked at my watch.

By 9:10 p.m., Boaz and I were in P. J. Clarke's. He expressed a desire for a nosh at the bar. I was unsure if I iterated I was not Jewish. Do non-Jews say nosh? Should I ask for an extra schmear on something? I hate eating at the bar. People always look hurried, and I want to digest the contents of my meal with feet planted firmly on the floor.

I said I have no problem with a nosh at the bar.

Boaz is an MTV VP. I asked what happened to the videos. He asked what happened to my youth.

Boaz wanted to know about light beers from the bartender. None of six were acceptable. An incredible fuss ensued. I looked up at the tin ceiling. P. J. Clarke's was established in 1884; the air ducts, I decided, were last cleaned in 1887.

Boaz ordered something regular on tap. Once our order had been taken, Boaz asked to see the pad. The bartender handed it to him. Boaz removed a silver stamp from his coat pocket, quickly hit our order with it, then returned it to the puzzled bartender.

Boaz was quite pleased with himself. This timestamp will ensure our plated food won't languish under heat lamps if the bartender finds himself in the weeds, he informed me. "We look like Secret Shoppers." We're spies from corporate, or the competition. The idea that we've teamed for a covert operation delighted him and chilled me.

The food arrived promptly, though, and that our meal obviously wouldn't be comped turned James Bond into Miss Pinchpenny. He was like a petulant baby now, in an adult highchair. Between sips, Boaz began to berate the bartender again about their pathetic variety of light beer.

I took a sopping bar rag and twisted it into his mug. "There. That ought to thin it out. Now your beer's fucking light."

At close to eleven, I met Piers at Birdland on 44th. He was enthusiastic about a late booking of an Italian jazz quartet. Piers and his weak chin moved recently to America from the UK. No surprise, since I don't know anyone born in America named Piers. Or Sinead. He spoke in Euromumble, like some Brighton ventriloquist. I tried not to pick up his accent. After *Steel Magnolias* I became Olympia Dukakis for three days and everything was a cuppacuppacuppa.

Piers's goal was to delineate for me the vast differences between the two countries, with the United States inevitably shite. After he was done natting about his inability to find a proper English breakfast in Manhattan—a man who considers each and every part of a slaughtered pig edible—he started in on America's obsession with teeth.

"Everyone's got braces, had braces, wants braces. What is gum health? And teeth bleach! Every toothpaste is whitening, every gargle is smile-enhancing. I can practically see through yours."

Piers smiled broadly to take the edge off his dig, oblivious to the fact that his own choppers looked like blue cheese. "Cheers!"

A CYRIL responds to me a day later. His name sounds British too. I ignore him. I don't want to hear again how BBC America is not the BBC.

YOU'VE been on your computer too much when your dreams begin to have desktop launch buttons. Yet I find myself rushing through tasks to grab computer time. It's like the bleakest 1040 imaginable, and I am determined to find some gains to offset all of these losses.

I amend criteria. I'll go out with you if I like your name.

Caleb, Dom, and Ryland make the cut.

But who would christen their son Chelly, especially when their last name was Temperosa? I won't go out with someone named Chelly. I just can't.

CALEB and I spend a warm lunch hour strolling through Central Park. Winter has been completely chased away. Tulips and daffodils stretch toward the sun. The trees have noticeably swelled. I think how the French lilacs are going in bud around our pool and how, this year, they won't be immediately cut for arrangements; they'll get to open and send their perfume into the world.

Young marrieds push prams at Bethesda Fountains. Joggers trot along the roadways. Two ducks paddle in a glassy pond. This is nice. Then, at the ornate Central Park carousel, as we watch the three-and-a half-minute ride, an ill wind suddenly kicks up.

"I want to get something out of the way," Caleb says.

He pops off a digit.

"This finger, it's fake."

I want to mount one of the fifty-eight hand-carved horses and gallop away.

Caleb tapes his finger back.

Not far from The Plaza, I see a male couple in line for tickets at the Ziegfeld Theatre. Andy and I once stood there like that. I wonder how long they have been together. I wonder if they have twenty fingers between them.

DOM is what Potsy called gay man white meat, the desirable and healthy cut. I like the setting, Prime Burger, on 51st near Madison, his suggestion for breakfast. I relish the paneling, the conical ceiling lights, the type of joint you expect to see Oscar, on a counter stool, harangue poor Felix into an asthma attack, maybe even calling him "schnook."

But it's me and Dom that are the odd couple, I discover, as we stand afterward outside the NBC windows to observe the final few minutes of TODAY. We watch workers complete the seasonal closure of the Rockefeller Center skating rink. This reminds me to set the sales floor wall clock forward tonight, after closing. I wish it were that easy to spring ahead.

Dom supposes today might be the day he catches Lorne Michaels and can pitch an idea. Under the golden watch of Prometheus, Dom opens his rich Tumi attaché and shows me a stack of proposed SNL sketches. Then he begins to perform one. Not part of it, all of it. He is every character. This is way worse than DeWayne's song. Dom affects voices ranging from a Russian spy to a Valley girl. People stare. I hope Mr. Michaels slept in.

When the metaphysical Applause light extinguishes and the soundless audience laughter recedes, he takes out a black leather mask from under the scripts. "My safe word is 'Don't hold back'."

"That's three words," I stammer. "How would anyone hear you properly if you're wearing that?"

He pushes the mask toward me. "What do you think?"

"First reaction? Clogged pores."

He touches the zipper mouth. "You will unzip it just enough to make me drink your—"

Prometheus just gagged a little. I don't let him finish. I jump up. Dom is warped and unplayable.

RETURNING from the men's room at Peter Luger's Steakhouse, I pass through hobnobbing Ivy League graduates saying things like "that would be a blast!"

I pull my chair back from the table. Ryland has undone his tie, which tells me that at least it's not the clip-on I thought it was. Too bad his hair is. Where crown doesn't quite meet part is the follicular equivalent of the equator.

As I find my napkin, Ryland asks angrily, "What in the hell do you think you're doing?"

Something soured his mood while I was away. It happens. "I'm sitting down."

"Someone's already sitting there," he points out.

"Who? Peter Dinklage?"

"Did you not hear what I said?" Ryland demands edgily.

It is suddenly very dark. I stand back up. I should have known, when he made that big deal about actually having a Peter Luger charge card when we claimed our reservation.

"Wait! Wait! Is that you, Barry?" he then asks. "I thought I'd memorized your voice. I should tell you that I suffer from something called face blindness."

Aunt Sarajane, if she actually got a whiff, would salivate over this one.

Ryland continues. "What happens is I don't recognize people when they walk away."

So he probably didn't notice that I just did.

JAMESON suggests Bowlmor Lanes, near the shop. He has a ball, shoes, and a lucky shirt. It sounds noisily competitive and not very fun. I think of Caleb in Central Park and find myself telling Jameson that I have no fingers. He's not so keen on the date now but wants to know how I type. Breath-activated keyboard. What happened to my fingers? I think of my grandmother. Frostbite, I reply, a long sad story. He veers into the sexual. Can you rub one out, he wants to know, and how? I've gotten good with my feet, I say. What's left of your fist must be like a penis, he types back too quickly, adding *I'M INTRIGUED.* I tell him I am tired and tell him I need to go while I can still blow.

This could be fun, hiding behind a false identity, fingerless, playing with people. I can lash out at fools too. When someone says he's a doppelganger for Mick Jagger, I write back that I look just like Keith Richards.

This is living the fantasy of plowing into every careless driver because you're in a worthless clunker and you can.

Sebastion asks almost immediately how often I bathe, because "I like the real scent of a man. It is my ambrosia." And, tersely, "no femmes!!!"

Using a word like ambrosia, then "no femmes!" seems a little contradictory. I dash off that I stink like a barnyard but I'm wearing a gingham sundress. Does one cancel out the other? He types back: Are you leading me on? Being a cocktease is a violation of terms of service, he'll have me know. We're having our first big fight and we've never met. I hang up on him, or, in this case, slam down my mouse.

My very next e-mail cares very much about cleanliness. He, in fact, wants only to bathe with me. He writes, "It can be a very nonsexual bubble bath we share by candlelight. I can, of course, at your indication, gently suds up your penis, but you need not feel compelled to acknowledge mine."

Andy would love that someone has just offered to bring me off into a warm, soapy bowl.

I can also opt for a tongue bath, another correspondent offers. "I eat amazing ass. And you may break wind if you wish."

Jake starts in on sober living. Spill forth about your sponsor and it had better be because you're PBS programming, or you can take those twelve steps out of my line of vision. I will not ask for a doggie bag for my chicken parmigiana because someone has jumped up for a meeting they forgot about. I send him away by telling him I've been on a three-day binge and that I am, in fact, typing completely smashed.

Wynn is a sex addict in recovery. He confesses to having driven over four hundred miles, without stopping, for dick. I would not drive that long to see the Red Sea part. I consider telling him about Captain Reg, but I would feel guilty if he fell asleep at the wheel driving all night.

I COMMIT to memory Gymrat's nutritional and fitness regimen, in case there is a quiz. We've discussed the good fat of salmon longer than Perricone ever has, with egg and avocado right behind, and I know he keeps his supplements in a fishing tackle box. He probably cums in pill form. Gymrat is so obviously juiced. I can't ignore the cystic acne plums on his neck and forehead, the simian jawline that suggests he came directly here from the makeup trailer of *Planet of the Apes*. I've fished a literal Monkey out of the Barrel.

Now he is telling me the calories of my crème brulee and when I could, in good conscience, order dessert again.

Adding to his allure, a button pops off Gymrat's shirt and skims off my dessert plate.

BY THIS twenty-first day, I debated not even following through on the last one scheduled; I myself have been stood up twice. But the dinner reservation he handled for La Grenouille sounded promising. And now John Carradine, or his older, more reptilian brother, is winking at me. Maybe it's a twitch. One wonky eye looks upside down and sideways, like he's had a stroke.

"I'm sure I mentioned that I was seventy-three." His breath smells like earthworms.

"I think maybe you transposed the number," I tell my antique seventy-eight rpm.

I HAVE experienced vinyl rot, mislabeling, bad scratches, defects, and missing content. I have Notched and Drilled until I am calloused. In computerese, a more apt description might be Dragged and Dropped. I empty my mailbox of more replies, and after a series of opt-out procedurals, I have finally deleted the screen names I chose, or I hope I at least disabled them.

I read aloud from a profile that catches my interest.

"I'm free of the 3 D's: disease, drugs and drama." Alliterative, balanced, very nice. "I'm determined without being dumb." I scroll down. "I love dogs, Dewar's and David Sedaris." I click to the next window.

Andy's face fills the monitor to announce "Here's the damn dilemma: I'm dead."

My dream pixilates into the collapse at ColonyScape.

Chapter Fourteen

Fast Friends

"YOU slimy son of a bitch!"

I hear Dee's screams of laughter from the bathroom. She has seen her foggy portrait on the toilet tank. She and Potsy just arrived. I called in sick, knowing that Marjorie will probably ask me to submit to a saliva swab. I had to immediately give Potsy a box of frozen spinach for his crotch; he traveled commando and a patdown resulted in one of his testicles being squeezed until he nearly blacked out. He's still groaning on the sofa. Dee emerges from the bathroom, struggling with her jeggings. Her face seems fuller. Is it possible she's eaten something since I moved?

I don't so much give a tour as I have them turn their heads side to side. What a comedown, their body language seems to impart. He probably eats leftovers. Six bedrooms, five bathrooms, and now he lives in Harry Potter's cupboard.

"Is there a Murphy Bed?" Potsy wonders.

I gesture. "That would require wall space and enough floor for it to rest on."

I offer to take the air mattress and give them my bed to share, sure they'll recoil, but they accept. It's only one night; their visit has been truncated by a last-minute closing for Dee.

Dee is delighted to discover how close the Crate and Barrel flagship store is. She wants to go look at picnic items she saw in a summer preview catalog. And a wok, don't forget a wok, Potsy reminds her. I may peddle ball caps with stitched logos, but shopping for housewares always felt like a busman's holiday; knowing the markup, I could never bring myself to pay full price for anything KitchenAid. Now I have a downright aversion. I walk past Gracious Home and get dizzy. I'll be right outside, I volunteer, on the ledge.

As I wait, I brush away like a mosquito an image of my father, patiently waiting on a mall bench as my mother meandered through department stores to emerge with absolutely nothing. They too come out with absolutely nothing.

We stop at Anthropologie on 5th. This time I go in. Dee gushes over and grabs handfuls of cloisonné doorknobs and jewel-tone drawer pulls, just perfect for home-buyer thank-you gifts. They will make her suitcase weight exceed the limit. I want to tell her Iz could obtain these at wholesale—the manufacturer frequently called on us—but I don't.

We come to Times Square. I beckon them both. "Come over here and see my little girlfriend."

The girl puts Ariel through gymnastics—Pogo Ariel, now, since the fin has broken completely off. When she sees me, she bleats out, "Pelmehemel," and her smile reveals a missing front tooth.

"She's cute," Dee says.

"She's illegal," Potsy says.

"Listen to this," I tell them. "It's become a game. No school today?"

The newsstand worker focuses on his cashbox. "Teacher not show up for class."

"She's never in school. What do you think that's about?"

Potsy dismisses me. "Slow. Or mute."

"They have schools," I remind him.

The girl gingerly traces her gums where her tooth was, curls her tongue through the gap.

When I point out Theatrilicious to them from a distance, I detect disapproval. It *is* a little rough-looking. From this angle, mold the shape of Texas is visible on the awning. They lower their heads slightly, like they're looking for the marbles I've lost. Their careful smiles still say Barry, oh Barry, this is beneath you, why are you not affiliated with Arne Glimcher and PACE Gallery, why are you not consulting at ABC Carpet & Home? Why this dump? I spare them any half-swallowed enthusiasm by making a joke.

"There it is. Where the Miranda Priestly of *Mamma Mia!* keychains holds sway. Actually, more like Rotunda Beastly," I observe.

"She swirls in late afternoon in her goddamn Shroud of Tourism like a matador at a bullfight. Except I'm the one who gets gored. I try to get her to look at sales numbers, which are atrocious, and she becomes a superhero—Wander Away Woman—and vanishes. Hell, maybe she's freelancing as a tablecloth at Sardi's."

"Florence Nightingale wore a cape," Dee says.

"And she was always sticking something up someone's ass too."

We pass through groups photographing the jumbo Times Square TV screen, other clusters inspecting goods on tables, and walk to the Village. I ask about Kerrick, whom I haven't heard from. Did I not know Dee had a falling-out with him over a catering calamity? I did not. Dee had referred a new client, a boating enthusiast. The buffet Kerr set for a local club had an aquatic-themed centerpiece—a series of large brandy goblets, the length of the table, each with a live goldfish. One attendee mistook it for a water with an orange garnish slice and downed not one but two. The client now won't return Dee's calls, so she won't return Kerrick's.

Potsy and I leave Dee at Uniqlo in Soho, where the employees— excuse me, *advisers*—fold Oxford shirts like automatons and the music is too global. Potsy and I find a men's clothing shop. Potsy holds up a clubwear shirt that would barely cover his ribcage. "Are we in the Gay Toddler section?"

"I think it's the clothing for their dolls," I say.

"We now know where Stan imports his clothes from," Potsy observes.

Dee has found us and is rifling the gay rags in a front rack. She flips to the back pages of *Next*. "I guess anyone can be an escort nowadays. Look at the mug on this one."

Potsy refolds teeny jeans. "Did you see the rise on these? The fly is an inch long. Who can wear them? Eunuchs?"

We veer off into a haberdashery. Dee insists Potsy needs a rakish chapeau now that he's had Lasik. Watching him try on various hats as Dee sings "Smooth Operator," I am startled to realize Potsy is *not* wearing glasses. He'd never mentioned to me that he was considering eye surgery.

I will soon discover this is not the only thing that hasn't been mentioned to me.

WE SIP Andy's sangria recipe, which they always begged for, on the rooftop terrace.

"Don't lean on that railing," I caution Dee, who keeps inching forward. "A balcony in Beacon Hill gave way last week, and the owner fell to his death."

This is my first time up here. After Andy, I've developed a creeping mistrust of things in the air. I find myself walking head back, like a nested baby bird awaiting the worm, newly aware how much is temporarily attached to the tallest reaches of buildings. We look up but we don't see the window washers on ledges. Or those tethered to sandblast a high-rise façade. The mid-air HVAC modifications. All of it cabled to something else that wasn't probably engineered to support extra weight or motion. It's not the city to dwell on disaster in, but I don't want my head to be separated from my body by a dropped pail.

Dee shakes her head at Broadway's traffic, foot and vehicular, even at this hour.

"I don't know how you'd meet anyone, much less trust them."

We revisit my drilling and my notching and we laugh. It's like old times, without invoking He Who Shall Not Be Named.

"All you learn from online hookups is everyone's weight is *not* proportionate to their height." Potsy bemoans all of this textual intercourse. "Let that Artiesmartypants Twitter on the shitter with his 140 words or less. Jesus! It's like reading someone else's fortune cookie! And shut him down if he brings up Grindr."

"He already did. I told him if I wanted to be located via tracking device, I'll break a law."

"Seriously." Potsy points at me. "You've licked your wounds. Time to lick something else. You need dick in your diet."

"I was just trying to meet someone."

"Reintroduce yourself to The Semens! You remember them: they're swimmers by trade and sometimes they show up too early at the party?" He perfectly rolls a spliff. "It doesn't have to be the kind of sex that involves an odor. So they don't park in your garage. Just let 'em play in the front yard."

"Even your analogies are vulgar," Dee sighs.

"Get thee to a peepshow booth!"

"The city closed most of those with their sixty/forty rule." They look at me blankly. "The proposal was more than 60 percent of walk-in sales had to be mainstream movies. No one buys porn anymore, anyway."

Potsy slaps his forehead like a cartoon character. "Not the one at 8th and 45th!"

"I walk by it almost every day. Vacant. Except for a Jeff Stryker video poster they couldn't blowtorch off a window."

Potsy mellows with his doob. "Then head to Saks and assume a wide stance."

Dee carefully returns to the railing. "Talk about sensory overload. It's utterly overwhelming, wave after wave."

"Like the ocean, the traffic lulls me to sleep," I say.

Serenity is found when wading into it, I want to say. The water never trespasses above the waist, so you're a little adrift and a little slowed but still capable of movement and it's not too tiring.

"It's daunting, all of it," Dee insists.

"You make the bigness small. The same newsstand every morning with the little girl, the bartender who knows my drink, a regular Chinese take-out place."

"See many famous people?" Potsy asks.

"All the time." I try to sound blasé. "Matthew Broderick, Sandra Bernhard, Liza, Al Pacino, Karl Lagerfeld."

"Karl Lagerfeld?" Potsy shrieks. "How severe was *that*?"

"Severe."

Dee is biting her fingernail, which is quite unlike her. Her manicure is as highly prized as a me/me real estate sale. She drains her goblet.

"I have a buyer." She says it so softly I ask her to repeat it. "I have a buyer."

A breeze extinguishes the flick lighter I am holding over a candle.

"For what?"

"Your house."

"I'm confused. It's not for sale."

"Say if it were," Dee furthers.

The quick look between her and Potsy doesn't escape me. "Your version of coy transcends obvious," I announce.

Potsy offers the joint. "You need this kind bud more than me."

Dee takes it. Thick bangles on her wrist collide. "It's me and Pots, Barry. We want to buy your house."

If my mouth hadn't gone dry, this is the time for a spit take. "As an investment? Like you'd rent it?"

Dee squirms on the hot coals of disclosure. "We'd live there."

Now I have a brain freeze. "Together?"

"We've been hanging out," Potsy says.

"Some," Dee tries to minimize.

Even traffic defers to silence.

"Say something," Dee implores.

"I feel like I've been tased."

Potsy gestures for his joint. "Now you're hurt."

"Come on, guys! I've only been gone two months, and you're debating sheers versus tiebacks. That's not hanging out *some*. We talk or text almost every day, yet not a word? That's called the sin of omission in most quarters."

"You have always been the one thing we have in common," they both say, connecting each other's thoughts.

"Would've been nice if you'd realized it when we all lived in the same state," I retort.

"We haven't changed," Dee protests.

Translated: I did. I moved on but didn't anticipate that those who stayed would do the same.

"I'm not some possessive adolescent, but I have to ask: Is that why this visit? To make a face-to-face offer?"

"That's pretty passive/aggressive," Dee says. Potsy adds, "Now he's shitty. We just got moved to the air mattress, Dee."

Right now I hope that it's as comfortable as an inner tube and the stem finds their eye.

"Can I not take this in out loud? I understand. Why not? It's too nice a house to sit empty. I'm not mad. I'll seriously think about it." I want more sangria, so I take Dee's. I recall Dee's lumpy shopping bag. "That explains Aunt Clara's ben-wa balls. I'm terribly sorry you don't like our doorknobs."

"Those really *are* client gifts!"

I look around them both, wordless. Other people in other buildings look out too, pacing terraces, silhouetted in windows, wondering what surprises tomorrow holds.

Chapter Fifteen

Stargazing Through a Veil

SOMETIMES it holds a celebrity.

I am opening my umbrella when there's a rap against our rain-spattered front door. Through the glass, a man insists, "I'm late but expected!" I let him in. "Thank you! My shoot ran over at Silvercup, and it's already pouring in Long Island City. I'm supposed to sign something before Memorial Day weekend." His damp hand accepts mine. "Chaz Stewart. I'm an actor."

"Barry Grooms," I tell him. "You're here about the poster for the Broadway Cares/Equity Fights AIDS fundraiser."

I don't need to tell him everyone else has already been by, since their names crisscross the show card. His laugh, head back, is the kind only a trained stage actor could get away with. "My costars upstage me even in charity!"

"We saw this last spring when we were in town," I recall. "We said the second act needed more of you."

"Well, the author felt too much of the character would dilute his effectiveness. I'd sit in my dressing room on my Mac and search for my name in theater message boards until the last scene."

"What'd you learn?"

Chaz howls. "To stay the hell out. Those people are hateful."

I know this to be true, from surfing those venomous forums myself, but I find it hard to believe that this affable man really flung the wrong brand of throat lozenge into the face of a stage manager, or called in sick at half-hour because of a snarky Reidel dig in the *Post*, or locked himself in the Orso men's room with two male fans, as a Billy Masters column inferred.

"Now you guys live here?"

"He's deceased." I touch my bare ring finger. "He was killed in an accident last summer. I moved here."

"I'm so sorry. How long were you together?" he asks.

"Since college."

"Just like Mark Badgely and James Mischka," he comments, like he knows them, which he probably does.

I study his flowery handwriting on the poster and change the topic. "You could have been a calligrapher."

"Actually, my mother does just that—invitations, place cards—for not-for-profits back home. Naperville, Illinois," Chaz says.

"I wish my mother did something so Red Hattish." I briefly describe the stalking and the trespassing of the Bright Spotters.

Chaz's laugh is long and, this time, real. "Do they not get the rude connotation? 'Hi, ladies! Still spotting?'"

I slide the poster into a reinforced sleeve I'd already prepared for transport. "Shortened, it would be the BSers, which is worse, yet apt."

"Where are you off to?" he casually asks.

"I'm going to scope out this empty space a block over."

He looks around. "Are you running out of room?"

No, the landlord is running out of patience. This month's rent is also apparently past due; I dodged the courier and had Artie redirect his hand-carried envelope to Marjorie's address.

"A preemptive strike. We could use more square footage," I answer.

"Then where to?"

"Then to home."

"Where's home?" he asks. When I tell him, he marvels. "You have a better address than I do!"

We watch those not in theaters scurry for cover as fresh thunder fires a warning shot, pounding and grumbling.

"Actually, I think that was my stomach," Chaz says. "HBO's idea of craft services is beef jerky and Gatorade. Would you like to maybe get a bite to eat? We haven't made fun of our fathers yet."

My surprised gulp must have sounded like a sink unclogging. I have just been casually asked to dinner by a noted Broadway performer who has delivered two brilliant Tony acceptance speeches, an actor who bravely admitted in a national weekly magazine that yes, he was dating that equally out reality-show host, a star who could approach complete strangers at TKTS and fill a banquet hall table with dinner companions. Why me, of all he could have chosen from tonight?

Well, why *not* me? I'm due for something good. I don't want to fawn, but I also can't ignore his celebrity. I shouldn't correct mispronunciations. I can't roll my eyes. I will watch my step with disparaging theater criticism; I don't know who's friend or foe. I should probably seal my mouth with the masking tape.

Big raindrops pelt the windows. While we wait out the storm, I clean up. I feel him watch my ritualistic sweep of the work area. I can't do much about the work jiz that coats me after taking money and Marjorie's grief all day, but I vanish long enough to rub my hands, arms, and neck with rubbing alcohol from the first-aid kit. I at least smell sterile.

When the rain quiets to plinks, Chaz smiles. "Shall we?" Just two words sound so urbane. He sprinkles a word like "phenomenal" into commonplace conversation, as all performers seem to. And Chaz is intimidatingly handsome, indifferent to it yet completely confident the room watches, just daring anyone to look away. His inflections and timing have been compared to a young Jack Lemmon, but something about his carriage reminds me of Cary Grant.

It's intermission outside the Music Box Theatre, where I collide with Tracy and DoorMatt.

"Tracy! Matt! What are you guys doing in town?" I blurt.

DoorMatt scrambles. "It was last-minute."

"We heard you moved here." Tracy blushes, the same color for a minute as her hair. "We love you in everything we've ever seen you in," she babbles at Chaz. "I'm Tracy Lawrence. This is my husband Matt."

"Chaz Stewart." Chaz shakes DoorMatt's eager hand, then Tracy's, after she wipes it on her *Hang In There, Baby!* cat sweatshirt.

Tracy, never shy, now is. The gotcha! of it all has strangled the meow right out of her. "I'm trying to remember the last time we saw you was—"

"You were with Andy and me," I interject. "Chaz was starring in *Things To Aim For*."

"How do you two know each other?" DoorMatt asks.

Chaz takes my arm. "Barry's one of my best buds."

They're impressed but miserably silent again. What I think is a tambourine somewhere is DoorMatt, playing with the silver in his pants pocket. I guess it's up to me. I try again. "So what do you think?"

"You look really good, Barry." Tracy nods.

DoorMatt adds, "You must walk a lot."

I'd meant the show.

We vow to stay in better touch. They walk briskly into the theater, rehashing and damning their clumsy cover-up, I'm sure. Last-minute, my ass. Ticket demand is such for this show that the cast can't get seats for their parents. *Heard* I moved to New York City?

We walk along 45th Street. I thank Chaz for his kind rescue.

"You handled it very well," he compliments.

"Tracy's assymetrical henna hair has gotten so tired. Did you catch the husband's eyeteeth? I swear they're spring-loaded. He'd lose one, another would push forward," I snipe. "I'm glad they've written me off."

"*Did* handle it well," Chaz uncompliments.

We cup our hands to the windows of the storefront formerly known as World of Hotness. It's larger, for sure, and more visible, but I can't tell what remains inside.

Chaz chucks Jeff Stryker under the chin. "I don't have to tell you what went on here. Bring bleach."

I step back, silently repeating the leasing agent's name, memorizing it. "We'll see. Marjorie doesn't like change."

We drift down Restaurant Row.

"Marjorie, she's the owner. I'm recalling yards and yards of linen," Chaz reflects.

"Sometimes we project movies on her back."

"And a lot of scary hair."

"She's a tent with a Medusa weathervane." I like making him laugh. "So your cable thing, is it a good part?"

"If the pilot gets picked up, it'll be a consistent paycheck, so that's good."

He gestures me down into the alcove of Joe Allen, telling me how he regrets outing himself the way he did. "It was as about as big a shocker as Ellen's yep, I'm gay. Maybe I should've declared yep, I'm a white supremacist." He waits for me to shake and close the umbrella before continuing. "It's kinda eye-opening to become typecast as Broadway's go-to queer, the homo dishing in his penthouse. When you're too old for a revival of *Boys In The Band* and too effeminate for Aunt Eller, I guess you become Nathan Lane."

He takes for granted I'll get three sequential theater references, and I appreciate that. He speaks with the gatekeeper. I assume he wants secluded seating. What was for decades an actor's restful post-performance hangout, Joe Allen has become overrun by tourist starfuckers stalking actors resting post-performance. Those who still come here prefer a table near the back of the main dining room, away from Kentuckians. I assume we are bound for this unapproachable zone.

We are not. Chaz points to forward seating, at a two-top just readied against an exposed brick wall of framed theatrical musical flops (the only Broadway shows Joe Allen displays,) like *Nick & Nora*, which I saw, and *Moose Murders*, which I wish I had. I slide into my chair under *Dracula*, *Lestat*, and *Dance of the Vampires*.

Chaz whips a napkin into his lap. "My long-term career objective is to *not* have a show card in here."

He orders the La Scala Salad, as do I. I hope he doesn't think I'm mimicking him.

"You're a Chita too!" he exclaims, then he explains. "The owner, Joe, concocted this salad for his girlfriend at the time, Chita Rivera. She wanted something light after a show."

Whether this is true or not, I don't know, but sure, I'll be Chita.

It doesn't take long. A male fan nervously offers a pen and a copy of his meal receipt to Chaz.

"When will you see you on Broadway again, Mr. Stewart?" he admiringly asks. "You're not forsaking us for TV, are you?"

I hear frustration in his sigh. He's a theater luminary who won't count himself truly successful with *Law & Order* or a secondary sidekick voice in a Pixar movie. It's why he probably turned down the overpraised Charles Busch play transferring to Broadway. He would have been playing some flame-y detective; Charles would, of course, be in a turban. He wants more, in every medium, the leap from Broadway that doesn't happen often.

"I'm focusing on film work right now, but you never know," I hear him say. "I'm married to the stage. Anything else is a mistress. Or masteress."

The fan practically shivers at Chaz's frisky eloquence. This is how swoon turns into poon.

The fan slides pen and the receipt to me. "You too."

I assure him I'm nobody.

Chaz slides into baritone: "'You're nobody... 'til somebody loves you.' It's the actor's mantra. Just sign, Barry."

I do, with a flourish.

Chaz regards me with bemusement. "Someone's practiced."

"Who doesn't, as a kid?" I mumble. The fan scuttles away, whatever memory this represents notarized in duplicate. "Are people usually nice?"

Chaz nods. "Theater fans are very polite. They see me on the stage, moving, talking. I'm not on a fifty-foot screen. I'm a person at their level. My physical presence isn't as awe-inspiring."

"When you're in a mood, have you ever said 'I'm not that guy'?"

"Actors don't leave the business, the business leaves them. So, no, never." He refills his martini from the sidecar. "Have you?"

"Have I what?"

"Not wanted to be that guy?"

"Not until the last eight months." That was more than I wanted to say. I help myself from the sidecar. I fill my martini like an infinity pool. I tell him how I'd pursued acting in college, only to be told my line readings were stilted and false by an instructor who spoke with the aristocratic accent of an RSC veteran but was born and raised one county away. I was dismissed with "Try writing." In theater, the playwright is king, but it seemed a lonely crown from the aspiring writers I knew at college who ate cigarettes and sipped herbal tea, as opposed to the acting students who bummed cigarettes and guzzled Long Island Iced Tea. I found my strength in set design, lighting, and costuming, which I parlayed into the study of Visual Merchandising and Store Design. "So I settled for saving every program of every stage production I've ever seen, sealed in clear collector's bags."

"And you never open them." Chaz leans in to confide, "Me, neither. Even the ones I was in."

"Somewhere I still have audio cassettes somewhere of the Tony Awards I recorded before my family had a VCR," I admit.

Chaz touches his glass to mine. "I would take pictures off the TV screen and get them developed."

"You grew up and won two. How cool is that?" I sound like a fangurl. I bring it down. "Where do you keep them?"

"They're bookends in my kitchen. All of my Barefoot Contessa cookbooks are between them. I love me some Ina."

We both laugh explosively. His hand, his napkin, something, slides across my knee.

"I present this year," he says. "Best Original Play. I love that New Yorkers buy tickets because they respect the playwright, not just because some sitcom star deigns to stretch themselves during their summer hiatus."

"Yet you're doing TV," I remind.

"Therein lies the rub."

By the time dinner is cleared even our glasses, when they clink, sound drunk. It occurs to me no bill is presented. He suggests we head elsewhere. I suggest Don't Tell Mama's, a piano bar across the street.

"You mean Don't Tell My Weight," he says with a giggle, referring to the array of singing, slinging perennials whose waistlines, but not theatrical careers, exploded.

We settle on directly upstairs, at the Bar Centrale offshoot of Joe Allen. We're slow to be seated because Kevin Spacey says hello, then Andy Cohen; the gorgeous producer Barbara Manocherian wants to talk to him about a revival of *The Elephant Man*; and Joe Mantello wishes him well with the HBO series. I'm still breathing the rarified air as he apologizes.

"Broadway is really just community theater with powerful unions," Chaz says, grinning. We settle into a small booth. "So. You. Tell me about your last eight months. You can narrow it down. Yes, do that. *The* biggest, most daunting thing."

"How do I say this? It's like I'm stuck wearing a permanent veil," I begin.

"If you mean by that you're a widower, the loss you've had... people you meet don't know, so don't feel defined by it."

"No, I mean a veil like I'm watching my life through a window screen." I can't believe I'm being this honest, vulnerable. I struggle to make sense of it for both of us. "Neon to you is pastel to me. Shiny things are dulled."

"What do you think you're missing out on?"

I touch my chest. "Me. *I'm* missing out on me. I just wait to go elsewhere but I get there and it's the exact same dusk."

"Try dressing more upbeat," he suggests. "Black anticipates doom."

I look down at myself. "I thought everyone in New York wears black."

"Everyone's clothes *turned* black."

"Dressing like a roll of Lifesavers isn't going to upend my pessimism."

"I read about this farmer," Chaz says earnestly. "In another country. He lost his arm somehow, and then it began to grow back. First, this nub. Then, a little bit at a time, what was very recognizably an arm in pictures the village doctor took."

"Like that *Night Gallery* episode," I suppose.

"*Green Fingers*! Elsa Lanchester! Exactly!"

I want to do a victory dance. He got, he even completed, a pop culture reference.

"Maybe the photos were doctored. A lopped-off limb can't regenerate," he acknowledges. "But nerves can. Feelings can. Maybe there's no Eureka! moment. Maybe it's incremental. Maybe one day the veil's gone and the sun's on your face again."

I hope my "maybe" doesn't sound as unconvinced as it is.

He leans back. "You are so open." I know he means it because he doesn't toss in "phenomenal." I mumble thanks. "This may seem really random. In just this short amount of time, I feel this connection. I'm not imagining it, me and you, this, am I?"

"Imagining?"

His palms turn up. "Us."

I sit up very straight. "Okay."

"Doing it all by yourself... all this... life... details, minutiae... it's so wearing, you know? Of course *you* know," Chaz says.

"My learning curve has had more squiggles than I counted on, Tracy and Matt tonight being the latest. I hear you," I reply.

"Am I moving too fast?" He shakes his head. "I'm moving too fast."

Actually, we're circling each other, yet remain still.

"What's too fast on a planet that's melting?" I try to joke. I have obviously run out of empathetic things to say. The learning curve bit was bad enough.

He pauses. "You're adorable. But you know that."

No, I don't know that. That's very whole-package. Tell me again.

"I'm not doing this very well. I blame the Grey Goose."

I drain my glass of water.

"God! I've unnerved you with this verbal foreplay."

I wait.

"I am so not pulled together. We actors, we're not all that bright. I hope you know that," Chaz elaborates.

Don't unsell yourself, I think.

"One look at you, and I said to myself: this is a man who can bring you some peace, Chaz."

I hope he can't see the pulse in the soft of my throat.

"Two guys... one mutual goal. There comes a point when you want someone you can trust." Chaz smiles. "Not just want. *Need.* On your side. So I'm going to put this out there and see what happens. I'll just ask."

Where is Cindy Adams? Only in New York, kids, only in New

York. This is amazing, like predestination: my hasty move, Theatrilicious, his charity poster. He's a catch. He thinks I am a catch.

His hopeful smile actually makes my toes curl, which makes it all the more laughable.

"Would you be interested in being my personal assistant?"

"OUCH!" Walt winces.

Walt is black and buff, a Broadway dancer who's no longer cast often. I could tell him why. Downtime between jobs gave him too much weightlifting opportunity and now he's too thickly muscled to appear graceful. He's the bartender who knows how I like my martini. During one of my circuitous strolls homeward after leaving Theatrilicious, I found him and this lounge on 9th, drawn by the bizarre window lineup of Rock 'Em Sock 'Em Robots games—the mid-1960s issue, not the update where the head doesn't scream as memorably when popped up. The ginmill is called Knock Yourself Out. That is what I am now doing. More than two, Andy would warn, made me mouthy. I am on my way to becoming a PA system with feedback.

"Arrogant turd!" I eat the maraschino cherries from the garnish tray as fast as he can replenish them.

"He led you on," Walt agrees.

"Me! I'm the arrogant turd! The biggest ouch is I fantasized being at my high school reunion, which, by the way, I have never been to, showing off the famous actor I snagged."

"You know the saying: a watched pot gathers no moss," he theorizes.

"A watched pot *never boils*, Walt," I correct. I want to tell him I already had my pot with its damn lid, but he won't get it.

He flips the tabloid pages of a Hell's Kitchen monthly. "Next week you'll be juggling seven different dudes. It's always feast or phantoms."

I eat just one more cherry. "Feast or what? Did you say phantoms?"

"Yeah?"

"*Famine*. Not *phantoms*. Feast or *famine*. Do not, Walt, ever apply for a job writing bumper stickers."

I look around critically. Whoever carried the name inside went apeshit. I can live with posters from *Rocky*, but it's hard not to be annoyed by the door knockers mounted everywhere, inviting tipsy patrons to rap endlessly on walls like no one's ever thought of it before. Punching bags, just begging to incite a brawl, are everywhere, and boxing gloves have been rewired as suspended lights. They're not much better than false teeth.

I stand, wobble, hold up a finger. "One more TKOtini, Walter. First, I tinkletini."

The ladies' room is identified by the framed cover of Rusty Warren's *Knockers Up!*, the men's by a still of DeNiro as LaMotta.

I pee with eight by ten glossies of Jack Dempsey and Chesty Morgan, chuckling to myself. "Feast. *Phantoms*." I don't even notice that someone stands alongside me at the other urinal.

"Sir, if you're gonna mark your territory, piss on your own shoes."

I look over at Nathan Lane. "Sorry!" I redirect my stream away from his suede loafers, back to trying to melt what's left of the urinal cake.

I cackle in the mirror. I'm so drunk I can't button my fly. I read what someone's written on the wall next to the condom machine: *The gum in this tastes like rubber!* I study Pride handbills on cracked tile walls. I tear off a pull-tab flyer and read aloud: "Nudercise. Cum work out… without! Special Pride weekend pricing!" It sounded like a VHS tape Andy and I once ordered from the back pages of *Playgirl*: low-rent Chippendale dancers doing naked calisthenics to disco music, $29.95 and forty minutes we'd never get back.

When I can only get part of me onto the stool, Walt helps me decide against a nightcap.

Nothing is more abjectly pathetic than returning to your home alone late in Manhattan. It is the Walk of Shame flip-flopped, scissor turns of hindsight at every corner. Did I present as that subservient to Chaz, alluring only as a Gal Friday?

Bunches of jittery people are lighting cigarettes, smoking cigarettes, extinguishing cigarettes outside a brasserie. They're like the unavoidable perfume spritzers at Bloomingdale's. It's nice that patrons of smoke-free bars no longer have to Febreze their clothes when they get home. Too bad those who pass them outside, however, do. I cross the street to avoid them. A man with no legs, pants bound above the knee with twisty ties, rattles a container at me. I ignore him.

"Ooooh, he's shy! That's it. You're Shyguy," he mocks.

I whirl around. "No goddamn legs, and you call me a name?" I bellow hoarsely. "Get a really thin dog if you want to make money begging, Stumps!"

His taunting, cracked lips turn to fearful, wide eyes. It's a low moment when you misdirect wrath at two-thirds of a person who's probably been victimized before. He can't run, so I do, feeling incredibly foolish.

The sprint back to the apartment didn't sober me up.

I know what will.

Chapter Sixteen

Inventory

I STRIP.

How long as it been since I objectively inspected my body as a means to an end? I had achieved the end: Andy. I could enumerate how many bags of unsold potpourri the gallery had the day I left, I gleefully catalog friends, yet I have woefully forsaken the Dewey Decimal of my own bits 'n' pieces. Could the midforties elasticity of my means snap back? To compete in events of the flesh, I need recertification. So how old *was* Miss Brodie, anyway, when she was in her damn prime?

I stare at myself in the three-quarter-length closet mirror. My people have an allergic reaction to the neglected physique. Backfat intolerance, it's called. I tie a towel low around my hips. I turn in profile and twist, a photo trick that whittles the waistline but will be impossible to maintain during a workout. I gave up on *Men's Health* magazine three years ago. Inguinal ligament close-ups especially sent me into a rage—Hercules's Girdle, or Apollo's Belt, or what Potsy called cum gutters. As lean as I was in my twenties, I was never cut like that. Now I'm pleated. I could claim that an ill-prepared surgeon destroyed my abdominal muscles like Mom had always blamed Caesarean delivery on her midriff jiggle.

I retie the towel higher.

This doesn't help. A few more pounds and I'll be a backward S, a pygmy. With all the strides made, it seems someone should have a flesh lace-up along the backbone that I can tighten, like a corset. If I wear the sheerest Spanx available, will that count as nude? I knead my love handles (although I challenge anyone to actually carry me by them). Only when I inhale until it hurts do I locate my ribs, comfortably resting beneath pinchy folds. After applications of Mederma, my gallbladder scars are barely pink and they're hidden within the softness of my torso.

My nipples used to be Hershey Kisses. Now they're sun-dried tomatoes. Maybe I should go boil some water and macerate them. Andy had a gym buddy whose nipples were like pepperoncini from his foray into titpigdom. It was way too much pulling for my liking, but they sure made a statement. My breasts have begun a doughy slide into my armpits. I can't see, but I wonder if I have hot dog neck, overlapping pink bands plumping on the back of your neck. Add some baked beans and gnats, I'm a picnic.

I have old hands, my mother's hands. All of those refinishing solvents, that's what did it. Old *and* dirty hands. I must have the shabbiest fingernails of any wealthy person I have ever known, in need of a good cuticle push.

"Well, you could stand to be thinner," I announce to my reflection. I drop the towel and look down. "And *you* could be fatter." Here's where I'm supposed to swagger that "I ain't had no complaints...." All cockbluster aside, I wish it looked better in a communal gym shower, but it's an average penis, not the serious sizemeat that lends itself to puppetry but also not the bite-size God saddled some with.

I cup my stuff with my old, dirty hands—my tenders, as a friend taught her young son to precociously call them. Well, my tenders aren't so high or so tight, but they also aren't trussworthy. I don't yet have to completely hoist my sac to just cross my legs the way I watched my dad's dad do. I also remind myself of the online profiles that idolize low-hangers and that one guy's e-mail address: LOVE_THOSE_EGGS!

When did my legs get so puny? My calves were once sturdy from endless gallery walk-throughs. Why does a knee now look like a witch's chin?

I turn around. My flabby ass looks like a baseball mitt. That was left out in the sun. After being run over by a car. I turn back around.

Skin tags. What are they? Why are they called that? Tag, you're it, here's another for your left inner thigh. I find a constellation of them near my collarbone. I'm turning into an antislip mat. What is it Mom said about these, something about a string trick? Tie a bit around each, it cuts their blood supply, they'll wither. Drawing attention to each dermal growth with a bow... sounds like a winner. I stop feeling around. I don't have enough curling ribbon.

My eyes aren't as blue, my temples are teased with gray and flecked with hyperpigmentation, my earlobes grow goatees if untended, and I'm getting those downturned lines around my mouth like Ray Bolger in *The Wizard of Oz*. I stick out my tongue. It looks gouged. Geographic tongue, my dentist called it when I asked, rough terrain and denuded but nothing to worry about, maybe try taking zinc. I stared at it for a few days, then forgot about it, since it didn't impede talking or swallowing, and Andy never mentioned that I'd left part of it in his mouth.

I remember how Mom, when Olivia was always smelling like sour milk, tried to bolster her: "Look around, you're cuter and have a nicer figure than 98 percent of the people here, what's the problem?" And Olivia's monotone reply: "The 2 percent, Mom."

I remember Captain Reg and the way he greeted complete strangers with his named penis.

WWAD? This seems to be the ticker symbol dashing along the bottom of my brain's frame. What would Andy do? I remember him quoting Wallace Stevens: "Sometimes you must go too far to see what would suffice."

What the hell. I left my dignity at the legless man. What is clothing but armor? I am going to Nudercise.

Chapter Seventeen

Jarod Is a Lot of Things

AFTER I do three gazillion crunches—cleaning the house right before the housekeeper arrives—I am in a hot shower for about an hour, hoping I'll lose weight in the steam. I rinse my hair in the shower with the coldest water I can bear. This, I have heard, imparts extra shine. I need to shine extra.

If I mix up a pitcher of Master Cleanse right now, I wonder how much weight I can lose by noon. Damn it. I don't have cayenne pepper.

I quickly call Marjorie, who's paged me three times. She tells me that, on an early walk, she stopped in Theatrilicious at 7:30 a.m. "Why did the workroom smell like falafel?"

Damn. This is the third day of an epic heat wave, and Elaine and Desliles, without A/C, asked if they could sleep in the store last night. I said yes, but clear out by sunrise. They did, but their garbanzo lingered. I explain this. We have a sharp exchange. She ends it by declaring she has no intention of becoming the Leona Helmsley of hostels.

"Do you hear me, Barry? On this, I'm putting my foot down," she screeches.

Please don't, Marjorie, I think. *It'll topple the building and I'm not confident we're insured.*

On the elevator, I jog in place and flex my paranoia. What if Nudercise is All-Welcome? The poster didn't specify gender. Or did it? It *was* in the men's room. Maybe it was in the ladies' room too. Knock Me Out isn't exclusively male.

Floor 14 boards. As I observe him drag a dry disposable razor under his jaw and jam it down into the sand of a lobby ashtray, I think I should have waxed my chest. Is body hair in, now, or out? When Potsy's temples had receded, he shaved his head; when his abs receded, he shaved his pubes. He rationalized both by stating great scenery needs no valance. This is so confusing. Maybe I can pluck the weirdest, longest hairs in the cab.

THE first thing we are told is "don't be ashamed if you pop a boner."

There it is, that word I hate. I won't argue the merits of a good stiffie, but my visual of boner is a drumstick gnawed meatless. It's intended as comfort to us newcomers, but I am more concerned about terrified retraction.

And splinters from the wood warehouse floor of this purposefully hot room West Village workout space.

Our overtanned, overnude instructor is undergroomed, black curly chest hair tufting down to an acorn.

"Pride starts with the penis, and this weekend celebrates that!"

There are maybe thirty of us, total, by head count, pun intended. I stand in the back, looking at floor-to-ceiling windows that provide an eyeful to surrounding buildings.

The guy next to me, also still clothed, seems as reticent. I whisper, "Think they hang sheets?"

"First time here too. I don't even think we get mats," he replies.

Why didn't I think of that? I could have brought my Minduka towel. It's suedelike and sustainable. Right now I'd be grateful to get a potholder for my taint. What was it Potsy called a sweaty taint? Duck butter, that was it.

"I like your kicks, man."

He's talking about my shoes. Damn it. I didn't check out my feet. If Mom's were deplorable, mine are condemnable. If I leave my socks on, will that count as nude? I look down at his. He's wearing those peculiar split-toe shoes. I don't get this whole foot-glove trend, but at least he has all his digits.

My thumbs strum the waist of my shorts. "This sure was easier at home."

He isn't wearing a belt and so his Wrangler jeans drop easily. I try not to watch. He isn't wearing underwear, either. He's so carefree. I feel provincial. His penis has that much-desired arc down and over his balls. He is perfectly proportioned, plumbed to please. He's that 2 percent. He places his shed clothing in a battered satchel of his own. He's gotten it over with. I still have to slide my briefs over my witch chin knees.

Dark crevices begin to plop down. We both flinch.

"I'm Jarod."

"Barry."

Barry, who worried about skin tags when the dude to my left has one on his back like a dorsal fin that I could grab and ride to the Jersey Shore. If he doesn't eat me first; he also has the triangular teeth of Jaws. Barry, wondering how long scabies can actively inhabit the laundry drawstring bag I was supplied. Barry, who stares forward, inhales deeply, and slips out of his Jockey shorts.

General stretching commences to music. The class uniformly effects a downward facing dog yoga pose.

Most can't achieve the stance, so I am faced with a stupefying and literal half-assed backstage vantage point. One especially long scrotum is like a stalactite. It's like I've been slipped a hallucinogen and can view everyone's tonsils from the opposite end. First Grapple, now dodgeballs. I am *so* not good with a roomful of strangers.

Jarod sees what I see. "Not a lot of anal bleach devotees among us," he whispers.

The instructor exhorts us with motivational phrases.

I try to duplicate the unflattering poses. I stand on my tippy-toes, as Jarod does. I see a birthmark on the man in front of me that only his lover has probably seen. I hop on one foot. I hop on the other foot. Everything is slapping. I am poaching in my own fluids and I hope no one slips in it as it washes over my ankle bones like broken downspouts.

The plump fellow with a walrus mustache next to me looks like Wilford Brimley. He isn't doing much but cracking his knuckles. They are misshapen by the habit and look like mushroom caps, which complements his dick, which looks like a green bean.

I make an X of my body. I lay back down. I am horrified when my body makes a suction noise as I adjust. My toes cramp up. I fan them out with my old fingers. We are directed to take a moment and cough as hard as we can. This, we are informed, will stimulate spinal fluids. Where it then goes is unexplained.

Disrobics. That was the name of that VHS tape. It wasn't in scratch 'n' sniff, not like this, where foot is the best thing I smell.

What I hear is unmistakable: the sounds of onanism.

I glance over. Walrus Brimley has gripped his haricot vert with both hands to milk it robotically, like he's trying to extract an additional segment from his pudendum.

"Cut it out!" I tell him.

His mustache wriggles with sweat.

Maybe he didn't hear me. The instructor, at the same time, exhorts us to "breathe from our butt!"

So I say it again: "Please stop doing that right now."

Walrus Brimley stares right at me, breath labored, as though I'm supposed to fall into cockstep with him.

"Come on! Nudercise or something!" I tell him.

Whatever I'd expected, this isn't it. My innocent little fantasy has dissolved like an antacid. Nudercise was supposed to be my Phys. Ed. locker room, just a little more salacious, and I wouldn't be shoved around. My Phys. Ed. locker room did not include gray pubes, genitals lassoed with metallic or leather, and one Prince Albert.

"The penis is our center!" the instructor chants.

Toenails as orange as Cheetos curl as Walrus's arm rivals a jackhammer.

"The penis is our king!" the instructor yells. "Let it reign!"

"I didn't bring a rain bonnet," I yell at no one. It doesn't quite muffle the ecstatic, prolonged moan of Walrus Brimley as he shoots ropes of ejaculate. It just keeps coming, like string cheese, just a little less yellow.

I dress quickly and bound down the warehouse steps. I hear "Hey! Barry! Wait up!" from the top of the stairs. Jarod too has dressed and fled.

"Fine line between edgy and yucky, huh?" he says.

"Especially when the dude next to me draws it with his sperm," I point out.

"And I missed the *Doctor Who* marathon for this." He shakes his head.

"I feel exactly the same. Except the part about *Doctor Who*," I reply.

He suggests coffee from the nearby La Bonbonniere. Jarod tells me he's a limousine driver. The company he works for specializes in high-maintenance stars. "It's recession-proof," he explains. "These are people who can't take a train or ride the bus." I ask like who. He cites a confidentiality clause, but tells me about the talk show hostess who urinated all over herself; the hip-hop star with multiple arrests who urinated all over a groupie; the pop singer with clothing, furniture, and lite-meal lines who handed him her autograph on a peeled-off water bottle label as a tip after an evening that ended at 9:28 a.m.; the actress who disabled her film career by playing Joan Crawford, threw her cell phone out the window in a pique, then demanded he pull over and go search for it. This all makes him feel like Travis Bickle after some shifts, he says, God's Angry Man who believes in strict gun control. Who else, I persist. He finally cops to Alexa Ray Joel, the daughter of Billy Joel and Christie Brinkley. "She's polite, and her dad gets direct billing. She performs at small clubs for, like, $1.89."

I easily tell him about Andy and the accident, and he says, "That was pretty high-profile. I remember it from one of the cable networks. Caught on-camera, right?"

This reawakens my resentment. "Sharing that visual still upsets me. Some stranger on his couch experienced the worst day of my life."

"Six degrees," Jarod says.

Maybe his stride is faster than mine or maybe I've slowed down because I'm actually enjoying this as we make our way to Pride festivities.

Fanfare directs us to our tribe, the Village People who favor a glass pipe over a peace pipe; chanting "guuuurrrrllll" like it's a rain or a golden shower dance; who, in their various states of undress, bring the block close to one big Nudercise. We decide on a corner and stand behind those who snagged positions early and zealously guard their space. I am growled at by a man in a nightie, hiked up enough to expose his jockstrap, for daring to tread upon the hemp blanket he's sitting cross-legged on.

The parade is what you'd expect: processional banners, Dykes on Bikes, a drum-and-fife corps called The Flaggots in S/M heels and corsets. Jarod gets fidgety very quickly.

"I don't see antagonism. I see a Manhunt.com float. Rainbows magically appear on hetero businesses and come right back down Sunday night. Wouldn't our 'community' show more clout if we actually came together on the same day, same *hour* all over the country?" he asks.

I don't disagree. I've always thought a circuit party sounded like a kegger thrown by electricians, and Pride, at least in Key West, was seven days of foam parties in which people fell or urinated to compensate for the tourism lull after Memorial Day. But something about Jarod's distaste makes me challenge him.

"There's more to it than that, bucko. Pride also empowered those who felt powerless against people like Jerry Falwell."

"Tell the people of Darfur about powerless... bucko."

"Jerry Falwell destroyed lives," I remind him.

"Not mine. He's an asterisk." He pauses. "All I'm saying is I won't be segregated to Fire Island. I do what I want and go where I want. That's *my* Pride."

"So where's the absolute gayest place you've been?" I challenge.

"Dollywood."

Flotilla speakers blare a tired "Proud." Heather Small is on her way, can't stop her now, and she'll be on her way for another twenty years until a new anthem emerges. We sing the final line together: "What have you done today to make you feel proud?"

A hand squeezes my thigh. My pocket is being picked in broad daylight in egregious gay-on-gay crime. I realize it's Jarod. He's trying to find my belt loop to hold.

"Let's go do something that makes us feel ashamed."

He doesn't mean the post-Pride pier dance. He is inferring a sex act, or plural.

I went to Nudercise hoping it would lead to more.

More is at my door.

Or, more accurately, at his door, since we are descending into the subway station bound for his Brooklyn apartment. At the platform, we suddenly have nothing to say to each other. I see a pearl necklace—a real one—looped around the customer information screen. Our train will be here in nine minutes.

Jarod points to a poster that has been defaced into protesting the presence of ROTC on state college campuses.

"I did that."

"You're a vandal?"

No, Jarod is apparently also an artist or, more specifically a subway artist, which is actually anti-art, he explains, because the purpose is to subvert the output of another. No poster advertising a department store, city service, not even Saltines, is safe from his jigsaw composite. Where there is no subtext, he creates one. He scopes out a train until it leaves, and then, using his razor blade and glue stick, cuts and rearranges, peels off heads, floats other body parts, moves words or just letters like a ransom note. Mostly, the MTA employees rip them down, his and many others', within the day. He draws, or rather slashes, the line at obscenities, which cheapens the effect, and "at goons who write plot spoilers on posters for new movies, shit like 'he dies at the end!' It's counterproductive. People end up resenting your art, you know?"

I nod as though I comprehend.

Standing in this overfilled subway car, en route, we sway and trade bits of information, mostly benignly sexual.

"A youth leader in church kinda molested me when I was eleven," he says. "I actually seduced *him*. But he should've known better. What was *your* first sex with menfolk?"

I admit it was Andy. This is the first time I have ever told the truth. I even kept it from Andy. Beforehand, I didn't want him to get all responsible and careful. Afterward, I didn't want him to have bragging rights.

"So who pursued who?"

"Him, me. He lived in a frat house. I wouldn't even *walk* by a frat house. He was a year older, finishing his master's early in business administration. He was pretty bold. He introduced himself in the student union building one day—'Andy Morgan'—and immediately added, 'I put the *More* In *Organ*'."

"Did you say 'I love you' a lot to each other?"

How he just goes there is disarming.

"We certainly did." Then I fold. "I wish more, now."

"It's never said enough, starting with parents." He lifts my left hand. "You never married?"

I feel uneasy that I removed my ring.

"Neither of us were big on rites of passage."

He frowns. "It's a statement."

"A statement that a referendum turns around and nullifies. We covered ourselves legally."

"Ever almost marry a woman?" Jarod asks.

"Never."

"Ever lay on a woman?"

"Once. She actually popped my cherry," I recall. "We were sixteen. She had a glass eye."

"Is that relevant? Did she take it out so you could fuck her socket?"

"I'm detail-driven." I also know it's an anecdote that was always guaranteed to elicit shocked titters, so I continue. "She lost it in a game of Jarts."

He asks what the hell are Jarts. I explain how the lawn game utilized large, blunted darts aimed at a faraway plastic circle.

"Unsupervised kids just flung them toward each other's eyes?"

It does sound ridiculously dangerous in an era when toys are recalled and parents panic because of lead paint traces.

"Lorraine and I went at it on a chaise lounge missing most of its webbing. She put my hands under her blouse. I jiggled her tits a little. She took one hand out and started inching my claw down to her waist. I came upon a thatch of coarse hair. I think we're heeeeeere. It was just her navel. She was Italian. Then I hit the real thing. 'See how wet I am?' she bragged. It was like a water slide, so slippery my hand slalomed down to her knee. I petted a seal once at a zoo, and that's what this felt like."

A man in seven-inch heels, pasties, and a bathing cap, set loose from Fellini's Macy's Parade, boards our car to immediately slump unconscious onto a seat.

"Pride just up and died," Jarod observes.

"My turn. What's the worst guy you went out with?" I prod.

"The guy who wanted to squeeze the blackheads on my nose took the prize until Harrison. All he ate was white or clear foods. I never determined what the hell was clear besides aspic. He lived on Minute Rice. Marshmallows, whole onions. I watched him eat a cup of mayonnaise once. The final straw was when he wouldn't eat the fettuccine alfredo I cooked because I used black pepper. Who keeps white pepper around?"

"We all have food issues," I say. "I don't like wet bread."

"Wet bread?"

"French toast, pancakes, Stove Top stuffing."

He's still in disbelief by the time we've reached the Congress Street stop. He won't relent on the wet bread topic.

"Not even biscuits and gravy? Soppin' up is the best part!"

The interior of his apartment building is even less nice than the ravaged exterior, which proves in reverse that you can't judge a book by its cover. He can tell what I'm thinking, because he says, "This place is loads better than my last. There, I was broken into so often I started listing 'Today's Specials' on my door when I left in the morning." He's moved a lot, he says, living on handmade streets with handmade signs that get no sun. His last roommate, Shari, "I called Poopshari because she was always asking when I came back into a room 'Were you pooping? Did you poop?' Sometimes she'd stand outside the bathroom door and sing softly, 'I know... what... you're... doiiiinnnng.' Made me nuts. She was an improvement, though, over the one who kept the bass on the stereo turned so high my plants worked their way up out of their pots." This is his first time alone. I am happy now I didn't pursue a roommate.

He checks his mailbox in the lobby. I'm startled by a series of bellowed profanities and loud stomping. Snack food cellophane litters the flights we trudge. It sounds and smells like what I suppose the New Orleans Superdome did after Katrina. The gentrification of Brooklyn skipped this building.

We stop at his apartment door so he can declare, "Tell you right now: I'm not the housekeeper you probably are." Two hours of solid conversation, and he's apologizing. Again, I'm Mr. Homestore.

Before I can tell him it doesn't matter, his sudden kiss sends me reeling back.

"Um, okay, it's still light out," I manage. "Maybe we can just fool around with our clothes on."

"I've seen you naked."

"That was meant to sound playful, but it sounded like a plea, didn't it?" I mutter.

He kisses me again. "It was a *little* nasal. Are you nervous?"

I pull back. "Very. It's been so long since I've had sex, I'm afraid my sperm will be like lumpy hummus."

Jarod laughs. "You're so silly."

"I am also double your age. I have a hair pick somewhere older than you."

He tries for a third kiss. I won't allow it.

"Really. I get your physical being at, or close, to, its finest. You get mine in meltdown."

"Your dick is still pink. It's not gray, like worn pavement, the way they get over time."

"You stared at my old man junk!" I feel very exposed. He clinically studied my nakedness. I'm like a great felled tree, the circles on my exposed trunk being tallied. "Well, you had half-a-hard-on."

He taps his rolled mail against my chest. "Did not."

"Did so."

He kisses me again.

My hands, which I've kept at my side, creep up to his shoulders. This feels very natural. "So it's always that springy?"

He yanks one of my hands down to his crotch. "Find out."

His own hands are in my pants, tugging. I tell him to slow down. His mouth seeks mine again. Whatever inhibitions I've had, however I have ever defined seedy, it's all forgotten as we chew each other's lips off in that hallway. My body speaks. Actually, it's ready to shout itself hoarse.

I AM standing in Jarod's kitchen. My upholsterer's van was larger than this. If my place is no more spacious than an ice bucket, this is an ice cube tray. I look at a cooktop, a single-cup coffeemaker, and a shower curtain. The kitchen and bathroom are both essentially a latrine with burners. He literally shits where he eats. Based on human anatomy, Jarod must slightly stand inside the refrigerator to pee. And I cannot find a sink anywhere. He must do dishes in his tub, which, if it were a human, would have the biggest port wine stain documented.

I sit down on one of the two mismatched rescue barstools and decide to call Potsy. It was never my intent to let their interest in my house become a real rift. I've let them boil while I stewed, but once all heat was removed, I don't feel betrayed anymore, just sore. Besides, I'm eager to prove that my monastic retreat has ended. What better way than to tell them I too have moved on than my inaugural sixty-nine with a smoking hot twenty-four-year-old I met during a boner-filled naked workout?

Potsy is in a stinking mood. His is the city's largest hotel and hosts any event not cost-effective enough for the convention center. He despises "conference trash, all proud of their corporate credit card," but it's had its benefits. He captivated dinner parties for a year with his memory of JonBenet Ramsey at a prepubescent pageant held there. Her mother Patsy was "vapid but dear," he'd embroider, "not at all the murderess type, with that headband. But it felt like those little girls were being publicly deflowered."

This time it's an annual Womynfest, or the Rubyfruit Jungle, as he calls it. He is spending most of his desk time either asking "these cagefighters to extinguish their foot-long cigarettes or bribing terrified locals to caddy for them." On a roll, he observes, "They might be dressed for success, but every one of them has a dirty neck."

"That's incredibly specific." I demand explanation.

"Well, maybe not dirty… more like ashy rings that their all-natural soap-free soap can't get at. All empowered with their muesli breath, strutting around like Suze-fucking-Orman. I liked 'em better when they were all LezbyAnns covered in chalk dust."

"Potsy," I gasp, "if you had a drag name it would be Miss Ogyny. Can you conference in your new sissy sidekick?"

"Do I look like Ernestine?"

He probably does, or close, on the ornate desk telephone he insisted upon at his first salary review. Potsy is very Patrick Dennis that way. It was this rotary phone he was photographed dialing with a number ten pencil when I, Dee, he, and even Dr. Steve landed in that magazine's picks of the city's finest. It would have been a quill if he wasn't allergic to feathers. As it was, he wore spats.

Dee's now with us, driving somewhere, on her headset, audibly applying lipstick. I update them both about Nudercise.

"Coincidence is, we have some group event here called Cootersize. It's being held in our Clitness Center," Potsy jokes. "Dee! Come down, bring your Kegel, see if they can't tighten up that jaws of life!"

This, she ignores. "Describe Jarod for us," she says.

I got no further than "thin" when Potsy interjects, "Like Anne-Frank-after-someone-squealed-emaciated?"

"Lanky."

"What does he look like?" Dee asks.

"He sorta resembles a young Bruce Springsteen." From here, through some unidentifiable country's flag that is a dividing curtain, I can see the young and naked Springsteen, asleep or, I proudly decide, completely fucked out. "He's still in bed. It's so cute. It's a twin."

"He's a twin? Like Andy? This is weird!" Dee exclaims.

"The *bed* is a twin."

"That's even worse," Potsy claims. "What does he do?" He moans when I say. "He drives around bachelorette parties?"

Dee pauses. "Potsy, you *validate* parking."

I hear Potsy rifle his desktop. "Fuck, you're right. I am a Welcome Wagon lady with discount tickets for Anne Murray."

Dee continues. "How great that you became a cougar before I could. Just proceed with caution, Barry. You're a man of means."

"One fuck doesn't make me reckless."

"You only did it once?" Potsy screeches. "Did the cougar need a catnap?"

"Pots, lay off. He's still mulling over the house deal."

Potsy begins to sing. "Barry and Jare-y sitting in a tree… K-I-S-

S-I-N-G. OMG! It's kinda like Gregsquared!" He rushes in one more dig before we all hang up. "Well, enjoy your Roman spring, Mrs. Stone."

I pass a hand over Jarod's mail, still curved from when he rolled it. I'm not snooping, I'm being helpful, I'm flattening it out: stickered postcards hyping a new raw foods restaurant and reminding about a change in garbage pickup, a personal letter postmarked from Philadelphia, an envelope from the Internal Revenue Service that doesn't look promising.

Jarod's last name is Pugh, which I hadn't thought to ask.

I creep back in, ducking under the aluminum Sedona bike that hangs from hooks, like someone's parked on the bedroom ceiling. Sliding into the bed will wake him, but there's only one chair, under today's clothes and those of yesterday too. I remember when we dressed from a chair like it, when the clean clothes never quite got put away and we'd finally take it all back to the Laundromat and start over. His doorless closet is narrow, more like the pantry his kitchen doesn't have. In it, a series of knobs wear bracelets, a diving watch, a charcoal-gray chauffeur cap, do-rags, a fastened black belt so thick I don't know how it passes through loops. The splintery rod is empty. The sum of his wardrobe seems to be on the chair.

His eyes flutter in instinct that someone is watching. The placement of a mole on his right cheek, parallel to his ear, is the perfect beauty mark every 1930s starlet had. I spy one gray hair at the temple. *Just wait*, I think. It will replicate itself and be of a new texture that resists a flatiron and, suddenly, you're being told you resemble your father by those who knew him at your age. I softly kiss the cupid's bow of Jarod Pugh's upper lip. I stare at the beauty that comes automatically bundled and unappreciated with youth. I can't be this anymore. What I can be, biologically if not rationally, is *his* parent. And a parent shouldn't act like this. I am rock hard again and I want more. I wonder if he'll wear the chauffeur's cap if I ask nicely. I have low-to-no expectations, but on this late Sunday afternoon, I feel so renewed I wouldn't even care if my Roman spring called me Mrs. Stone.

Chapter Eighteen

Jarod Is a Lot of Other Things

"If he doesn't know who Carlton the Doorman was or never washed his hair with Body on Tap, Jarod is a Protégé. Period."
    Potsy, 12:18 a.m. Tuesday

ANDY and I, when things were especially crazy work-wise, would half-jokingly resort to scheduling appointments with each other. I'd write *Face Time* in his Franklin Planner, or he'd leave a snide *Warm, Soapy Bowl*, underlined many times, on my calendar.

But time operates oddly in New York. Your Monday is someone else's Friday; your free evening is someone else's commute. Jarod's schedule largely runs counter to mine. His night is my day. Saturday works best for him, because he can pick and choose from the many limo reservations on the books; for me, Mondays are better, since many Broadway shows are dark and the store is less populated, Marjorie cameo appearances notwithstanding.

So the next time we get together is the following Saturday. Jarod is a cyclist. I already know this from the tread stenciled on his ceiling. In what amounts to our first, planned date, he's invited me to accompany him on a ride.

He's borrowed a bike and helmet from Bicycle Habitat on Lafayette, from Charlie, the owner. He's gone to trouble. I am flattered, with some trepidation. In Central Park, I have seen the Spandex whooshing by like they're in the Tour de France. It's not that I need training wheels—I rode some with Andy when he trained for the SMART Ride but always fell by the wayside after a couple miles—but today could amount to an endurance test and/or obstacle course that I'll humiliatingly fail. It's also the beginning of the weekend, and the city will be busy with country homeowners vacating for the Hamptons and New Jersey flooding in looking for a fight, and I have read how dangerous the Queens/Midtown Tunnel and Williamsburg Bridge are for bicyclists.

He explains, as we depart from the Village taxi garage where his limousine is kept, that we'll be paying respects to Ghost Bikes.

"Ghost what?"

He takes off. If I can't outpace flesh-and-blood cyclists, how will I keep up with specters?

As I am still adjusting my chin strap, he further explains back at me. It began in St. Louis, that rare instance when Manhattan's ego deigned to embrace someone else's trend. When a cyclist among the five boroughs is killed, the New York City Street Memorial Project, to which he belongs, takes a bike—not the bike the person died on—and coats it thickly with white paint and chains it to a sign post near the accident. It is rare that anyone from the Project personally knew the victim, unlike those artificial highway wreaths and makeshift crosses a parent labored over. A small sign factually offers the name, age, and date of death. The epitaph is always the same: "Rest in peace."

Knowing my immediate history, it's a questionable choice, taking me to what are essentially tombstones of the fallen. I want to interject the obvious: Why are we doing this? Is there something more? Is this his way of breaking to me that he ran over someone with his limo?

We come to our first, at Houston and Elizabeth. Plastic flowers are in the spokes; this, or wound around the handlebars, is common, I will see. The whiteness of the bike makes the flowers vibrant, no matter how sun-bleached, like a black-and-white movie where one thing was selectively colorized. It almost looks edible, like a pretzel dipped in white chocolate.

There's some presumption in this, that the dead seek immortality in some quasi-public art installation. If this were the norm, I don't how I would meaningfully designate Andy's death at ColonyScape. His Tommy Bahama shirt, sewn onto a girder? Mercedes Benz ornamentation? I voice this wariness.

"Some people do hate them," Jarod agrees, yelling back at me from ahead. "And others see them as an anti-biking scare tactic."

I pedal faster. My bangs are drenched. I ask to slow at 17th to inspect what Simon Doonan's up to with Barney's windows. I am the recipient of a look that could snap a spine.

"Barney's is owned by the Dubai government!"

"That infusion of cash kept them open," I inform him.

After our fifth Ghost Bike at Third Avenue and 17th, Jarod insists on treating me to a lunch at a ground floor diner in the only building of height around. A dialysis clinic is also housed here, so we will potentially dine among those with freshly cleansed kidneys.

"It's no Pastis," he warns as a booth is readied.

I'll say. The small restaurant is mostly plastered with religious paintings, Coney Island postcards, and ragged sports pennants. The linoleum looks like a bunch of unmatching plastic placemats fused onto the floor. Some restaurants offer a tie to dine. This one would give you a roach motel. I'm game for anything, but I swore off slumming years ago when a coworker of Andy's, eating in a dive, stumbled into a nest of brown recluse spiders in the men's room stall and was hospitalized with an IV drip for ten days.

A line cook exits the unisex bathroom. I didn't hear a flush or water running. I don't know what he was doing but I don't want traces of it in the apple cobbler Jarod just swooned is "rhapsodic. It exemplifies the city I want to live in, really flaky. You won't ever see paella on this menu," he boasts.

The reverse-snobbery ticks me off. "Because they can't afford saffron?"

"You'd rather wait in line at Shake Shack?"

"Danny Meyer knows what he's doing."

"I come here whenever I can," he enthuses. "If I had to choose the one place that means the most to me, I would say this." He sees my skeptical face. I am waiting for him to completely break down and weep that it's honest food. "Steve Buscemi ate a gyro right over there last week."

He orders a hodgepodge to share, but I just want water with a lemon that hasn't been fried. Old cooking oil has replaced oxygen here. I will have a nose full of huge black boogers.

"It's all yours. I'll chew the air for my transfats," I assure him, thinking a neighboring arterial flush clinic would be more complementary.

A man in a stained apron, presumably the owner although we're not introduced, scuffles to our booth to tell Jarod he has lost his lease to an incoming Whole Foods.

"This is a travesty, Sasha!" Jarod yells. "They're carpet-bombing the fuck out of downtown with their fifty-dollar artichokes!" He assures Sasha they'll talk before we leave, then lifts up his bag by the strap.

"What's in your murse?" I ask.

"Murse?"

"Man purse."

The way he looks at me, I feel like Quentin Crisp.

"I keep my passion in it."

Jesus, I cannot handle another bondage hood.

"I'm a wingless carrier pigeon. This is my portable desk." He shoves his hand in and yells, "Ouch!" Maybe vermin that have nested in there bit him.

"You need a bag with compartments."

"It was an X-Acto knife." He sucks his finger. "Life doesn't have compartments."

"Don't kid yourself. Niches and cubbyholes contain us," I reply.

He tosses me a wrinkled brochure touting his employer. Jarod is pictured on the front, opening a limo door.

I return it to him. "So you're a print model?"

He passes to me a surveillance dossier of buildings marked for demolition. "Here's what I wanted to show you."

Leafing through the hitlist, all I see are unlivable tenements and inhospitable flophouses, crumbling masonry, scrambled fire escapes. These are not quaint, they are downtrodden. Safeguarding most of these would be criminal endangerment.

Jarod is a preservationist.

"In the past fifteen years, 76,000 new buildings have sprung up, 44,000 were razed, and 83,000 were radically renovated, no thanks to the Landmarks Preservation Commission, who are either on the fucking take or working off a monolithic favor bank."

I tell him how I melded past and present with my gallery, and all he can impatiently say is, "That's Ohio, or wherever you're from. Intelligent, adaptive preservation is not what Manhattan Yunnies are all about." He pauses. "Young. Urban. Narcissist."

"Listen. I'm no fan. My husband died because of new construction and piggish shortcuts." I close the spiral book. "Prosperity typically yields great variety in urban architecture."

"Twenty stories of people with no stories! And when the economy tanks again, The Standard will become The Sub-Standard, the luxury high-rises will be at 30 percent capacity, we're stuck with ugly and uglier." He gets loud. "It's Bohemia Nouveau. God, if Jonathan Larsen wrote *Rent* now, it would be called *Maintenance*! Don't get me started on how NYU is gobbling up property. Why can't they see the city itself is already the best campus in the world?"

"Change is inevitable. It can even sometimes be constructive."

"A guy I know working on an anecdotal documentary has some phenomenal footage of what's been lost. He has Woody-fucking-Allen on-camera call it 'the progression of opulence'."

"And Woody-fucking-Allen solemnly pontificates this from Central Park West," I say. "Everyone has a different Manhattan. His is all-Gershwin with a Windsor Light Condensed font. In Spike Lee's Gotham, no one gets along. Documentarians have agendas."

Jarod picks up a loaded potato skin. "They're turning Bellevue into a boutique hotel."

"Where Kris Kringle stayed?" I joke. "*Miracle on 34th Street.*"

Archaic Me gets a "Huh? People paying a grand a night for a suite haunted by pain. The restless moans of the criminally insane pouring out of new brass bathroom fixtures." Jarod shivers. "And look at Harlem, its whole 'Renaissance'." He brackets the air. "Nothing but a bunch of new brewpubs. The darker the beer, the whiter the resident."

Now I think, *Wait a minute.* He objects to repurposing as much as he does teardowns. This is no-win. Jarod would have picketed my gallery expansion, catcalled the loudest.

Sasha motions to Jarod, who excuses himself, swinging his knapsack over his shoulder.

What Jarod says is true. New York still holds wonder but it's changed, and is changing more. Every poet and prophet says that. They will say it a century from now. My own New York blossomed like a kaleidoscope at twelve. All that Earl Wilson used to write about in his column—a syndicated portal into a New York of Toots Shor and Ted Hook and sightings of Garbo in Turtle Bay that I read and reread once Dad finished the newspaper—those were gone even before I started coming in the late eighties. Windshield washers holding you for ransom, all-night grindhouses unspooling European bloodbaths and unwatchably watchable *The Robin Byrd Show*, that's the New York I got. I would wander away from the sameness of the accessories market and head to Chinatown, where I'd snap up cricket cages and have them shipped to the store, then listen to the sitars on Indian Row, or I might drunkenly go to The Gaiety strip club with other buyers.

Then, through condemnation, rezoning and eviction, what felt like a really big tented carnival was dumbed down, fingerprints erased, and the slaves that Tama Janowitz wrote about got their emancipation papers. The punk rebellion of St. Marks Place was reborn, now with kids in fingerless gloves spare-changing tourists; to them, CBGB is just something they might need ointment for. The Gaiety closed. Mondo Kim's, where a film buff could lose his mind, closed. Penny Whistle Toys, gone. The Variety Arts Theatre on 3rd at 13th, where we saw the atrocious *Annie Warbucks* sequel (which Marjorie is glad she was shut out from investing in) has been replaced by a cube. The Promenade Theatre is a Sephora. Broadway theaters are being renamed overnight after janitors and producers like Will Smith and Bette Midler are more likely to be above the title than the star. Nancy LaMott died with no one coming close to replacing her. The Algonquin's Oak Room is gone. A Saturday night's entertainment is about how comfortable you want your chair and shoe to be; I can pay $125 plus a two-drink minimum to see Betty Buckle at Café Carlyle, or I can see the same set, including Kenny Werner, in the performing arts center of a Midwestern high school for thirty-five dollars. We watched the methodical renovation of Lincoln Center, negotiated its labyrinthine, plywood corridors to get to the Vivian Beaumont; Andy didn't live to see the result. Then O'Neal's across the street went out of business. The new Plaza Hotel? A repulsed Eloise moved out when she saw the fiberglass moldings in the refurnished rooms. It's too late for me to be shunned by Elaine Kaufman, but I can have Eli Zabar's sourdough rye bread overnighted to my dinner table anywhere. Why haul my ass to Rao's after a ninety-day reservation when I can buy their pasta sauce from any grocer?

When Midnight Cowboy became The Naked Cowboy, with a trademark, and when Rupert Murdoch bought *The Wall Street Journal*, New York became every major city. Or the other way around.

Jarod returns. "I offered to work on an e-mail blast for Sasha. Raise awareness, rally the troops. If he feeds them, they will come." He pounds his chest in worshipful regret for the yellowing photograph of a New York City he never posed in. "It's just heartbreaking how Yunnies are relentlessly desecrating our heritage."

"Our heritage?" I chuckle. "Didn't you tell me you moved here from Pennsylvania less than two years ago?"

"Historians don't have to live in a certain region or era to defend it."

Now he's a historian.

"What constitutes defense? Do you squat in buildings as they're being leveled, or do you just throw bad fruit at hardhats?"

"Rocks, baby, rocks."

"You'll get arrested for that."

"Been there."

Jarod is a jailbird.

"Your parents must be thrilled by some of the windmills you tilt at."

"I am a complete letdown to my parents."

Devil's advocate is one thing, but strumming an exposed nerve was not my intent. I try to neutralize. "Due to your activism, because you're gay?"

"All those. Keep going. Everything from their youngest son being left-handed, and no else in the family *ever* has been, to the chauffeur's license when he should have had a degree in sports medicine."

Jarod is a college dropout.

All I can think to say is, "We all disappoint our parents in some way."

He looks at me for a long time, then admits his mother is a state senator.

Things become a little clearer. I recognize who she is. The name Pugh is just different enough I should have made the connection. Jarod is the son of the outrageously conservative Senator Marianna Pugh.

"Senator Makemewanna—?" I stop myself before I say Puke, which is what she's mocked as by most liberal, or thinking, persons.

"*Puke*. Say it. Projectile it."

"Sorry. The Makemewanna probably gave me away."

"Growing up Jarhead Pubic or Putrid or Poopstain is bad enough. Around the time the line between church and politics blurred in this country, Mom ran for office. Then I became Jarod Puke, Pukefest, Pukesmell." He rummages through the jumble in his bag. He may not have Mary Poppins's floor lamp in there, but I bet he has the means to wire it. From other diatribes, screeds, and tracts, he produces her stapled press bio. "Funny, you might miss the mention of youngest son Jarod on Page Two." He squints. "Right here. I'm mentioned under her helpful tips on how to build a waterboard."

From Utah wealth, she's the heir apparent to Phyllis Schlafly, queer son and all. I know this because she was one of the Proposition 8 champions Andy and I wanted to punch in the nose. (She wrote that notorious op-ed for *USA Today* called "What's So Great About Diversity?") She's about as photogenic as Dick Cheney; her Latter-day Saintly face is the countenance of someone who accidentally chewed an entire jalapeno, and her mouth is a nail gun in matters of deporting immigrants. She, along with a realistic Romney scarecrow, was burned in effigy in New York, probably not that far from where we sit. Some of the protestors wore temple undergarments in provocative ways.

I have to ask. "Did you participate in that, um, incredibly warm salute to your mother in the Village?"

He shakes his head no vigorously. "I told them where she buys her pantsuits, though."

"Do you even speak?"

"Not after she sent me a Joseph Smith mousepad for my last birthday."

"What about your dad?"

"He tries. I hear from him when she's in Washington. He's pussywhipped yet pussystarved."

It makes me appreciate my own parents a little more. They were at least enlightened enough to see gay people were as misdirected and sexless as everyone else.

"It's bad Maury Povich. Or something more long-form, a reality show. *Medea and Me and The Angel Moroni.*"

"If it's any consolation, I hated *The Book of Mormon*," I say.

He grabs my left hand. He doesn't release it. We are holding hands. Andy and I seldom did this. His thumb taps my palm, then my wrist, like he's checking my pulse, then he strokes my fingers singly like he's trying to coax tumescence from each one.

Finally, he suggests we return to ghost-chasing on our bikes.

On the West Side Highway and 38th, a stuffed velveteen rabbit is lashed to the handlebars like collateral damage.

"They've seen real coyotes along here," he exults, "which is better than some fucking Coyote Ugly saloon chain!"

We ride on. For several minutes at a time, our ride is pleasurable. New York has more designated bike lanes than it has pomme frites, but every time we detour for a new Ghost Bike, we enter a treacherous vise. Jarod can intuit safe space from driving the limo, but I am very aware of the yellow cabs and delivery trucks squeezing me closer and closer to the curb. I've seen riders get doored. There's no gracefulness in it.

The Ghost Bike at 40th and Broadway especially reverberates. I've walked by it many times and I guess I just chalked it up as a midtown peculiarity. If it had been a white horse, I might have at least speculated about its grooming, but this albino bike never even registered. The victim was a man of seventy-two. I hope I'm ambulatory at seventy-two, much less darting through city traffic on a two-wheeler.

"This is the one. It's my turn to do touch up," Jarod tells me. "See the chipped handlebars? Silver is showing."

Now he's unscrewing a small jar of white pigment, a fine brush clenched in his teeth. It's an art supply store, too, his bottomless bag: blades and rubber cement for his subway art and, for all I know, wet potter's clay. He carefully covers the silver reasserting itself and thoroughly examines the frame for other hints of color he will squelch.

Jarod offers that he has bigger plans for white paint. I am hoping it isn't as a mime. A physicist he cannot remember the name of, he tells me, believes that replacing sidewalks and roads with white material would reflect the sun rays and have a massive Earth cooling effect. Buildings with white roofs could be up to 30 percent cooler in the summer.

"White paint could save our planet," he enthuses. He wants to gather a salon to strategize.

Jarod is an environmentalist.

"I thought the treehugger trend was to haul up soil and turn roofs into community gardens."

"Most building engineers won't OK the weight-bearing limit."

As close as we are to 42nd, I ask if we might stop at the Disney Store. Ariel looked like a big eraser the last time I was at the newsstand, and I want to give the little girl one brand new.

Jarod points out how misguided my good intentions are. "Kids get attached. She doesn't know or care that it's ratty."

"I do."

I'm hoping he didn't hear my moan as I got off of the bicycle. My calves throb.

Just the sight of mouse ears prompts a "Goddamn Guiliani! Goddamn Bloomberg! Their pitiful stewardship is to blame! You can't even buy a counterfeit Fendi anymore."

"Sure you can." I cross the sidewalk to a table of street ware. "Plus plastic Dolce and Gabbana sunglasses and questionable Justin Bieber autographed merchandise."

Jarod tells me he is a Libertarian. This means he campaigns for the unelectable. When I point out how Independent candidates always leech critical votes away, he becomes apoplectic.

"We should be content with status quo and ignore the moral alternatives?" He chains our bicycles together near the curb. "I get it, let's just all write SOS on the ballot. Same Old Shit! You probably voted for a second term of Bush."

Jarod is a provocateur.

"And you voted for? Oh, wait. You were thirteen. You were playing with your own hanging chad."

I don't know why I bother. I am borderline apolitical. If I were elected president, there's only one thing I really want to know and that's who really killed Marilyn Monroe?

I pay as Jarod intentionally knocks over *Shrek* merchandise. When he sees I'm annoyed, he smooches me. It's an act of defiance that goes unremarked upon. I know he wanted a floorwalker to tell us it to "tone it down, boys" so he could then push over a display of Buzz Lightyears.

Jarod makes various noises of indignation when we reach the newsstand.

"Those in power have made Times Square the center of nothing. A kaffee klatch is what it is! It's a pedestrian plaza, all right! Bleachers that glow red and resin chairs. Utterly pedestrian!"

"The preferred word is piazza. Pedestrians are safer."

"Really? Bike injuries have spiked 10 percent."

"Because they added more of your beloved bike lanes. It's basic math."

Jarod stays back as I approach. It's rare that I've seen her at the end of a workday and rarer still that I'd stop by on the weekend, so it's no surprise she's not there, just her father. I return to the bikes with Ariel. I want to ask him to hold the Disney bag; I need both hands. But he'll probably pitch it at someone's hardhat, so I don't. I hold it in my mouth or under my arm.

We pass Grand Central Terminal.

"Thank God for Jackie O. She saved this place from demolition," Jarod says.

"Your mom would have your nuts for commending a liberal," I joke.

"She'd just put 'em with Dad's and my brothers'."

Jarod has a booking to ready for. Except for him to point out that Greene Street has the largest concentration of cast-iron buildings in the world, we don't really speak. The aftertaste of Senator Marianna Pugh seems to be the playing card in our spokes.

IF ALL variables cooperate, Jarod can come from the Clark Street station to Times Square in thirty minutes, and vice versa.

While bonding time is minimal, we have fun generating the sticky adhesive. For Jarod it's less about the act and more about the anticipation. The duration of foreplay, with him, is like *Nicholas Nickleby*. I don't know when or if Andy and I indulged like this. Jarod makes me feel desirable. Andy made me feel like a box needing a neat checkmark in it. I was no better. If we did put an egg timer on the buildup, it's because we always had to be somewhere or be asleep for the next twelve-hour day. Jarod will lie in his own fluids. Andy and I sought quick cleanup and closure. I love you, now hurry.

I feel like sheepish Hermie from *Summer of '42*, laying down prophylactics in the new Duane Reade, which is just like the old one. Condoms haven't been a concern for a long time. Cleanliness, not safety, dictated when Andy and I used them. I recall him grabbing one from a drawer so vintage it had hardened: "Look. A poker chip with a reservoir tip."

I toss in Altoids to lessen the sting. This is probably a great pharmacy secret: customers buy at least one more item to populate a checkout receipt with something more than rubbers.

I have a missed call from my Aunt Sarajane, which concerns me until I see my next message is from my mother.

"It's just me." Mom sounds like she has summer allergies. "Happy Independence Day. I hope you're out having something flambéed tableside and not just mingling with people you doodled on a wall, Mr. New York scenester," which she pronounced like "semester." "I hope you're not at that museum exhibit of sculpted feces. I read about that at the doctor's office, buddy. I've heard of shitty art before, but…."

I haven't been to the Whitney or MoMA, neither a cabaret nor a concert, and though I work in Times Square, I've yet to see a Broadway show. I would never admit this. I don't want to hear her exasperated, "Then why did you move to New York?" I especially don't want to tell her that I've hooked up with a man half my age with whom I'm trying to make an actual connection.

"I heard what I am sure were gunshots in the woods yesterday, and then today. I hope someone wasn't hunting my deer. I called the sheriff's office. If it's kids, I hope they shot themselves and they're all sprawled, suffering and bleeding out, flies on their lips, that's what I hope, like a deer would have to, laying there, that's what I have my goddamn fingers crossed for. Over and out."

I should call her back. I'm still trying to atone for the fact that I completely spaced on Mother's Day. That was a mea gulpa low moment when, on Monday, I realized what Sunday had been. The Prodigal Son became Bad Barry. The blame, my preoccupation with Theatrilicious, was all mine; even Olivia, remarkably, acknowledged Mom. But I am tardy in meeting Jarod and his friends to watch the East River Fourth of July fireworks. I save my mother's cheerful death wish for young people and promise myself we'll have a nice long talk full of my bouquets and her bricks.

I am late to South Street Seaport. Purple, orange, and yellow are already sizzling in the sky, drifting down like Skittles into the river. I see Jarod before he sees me. He's wearing the tennis shoes I bought him. I'm pleased. He had so fumbled his thanks, I couldn't tell if he actually liked them, even thought they were the same Saucony ProGrid Paramount 3's he had admired on me at Nudercise.

I immediately dislike Brent. I didn't know anyone who doesn't appreciate a well-produced aerial explosion until tonight, but Brett gripes that the drift of sulphur makes his eyes water. He's prissily familiar, the one who calls everyone "hon," the type I would have fast-tracked into The Drilled And The Notched repository. Scotty, shirtless in a vest, is a hairburner at SuperCuts. This I know: he needs to put his own tweezers down. Anthony is wearing a porkpie hat and looks like he belongs in a tattered Mickey Spillane paperback.

Afterward, everyone wants pizza. Jarod's entourage carries theirs to a booth as he pulls wadded currency from his pocket.

I hand over cash. "I've got it. Go ahead and sit down."

Brent, a slice folded into his mouth, calls across the pizzeria, "Thanks, Dad!"

That kind of courtesy can get a boy killed.

The rest, including Jarod, are intensely texting by the time I sit. It's like eating with court reporters who have sunglasses on their necks. I gaze into space.

I hear someone say, "Farmville." A bite of pizza stalls in my throat.

Jarod mentions clubbing. I assume it's about baby seals. I've given up tracking his causes. He must have an Affront of the Day app.

Scotty says something about a portable party, which I mishear as portable potty and I think of a commode. They're talking about the weekend, going to some party. I'm even less interested. Anthony proposes they all first converge at a public pool to ogle straight teenage boys.

Brent says, "What we'll do is take the free water taxi to the Red Hook IKEA and then fuck IKEA!"

"You up for swimming Saturday afternoon?" Jarod asks me.

I indicate no.

"Too good for a public pool, hon?" Brent asks unpleasantly.

No, hon, just too good to listen to your drivel. I cite work, then add to Jarod: "Didn't you say you'd do that greeter thing at the LGBT Center Open House?"

"I'm bagging that. Bunches of people volunteered," he says.

"Dick trumps docent, hon." Brent smiles.

Jarod is clearly unreliable. A couple days ago, when I'd asked if anything was happening with Sasha and the diner and the rally, his stupefied look said "What?" His irritations and inflammations seem to be easily calmed by the unguent of time. And by "time" I mean a short catnap.

"Then, that night, you can come hear your man and me make music," Anthony nudges.

I turn to Jarod. "You're in a band?"

Jarod is a musician.

He says he plays the occasional snare drum for Potassium Anime. Anthony plays the ukulele. Some girl plays the harp. The music sounds about as unappealing as their name, which isn't much better than Theatrilicious. I ask its origin.

Jarod hunches his shoulders. "Two of the best things life has to offer: a beautifully speckled banana and Japanese cartoons." He pauses. "If you had a band, what would yours be called?"

"Gertie Noel," I announce after thinking.

I TAKE Ariel out of my pocket. Again, she's not at the newsstand. I put Ariel back into my pocket.

"I hope your daughter is doing something fun today."

"What daughter?"

I consider this. My misinterpretation of her proximity and his presence, maybe. "Did she go away for the summer?"

"She who?"

"The little girl that's always here."

He looks at me. "No little girl."

My eyes shift to where she was trussed, but there is no strap, just a beam that shows the same wear as any other support.

"Come on. You keep her right there. Where's she at?"

"Keep no one, ever."

"That's not true," I say, shaking. "Do I look stupid?"

"Didn't say stupid. But I tell true."

"Sir, you are making me nervous," I say.

"No reason for nervous."

"Then why am I?"

"I don't know. You are thinking of another place like this." His manner is cool, but his sneer is quite clear. "Lots of us look the same."

"That's a convenient self-racism card to play."

I see Ariel, by now faceless, tucked between two kiosk planks.

"No! Right there is her Little Mermaid! You're a damn liar!"

I slap my flat hand firmly down upon his and I am warned, "You will stand back. You cause trouble when there is none."

I don't know what to do. Begin yelling? For help? Help for what? I continue to Theatrilicious but, troubled, I continue to look over my shoulder. I see the worker watching me between transactions.

THAT same night, I am hosing the black-and-olive mold off the Theatrilicious awnings on an unsteady stepladder as a man who looks like he was in ZZ Top offers to hold it still for a buck. I give him my last five to get away from it. Something very close to overcooked spinach flops to the ground. I expect the many splats to regroup and pull itself toward the subway station steps like The Blob.

I join Karen to labor within the windows. The encrustment of soot was so dense I had to hand out an antihistamine when customers got too close. At my direction, supplied with a surgical mask, she's stripped them bare.

Karen first sees Marjorie, all in crimson.

"Here comes Big Red Riding Hood!"

Karen leaps out like a gazelle to refold Broadway towels. I hear Marjorie's phlegmatic intake of breath through the glass.

"What was wrong with my displays?" she huffs.

I snap the bunched damask that served as the backdrop. A spore talc gradually settles. "If our country suffers a pandemic, mark these words: it ignited here."

"City grime that every shop window has," Marjorie poo-poos.

"The merchandise was also more sun-damaged than Jan Brewer."

"So at last you're blowing me shit," Marjorie crows.

"It's more like backing up. Karen, get me a plunger." Karen dashes behind a rack of sheet music like she might actually find one there. "That was figurative," I add. "Take cover in the storage room." She runs, still wearing her mask like she's fleeing the infectious, which she probably is.

Marjorie studies a pewter watch on a chain deep in her crepey cleavage. "I'm going to be late for the eight o'clock curtain."

Marjorie's a bully. Hit back.

I've bitten my tongue for so long it's perforated. I reach in, tear off a section, and slap her with it.

"Marjorie, you *are* the eight o'clock curtain." I flick her cape. "And from the looks of it, it's a Druid sacrifice."

"Whaaaaaat?"

"I'm not pulling fourteen-hour days to rearrange *Rent* swizzle sticks and *Priscilla Queen of The Desert* press-on nails," I continue. "If we burned this place to the ground, the ash would still be cluttered."

Startled, she shuffles back.

"You either let someone merchandise and grow this business or you don't."

"I'm very hands-on!"

I advance. "Equal parts interference and indifference."

"You're talking about my legacy!" she protests.

"I used to think in those terms too. A store is an organic thing. Like people, it has to evolve. And occasionally be rinsed off."

"Who do you think you are?" she bellows.

"Neither your assassin or your goddamn Swiffer. You're like listening to a cheap blender. Once it starts all you can think is, when will this be done?"

Now she's wheedling. "You know I'm bipolar."

I step over a Dirt Devil cord and out of the window. "And lady, both halves are nuts. There's a pull-quote for you."

"So that's it? Like everyone else, you walk out on me?" she demands.

"To some, it would look that way, Margarine." I smile. "I'm walking at a very deliberate pace to an ATM. I promised Ruby Foo to Karen if she'd stay late with me. We *are* changing out these windows." I pause for effect. "We'll also be changing store hours. Analysis of sales makes it obvious we need to rejigger things to align with Broadway. We should stay open until midnight Friday and Saturday, 11:00 p.m. through the week, except for Mondays, when we will be closed, like most theaters. I'm done carrying your water. Here."

I swing the pager, still suspended from her unbreakable hair, at her. She's a good catch.

That felt good, leaving her in a combination of aggravation and fascination. I opt for an ATM within the Marriott Marquis, but I'm distracted by the sounds of law enforcement: four cars, a handful of officers. Times Square arrests are as common as twofers, so I don't acknowledge it, not until the resistance becomes profane, the scuffling explosive.

I rush through a small crowd to see the police loading the newsstand worker into the back of a car, handcuffed, kicking.

Another officer has just finished dusting the newsstand ledge for fingerprints. Another officer brings down the metal door. The worker rages, most of it indecipherable except for "No one will never see her again!"

FLOOR 14 boards the elevator.

Holding his hand is the little newsstand girl.

She is completely naked.

This is not the worst part.

Blood is spattered all over her pale belly, so thickly concentrated on her pudenda I cannot tell where or what it is. What hasn't clotted is trickling down onto her scraped knees. Her small hands are stained from holding the desecration of her lower body. Her gaze accuses, and her words are a spooky croak.

"I was saying 'help me'."

What looks like a purple, overripe plum begins to emerge from her mouth, like a gimmick, and this bubble of blood bursts right on her eyeballs and fills them.

As Floor 14 begins to lick the blood off the Ariel he violated her with, I wake myself.

There is no cool part of his pillow. Jarod is so hotheaded, it feels like it's been popped under a broiler. I ease out of the twin bed to sit on his closet/chair, not quite crying.

Jarod is now awake, asking, "Is that you?" on an elbow.

"How embarrassing. Yes, it's just me," I say into the moonlight. "I seem to have traded old nightmares for new ones."

He scoots closer. "Maybe in a way that's a good thing?"

"I'd prefer none."

"Was it work shit, your old life?" Still in recline, he cannot quite touch me with his extended fingertips. "Or the newsstand girl?"

I nod, reaching out to turn on a crooked lamp with a hairy lightbulb. I have scanned newspapers and watched local newscasts. A captive little girl suddenly missing warrants coverage, even in jaded Manhattan. There has been nothing. I wasn't family, I didn't even have a first or last name, and, when I stopped in the 43rd and Broadway precinct, I didn't like the way the desk sergeant looked at me when he asked, "What's it to you?" I'd seen enough wrongfully accused movies to feel paranoid. It wasn't officially a homicide, I was told. Whether the newsstand guy was still jailed was not disclosed.

"That little girl was never ever in school, and I let it become a lame morning ritual," I say. "She wasn't in obvious crisis. I only hope it was a custody mess." My shudder courses downward. "I hope she wasn't being abused. I hope she wasn't something he bought, like a child sex ring."

"He wouldn't have had her out in the open."

"I disgust myself. I did nothing."

"They'll find her, if they haven't already."

I wave him off. "Forget it. It's not you. It's me."

He sits up. "Oooohhhh boy."

"Oh boy what?"

"Oh boy in that I've heard 'it's not you, it's me' before. Next thing, I'm invited to immediately leave."

"This being your place, I won't ask you to leave," I promise.

"It's happened."

I manage to laugh. "Really. It's just me. All of it. Everything. Me and my old life. Forget it."

ALTHOUGH I didn't know it at the time, it started with the sheets. I am about to discover it's not about with whom you sleep, but on what.

I pretend that I am checking on how Rooms Great and Small is faring, but I'm really calling about bedsheets. I've now spent enough nights at Jarod's that I require something better than what is on his bed. His white fitted sheet looks like a Rorschach test, the topsheet has its own birthmarks, and the light blanket is tie-dyed. I am come undone by the conjecture of how all of these stains originated.

Jarod narrows his eyes at me when I point it out.

"It's not like they're from a dollar store."

No, I think, *that would be the childlike boxsprings.*

"Does my thread count offend you?"

There can't be a thread count when there is no thread, I think. "These get better every time you wash them."

They are bamboo sheets from an organic line free of chemicals and off-gassing we carried, and that's why I telephone Isaac, to FedEx me a complete set.

"Twin?" he repeats. "Are these for a dorm?"

Yes, I say.

Isaac doesn't have to run anything by me, but I'm glad he does. He's brought in a chocolatier, with bonbons made in full view of customers, truffles and low-glycemic caramels. I congratulate. A niece and nephew of Mr. Albanese have been making and selling ice cream on the weekends, just three flavors. I say yum. The small cigar boutique that we gave a stall to last summer, however, is a complete bust. No one wants to pay $10,000 for a humidor. I counsel. Go easy on him, give him until Labor Day to secure space elsewhere. Amends have been made with Moberley's, the coffee house that saw our cappuccinos as competition; they are going to build a roastery in some of our unused space and sell their coffee in bulk. Pies too. I commend, but I am imagining all of our polished woods blurred by a thin film of lard. And one other thing: the store has had another diversionary fire, staged in dead space near a drinking fountain. It was a bold but odd theft this time: a bunch of imported Cire Trudon candles.

"Let me guess. The triple wick?"

Yes, Isaac says, those, the ones that retail for $375 each.

Customers reported two individuals sitting in a parked, running car in our overflow lot, usually empty except for holidays, before that. I knew, unfortunately, that our security cameras didn't extend that far.

"The smoke also caused a kid in the store to have an asthma attack. What pisses me off the most is the police said they used store matches, a book from our grand reopening!"

Then he reminds me he and a few others are bound for market in Manhattan in a few weeks and that drinks are in order.

I say I'll be around.

My tone says I'll be busy.

I ask when I can expect my sheets.

ON THIS Tuesday, Jarod calls to announce that he has deposited the overbearing, media-whoring Momanager of an overrated teen actress at a buzzy, exclusionary Village club. Giving him a grin of veneer her daughter paid for, she wink-winks she'll find a way home, but "keep your cell on vibrate in case the paparazzi catch me with my dress up over my shoulders." He tells me to meet him at nearby Splash, on West 17th, for Twink Night.

Is Jarod a twink?

"Beige was better. 'Course, it's fucking gone." He's talking about the now-defunct Tuesday night dance party at B-Bar, at 4th and Bowery, where Amanda LePore, or people who wanted to be her, could be found. "The fuckstick residents of 2 Cooper across the street bitched about the noise and poof! Beige goes translucent!"

"I read the real reason is B-Bar wanted to expand restaurant service hours."

"Spin, spin, spin! The Olsen twins are giving us an urban lobotomy!" Jarod continues to ignore the paradox that he drives many who populate Lower Manhattan.

I am not really in the mood. My head is elsewhere. The same man has been in Theatrilicious twice, throwing around a tape measure, and not very discreetly. When Soapsuds asked what he was doing, the man, who she said was shaped like a molar, answered drily, "Making sure the ceiling meets the floor." I may not be down with the whole foreshadowing thing, but even I recognize that Theatrilicious no longer pleases the palate of the landlord. That's why I requested, without Marjorie, an exploratory discussion with the owners of the vacant 8th Avenue porn shop. We met yesterday, with agreement to convene again, also without Marjorie.

I eye recent clothing acquisitions. I'd crept back, feeling like a hypocrite, to the store on Macdougal, piling attire I once made a face at in my arms. I rationalized it as a uniform of sorts. I'm playing for a new team, The Nightlife Fireflies. I regret that damn tarragon chicken salad wrap. It will make the difference between a fitted and fatted shirt. Yet my will is still strong. Some things I won't compromise. No popped collars, ever.

I have no idea to what we're dancing since there are still no lyrics, but between the crossfades, the intros and outros, if they played a remix of "God Bless America," even Kate Smith wouldn't start singing for six minutes. Gay clubs are ideal for the sensory-deprived. Can't hear, can't see, not much to say, and you won't want to smell, either. Save your taste and touch for last call. The dance floor vibrates with the self-medicated and the self-deluded. It seems every clubkid's shirt has been zapped off by lasers. Jarod's too... his is tucked into a back pocket as he exhorts, "Get fucked up!"

The tribal "yeahs!" confirm most already are. One admirer gropes Jarod's ass.

"He'd be hot with us," Jarod suggests.

The admirer twists Jarod's nipple like he's trying to remove a screw. I am nonplused by his audacity and Jarod's appreciation of it.

"Like you and Andre didn't do three-ways," he confronts, nipple still engaged.

"Andrew. *Andy*. No, we didn't," I say.

Which isn't true, but bringing in a third was an exotic appetizer that always resulted in heartburn. Like an *American Idol* group number, they never meshed. No matter what deal-breakers are negotiated upfront in a ménage, someone always ends up freaked out in a wicker chair across the room. Which of us that usually was, I choose to forget.

"If we did, it was only on vacation," I admit.

Jarod either laughs at my disclaimer or at the admirer who nibbles his neck. "So would Andy have let you pick me up?"

"It wasn't an open marriage." He offers me that look I'm coming to recognize, the one that brands my thinking prudish and obsolete. "The one thing open in any long-term relationship I have will be the door," I announce stiffly. "As in, leave through it if someone else catches your eye."

Point taken, Jarod untangles himself from his admirer's clutches. We move toward a gap at the bar. He orders two sugarless energy drinks with vodka.

"I work tomorrow," I protest. And the taurine in Red Bull makes me feel like I have bedbugs.

"The best parties happen on a school night!" Jarod grabs our drinks from the bartender. "A bunch of people are heading to The Box."

The Box is a tawdry Lower East Side club with an after-show of avant-garde performances and human oddities that Jarod thinks are awesome; I think the wait to get in and drink prices are. While I enjoy degeneracy, I do not, at 2:30 a.m., want to watch someone in a gorilla mask wearing a giant chrome dildo drink something from a pail and then spray it over the crowd. I pass with "I just say no to hepatitis."

One clubgoer in leg warmers near me yells out, "Why do I hear 'Everything's Comin' Up Roses'?"

I am so startled as I reach for my cell I drop it. "That's me, that's me!"

Leg Warmers makes a go at this. "I'm a pretty gurl, Mama."

Gurl, now is not the time to deconstruct musical moments. This can't be good, not after one o'clock in the morning. The Theatrilicious alarm has been tripped, Testosterina didn't unplug the curling iron and burnt down the house, Sarajane's ass dialed me again, Olivia has a sty, something. I kneel frantically. Jarod finds it among the sandals and tablets carelessly dropped.

It's a local number. I plug my ear. "Hello? Hello? Luke? You're what? Where, Luke?"

I hop into the front of Jarod's limousine, parked one block away. We make our hasty way toward midtown. The streets glitter like they're paved with crystals. We pass a Ghost Bike, milky and aglow at a lamppost. Its planes vaguely suggest a skull-and-crossbones X-ray.

"Luke's parents found guy-on-guy pictures on his computer," I explain, "and it apparently all went downhill from there."

We're going to get every stoplight. We slow. A silver grid lies across the windshield, a reflection of construction cranes, as investment firms blend into Times Square.

"Nothing like an AMBER Alert to sober you up," Jarod notes.

I see the shuttered newsstand, crime scene tape still clinging to its planes.

"Shit! Don't say that! What if there is? Oh my God!"

LUKE emerges from the dark alcove of a currency exchange shop. He's the walking wounded—sour clothing, unwashed hair, a suitcase missing a caster—but he manages a wry grin at the limousine.

"Is this how you get around, Uncle Barry?"

"First things first. Your car is…?

He flips his hand backward. "Down by the Dave Letterman theater."

We all go inside to my apartment. He has to pee, and bad. I softly scold him outside the bathroom door. "Luke, there are ways to reach out to me that don't involve running away to New York City. You're a minor." I get "I'm sorry" over the flush. "Why a pay phone? Where's your cell?"

"They took it from me."

"Are you hungry?" I open the refrigerator and read what I've written on Styrofoam. "I could warm up fried oyster sliders. With pickled okra relish."

Jarod grunts at how stupid this sounds. "Yeah, a bivalve sounds real good to Luke right now."

He's fine, he's eaten. To prove it, Luke takes an empty Sbarro sack from a pocket of his suitcase.

And he is walking, wounded. His arms are mottled with bruises shaped like fingerprints. Jeans lowered, we both see the small cuts which run parallel to his spine, all the way to his asscrack, visible like a coin slot. When he turns around, his treasure trail and pubes are almost exposed. The casual exhibitionism makes me uneasy.

Jarod asks, "So, on a scale of one to ten, how bad were these gay pictures your dad found on your laptop?"

The mind boggles at what a ten would be. I am relieved that Luke holds up only six fingers.

"Luke, were they of you or did they involve you?"

"No, Uncle Barry!" Luke exclaims.

"So then your dad, he whaled on you?" Jarod continues.

"He blew his top and stormed out. Mom came in and said it could have been our secret, and now I'd ruined any chance of peace and maybe the marriage. Then she started. I knew not to fight back."

"Wait a minute. Mindy did this?" I ask in disbelief.

"She was yelling, things like maybe my sissy ass belonged in the military," Luke says. "Then she'd wallop me again. When she let up, I took off. The first place I thought was here."

ONCE Luke is asleep on the convertible sofa, Jarod and I go into the bedroom, where the window air conditioner will filter our discussion. I open my cell phone. Jarod snaps it shut in disbelief. "Tell me you're not calling his parents!"

"Of course I am."

"Why in the hell would you do that?"

"He's their son."

"Please wait, just hold on!"

I do.

"You'd tell him things get better, ship him back, and condemn him to more red state sameness?" he demands. "Clearly, he expects to remain here."

"Clearly, that isn't going to happen."

"If he can't seek refuge with you, where, then? That kid looks at you like a puppy dog. Where is your sense of solidarity?"

"This isn't a protest rally, Jarod."

"No, it's a one-man war. You've got to yell for the voiceless!"

"I am going to return him personally," I say.

"If you don't want him, I'll take him to the Ali Forney Center. It's in Chelsea. They have emergency housing."

"It's not about wanting him. And he's not homeless."

"I'll hook him up with the LGBT Center. There's a support program called '20something' for queer youths," Jarod continues.

"I don't know anything about the Center," I reply.

"Because you've never truly assimilated."

"Just maybe not in the way you'd prefer. And, by the way, Luke is seventeensomething," I tell him.

He's still planning. "He could seek legal emancipation."

Jarod is a family lawyer.

I frown. "Not exactly realistic."

"There's this great group called FIERCE for underprivileged gay kids."

I wave this off. "He's not underprivileged, he's just not understood. And that name."

"It stands for Fabulous Independent Educated Radicals for Community Empowerment," he snaps.

"Fabulosity. Radicalism. What a schizo juxtaposition. Do they wrap their pipe bombs in leopard print?"

"Forget that," Jarod scrambles. "He works a great look. I occasionally drive this big-deal guy from the men's division of Ford who might be able to hook him up."

Now Jarod is an agent.

He paces. "You're prepared to deal with the brother?"

I restate my position. "Alex is Andy's bookend. Luke is part of Andy. I am obliged to do what I can."

"I should go wake him and tell him to run for it!"

"You'll do no such thing."

I open my phone again. Jarod grabs and takes it.

"I don't understand you!" he blurts. "Don't you see? This is karma offering you a way to reclaim what you lost!"

"Someone else's son is not mine to lose."

"Neither was that newsstand girl."

"And I did nothing."

"Then become Luke's guardian!" Jarod pleads. "To be seventeen going-on-hot-little-number, without straight boundaries. How fun would that be, taking him to his first club?"

Jarod is a father figure.

"Mentoring is more than sneaking him past a bouncer. And you're way too young to give me advice."

He stops. "That is it, isn't it?"

That *is* it. Jarod is a lot of things, but Jarod is mostly young. I understand the pain refracted by his drive, but it still does not make a match I can work with. He wants to be pretty *and* gritty, this octopus wrapping his tentacles around everything, each little suction cup dangling a different cause, trying to determine what will hold, and when a seal is broken, it grabs something else. All I am is the next thing he picked up trawling.

"Yes," I admit, "you're seven years older than Luke, barely. But you're also very quick—"

"Like in fetch?!" Jarod interjects. His slight underbite prepares to lunge and do battle.

"Like in I admire your energy."

He paces. "*Admire*. That's pretty nonspecific. Is it so distasteful that I agitate?"

"Not if you're a washing machine." I carefully continue. "Aspire isn't the same as inspire. Those anxious to sign up first usually back out first."

"*The Voice* didn't think so. I showed you my essay they published."

"They printed a letter. That isn't the same as published."

"Because I'm still finding my way, I'm a poseur?"

He said it, I didn't. It's like what Maria Callas barks at an average student in the play *Master Class*: "You don't have a look. Get one!" Jarod has too many outlooks. Choose one.

"You mouth all the right things, but do you believe half of what you say?" I ask.

"Did you say 'trite things'?"

"Clean your ears. That's maybe what you heard, but I said 'right things'. You tend to misread and then you overreact. I find myself being careful around you."

At that, he begins to gather from my bureau items he sometimes leaves behind: sunglasses, lip balm.

"Sorry you bloodied your feet walking a tightrope of barbed wire." *More like a series of annoying paper cuts,* I think. "So apparently someone my age can't voice strong opinions yet have contradictions. I'm just someone who has past-due bills rolling out his ass."

"How is this suddenly now about money?"

"As *quick* as I am, I've been aware from the very beginning that I can't keep up."

"Andy and I had our struggles. We sawed through a lot of cube steak that tasted like rubber bands drowned in A1. I won't apologize for not being destitute."

"I don't recall saying I was destitute or felt it. You did. Your houses, your investments, they mean a lot to you," Jarod challenges.

"You diminish my life when you say something like that." All of these references that I'm financially flush makes me suspect he looked at bank statements in my laptop case. "Out of curiosity, Jarod, why did you cruise me?"

"I didn't cruise. I spoke."

"You followed me out to the street. So why *were* you at Nudercise? Why were you willing to miss *Dr. Who*?"

"Okay," he concedes. "I went to get laid."

"And I was the best of the naked jumping Jacks."

"If we're being totally honest now…"

He is locked and loaded for retaliation.

"…I'm just not ready to be someone's trophy wife."

I want to instantly come back with that he wouldn't even justify a runners-up certificate, but I don't.

"My heart sunk when you made such a big deal about those sheets, those eco-friendly, wallet-unfriendly sheets. That's when I knew that style over substance defines you."

A sublime revelation, that the tipping point was a decent set of sheets, and not even Porthault.

"Exhorted from your $2500 bike," I shoot back.

"I'm surprised you haven't paid it off somehow. This rain of gifts has been a very cold shower."

His arrogance, that he's being slowly acclimated to a different hemisphere, is a punch. But I fell into a trap of my own composition. Mrs. Stone *did* give him things, something new for his closet, something new for his bookshelf, was it to camouflage the something old in his bed? Well, he's for sure not getting the panini press I bought for him.

He's far from done. "This is your version at starting over until you face the co-op board and move in next door to A-Rod at 15 Central Park West and you rejoin the cognoscenti. That sad kid asleep in there doesn't fit into that. You aren't going to give up a thing."

"I should put everything into a blind trust and start from scratch?" I demand. "Life's complex. Walk a mile in my shoes!"

"I have, remember? You bought me the same exact ones."

I made that too easy. "I would pile high every one of my material comforts for just one hour with Andy! I would surrender every cent I will ever have to bury my face into the neck of one of my dogs! I also know my wishes can't come true."

"Because you're the grown-up here," Jarod replies.

"Enough to know I'll never recreate the brand of happy I had!"

"Which makes me, every guy that comes next, the generic placeholder," Jarod decides.

"Exactly who is you, Jarod? Besides the rebellious, defiant black sheep?" Then I hear myself say, "Because you are your mother's son. You're a lot like her, so quick to separate the black hats from the white hats. Everything needs Occupied, everything's a polemic, it all sucks, danger lurks."

He is trembling. "Your armchair may be Bedermeier, but your psychoanalysis is strictly Lego."

High marks that he knows Biedermeier. Points taken for mispronouncing it.

Then it gets really ugly.

"Funny how your disapproval of me doesn't include the way I Occupy your ass."

I point for him to get out, immediately, right now. That his keys remain on the bureau spares me asking for them back. It's a grim walk into the living room. When he starts to say something, I point to Luke and motion that he should keep it down. He opens the door enough to slide out. I chain it as quietly as I can.

I stand over Luke, still asleep or pretending to be. I couldn't stop Andy or the newsstand girl from getting on the Crazy Dipper, but I sure as hell can slow this boy down from showing his string bracelet to board.

Due to the lateness of the hour, I text Mindy from my bedroom that Luke is with me and safe, and that once I call Northwest Airlines, I'll follow up with arrival information.

I get back THX.

Chapter Nineteen

New Fault Lines

WE ARE in the air one minute before our scheduled departure. This is a good omen. Then I realize that, in our rush for the first available flight I left Andy's grade school picture in my other wallet. Now I'm uneasy. This trip is entirely about and for him and he isn't accompanying me. I close my eyes. Maybe I'll awake to discover Andy instead beside me. We're on Oceanic Airlines Flight 815. We're just Lost, that's all.

I hear the woman ahead of us snap to the male stranger next to her, "Please refrain from touching me in any way with your knees or elbows." Or maybe they're married. Hard to tell.

Luke is asleep. I muted his protests at returning by promising to be his advocate. We have options, I told him, emphasizing *we*, and I fumbled through some of the acronyms and jargon Jarod spat out. Luke seemed mollified. His biggest concern was why Jarod didn't deliver us in his limousine. Before I could honestly tell him that Uncle Barry screwed us out of a comfortable ride to LaGuardia in rush-hour traffic, he had grinned. "He's a keeper. Really cute. Major boner fuel."

That word should be banned.

From up here, I see the cemetery where Andy lay. I see the parking lot is gratifyingly full at what was once Great Rooms! I see a familiar neighborhood. A rectangular swimming pool, covered. The place I called home.

I don't recall ever being as acutely aware of geography changing as now, from up here, how the planes of Pennsylvania valleys smear into flat Midwest farmland. Down there are failed levees I'll never endure, car dealerships I'll never haggle at, people I don't know and will never know, people who are waking or retiring or sleepless or dying and don't know it yet, making choices, agony, reparation.

"Need anything? Is everything good?" a flight attendant, frighteningly cheerful, comes by to ask.

"It's all good from up here," I tell her, wishing it were true.

At landing tones, I wipe away Luke's drool and tap his arm.

BEYOND Security, in cut-offs, Mindy's welcome to her son is emotionless and flat. "It's good to see you. How was the flight?"

"We sat in first class."

"Welcome back to no class."

This is what I returned him to?

"Your dad's circling in the truck."

"I checked a bag. Let's walk as we talk," I suggest.

"We don't need outside mediation," Mindy tells me.

"It can be me or it can be a higher power, Mindy. Luke has legal options beyond being beaten down."

This startles her into silence. That the moving sidewalk we jump on won't actually move contributes to the pall. We closely space our steps, suspicious it will chug into overdrive and catapult us into a Wolfgang Puck kiosk. Everyone else on this treadmill thinks so, too, resulting in a very strange procession.

Mindy suddenly snaps her fingers. "For ignoring our three-zillion frantic calls, right now, surrender your cell."

"I lost it," Luke says, as I remind her, "You took it."

Mindy gives me the first of what will be many bewildered looks. "Someone's misinformed."

I ask about the sexual computer images.

"Are you talking about the gay stuff? The Geek Squad found it a year ago when we took the computer in because of a virus," she remembers.

"A year ago?" I turn to Luke, who is pounding the nonmoving handrail as he walks.

"More than. The pictures came from some naked athlete site. So did all the spyware. Alex was less than thrilled, but that's old news." She swivels. "Apparently Luke recycled it."

I am unsettled. "So this really bad scene with Luke... getting physical?"

"Are you talking about how Luke shook Duncan? That he shook his little brother so hard it dislocated his right shoulder when he turned over a glass pipe he found?"

"Wasn't mine," Luke protests.

"Whose, then?"

We all get on an escalator which *is* functioning.

"That's when he ran, after he hurt his little brother. But not with the bruises and the scratches. You do that yourself?" Mindy asks.

He snorts. "Yeah, right."

Momentarily, Mindy and I share an escalator step. She takes a step back to occupy Luke's. I awkwardly ask behind me, "What would Luke gain, coming all that way and lying?"

"Sympathy. Attention. Cash. It's common knowledge you're a very rich man now," is Mindy's answer. The green of her envy clashes with her ridiculously brown skin.

"Maybe he was looking for safe harbor," I suggest.

"Right! They don't want me to be who I am!"

"Not what you're *becoming*," Mindy snaps at Luke.

I steer them toward baggage claim. "Luke isn't *becoming* anything, Mindy. Luke *is*. Let's face it: your husband—"

"—is just one of two voices!" she interjects. "Maybe I come across to you as this bleached blonde ten steps behind—"

"—Mindy, I'm not claiming *you*—"

"—you all talk about being demonized yet it's okay to paint people like us with the same brush. We know that gay is not a choice. We are not writing our son off. I've looked into PFLAG. Maybe I can get Lexie to go, maybe I can't. We're more upset about the drugs, truancy, stealing. Those aren't genetic. Those are conscious choices he's making."

I feel very sick. "Luke, what's going on?"

"You're falling for it too!" is all he can manage.

Those anxious to grab their luggage curve around us.

I cross my arms. "I'm ready for some rebuttal here, Luke." He stares at the suitcases bumping by. "Don't turn sullen on me."

"Why? You've turned over!"

"Luke wouldn't know where to start a defense. He quit the debate team last year. Along with everything else," Mindy says.

"Lies!" he shouts.

"Go find Dad. Go!" Mindy tells him. "He's in a loading zone out front."

Luke stomps through the automatic doors. I turn back in time to pull my bag.

Mindy's burnished skin doesn't square with her exhausted, red-rimmed eyes. "We're heartsick, Barry. He's lifted out of other folks' medicine cabinets, which we barely smoothed over. I hate to say this, but check yours when you get back."

"And school?"

"I'm not implying he's like Columbine," she insists. "When he shows up, he excels. When. Missed days that are mostly unexcused, mouthing off, those things don't play well when colleges check transcripts. His best friend Dale—maybe his boyfriend, we don't know—he was expelled after he got arrested for stealing farm fertilizer."

I finish this for her. "Which makes methamphetamine."

"Dale's out on bond. We think Luke skips to be with him. God knows what else they're up to. We've also found unexplained things in Luke's bedroom ceiling," she explains.

"In the ceiling?"

"We separated the boys last year and put Luke in the basement. We did a tile/grid thing to cover pipes. I know what you think about stuff like that." I wave her on. "We had a leak and took panels down and it was like contraband."

"Contraband?"

"Stuff that makes no sense for a kid to have, even if they were trying to furnish a place together. It would smell good and they'd know the time, but that's about it."

"You lost me."

"We found a fancy clock, a bunch of new candles up there."

I flush. It's not too dramatic to say that my eyeballs are seared by the self-igniting flames of diversionary fires.

"Luke's explanation was so drawn-out we knew it couldn't be true. Wherever they came from, we assume he was going to trade or pawn them," Mindy concludes.

I am numb, no feeling in my hands or my feet. I hope it extends to my face, which I am trying to keep unreadable. I weigh whether to tell Mindy, what the ramifications might be.

"Mindy, I just wanted to help," I stammer.

Keep my mouth shut, I've enabled. Tell, I could toss him into the legal system. He's just old enough that a criminal record will snap at his heels for a lifetime.

"He's home. That's a big help," she says gratefully.

I can speak up later if the situation worsens. If I *know* it's worsened. How will I know? More doubt. I focus on what I can control. "If you get me the keys and parking garage ticket, I can at least figure out a transport service to return Luke's car."

Mindy clamps my wrist as she delivers her final jawdropper sympathetically:

"Barry, his car *is* here."

From within the Hertz rental hub, I see Alexander's SUV merge into traffic. I wonder what sacrifices Luke made to reach me in New York City, if it explained the battering his body obviously took, and I wonder what animal would take glee in doing that to a seventeen-year-old. I shake my head no to the rote upgrade, insurance, and fuel options the counter help is miserably forced to recite, and accept the keys. I see Luke, unreadable, slumped in the backseat, maybe already planning the next diversionary fire. I can't tell from Alexander and Mindy's disquieting smiles if the Crazy Dipper crash landed or if it stopped just in time.

IT WAS a long drive. Impatient, I give up on my mother's doorbell to look around. The irrigation system is spitting, like a thousand snakes, around the community vegetable garden. Someone has grown a crop of enormous sunflowers, as tall as young trees. They're doubling over from their own weight. Just past climbing rose bushes, I see Sarajane, in the familiar denim gauchos I've watched fade through the years, stepping backward. Watching her from a distance, it's like a projectionist threaded a film on the sprockets while really drunk, not just backward, but slightly accelerated, like every other frame is absent. Hayley is obediently walking behind her.

Or is that in front of her? It's so confusing.

I greet them both. Hayley barks and saunters toward me.

"Well, hi, Hayleygirl. Mom not around, S.J.?"

"Jeanie said nothing about you visiting."

"I flew back to take care of some personal stuff, so I drove over as a surprise."

Sarajane points. "And that's the car you rented! It stands out from the fixed income junkers around here." She looks down woefully. "Her place isn't picked up."

"I haven't been in. I didn't bring my keys. Where *is* Mom?"

Hayley looks at me, then at Sarajane.

"Damn your mother, she's left me in a terrible position."

"Left as in *left*?" I'm confused. "I just talked to Mom three or four days ago."

"It was longer than that, had to be."

"Okay, a week. Sarajane, what's going on?"

"Jeanie was doing okay then." Sarajane is bordering on frantic.

"Tell me where Mom is *right this second*."

"The hospital," she whimpers. "The chemo really kicked her in the booty this time."

"Back up! Chemo, as in cancer? This time?"

A trillion times, that's how often Aunt Sarajane considered telling me, she cries. I tried hinting to you. I called once but hung up. "Hiding this from you left a blister on my soul! But when a friend asks you to keep a secret, you do it," she chokes out.

"She's not a friend! She's your sister!"

"She's my *best* friend!"

"*She's my mother!*" I do not mince words. "For your absence of shame and all this subterfuge, S.J., you are on my shitlist."

Her wet eyes go icy. "You're on mine. You kids should live closer."

"Like your only daughter Clem who's shacked up in New Zealand with, what, a hobbit?" I ask.

"She was a personal assistant to Mr. Peter Jackson on those movies and stayed!" She exhales. "Did you ever notice your mother was mostly on speakerphone? She was flat on her back for weeks!"

"I thought it was a bad connection," I mumble.

"Oh, that's what it was, all right, buster."

"S.J., I don't care about any of what we're saying to each other!" I am screaming. "*Where is my mother?*"

She drops her head into her hands, names the hospital, which is within walking distance, "only a half mile away."

I HAVE never run so fast in my life. I fall on the exterior second step of the hospital. The knee of my jeans soaks with blood, yet it's somehow not torn. I am quite the sight, hopping to the curved reception desk and asking how I can locate my mother, Jeanine Grooms.

Room 2012 in the Oncology Unit is identified as an occupied double "so please have some sensitivity and speak softly."

Like hell.

I expect a mouthy woman in a backless gown, defiant butt exposed; I don't expect a Mom that doesn't look like Mom. It is like a Madame Tussauds workstation, where the in-progress wax figure is covered on a slab. The realization is uncannily accurate, you oooh and you ahhhh, but you're not fooled. The hand-tufted hair has too much volume, the skin is too pallid.

"Why are you limping?" my mother asks. Sarajane got to her, and she is trying to stoke her own diversionary fire. "What's up with your leg? Is that blood? You should see someone here."

My hope is my body language speaks volumes. I can't find it within me to utter one word.

"Honestly, honey, I was getting ready to call you," she explains.

"I'm elated to be on your speed dial. Is my sister in on this?"

"I just called her."

"Now that you're busted."

"If it's any consolation, she hung up on me."

"Can you blame her?" I ask in disgust.

Mom shakes her head. "She's on her way. She wants to not speak to me in person."

"How could we have known you took 'it's just me' so literally?"

"Say this was you. Would you have told me?"

"I'm not playing What Would Barry Do?"

"You might not have."

"Of course I would!"

"Even if I broke down every time I was in your presence?"

"Yes!"

"Me, petrified and helpless that my son was so ill, you wouldn't have downplayed anything, delayed?"

It was only my gallbladder, I tell myself.

"Why would you go through this alone, why?" I demand.

"I always had S.J."

"You have two children! Knock it off!"

"All I needed was someone to drive when I couldn't."

"With the car in R all the way?" I throw up my hands. "We go from bad to worse! Why, Mom, did you let me move?"

"I was not going to use my cancer as rock paper scissors. You would have just stayed for all the wrong reasons," she rationalizes.

"Cancer is not a wrong reason! You played God."

"I played Mom," she states. "Watching your dad slowly turn into a trembling bag of bones was enough to last you and Olivia's lifetime. I wish my own mother had been able to spare me."

"She couldn't. Grandma had Alzheimer's."

"Honey, it always comes down to apples and oranges. But the baths she let run over, when she baked her hearing aid into a cake, pounding on neighbors' doors at four in the a.m., the large checks written to herself and then the missing cash, they still had to be dealt with."

I repeat what I remember from that period. "Grandma Lola has plaque on her brain like you get on your teeth."

"And, at seven, that's all you needed to know. Neither me or S.J. took her in because we didn't want our children exposed to their grandmother topless or peeing on homework. We couldn't handle her. We knew she'd be well-tended."

"Until they forgot Grandma's after-dinner lockdown. Mom, I can handle you. I want to. I have always been more than willing to help you or take you in—your words, not mine! You could've come to New York."

"What about my treatment?" she asks.

"There's a great cancer center at NYU, Langone-something. You could have had access to alternative medicine and research specialists."

"There is nothing special about my cancer." She smiles. "It's just your run-of-the-mill-say-howdy-to-new-lymph-nodes-cancer."

"Enough with the smart-ass remarks!" I snap.

"What made you show up?"

"Never mind that. What if I hadn't? Would a hospital representative ring me up, like Andy? Or a policeman knock on my door and tell me Grandma's in a snow bank?"

"You shield your kids. You didn't need more stress—"

I stop her. "Don't piss me off any more than I am!"

A quavering voice comes from just beyond the shielding curtain.

"Show your mother some respect, young man, and try to see her point of view. She's very sick."

My punch sends the aluminum rings clattering.

"Show some mind-your-own-business! The very sick point of view is brand new to me!"

"Sorry, Ruthie," Mom offers to the curtain.

"That's okay," the curtain acknowledges.

"Do I track down your doctor or can I get some truth?"

"My left breast came off last May," she begins evenly.

"That's almost five months before September 19!"

"It was a mistake, me waiting. But it's human nature to believe you'll prevail. I thought I'd be able to announce that all's clear! Whew! talk about a scare! I was in the middle of chemo when you lost your Andy. That wig was so goddamn hot. Then I had radiation. Four months ago, they found more cancer. More chemo, good-bye to my regrown hair you thought was so short and sassy. They stop chemo. It's counterproductive. Herceptin didn't agree with me, so the doc said let's try Interferon. That's actually what ran me down and landed me here."

"Now they're treating the treatment," the curtain says.

I fumble with what little terminology I know. "At what stage are you at?"

"I am beyond a stage." Mom says this calmly. "It's more like a coliseum. It's metastasized everywhere."

The magnitude punctures my outrage. It's as quick as an auction paddle: fury, back to sorrow. I can barely manage, "Oh, Mom."

"There's an inoperable mass on my liver, which explains why I'm the color of Dijon mustard, and a new, suspicious smudge on my thyroid, which means I could die fatter than I've ever been, but at least I'll have this tan."

"Does it hurt?" is all I can manage.

Ruthie pipes up again. "You're sure not helping."

I want Mom to shake her head no, but she nods yes, and then she implores, "Ruthie, please."

I say as loudly as I can toward the screen, "Mom, I didn't even know hospitals had double rooms anymore. We'll get you a private one." Then, to her: "Nothing screams success like a boarder." I need her to exclaim "Touche!" but "I'm fine here" is all I get. "Are they doing anything for pain?" I ask.

"Of course... oral... said no to a drip, not yet. Your brain goes abroad and doesn't want to come home." As if on cue, she seems to lose her navigation. She repeats those last two words, "come home," three times. They're a brutal, if coincidental, accusation.

I offer, "We'll get all of your scrips when you're checked out of here and—"

My mother jumps back into coherence.

"Be realistic." She doesn't hesitate. "I'm not leaving." She closes her eyes. "Rub my feet. They sting. Chemo brought on neuropathy."

Through the sheets, I squeeze her toes. "Remember me and Livvie doing this after you stood all day?"

"At the carpet stuporsnore."

"You'd give us fifty cents apiece."

"My purse is here somewhere." Mom's eyes remain closed. "Remember brushing Grandma Lola's hair when we let it down long?"

"Vaguely." I repeatedly press, then release, her feet. "I love you, Mom."

"Get a load of that, Ruthie?" she calls out.

Ruthie plumps her pillow loudly. "You said he was a good guy."

Then my mother makes a special request of me, telling me where the nearest Hobby Lobby is, and that there is a 20-percent-off mailer on her counter at home and that I should hurry, it's time-sensitive.

All I can think is this is my payback. I shouldn't have been so contemptuous of *Year of Magical Thinking*. I brought on the parallels. Joan Didion's husband, then the daughter. My partner, now mother. Where does it end? I'd better warn Olivia when she gets here.

Chapter Twenty

Hell

MOM is right. She will live long enough for at least one hospital administrator to imply they will need her bed, but doesn't live long enough to be moved to hospice care, which Olivia and I dread, since the town has only one facility and that is where our father died. She never leaves the hospital.

HER rapid decline begins with general discomfort. She cannot find a position to sleep in, no matter the degree of her bed's elevation. The neckroll Olivia puts under her head makes it worse, she complains. We ask an RN, who supposes that a tumor has invaded one or both of her hips.

"Mrs. Grooms's form of cancer is greedy."

Without additional tests—Mom refuses another MRI, and we ourselves reject a fine needle aspiration based on how it sounded— there is no way to be sure. If Mrs. Grooms's outlook were better, the RN tells us, a hemipelvectomy was a surgical option. This is when they amputate the limb, or limbs, from the top of the pelvis down.

Our mother's greedy cancer wants her legs.

Olivia, myself, and our Aunt Sarajane coordinate so that one of us is always present during rounds, but our questions dwindle. The answers become one answer, the only answer. Mom is shutting down. What time she is fully aware is spent debating the next plateau of pain management. Those two words indicate surrender, so she says no no no, I don't want to go to that place. Then comes a spasm that she can't get away from, so agonizing Ruthie weeps until Mom nods to bring it on.

"I guess I don't have the serenity of Elizabeth Edwards," she gasps.

In comes the pouch of clear fluid imprinted with different words than the last, with new side effects which cruelly rob Mom of her one pleasure, that of rainbow sherbet. It now tastes like aluminum foil, she says.

We don't know what short-term memories she carries forward, so we start each day anew and let her do the tweaking.

If she says, "God, you kids told me that already!" we smile at her blessed impatience.

At times, she's so in the moment it's startling. She demands catheterization. The constant influx of intravenous fluids make her pee constantly.

"You just think you have to urinate, ma'am," the doctor insists.

"Sir, you try lifting up onto a bedpan. It's a mess," is how she dismisses him. "Intubate me!"

She mixes yesterday with today until even I'm confused, unsure how to help her find solid mooring. She greeted my arrival Tuesday afternoon with, "Oh my God, Barry, I had the most awful nightmare. In it I was full of cancer." I say or do nothing to remind her she is. "I was thirty-five, and you were just four," she continues. "I had cancer and I wouldn't be around for you kids." She sips from what I offer. "If this had to happen, let it be now."

Mostly, she is bewildered why her adult children are present, standing among tubes that beep if crimped or why oxygen has been plugged into her nostrils. We have brought effects to personalize the room and somehow ground her, but their appearance seems to further confuse, even irritate, her.

"I don't like you moving my things," she says hoarsely of a substantial peace lily she nurtured from a six-inch pot. "Put it back by the fireplace tools." I scoot it close to nutritive equipment that has joined the collection of medical paraphernalia. "There. That looks better. Thank you."

It is easier for us to believe the past grueling year of treatment have scrambled her brain. Nothing else can explain her nonchalance about slipping away without acknowledging her terminal illness to either of us. It doesn't make sense. How could she have not foreseen the gnawing guilt, the anger we would never be able to accept?

I AM quick to fulfill Mom's request. I recreate Tome Village in her room. With that 20 percent savings, I bring back to the hospital more lavish and varied supplies than I ever had as a kid: dried cattails, polished pebbles, acrylic beads, foam forms, clay and ribbons. I transform one corner of the hospital room in what looks a little like a daycare workstation: fabrics, rubber cement, crayons, art gum.

With the floor administrator's permission, I take down a dry erase board and a watercolor of a lighthouse. When I first unroll that oyster craft paper against a wall facing her bed, my mother's colorless lips raise in a smile. It is as much for me as it is her, this stylized alternate reality. In Tome Village, cancer doesn't suddenly spread to the esophagus, as hers does, and renal failure is a diagnosis their people, but not my mother, can genetically defy. My wish is to somehow animate it. My mother's dulled eyes still track movement, and if Tome Village actually bustles with productivity, it might hold her interest. So I construct some characters independent from the mural, of heavier card stock, so they can be moved around in forced, dimensional perspective. What I don't have I improvise, careful that it isn't too heavy. The women's bonnets are forged of white washcloths snagged off a hallway cart. Bendy straws simulated piping that pumps from the reservoirs bordering their town. Hut roofs are inverted Vs made of cafeteria toothpicks. My many suns have an undercoat of sugar granules. Crude, maybe, but the opposite ends of life's spectrum tend to be attracted to the same sparkly things. Each day brings a new, active feature. A village ceremonial dance. Or a crop of Sue Grafton mysteries, Mom's favorites, husked for harvest.

Not wanting to spend Mom's few lucid moments with my back to her, I do most of this work in the late hours, once the room is as quiet as it gets. The machinery makes very little noise, but the hospital staff makes a lot. Vitals are endlessly being taken. One nurse whispers sympathetically to me when I scowl at the intrusion: "A person has to check out of a hospital to get any quality rest."

I am concentrating on my handiwork when Ruthie's snoring

stops. When something like snoring stops in a hospital room, something with a direct correlation to breathing, you get anxious. I freeze. Please, not Ruthie, not on my watch.

She groggily asks, "That you, Olivia?"

"It's Barry, Ruthie. I tried not to wake you. Olivia went back to Mom's condo."

"Would you open my curtain so I can admire your painting?"

"All the way?"

"It makes the room feel full even when it's not."

She has forgiven my confrontation with Mom and my combativeness with her and happily tells me that she knew and liked "many of your type from my Avon days." She is mending from multiple surgeries, from what she calls "cherry picking."

"That's when they go in and take out individual tumors," she explains.

I flinch at the imagery: migrant workers in scrubs in bucket trucks grabbing at chicken fat.

Ruthie's recovery has been slowed by an allergic reaction, then a blood clot, but she is hopeful she'll be home by Labor Day.

Our watch is so relentless that Olivia and I gratefully latch on when levity, no matter how tiny, presents itself. We laugh at things we know better than to, like when I step out so Olivia can bathe Mom. Once finished, Olivia joins me in the hallway. "I'd forgotten how generational bikini waxes are."

I beg her please, go no further, but she's gotten this visual by the hairs not so short and refuses to stop.

"I lifted the covers and for a minute I thought Willie Nelson was hiding under there."

We are so doubled over we actually awaken Mom, who demands, "What's so hilarious? Don't make me come out there!"

I want to make up something and hear her laugh. Olivia and I always vied for her hearty laugh, not the courtesy laugh she used around Dad's business associates. Her real laugh represented approval, and more than ever, we both could use some affirmation that we are doing everything right.

I AM looking through the *New York* Olivia brought me from the gift shop, reckoning I might be homesick. I marvel at the photos, all sorts of people young and old dressing oddly just to be noticed. I wonder where this fun town is and how I can get there. It doesn't seem to be the same place I decamped to for ninety-hour workweeks.

From whatever dark, warm water she is sinking in, Mother bobs back up.

"Barry? You know what you have to do?"

I lay the magazine aside to join the neglected others, which neither of us can muster the energy to even finish the table of contents, much less completely read an article.

"What do I have to do, Mom?"

"You have to get the next one out of the way."

"Next one what?"

"The one after Andy. The Next One." I've never mentioned Jarod to her. "Only when you get that fellow out of the way will you recognize love again."

"What does love look like the second time?" I ask her.

"You're asking the wrong lady, honey. In youth, you want someone to build a life with. After fifty, you just want someone who can handle salt." Her smile is weak. "Your dad was it. Love is not the miracle. Lasting is."

Her meal has gone mostly untouched. I mindlessly comment on how tasty the chicken pot pie appears.

"Then eat it," Mom offers. "Order a second. Insurance will pay." She pauses. "It's pure shit that I won't be around to help you through your birthday."

"That's hard to hear."

"It's hard to say," she responds. "But not as hard as looking at that tight, angry mouth of yours."

"My partner, my dogs, now my only living parent? I can't be miffed? At all the things left unspoken?"

"It's all been said. I'm okay with this." She gestures with her chin. "You need to be okay with this. Listen to me."

I gulp.

"I don't want a pointless calling or to be shown."

"We know."

"I *do* want to be buried in my fur whatever-you-call-it."

"Shrug."

When she does, we laugh a little.

"You made me say that so you could do that!" I accuse her. "I'm glad you like the fur that much."

"I'd like to look nice when I see your father and Daisy again."

My throat constricts. I can't even gulp. This is going to get messy.

"Show it off to Andy too."

"Just imagine: I'll get to meet his mama."

And she falls back to sleep.

Mom, Mom, Mom, I think. *You're so wrong. You miscalculate that everything has been said and asked. Your death is imminent, and I need to know every truth before they die with you. Santa Claus, terminal illness, what else did you lie to us about? Should I search my birth certificate for white-out?*

The trivial: why did you not force me to play some sort of musical instrument? The sniveling: was it necessary to barter with me at sixteen that, if I wanted to borrow your car, I had to buy your Kotex, and did it have to be hospital-size? The shattering: did you cry in front of the doctor when told your cancer was terminal?

I have always wondered what Mom and Dad really thought of Andy. Did they think we'd last? Dad's remarks about Ted were mostly snarky speculation about his ample gut, or even a little competitive, the envy an older man has for the younger man's possibilities. I remember his observation at their wedding rehearsal dinner: "I just noticed how knock-kneed Ted is." Mom looked up from her vichyssoise to add, "With Livvie so pigeon-toed, any child they have will have to screw on its socks." But they were both grateful for the calming effect he had on Olivia.

If they thought Andy wouldn't age particularly well or couldn't tell a crackling story, if they mused who was the wife and who the husband without ever saying bottom or top, it was kept to themselves. They did not tread heavily on the queer issue; they probably thought it fraught. Dad never offered much except "Andy is like another son to me," which he also claimed of Ted.

Growing up without one made Andy blessedly clueless about Mom boundaries, so he treated mine like Jeanine, a friend. I skipped all that. I never had to pass muster with Andy's parents.

"Lucky you," he solemnized. "My dowry is that I essentially have no family, which means no in-laws, which means no reciprocal barbecues."

It didn't feel so lucky. It also meant that the Morgans would never plug the gaps of his childhood with unvarnished anecdotes. Whatever he shared was so self-sifted, everything just seemed to lead to the next thing, and life doesn't work that way.

I take my mother's hand. Her fingers, ringless, are like fireplace matches. I am afraid I'll break them.

I think about the secrets still being kept.

Like the Next One Mom never had, because Dad was *it*.

She actually had Simultaneous One. Dad wasn't *it*. There is the matter of August, or her extramarital fling with a man of that name, the affair only I knew she had when she was still working.

One weekend afternoon, when the phone rang, I had answered the upstairs extension, Mom down. She spoke a greeting first. I listened, careful not to breathe. This man's name was August, like the month. August asked what my mother was wearing. I wanted to jump in that it was something Diane Von Furstenberg licensed but would want no part of. August was worried Dad would find out, one hint that he's a friend or an associate of some sort. This was clearly a confirmation of a previously arranged rendezvous.

Maybe August was Gus, an installer Mom occasionally accompanied on larger projects. He had a German accent. This guy didn't. I hoped it wasn't Auggie, a jewelry store manager who always seemed to be staring at your watch or necklace. Worse yet, what if was that fellow known as Gusto, who'd opened squalid rent-to-own outlets after "sneaking in from Baltimore," the town criers sniffed.

Then August sang to her. He sang, "I dream of Jeannie with the light, brown...." I still cannot bring myself to repeat what of my mother's he described as light brown. What was said next was too nauseating to consider and too hideous to comprehend. I will only say August wanted to know if Mom was going to "treat him mean." Sexualizing a parent is uncomfortable enough. Knowing they are about to spend time in the arms of someone who's not your other parent is downright ugly.

Me, August, and Mean Jean all hung up.

Whoever Mom met that night, we were told she was going out with "S.J. and the girls, and I deserve it, so quit looking at me that way!"

One damage-intended blurt from the car backseat to my father would have altered family life forever. Cuckolded, and his kid knew it. Pride would have mandated a divorce with no retreat. I couldn't do that to the man who brought his oddball son drawing on cold basement walls a small space heater that glowed orange, who would then occasionally jog down to make sure neither I nor my drawing had ventured too close and caught fire. I was also shrewd enough to understand the adverse effect this would have on the comfortable life he provided. I didn't tattle and I never shared it with my older sister for fear it would become the crackling revelation in a contretemps with Mom.

Momless Andy didn't find much gravitas in it. This is what he said when I told him: "So the bitch had an itch." Then, more seriously, "Barry, obviously Jeanine needed something. Maybe this guy made her happy when your father couldn't. Who are you to judge? It didn't impact you."

But it did. It made an indelible impression on an adolescent boy who discovered his mother had unmet needs. Were there Madison County bridges or were they all trysts in tool sheds? What precipitated it and was it her first? Was he considerably younger? Was Mom, gulp, a MILF? Was S.J. as complicit as she was in covering up Mom's cancer? Was the relationship short-lived or did it endure into another decade?

These are a sampling of the questions I want to ask but won't, in the same way I had chosen not to pursue why Andy was where he was that day he was killed. Look for trouble and you will find it. A past employee of mine had installed spyware on her girlfriend's computer when she became suspicious of philandering. Then the girlfriend found it quarantined in a scheduled scan. The Trojan horse wasn't another woman; it was mistrust. They broke up. Andy and I knew each other's passwords. At any time, I could have signed onto any account to look for anything that portended disaster: other web identities, browser history, funky banking transactions, bookmarks, Mail Sent/Received/ Deleted. I didn't. Funny... I would have been the first to persuade a friend in a similar situation to root out the facts. I'd be Mr. Watson. I'd help sleuth and solve that mystery. Instead, I packed Andy's Mac into a travel valise, headed to the basement, and stowed it behind our furnace. Was it fear that a stored cookie might take me to MapQuest and a standing Saturday assignation with someone Andy needed? He was nearly the same age as Mom when she had her affair. I know I had been faithful, our own asterisk three-ways notwithstanding.

Did *my* bitch have an itch? I still don't really know what loose possessions were found on or around Andy. If among them was a questionable receipt, it had been hermetically sealed by the coroner as instructed. I didn't want my own Rosebud to ponder.

It wasn't just being Fernie's Secret Santa. If an imposter shared my life, he died unexpectedly, and that's that. I am more my father than I thought. We wouldn't have to forgive and forget what we never knew.

DEE and Potsy are en route when I contact them about Mom. I tell Dee to bring whatever transaction contracts are required to initiate the sale of my house.

"Are you sure?"

"I am several continents ahead of sure," I say, steadying her.

When they arrive, I'm glad to see they have also brought Kerrick. He and Dee have reconciled. She has, in fact, helped him buy Gyrate. Owner Joey skipped town when his liquor distributor threatened to break a bone for every bottle he hadn't paid for.

"If you take that literally, factor in each individual bottle of beer, and that the human body has 206 bones, the collection thugs would have to break each of his bones in several places," Kerrick explains.

This acquisition, Dee says, will represent an ancillary business. It will be called Party with Kerr. The main level will essentially remain a dance bar; the upper will become a banquet and dining room for private events.

"What about the denturelier?" I ask.

Dee cradles her forehead.

"I moved it to the entryway." Kerrick beams. "I had it refitted as a fountain."

"The water is blue, so it seems like the mouths of several Osmonds are rinsing and spitting," Potsy adds.

"If there's anything you need, please call Isaac," I offer.

"I'm on the lookout for a real electric chair."

Dee and Potsy gasp.

"Deactivated, of course," he adds.

"We don't canvas penitentiaries, so the chances are slim." I chuckle, imagining how Isaac will react. But I'm proud of Kerrick. His waitstaff might arrive looking like they just wriggled out of Comic-Con and he really could use a little less reverence for the early film work of John Waters and try to get more in touch with what Ivanka Trump would appreciate, but he is, unapologetically, what he is.

Potsy wants to paint Mom's nails an iridescent pink. Now that morphine has stopped working, Mom is barely alert from the injections of Dilaudid and Demerol, but my hope is, when she wakes, she'll register that our loving ministrations aren't limited to drawing ice chips across her lips.

I skim over most of my confrontation with Jarod but try to place blame equally. "He was Lance Armstrong, Andy Warhol, Gloria Allred, Harvey Milk, Ringo Starr, and Larry Kramer before I finally lost count. He could stump the panel for the entire half hour of *What's My Line*."

Kerrick nods. "You passed to Arlene."

"He doesn't know who Arlene was." I pause. "I have lived over 16,000 days to his 8,500. He has so many false starts and victories, setbacks and reversals ahead. Now *is* the time for him to try it all, do it all."

"Just not on *your* time," Dee observes.

Right, I agree. "As he marches, I'd be the one looking for a hand rail."

Potsy looks up from the tray he's preparing. "You just can't trust someone who's never chewed FreshenUp gum."

"Never mind *me* thinking I'm Stan," I say. "Jarod thinks I'm Stan, which is so much worse."

"And that mother of his holds the patent on cunt," Kerrick offers.

Dee nudges Potsy. "Tell Barry about your Tinker Toy Dumbass."

"That's what she calls the Log Cabin Republican he hooked up with at the bathhouse," Kerrick says.

"Pots? A Republican? You even *dress* to the left!" I exclaim.

"Potsy is dating a man who doesn't believe there's a hole in the ozone layer," Dee adds disdainfully.

"Bathhouse sex isn't much of a 'Meet Cute' courtship to tell your grandchildren," I point out, "unless your grandchildren are the Kardashian girls. You've always said your perfect boyfriend had to hate everyone and everything you do."

"He's not perfect, he's not my boyfriend," Potsy says, blowing on Mom's nail, "but he *is* my age."

Dee shook her head. "He's an ass."

"*He's* the elephant, *I'm* the ass," Potsy said. "We masterdebate each other."

Their banter now has no rancor. It's comfortable, safe. Still, Potsy doesn't shy from gallows humor. He gestures to Mom.

"How is your Aunt Sarajane going to compete? Terminal illness is hard to top."

He caps the nail polish, having even carefully double-coated the pulse oximeter on my mother's finger, which will displease the on-duty RN and Blue Cross.

I don't think Dee has ever looked so beautiful. Her hair is held back by sunglasses and she's in a sundress the color of lemon curd. I tap her foot with mine. "And you?"

Dee moves her chair closer, until our knees collide. "Alone, never lonely, busy enough, always ready."

I sign, initial, date, and surrender the final document.

A GROUP of Bright Spotters have come to visit. Olivia fluffs our mother's wig and powders her face as I warn these women in the lobby the fast toll the cancer has taken. They form a circle around her. Mom's eyes become active beneath closed lids. I hear prayer. Olivia's head is yanking insistently to one side. She either wants a word with me or daily exposure to Mom revived her tic from a thirty-five-year dormancy.

As we excuse ourselves, one BSer notes cheerily, "The room will be a little less bright without those beautiful smiles." The only way we were smiling is if we were standing on our heads.

Down the hall, Olivia blurts, "My God, Barry, do you recognize Mrs. Hasewinki?"

I didn't, but I sure knew the name. "Which one?"

"The one with the obvious bone loss," Olivia said.

"That poor old hunched-up thing? I thought she was looking for something she'd dropped. That's Crystal Hasewinki?"

She and husband Abel once owned Winky's, a cafeteria where Olivia and I both worked when Mom decided jobs were in order. Dad had protested to let us enjoy our summer but Mom, as usual, won. Olivia was proud of conquering her eating disorder and eager to show off by carrying food all day as a waitress. I inquired if I could greet-and-seat. Guiding patrons to a booth with an unctuous smile seemed as perfect a fit as the seersucker vest I mentally selected I'd wear most of the time. Crystal Hasewinki announced that hostessing was a position reserved for older gals with feet too flat for waitressing. I was told I'd need a clean white shirt and handed a gray Rubbermaid tub. I was to be the Winky's busboy.

"Mrs. Hasewinki seemed ancient. She must've been, at best, fifty," I say.

The BSers, after their short visit, speak to us about a public gesture they have in mind. Olivia and I exchange looks that declare don't you dare laugh. We give our permission.

We return to sit with Mom. We still have Winky's on the brain.

"Do you think the Hasewinkis ever found out about The Wart?" I speculate.

This about does Olivia in.

"The Wart! The Wart!"

I hadn't thought of the mythological wart in years.

To expedite orders at Winky's, a basic dinner salad was prepared by quickly dipping a wood bowl into a lined trashcan of chopped iceberg, carrot and red onion. Servers then plopped pink and tasteless hothouse tomato slices atop it. Plastic gloves were considered wasteful, so at the end of a shift servers still had bits of radish caught in their rings, under the nails. Since we were already violating every basic tenet of food prep and handling, Olivia didn't think twice about applying Compound W on a wart as big as a thumbtack head, wrapping it tightly with a Band-Aid, and clocking in at Winky's. Soonafter, she was paralyzed by panic.

"Barry, my Band-Aid came off when my hand was down in the salad mosh pit! Help me find it!"

I only had to toss this massive salad for a minute or two until I lifted out the limp, flesh-colored strip.

"Found it!" I announced.

"Thank God thank God thank God," Olivia chanted.

"Liv... the wart isn't in it." I ran to the small window of the pass-through door adjoining the main dining room. "Which are your tables?"

"Every one of them. I've been helping all the girls," she moaned.

I quickly enlisted others working the floor for an immediate game of 'Find The Choking Patron, Find The Wart'. I remind them about the workplace safety poster and to specifically refresh themselves on the Heimlich Maneuver.

As I stalked the booths, I overheard three widows heatedly debating. Dizzied by the cumulous cloud of something Estee Lauder, I watched one of them pass my sister's discolored and puckered wart, impaled on the tines of her fork, to another.

"I say it's an albino caper."

"More like a chickpea."

"It's a little crouton."

"Whatever it is, why would you get one and not us?"

Thank God for lettuce envy. I snatched the fork my sister's wart was impaled upon and then, for good measure, the woman's salad bowl.

"But that didn't get you fired. What did?" I try to remember.

"It was that creep I refused to serve."

I look at her blankly.

"The one who ordered Beef Strokemeoff!"

Now I remember. "He had a cleft-palate, Liv. You misunderstood. He was humiliated when you reported him."

"I know what I heard."

"I hated the lunch crowd the most."

"Me too. None of the maroons could even pronounce quiche. It was quinch. Or they'd overcompensate and call it kee-shay like touché," Olivia says. "My favorite was quickie. 'I'll have that Quickie Florentine.' How quick, sir? Should I run?"

Night closes in. As though over a campfire—without the flashlights under our chins, the campfire being our inert mother—we deconstruct and reconstruct. Our entire upbringing, it seems, can be condensed into one-word shout-outs. Two words, if you precede it with The, which sounds definitive and elegant, like The Wart.

We talk about The Telescope: the expensive Christmas gift that fell apart, then how Mom burnt dinner while angrily looking for the receipt.

The Reunion: a drunken family get-together that ended with a second cousin intentionally hitting ping-pong balls, quite hard, at people, and how one uncle suffered grave injuries after being flung from a rented mechanical bull.

The Red Fire truck. It was as reliable as Andy's Christmas cockatiel spiel. Hard times filled the calendar of Dad's upbringing. When he was seven, his favorite toy, a red fire truck, went missing at Christmas. He tore the house apart, emptied the toy box, frantic. Come Christmas morning, he opened his one gift. It was a red fire truck. It was the *same* red fire truck. The red was slightly different and had gotten on the tires. A dalmation had been glued to the back to differentiate it, but its size was out of proportion, like a spotted mutant terrorizing a fire run, Dad said. That's when he stopped believing in Santa's workshop, or at least the painting prowess of his elves. It was sadder each time he told it and it beat anything by Truman Capote about Sook and Buddy all to hell.

"Don't forget Dad and The Tool Kit," Olivia prompted.

After earning it in some incentivized sales contest, Dad began fancying himself a handyman. The Tool Kit was orange and tremendous. Even Dad strained carrying it, but carry it he did, since it came with the self-imposed tax of fixing everything. Our poor house endured so much. Turning on the fan he painstakingly installed himself brought most of our den ceiling down. He'd tinker with or rewire a faulty appliance until Mom replaced it, afraid of what he'd done. Adjusting the settings on the water heater, he somehow flooded the crawlspace. Mom finally spirited The Tool Kit away and bought our father a shredder. Satisfied to reduce a lifetime of hoarded receipts and warranties and policies into dingy noodles, he never touched an Allen wrench again. The Tool Kit, I told Olivia, was still in my garage somewhere. Mom had insisted I take possession of it when she downsized to a condominium in the same compound her sister lived in.

"Quick. What was Dad's all-time favorite movie?" I challenge.

"*Animal House*. Go figure," Olivia giggles.

Much is irretrievably gone. Complete years, inaccessible, a void. We can't access Mom's archives, "the family Jeanie-ologist," she called herself whenever we'd inquire or disagree about our upbringing or relatives. On which side of the sink in our kitchen was the garbage disposal?

"Honestly, I don't remember."

"Me either. It's nice, not remembering things together," Olivia reflects.

Finally, we realize we didn't even have a garbage disposal.

No, Olivia, it wasn't Old Lady Fuller who kept our badminton shuttlecocks when it soared over her hedge, it was Bird Legs Cunningham.

"How about The Clothesline? Hanging stuff in back of our house?" I prompt Olivia. That's where delicates were taken, next to a flower garden so that, as they dried, they absorbed their fragrance.

"We'd haul out that jambox while Mom hung up things," Olivia jumps in.

"She'd put clothespins on the ends of her fingers and clack them together like castanets," I add.

Olivia harrumphs. "Talons."

"We'd dance, we'd spin."

"We'd go inside smelling like lavender."

"Remember how that butterfly got trapped inside one of Mom's bras? She went to put it on the next morning, and talk about scream! Dad laughed and told her to enjoy it," I say.

"I've always had a clothesline," Olivia confides.

I smile. "Us too."

We trade faded Polaroids without anything changing hands.

How Olivia pulled a pack of cigarettes and a Playboy lighter from one of Santa's pockets as she was photographed on his lap.

How I went through a period of carrying around one of Dad's retied briefcases, stuffed with Archie comics. (I still maintain Jughead is gay with that notice-me-but-don't crown.)

Olivia spoke of her fascination with Mom's deodorant, called Tussy, that she would creep in at night to stare at what she was sure was a naughtily named vaginal spray.

We both knew which book Dad had hollowed out to hide a loaded gun, but we never opened it.

How, when Mom went on a tirade, our father would often respond to her pointed questions by repeating it exactly back without the punctuation.

We confess. I stole her *Official Preppy Handbook* from her room and appropriated her Aigner stickpin. She taped bottles of water to her shins under her wide-wale cords during therapist weigh-ins, when every gained ounce was a victory.

"This all makes me sorry Nina doesn't have a brother to support her through the hard times she'll have someday," Olivia says, yawning.

"What time do Nina and Ted get here tomorrow?"

"Depends on traffic." Olivia sniffles. "We should've had another child."

When she offers up nothing else, I know she is asleep.

IT IS past 2:00 a.m. when I drive back to the condo in Mom's Cadillac. I've been in Manhattan not even eight months, and already it's jarring to see no honking cabs, to pass businesses that darken for a respectable twelve hours, to marvel at how many gasoline stations people have access to.

Pressing through AM, I hear Styx twice, on separate stations. From the tubercular sound quality, AM is where The Drilled and Notched albums came to roost. I come upon shouting, as though someone with Tourette Syndrome has broken into a sound booth. I don't know much about the Fairness Doctrine but I wonder if any Scariness Doctrine applies to local talk radio. It is probably a good thing the streets of the town I grew up in are deserted; the call-ins send me into road rage. When I hear the name of Senator Marianna Pugh orgasmically bandied, I turn the radio off. No wonder I love show tunes. They are the only sane antidote to this mush-mouthed ignorance.

Hearing it is a tart reminder why I chose a university outside the state. That day at the crafts store, stacking what would become Tome Village at the checkout, a woman behind me had loudly marveled, "I ain't never seen a man in here before, much less with coupons." For a second, I felt the same shame when, as a teenager, I bought ostrich feathers and ting-ting grass. *You little queer.* It was the kind of indignity I'd kept quiet when I was growing up, convinced I'd somehow be faulted for bringing them on. Mom and Dad had their hands full with Olivia's empty stomach, shuttling her between a psychiatrist and a nutritionist.

Shit like that is why I outran my zip code. Even if Andy and I hadn't happened, I still never would have returned here, not to apprentice at Mom's floor-covering show world, at the owner's grandiose invitation.

It would be easy to rejigger the town I grew up in as something out of *The Last Picture Show*, but it never had that panoramic artistry. It's just drab, flat. It's been a very long time since I've explored it, but one of the BSers had boasted of their latest citation, so I divert to look. The street name is familiar, but most of the homes have no exterior lighting, so I can't see physical addresses. I give up.

I pass the scene of The Wart. Where Winky's was has been split into an ethnic beauty supply outlet and a Planned Parenthood. The movie theater is still across the street, but what was once a place has been split, too, into four screens. I hate the digitized marquees. After a Thursday night shift at Winky's on Thursday night, we'd wait for Dad to pick us up over here, watching grouchy employees pile the alphabet on the sidewalk. Down this same street is the ice cream shop where Mom, watching Olivia go from pudgy to barely budgey, secretly had yogurt scooped onto Olivia's cone. It is still here, once independent, now franchised.

This makes me hungry. I grab one of the empty bags from the floor, the fast food Olivia and I have been subsisting on. Seven cold french fries in a state of petrification drop out. I am not ashamed that I eat them.

I pass the empty lot, smaller than I remember, where the county fair was held, where those three kids became airborne. The grocery they crashed into has been gone a long time.

This next corner, yet another empty lot, is where the town's tallest building once was. It now provides space to county agencies. I remember our parents shaking us awake and herding us into the car. The tallest building in town was burning. They took us to watch the unstoppable flames as we sipped chocolate milk in our pajamas. I'd never seen water shot so high and for so long. When the ash settled like black potato chips on our hood, Dad exclaimed worriedly how he just had the car Simonized, and we left. The lesson of that night, I can't figure. Maybe how temporary everything is, how things we admire can tumble. Buildings fall. Cranes too. Maybe Mom and Dad just liked big fires. The only thing absent was Miss Peggy Lee.

A large moth joins the humid paste of insects on the windshield. I am reminded of Andy's caterpillars. I'm also reminded of my intent to have this car detailed for Nina and Ted to drive back. Mom wants them to have it. "Teddy's in outside sales, and it's a good fit for him." I knew from Olivia's polite refusals that she was actually pleased.

I drive by my grade school, that Land of Broken Capillaries where the chatter of children was drowned out by the sound of the tenured staff dragging their barnacles along hallway walls. The façade has barely changed. This is where Olivia and I spent our deformative years. How fitting that I made a career out of an elementary school I bought, refashioning seven dreadful years into a domestic domicile. I remember Nancy, my only real friend, our bond forged from the humiliation of never being chosen when teaming for recess kickball. Nancy's exclusion was understandable. She was missing her right leg. Her father had backed over it when she was playing in their driveway. Unbelievably, everyone, even teachers, called her Peg. A prosthetic left her with a horrendous gait that bystanders would move a silent distance from. Sometimes it froze. She'd make a casual fist to hit the knee like you hit a salad dressing bottle for the last dollop. When we had a fire drill, it was single file, everyone pushing. I was right behind her when her leg snapped off. Peg went down hard on her stump and rolled all the way down cement steps. They got her out onto the hopscotch grid, somewhat fittingly, where against chain link we watched her fit her leg back on her, and God! I wanted that leg to rear up, to take on a life all its own and stomp the stupidity out of everyone. What an extra-delicious *Afterschool Special* it would have made.

Mom saw her, years later, coming out of a check-cashing store. Peg had a little girl—red curls, just like her—and a wedding ring.

"So she'll never be a Rockette. She soldiered on," she said admiringly.

I cross railroads tracks in terrible disrepair. I hope the innards of the car don't spill themselves. These are the tracks I would walk, after dinner, looking for God knows what.

Jesus, what's that smell? I am not just on the wrong side of the tracks, I'm on the wrong side of the landfill. No Bright Spots here, just Dim Stains.

Among a spooky crisscross of dead ends and one-ways and unresolved potholes, I realize that the maintenance hub for city vehicles I just passed was once the hilly field where my permanently confused Grandmother Lola, seventy-seven years old, in a thin dress both backward and inside out, was found fetal-like and dead of hypothermia in a snowy indentation in the earth on Christmas Day. The temperature had dropped to a low of eight degrees, and several groups of searchers had fanned out, but it was a father taking his two young sons out with their new sled who first saw the black felt eyes of a Santa slipper protruding from several inches of fresh snow in a ravine. When he went to pull it out, a foot was still in it. It was as shocking then as it is now, but somehow inevitable, given her propensity for roaming into the center of night.

I pass the general area where her assisted living unit was. It too is gone.

I am within blocks of the house I grew up in. Mom said our old neighborhood had changed. Clotheslines are strung from necessity now. She's right. Even the fire hydrants look condemned. Yet the contours of familiar avenues and roads are all different, a lane added here, parallel parking where there was no parking at all.

You can't go home again, not if you can't find the fucking street, Mr. Wolfe.

This is something else I am getting used to. Andy and his uncanny GPS never made a wrong turn. I seem to make nothing but.

LAST night's sentimental glow has been doused. I arrive back midmorning to relieve my sister. She is crying so hard in the hallway she has the hiccups and is hyperventilating.

There has been a setback. Not with Mom. With Olivia.

Once I determine Mom hasn't died, I wonder if I should scare Olivia first, then get the paper bag, or let her regulate her breathing before screaming "Boo!"

"Mom told me that she hated me."

Olivia was wrapping a scarf around our mother's prominent neck bones and clavicle when she heard Mom say, "I hate you."

She is convinced of it.

I reason with Olivia. "Mothers may not like their children very much, but they don't hate them." The sentence, I continue, was obviously severed by a fresh surge of narcotics. The missing second half was "… both are going through this. Or "… will have to watch me die."

Olivia tries to belch, then inhales. "We've always been so *Terms of Endearment*."

I try to roll my eyes from the insides. "Except you had a brother and a father, we don't know any astronauts, and you're not the one dying. Stop this."

Olivia wails that the drugs are acting as a truth serum. Mother *did* despise her.

"She's hated me from the get-go. It started with The Tooth. Daisy would never have been so thoughtless as to be born with a fang."

I'd hoped we skimmed past this passage in our verbal memoir of the night before, but Olivia's discovered the index. This was an unhappy chapter: The Tooth, which led to the page-turning sequel, The Fistfight.

Olivia was born with a fully emerged and sharp front tooth. The Tooth represented an obvious hardship to a nursing mother. Because Olivia could bloody Mom's nipples within seconds, breastfeeding was abandoned, withholding what Olivia decided was critical, tactile stimulation, "not to mention natural immunities. Is it any wonder I was so sickly?"

The Tooth would drop out at five months, but Mom's stories of smearing Vaseline on the tips of her breasts, covering them with what amounted to medicated pasties, lingered way past lactation. She shared it like a no-fail recipe with her dental hygienist, her Scrabble partner. No one knew how it bothered Olivia until she was sixteen and the Bertellinis moved in across the street. Olivia heard Mom tell Mrs. Bertellini over iced tea about her Cyclopean baby tooth. For an extra laugh, Olivia claimed that Mom added, "And it was crooked!" My sister burst into the room. "Goddamn it, Mom, I wish it had been a whole set!" In front of a young mother who probably wondered what kind of neighborhood they'd chosen to raise their family in, Olivia then struck Mom with an open palm. Mom hit her back with a closed one.

This became known as The Fistfight (and, after separating them, the last time Sandra Bertellini was in our home).

"Livvie, Mom loved The Tooth. Other moms at a Longaberger party would relive walking the floor with colicky infants, and she could gloat, 'Girls, get a load of this story!'"

"And look what became of me," Olivia complains. "Mom's kept me in the time-out chair my entire life. I just wish she could acknowledge she did a lousy job."

"Have you done such a superior job with your daughter?"

Olivia is jolted. "What?"

"People are flawed. Mom was domineering, Dad was passive, but it was no *Running with Scissors*!"

"Who wouldn't develop an eating disorder when Mom constantly apologized for my weight by saying 'Livvie's just big for twelve'? And they locked *you* in the basement with crayons! You call our upbringing normal?"

"Mostly, yes! Don't get all revisionist. I was queer and lonely. You were weird and hungry. It wasn't nature *or* nurture. *We're* the ones who cultivated our abnormalities. Remember how we wrote CP on our palms for Cootie Protection in case anyone undesirable came into contact with us? *We* were the ones with the cooties, Livvie."

"Don't say I had cooties."

I take a breath. "Mom had a conference with my fourth grade teacher, Mrs. Hartman. After she filled Mom in how I held a flower and recited a poem like Henry Gibson did on *Laugh-In*, plus talked too much about Liberace and his dancing waters, she presented a movie still confiscated from under the lid of my desk. I'd taped it there. It was Sean Connery in that peculiar Borat sling from the movie *Zardoz*."

"You know this how?"

"Mom told Dad. I heard her. She was angry. You see, our mother was also informed I was sure to wind up a hairdresser or a suicide." I pause. "I'm still unclear which to Mrs. Hartman was worse."

Olivia lowers her head. "I do not want to fight about who didn't fit in the most."

"Me either. Let's just be honest here: you and I, we came with disclaimers. Mom and Dad did their best, like you've done your best. Home was safe."

Olivia nods. "This is why I wish Nina wasn't an only child. Everyone needs someone like you to talk sense into someone like me, especially when I'm all menopausal."

The arrival of Ted and Nina cheer her. It has taken them both awhile to finalize work and school obligations so that their stay could be open-ended, i.e. staying through the funeral. I expected Nina to be a Death Eater with mascaraed clots of sleep in her eyes, and she is. She's also instantly engaging and funny. In the hallway, Olivia and I warn her and Ted that Mom is especially fitful and might not be responsive. She might not even recognize them, nor they her, her weight loss is so drastic.

The coming together of grandmother and grandchild is bumpy. When Olivia whispers, "Your namesake is here," Mom's eyes pop open, and she rasps, "My name isn't Je-nine-ugh."

Nina crouches. "Hi, 'eenie." That's what she always called Mom. She'd intuited early that Mom might leave her in a dingo's care if she called her Grandma, but she had trouble with J's, so it was 'eenie. It stuck. I always thought Mom would have ultimately preferred Grandma.

Nina squeezes her eyes shut. "'eenie, I'm visualizing your cancer exiting your body."

We all do our best to visualize, but it's hard to ignore the claustrophobic stink, the metal, the cleansers, the disinfecting detergent embedded in the sheets. Those are the things no bedside vigil in a movie, no matter how stark or handheld, can impart. When my cell phone rings in my workout bag, I leave them.

It is Artie, a welcome break. Theatregoing dwindles in the summer. Several productions had closed after the Tonys—*My Bad Luck* fulfilled its destiny, winning none and losing multiple pensions— and so my absence has been easy to absorb. My offer to resign was pooh-poohed by Marjorie, who appointed Artie interim me. Artie tells me Theatrilicious is in receipt of a declaration from our chief distributor. We're being bumped to COD terms starting October 1. Artie clearly doesn't grasp the implication of this or he wouldn't be asking, "What do you think that means?"

COD means we're DOA. On-premise funds won't begin to satisfy their extended palm, which will, of course, be joined by others, a fan of hands. The noose tightens. I let Artie chatter on, concluding with him saying, "You know those bizarre mini-moans Marjorie lets out sometimes? Those 'umphs' we thought were disapproval? We're convinced she has a slave midget under her cape, standing on her shoes and sucking on her clit nonstop. We miss you."

I miss them. I even miss Floor 14. Maybe he's grown unkempt in my absence.

I take from my bag and sort accumulated mail forwarded by my building super and from Artie. He inadvertently included a registered, hand-addressed letter intended for Marjorie. *Urgent Action Needed*, it is marked. After our conversation, opening it, much less taking urgent action, is needless. This is show biz. We're a stale vaudeville act and we've gotten the hook. I go to my own. In with Teste's habitually tardy rent check—he always adds the late fee, even after I told him it was unnecessary—is a gleeful sidebar. His drag queen cursive is a lot like he talks, breathless dashes and conclusions drawn that have no grounding in reality. He has had three dates with Captain Reg. Cocktailed optimist that he is, they are officially a couple. They are probably registered with Payless Shoes and Orvis. Teste has taken a sabbatical from drag, at Captain Reg's request. This isn't capitulation, he reasons, but compromise; Captain Reg promised to keep Wessie submerged, and Teste is now going by Len. TesteLen is now working at a local male-only resort. I know the place: clothing-optional, shared baths, and room doors left purposefully ajar. TesteLen writes that he's had pink eye three times already, probably from handling the laminated day-pass cards, and you'd better already have a condom already up your ass if you sit anywhere, he concludes.

And the world goes 'round, I think. At least according to Kander and Ebb.

I call Raoul at home. He's surprised to hear from me. He'd heard I was globe hopping. Something like that, I tell him. He's even more surprised that I want to make a sizable investment in something called Theatrilicious.

"No," I explain, "it's not a start-up. It's more me putting the foot on the accelerator."

"It doesn't sound like this car has gas," Raoul warns, after I brief him on what I know about Marjorie's pitiful financial profile.

"I'll be the gas," I say. "And the battery. And the tires."

"What's your endgame?"

"Endgame what?"

"Is this a hostile takeover?"

"More a benevolent pitch-in."

Yes, I'm of perfectly sound mind, I reassure him. God help me, am I really considering getting into bed with Marjorie Lewis-Kohl? I rationalize that at least it already has the dust ruffle. Of course, she's wearing it. But I can't stand by and watch Theatrilicious, another touchstone in my life, trickle away to, at best, an eBay shop because of ignorance and negligence.

Mom would have admonished, "You have little to gain and an awful lot to lose."

I can also hear her placative, "But you'll be fine."

When I return to the room, Nina is alone with Mom, who is sleeping.

"Willy and Linda Loman went to the cafeteria," Nina whispers.

I take a seat. I'm glad she knows *Death of a Salesman*, sad she feels that way about her parents. She reminds me of Mom, except for the metal adorning an eyebrow. "Appreciate them while you got them." I say this softly. I don't think she heard, but she nods, then offers me some of the edamame she's munching. I decline.

I think about Luke, Alexander, and Mindy and how stifling their home was with shame, punishment, and lies; I think about Jarod and his senator mother who craved world domination; I think about my own, blessedly content to just dominate our household.

Nina puts on glasses that I notice are just frames, no lenses. She is studying Tome Village. "This is really good, Uncle Barry."

In a moonlight diffused by the shades, she sniffs one of my El Markos. I pretend not to notice when she puts it into her schmatte pocket.

SARAJANE arrives at the hospital for her shift with a stocking cap for Mom, which we're sure she originally knit as a cozy for a cookie jar. She draws close to show Mom photographs she's brought in her purse, the kind of evidence children pore over to verify if their elders ever looked or acted young. We recognize a few our mother also had duplicates of, like their stern mother, Lola, in a housedress she'd cut the belt and belt loops off of, and their father, Ernest, stout and sour.

"They couldn't even smile for their anniversary photo?" I wonder.

"Daddy was an honorable man, keeping his head down, loving us girls from his own distance," Sarajane says.

"Sometimes I wasn't even sure if he lived at home or just slept there for appearances," Mom comments.

"He worked in a pulley factory, and the metal shavings would work their way into his shoes, which scratched our wood floors, which enraged Lola," Sarajane remembers. "She castrated him into an empty place setting at our supper table."

"Daddy deserved better," Mom weakly manages.

Sarajane shakes her head. "How'd this get in here?"

We come closer. It is her husband, before drinking carried him away and she had the bastard legally declared dead.

"Did you ever find out what became of him?" Olivia asks.

Sarajane says yes but nothing else.

Other photographs we've never seen. We're in thrall. They're like movie publicity stills from scenes didn't that make the final cut. The people are familiar, the situation isn't. Olivia especially studies one of our aunt and our mom, escorted on a double-date by a couple of cheapos, we are told.

"How pretty the both of you were," Olivia murmurs.

Mom locks eyes with her sister. "I was prettier. Everyone thought you looked like Eleanor Roosevelt."

Sarajane meets her gaze. "You never had a waist."

Here's Mom and Sarajane, quite young, feeding a small, hairless robin, abandoned or lost, with an eyedropper. Whatever became of that little guy, Mom asks. Photographic proof that it outgrew and left its shoebox had been lost long ago, but Sarajane assures her it had thrived.

"You keep scrapbooks?" Mom asks us both.

In unison, we say we do. Olivia mentions a scrapbooking group she had belonged to until she'd either lost interest or her glue stick.

"Kids today, though, not so much," she adds. "They put their pictures and music on a keychain."

"Flash drive," S.J. clarifies, surprising us both.

Mom stops focusing. We assume she's upright but going back to sleep. This is common. I've returned to inking in the details of a farmer steering a wheelbarrow of books when Mom points at Tome Village, to the free-range llamas I drew on the roads, and says, "I miss my critters."

The feeders are constantly refilled and the slime is being scrubbed from the birdbath, I assure her.

"I love those birds but not crazylove, not the way Georgia Gould on Snapdragon Lane is. She keeps a mynah on her shoulder. She's got bloody pecks on her neck and ears! She calls them kisses." All three of us know Mrs. Gould passed away three years ago. "S.J., it's going to be tough to lure my outside friends to your lanai. Rufous hummers are especially territorial. And don't forget green apples for the winter."

Sarajane says yes to all of it.

"Animals, so fickle. They love whoever feeds them. Hayley loves you now because you give her tupper."

"You mean supper, Mom."

"I mean tupper. Call it that," Mom says firmly. "Tupper. Hayley says it that way too. Morning meal or night, that's her tupper."

I smile indulgently. I called my dogs puppets.

"I miss my little girl. Do you think Hayley misses her mommy?"

Of course, I tell her.

I didn't come through for the little newsstand girl, I struck out on Luke, I can't fix Mom, but I can make sure she sees Hayley.

When I ask, Mom's primary physician replies that domesticated animals pose an infectious threat to a body weakened by chemo and immunosuppressant drugs. I know that the HIV/AIDS-infected are dissuaded from puppies and kittens under six months because of a bug they may carry. I reason that Hayley is over seven, "which is actually like fifty, in dog years."

The doctor interrupts me. This is not the first time a patient, family member, or an enlisted veterinarian has asked, he explains rigidly. The answer has to be no.

"Even if a child with leukemia wanted to see their—?"

"No."

I remembered Dr. Steve once, over salads after gay tennis, talking about the recuperative power of animals he'd observed in his practice. My mother can't be healed by Hayley, but I call him anyway. He is immediately peeved by the uninformed thinking I encountered. I hold the phone out as his tone rises, knowing he will speed-dial his anger management guru after this.

"Anecdotally, spending time with your pet can be as powerful as medical treatment," Dr. Steve says tightly. "Tell that insensitive asshole that Christiana Hospital in Delaware *prescribes* in-room pet visits. Other hospitals have volunteers who care for the pets of patients. Anything that can reduce stress benefits recovery."

He offers to fax literature from the American Humane Association and CDC guidelines about pet-to-human disease transmission. I gratefully request he do so immediately, because there's not much time. Stoicism from attending so much death seamlessly glides him into a general, sympathetic wish for my sister and me. It's a strange conceit doctors have: focusing on treatment yet able to shrug off an unpleasant outcome.

The faxes arrive, so many an office clerk seizes power and charges me two bucks "for the paper."

My mother's doctor firmly says, "The answer is still no. It's way… way… *way* too risky."

He overshot his wad with that third "way."

I tip off Ruthie, who thinks she still might be allergic unless she'd outgrown it. She takes two Benadryl in advance.

Hayley is thankfully compliant when, after seeing that asshole's car gone from his assigned space, I smuggle her into the hospital within a workout bag.

I am as thankful to the aide in the hallway who hears and ignores the small yips from the bag as I measure my pace toward 2012.

I place Hayley, freed, on the bed.

Her foxlike face sniffs Mom's hand. She immediately lies down.

Seeing this is worth the heart palpitations and feeling like Jane Fonda in *Julia*.

I take Mom's hand to Hayley's head, which bobs with joy at the reunion.

"Will you please raise my Hayley?" Mom asks.

Hayley and I have mostly considered each other like two gunslingers on an endless final draw. I don't know that I want another dog, ever, and not someone else's.

"Livvie would, but Nina has that psycho cat she named Punjab—Punjab!—who would probably rape her," Mom whispers.

"Sarajane probably expects to take her," I say gently.

"No way. Hayley will end up walking backwards too."

"Hayley won't be enamored with a world view limited to an eighteenth-story window."

"She's easy! She likes people food. You should see her chew a piece of gum."

This, I've learned. Mom had said Hayley would steal my heart, but so far, all she's stolen is my breakfast cruller.

"If only I could see my little girl again," she then says, forgetting Hayley is right there on the bed, belly up. "Please, please, please take care of her," she mumbles.

My eyes flood but do not spill. "Of course I will."

I can't describe any more of this.

THE room is now a single. Ruthie was discharged an hour ago. Her belief is that she is in official remission.

Her daughter sadly confides in me that no, she isn't.

A secret, being kept. Parent protects child, child protects parent, no matter the eventual ramifications.

Ruthie wobbles to Mom's bedside. She looks alien to me in a cerise pantsuit after being covered to the chin most of the time.

"Jeanie, you've gone all Moms Mabley on us," Ruthie whispers.

It's true. With her partial plates removed, Mom's gaunt face is in final deflation.

Ruthie kisses her forehead. I can barely stand the recoil when she realizes how cold it is. I hear her say, "I'll see you soon, Jeanie."

I can't describe any more of this, either.

THIS is very bad. I am sure each labored breath is Mom's last. When her vital signs are checked by the on-duty doc, we are asked, "Are you both in agreement as her medical proxies?"

Olivia can't bring herself to say it, so I do.

"DNR."

Damn you, Andy, for not being here to steady me through a Do Not Resuscitate order for my own mother. This late in August is not so far from my birthday. Damn you, Andy. I hate you for making me this selfish.

I glance at Tome Village. Gunmetal-gray moonlight has generated a spotlight around one of my male villagers. His hand is raised, not in buoyant welcome but in resigned farewell.

I know I didn't draw him waving.

I approach the mural. It appears something was crudely erased from his grasp and manipulated into this wave.

"I didn't draw you waving," I tell him.

When Olivia asks what I am talking about, when the doctor asks who is waving, Mom's life ends.

We don't hear a death rattle or a spastic grasp of the bedrails. Mom goes quietly. It's a first. She sure never did before.

In less than one hour, the medical equipment is redirected elsewhere. I watch the bed being efficiently stripped. Like I'm listening to a garden seashell for the echo of her take-no-prisoners affection, I lay my head against Mom's cold pillow.

Chapter Twenty-One

Daisy and Oscar

WE FOLLOW the stiff bank attendant down a marble hallway of wall sconces and brass drawers. She treats us like we're the trashy relatives who outlived everyone else in the will. We look it. I'm in a pair of Nina's Birkenstocks; Olivia wanted a ponytail but settled for a knot.

We're left in a small private room. I open the deep, eleven by fourteen lockbox. We divide the contents, including sealed envelopes containing her will, details about her condominium, some QVC jewelry we both chortle over. Olivia's confused by what Medicare covers and what it doesn't. I offer to take the multiple insurance policies back to sort it all out; I know my way around this stuff by now.

Basically aware of Mom's worth, we are still taken aback by how she made do on surprisingly little. I mention what I'd like to do with my portion: endow a variant on the Bright Spotters' mission. It's hard to be a Bright Spot without a little Tarn-X. I could incentivize families of lesser means, help fund Habitat for Humanity, grants or low-interest loans, something. I want it to be more than patting someone's back because they kept their lawn jockey's eyes so white.

Something with more heft is stowed in the back. Olivia withdraws a puffy pink baby book, *Daisy* needlepointed on its silk cover. It still slightly smells of powder and lotions.

I hand it to Olivia. She acts like she's been scalded.

"Why would Mom lock something like this away?"

"Made her melancholy. Out of sight, out of mind," I decide.

"Maybe this was her way of ensuring it wouldn't get overlooked and that we'd accidentally toss it."

I make it to the first page, to our mother cradling her newborn, a little wizened face. "I found our obituary picture." I spin it toward my sister. This finally clarifies the gallery of dead faces in the newspaper.

No matter how easily mocked it will be by strangers, it's the last chance for survivors to reclaim when the deceased was fun, excited, at their best.

A small bracelet drops out that has each letter of Daisy's name on little blocks like miniature Chiclets. Olivia slides it over three fingers and cries. "You're so strong. How come you got her strength and I'm so weak?"

"Maybe I'm just detached."

She pushes her hand again into the back of the metal box.

"No man is an island."

"So I'm a peninsula. Only semidetached."

I think we're done but we're not.

"Something else is in here."

I wonder if Olivia has found an August-related stash, secreted away, a photo of him with the handle of Mom's prized tortoiseshell hairbrush up his ass. I think of the locked steel cabinet in what is now Dee and Potsy's basement that holds some homemade videos I would prefer remain private.

Olivia removes a DVD in a plastic jewel case.

I shudder. "So help me, I hope Mom didn't leave some remembrance video so she could have the last word."

She lapses into her trademarked unfocused look, but this time it means something.

She passes the DVD to me.

"I remember this. It's from the video company... Andy, that day. They brought this by. Mom wanted to keep it away from you."

My hands are shaking. "Remind me how strong I am." I lay it on the table and study the label: the Imagenation logo, September 17, B-ROLL. "Now I can see my husband get killed in the souvenir Director's Cut."

THE mausoleum is like an adjoining room to the bank vault, just a little less sepulchral. Interment is as stipulated: Mom's remains are consigned to the third and final crypt of a mausoleum our parents had bought or, rather, paid on, like a timeshare, when Daisy died. It takes longer to fill a gas tank than her eulogy does. Mom's name is mangled as JenAnn, and her full life is reduced to a quick syrup by the furious boil of a double-booked pastor, quickly gone in his Kia to the next burial. We actually see the anxious family waving at him from an open plot at the far side of the cemetery.

The best part is when the BSers erect a bunch of THIS IS A TOWN BRIGHT SPOT! signs outside the crypt, like they've barricaded a fortress. They've replaced the I in BRIGHT with a lashed eye.

Sarajane takes Hayley for a backward walk. Ted and Nina join her, on either side. Olivia and I remain, looking at Daisy's plaque.

Perchance, to dream you still beside us.

It's from Lord Alfred Tennyson's poem *The Daisy*, the *us* presumably modified from *me* to reflect parentage. I'm not smart enough to know this; the etched plaque gives attribution. Neither Mom nor Dad was that smart, either. The burial salesman must have picked it from a volume of death-appropriate quotations: gimme a name, I'll find you profundity.

"Why was no space ever added for us?" Olivia asks.

My sister's still busy being overlooked. At least she said us, not me.

"We'd have someone to be buried with, they assumed," I point out. "The natural order of things."

Olivia wants one more night with me, so she doesn't, as originally planned, head to the motel where Ted and Nina are packing. At Mom's, we separate what we'd each like. There are no real disagreements. A lot must go. We're just not sure to where. Olivia decides she'd like to keep the condo furnished, as a rental, then maybe retirement for her and Ted. I agree to it. Despite what I've done for most of my life, I could never discourage Mom from décor that looks freshly sneezed upon. You could go to knock wood for luck and three days later still be looking for something to pound. I happily give Olivia the laminates, black lacquer, and glass tops.

Together, we move Mother's wildlife accouterment to Sarajane's patio as she sorts through Mom's QVC largesse. I then take the gas grill and reattach the propane tank for her. I place it near the sand-colored fiberglass pyramid she had built after reading of its legendary restorative powers. Mom said she finally abandoned sitting in it when the kitchen knives she took out with her didn't sharpen (the pyramid also has sharpening powers, apparently). If her cutlery didn't glint, she knew, then neither would her complexion or mental acuity. For the first time, I recognize how similar my aunt and my sister are.

Yet I'm the oddball.

"It's that time of day. Do you two want to share my surprise martini?" Sarajane calls outside.

"What's in a surprise martini?"

"It's not what's in it, it's how it shows up. I shake one up midday and pop it in the fridge. I'll open it up after 5:00 p.m., never before, and go, 'Oh! What have we here? Who made me a martini?' Sometimes I'd split it with your mother."

Olivia doesn't drink, but she says sure, and our aunt divides the gin martini by three, which, in another surprise, is also excellent. Sarajane then insists on barbecuing. I wonder: will the meal be served backward and start with dessert? How far does she carry this?

I watch her set the table, laboring with an iron over the creased damask tablecloth. I show her how, after it's laundered, to roll it to avoid folds. She and Olivia listen, seemingly amazed. I promise to have Isaac send them both dowel hangers if they would prefer to store them that way instead.

To complement the surprise martini, S.J. serves a charred mystery meat. She tentatively asks for the many knitted cozies she gifted Mom back, "Unless either of you want them."

I assure her that my toaster already wore a very nice vest but that my can opener was an exhibitionist and eschews pantaloons. I bite into something that makes the exact sound of a knuckle popping. Hayley growls when I give it to her.

"Jeanine's clothes?" Sarajane wonders. "And her Vera Bradleys?" When told we plan to donate them, she frowns. "Oh. Jeanine's style was much admired here. I know ladies who—"

It is decided Aunt Sarajane will take possession and handle distribution of Mother's wardrobe and purses. The neighborhood will be awash in Jeanine look-alikes.

"Her wigs?"

I was going to send them to Testosterina for Elaine Stritch Night at Barrage. "Do you want them?"

"I saw in the paper where a cancer group recycles them for needy patients."

The town will soon be also awash in Jeanine hair-alikes. My mother has been absorbed by the town, and we didn't sprinkle a thing.

Sarajane asks for a final sleepover with Hayley.

"This isn't a custody battle. I know she belongs with you. Something could happen to me at any time."

"Something could happen to any of us," I comfort her.

I hear my mother's stridency in the way Sarajane brusquely shakes off what she hears as patronization.

"And probably to you first in that city! So-and-so had her full leather duster stolen off her back in a subway station. Visiting. First day there! At gunpoint!"

"I don't own a full leather duster, S.J."

"I'm surprised." She gestures with the wire grill brush. "What will you two do with yourselves your last night here?"

"Aim and click, maybe."

"Jeanie has HBO, the whole pricey lineup." She sighs. "That needs to be cancelled."

They've lived less than a block from one another for a decade, and all Sarajane has left of Mom are purses that look like quilts with straps, in which she will keep green apples. She outlived the sibling she grew up with and, someday, me or Olivia will be her. She is a gray and sad woman who surprises herself with martinis, who can't smell if her steak's done, and who has this baffling, undiagnosed medical condition that people stare at. At least she has her back to their laughs.

Olivia and I return to the condo, sit on the sofa together, and turn on Mom's dark Mediterranean console television, with distressed brass pulls on drawers that don't exist, to land upon a marathon of 1970s sitcoms focusing on moms, an era when they and TV signals were still analog. Ours had always rejected television mother templates with the kind of rage reserved for wartime politics. Some I barely remember from the promos flashing by. We see an image for one Olivia said she held some regard for, *Family*, but it didn't extend to the dour Sada Thompson.

"Mom would go on a rant. 'Who wears pearls when they dust?'" Olivia recalls. "Dad said 'She's got a lot on her plate. Her husband's going blind,' and Mom came back with 'Only through next week. TV Guide says it's a two-parter and no main character, the breadwinner yet, is going to carry a white cane'."

I recognize *One Day at a Time*. "She thought Bonnie Franklin was a cross-eyed jackass. *Alice* made her gag. 'Damn it, she's gonna sing!'" I think. "Mom said if she were Carol Brady, she'd run away. 'They have that housekeeper. They'll be fine'. I vaguely remember when Olivia Walton was stricken with polio, she said the actress with the man's name just wanted more money," I say.

Olivia smiles. "No one on television acted like her, she complained."

"I felt the same way until I saw Danny Pintauro on *Who's The Boss?* He was embryonically gay."

"Man, she hated Judith Light. 'Who has time to mess with hair like that?' she'd snap."

"I was too busy rewriting every episode so Tony Danza would discipline me to notice."

Olivia decides it's time for bed. She's leaving early, before me. Ted and Nina are picking her up for the drive back in Mom's Cadillac. We switch bedrooms for this final night, so Olivia takes Mom's. She isn't in there long when I hear, "Could you come in?" She can't figure out the alarm clock. As I set it for her, she says wistfully, "I suddenly feel like this is the last meaningful time we'll ever spend together. You sold the business, you're selling your house, ties have been cut. Barry, you're not an orphan. You know that, right? Orphans are in state homes and pray for one person to want and care about them. And that's not what this is, not unless you're determined to star in your own one-man show and be that person. Don't play it out that way. I care about you. So does Ted. So does Nina. Please, Barry, please stay available to us."

"I will. I will!"

Our embrace is more an awkward collision. My sister is in a nightgown I recognize from a hook on the bathroom door. I think better of telling her how much, in it, she resembles our mother.

She goes brrrrrrr. "Do you know how to work this digital thermostat?"

Oh: And how do I lower this blasted shade? Then: Why is the bathroom exhaust fan rattling? I get out of there before she asks me how to use those newfangled things called tampons. Small wonder Ted has such dark circles. He must get no sleep, always Olivia-proofing their house.

I remain up. I'll sleep here on the sofa. Mom's bedroom doesn't give me the creeps, but the guest bedroom does, because it's all blue. I scan through hundreds more stations and happen upon the new HBO series starring Chaz Stewart. In this scene, he's engaged in some exposition about the curmudgeonly building super. He spouts a bon mot that simultaneously unemploys Rip Taylor and posthumously shames Paul Lynde. If that's not enough, he kicks up a back leg so high the heel touches the vent of his velvet smoking jacket.

The Imagenation DVD sits on the coffee table. I don't touch it, but I stretch, like that might make it open and play like a hologram. I inspect the jewel case. It is taped shut. I impatiently break it apart. I let the player take the DVD.

Just hit play, man.

Broadcast color bars and tone segue to a countdown.

The canted video image finally stabilizes.

Andy is centered in the frame, speaking to a nameless Imagenation producer and an assistant who will be identified as Jill.

The focus pans past a Mexican restaurant, a banking center, then a zoom to Blend signage, a female clothier.

"...we're shooting a commercial for Blend. There."

Andy, off-screen: "I came from the pet store next to it. Chien Chaud et Chat Froid."

There is a pan to its storefront. "It means Hot Dog and Cool Cat," Andy translates, bouncing back into frame. "I keep telling my boyfriend his home store should be on TV."

From the freckles on his nose… slightly chapped lips… a shaving rash burnishing his Adam's apple… it looks like a live feed, that it's happening now.

"What's the name of it?" a woman asks.

"Great Rooms!"

"I love that store!" Jill squeals.

They stay on Andy's face. "It's a half-assed play on his last name, Grooms. Great Rooms. Grooms. It's okay. Absolutely no one gets it."

The producer requests, "Would you sign a release in case we use you and the dogs?"

"For a woman's clothing store?" Andy laughs. "I look *that* gay?"

"Get him a release, Jill." A case is flipped up, papers withdrawn. "People are buying into the whole urban shopping experience, so we're doing lots of lifestyle, quick cuts."

Andy takes the form, extended from off-camera by Jill.

"This is Gertie—Gertrude—and Noel. Here, Jill, hold their leash so I can fill this out."

The camera drops down now, to a cardboard box punched with holes and what Andy withdraws: a trembling pug puppy.

"Oscar is their new little brother. At least I think it'll be Oscar. Like in Oscar Wilde."

"Who?" they both ask.

Andy lifts up Oscar, who urinates in an arc.

"Oops! Pissing on your release! Grab it! Oscar is for my boyfriend's birthday today."

So this is what else Andy kept from me. He was adding a third to our family that would be killed any time now.

"I love pugs!" Jill shrieks.

Oscar's face, smashed up around a lavender rhinestone collar, fills the frame. Andy's hand chucks his chin.

"Yeah, but how shiteous do I feel, taking him away from all he's ever known, his mommy, his siblings?"

"But Oscar gets a new family!" Jill sings.

The image widens: Andy is cradling Oscar, who is looking up at his new owner.

"It's time to go. I couldn't tell if where I parked is allowed."

They all walk toward the demolition site not yet lethal.

Jill says, "Bye, Gertie, Noel, Oscar! Bye, Andy!"

It freezes there, a prequel of sorts to the apocalyptic main feature.

Which, I suppose, makes me the sequel.

I DRIVE back for the closing transaction Dee has arranged.

What they don't buy from the house, I give them. Basement storage, we all agree, can stay there until I make provisions otherwise. That's when I'll open it and know if Andy bought a little foil packet of aspirin for his post-party headache from a Village Pantry and I can cry over any other little discoveries.

I have my Oscar. That is all I need from that Saturday's chronology.

I provide handwritten notes compiled with such minutiae Dee at first thinks I am countering their offer. These recount everything I can remember, from the preferred floor buffing equipment to being so-so about the pool maintenance people. I even wrote down how to access the small secret room behind a false wall in the master bedroom closet.

This list is my Dear John letter to the house. I know it, they know it, and we all know it won't be looked at again. They feign gratitude and make a big deal about putting it in the contract folder.

Dee launches into a final disclaimer. "We won't change a lot, in case you—"

"It's yours." Their conservatorship will preserve memories without getting bogged down by nostalgia. "When I'm inspired to settle somewhere permanent in New York, I may come loot a little, but I'm not an Indian giver."

"Will you come back for a housewarming?" they want to know. Knowing Kerrick will handle it, knowing how literal he can be, I say yes, because I want to see if he lifts the house onto a gargantuan can of Sterno.

Despite their excited invitation to follow them and see if we can all fit into the secret room—we can, I assure them—I do not then go to the house.

On my way to the airport, I go somewhere else.

I do not go to Andy's grave. I know that the mound has settled and the grass has grown so tall that Potsy has sheared it back twice with hand clippers. I know this because he told me so in the title office. It's the first time he has mentioned visiting Andy's grave.

I go to where Andy died.

Which really isn't anymore.

I get it. I didn't expect the site to become my own Ghost Bike. I had heard Tarantella Demolition Contractors filed for bankruptcy, no surprise. A new developer has cleared the site and has a different vision. Proprietary dumpsters and Bobcat Versahandlers line the basic steel framework that has arisen. Signs indicate its combined office space and retail intentions for the following April and even lists a handful of tenants.

Hayley slaps her paws on the crate ventilation slits. I release her. She dunks her snout in a plastic bowl of water.

I'm glad I stayed in the car. A woman is pushing a man in a customized wheelchair on the sidewalk. I am sure it is one of the survivors, although I'd only seen them in the newspaper or on television. Obvious head trauma has left his chin resting on his collarbone. She crouches, points, and, with her help, he manages to look up at what changed his life forever too.

Chapter Twenty-Two

Short and Sweet

"I KNOW you. You were a grappler."

When I hear this, I am settling the car rental with a young woman either very anemic or terrified I am going to dispute my whopping final invoice.

A diminutive man, alone at a food court table, is waving at, then saluting, me. He looks familiar, but after Manhattan, everyone does. I sign wordlessly. Some of the color in the agent's face returns. I head toward the old man who, like most old people, is wearing too much on such a warm day.

"Iverson-comma-Shorty." He offers his hand without rising.

"Of course, sure. Hi, Shorty," I say, wishing my grip had been better. "Is there anything else I should call you by?" It fits but just seems derogatory, even though Shorty's unshaven gray stubble makes him even more like this miniature sage.

He looks puzzled. "Why? It's my given name. Guess my folks knew I'd grow into it. Or *not* grow into it." He looks curiously down into the pet carrier. "Someone's proud of her pretty necklace."

He's referring to Hayley's new lavender rhinestone collar. He withdraws his wagging finger when she bares her teeth. She's got a little bit of Mom in her.

"You coming or going? Let me guess." His eyes twinkle. "I say going."

I nod at his tray, which indicates he's lingered through several snacks: plates, orange peel, deflated bags of chips, ice cream boats, plastic pudding packs. "And you?"

"Neither. Mrs. Iverson and me used to take a city bus out after I flunked that damn DMV vision test. We liked to watch you all do the coming and going."

That explains the layers of clothing. He's been here since winter.

"You must see plenty."

"Faces slapped, good-byes that were more good riddance, but we saw some reunions that would choke up Mount Rushmore," Shorty recalls. "Kids of fifty/fifty divorce, they're the worst. Trying to be brave until that little lower lip gets to twitching. It's all I and Mrs. Iverson—Vera—could do not to sweep them up and find them new parents under the same roof."

So it all comes down to vicarious everything.

He plucks a miniature cup from the tray. "This was a five-bean salad. Vera especially liked these. She saved them for pill dosages."

It also comes down to small containers.

He slurps loudly from an economy cup of soda, and Hayley barks. "She won't go with the bags, I hope."

"The carrier fits right under the seat."

"Where to you heading?"

I set down my suitcase, then myself.

"New York City. Returning to. I moved there."

"Left it all behind to get better faster," he states.

I nod.

"Did you get better faster?"

"Not really."

"You retreated. You grabbed the low-hanging fruit."

Boy, did I, I am tempted to say, thinking of Nudercise.

"You get yourself into a group?"

I think about Nudercise again. "Kind of."

"Your pants are on fire," Shorty retorts.

When I admit no, I feel like I've let him down.

"Nothing wrong with a tune-up." Shorty begins to loudly hum, then comments on it. "Something you don't hear much of anymore, humming. You hear someone whistle a little melody every now and then, but never humming. It helps me think, like a gentle propellant." He hums again. Maybe his intent is that I join him, but I don't know the tune. "I'm remembering. You didn't part well with us, right?"

"Right."

"I hated to see you leave that way."

"How are you grapplers?" I inquire.

"Let's see," he thinks, then remembers. "We lost Janet."

"Come-To-Jesus Janet? Was it sudden?" I ask.

"Very much so. One night we just kicked her the hell out. What a mealy-mouth. Windier than a bag of assholes."

I don't even try to suppress my smile.

"So see? We weren't *all* bad." He looks wounded. "We weren't *all* evangelicals."

He's a little bit right. They didn't quite understand my particular loss. So what? Maybe Olivia isn't the only one who overreacts. I don't need this introspection, especially not while watching a delayed tourist wolf down a burrito as big as both he and his wife's heads.

Shorty slurps again. "Yuck. This has gone flat."

He bounces his chair back. I stop him and offer to buy something else.

"Refills are free. Here's my cup. Over there," he points.

I also take his tray. On one napkin is a mostly complete drawing of a flower. It's in blue ink, quite intricate, yet delicate. Before I can comment, he offers, "I was a botanical illustrator by trade. I worked for a seed company, did some work for textbooks. A dead art, like saying 'please' or 'thank you'. Microscopic photography surpassed it and retired me, but practicing the fine lines keeps my mind sharp and my hands from calcifying, or so I hope."

As I go to an island of dispensers shared by the restaurants, I turn over another napkin, expecting another surprise, which I get: something dark and brown, maybe a raisin if raisins grew hair. I fold it quickly.

"What were you drinking?" I ask.

"Vera always said surprise her," Shorty shouts, louder than necessary. "You choose. Just start me over. Anything but diet."

I upend what's left into a trashcan. "Was your wife artistic too?"

Shorty looks ahead. "Mrs. Iverson was my mother."

I refill the cup over the brim with ice. "Did anybody in grapple know Vera Iverson was your mother?"

"No one ever really asked. I lost Mrs. Iverson. What was the difference?"

Still floored, I hand him pink lemonade.

"You got the color right." He takes a long sip. The white straw turns rose.

"Did I, Shorty?" I sit back down. "You're gay and you said nothing?"

"Say what about what? I fought in Korea. I'm not fighting again. That's for your generation and the next ones to do."

"I guess not everyone gets their Stonewall."

"I remember Judy Garland dying, but I didn't even *know* what Stonewall was, where or why, until years later, when I saw a documentary. It didn't change my life much, or the lives of many who weren't in no position to throw a pie at Anita Bryant… much as we wanted to. It was simpler to be the tiny man with the billy goat facial hair and the Napoleon complex. I had my share of loving. I wasn't always the age I am now. Attachments just couldn't be made."

"I know men couldn't always live openly together, but by the nineties—"

"Don't oh, Shorty me," he cuts me off. "By the nineties, I was approaching sixty. An old man who likes other old men just makes people nervous." Another long sip. "Plus there was Mrs. Iverson. She came down with MS. My older sister was in Nova Scotia and passed there. As I saw it, as I *still* see it, it was up to me to care for my mother to the end, in my home, which I did. You would too. Same cloth."

My smile quivers.

From my phone, I insist on providing the direct numbers of both Isaac and Mr. Albanese. Maybe one or the other can use his talents. I don't have Herb and Arthur's numbers; even though they don't seem his type, I would have given those too. I think of a different world where he might go out with Stan, but in that world Shorty is twenty-three and he's still fighting in Korea.

I hope he didn't register my fast look at his wristwatch. I'm not sure how to end this brief conversation with a homosexual man from another era I'll probably never see again. "Have a good life" seems a silly send-off for someone at the end of theirs.

He's wise and kind enough to do it for me. Shorty looks at his cup thirstily. "Could you get me one more on your way to the gate?"

Chapter Twenty-Three

Curating Myself

I TAKE Shorty's advice. Jarod had, yes, gotten under my hood with his dipstick, but an oil change wasn't enough. I could use that tune-up. I call the LGBT Center and ask about a grief healing group exclusive of AIDS. Sure enough, there is, and it's tonight. "Was Us/Is Me." Confusingly, the man with the thick Bronx accent who answered the phone verbalizes the slash mark.

"I think the slash is silent," I say. "Otherwise, it sounds like a fencing class."

He gives a Bronx chuckle. "You ain't met these people. Then we'll tawk."

I make out my own name badge, which one member takes to laminate. Another who thinks I need a chin up recites Sartre: "Life begins on the other side of despair." Andy might have quoted Wallace Stevens right back at him. At best, I can maybe throw around something from Chelsea Handler.

Next year's resolution: read more philosophy.

The safety pin on my badge is loose. This makes my name topsy-turvy. People I meet keep cocking their head like they have neck pain. The room is very small. Seated participants' shoulders practically brush. I am directed to take any one of the free available folding chairs fanned out in a horseshoe. Like GRPL, I end up by the food platter, which aspires to be healthy, but everything contains sprouts and looks like edible Chia Pets.

There are a lot more rules than GRPL, delivered by a woman in overalls and no blouse, obviously from the Deep South because she bites into every word.

Do not talk over one another. No interrupting. Yes, raising your hand is an interruption. Making a face will result in expulsion. Forgetting or neglecting your homework insults those who did not.

Homework? I am galled, except I don't have the required organ for it. I listen but say nothing for the next seventy minutes as I picture myself in a dunce cap. The other freshmen and I are assigned to write an audit of where we think we are in the grief process.

"Sometimes you don't know your story until you write it. It doesn't have to be original. It just has to be real," drawls Overalls, who pronounces "real" as "rail." "You can write a posthumous letter to the person. Bring sections of your diary, if you kept one. Say what you wish the minister had said."

I am to bring this homework to my second meeting, the day after tomorrow. I didn't know what of meaning I would have to say. I consider a checklist. I'm good at the factual. Here's what I've lost:

- Andy
- Mom
- Three dogs
- An organ

and

- A little girl who was a stranger to me

What I've gained:

- Hayley
- An acting class, every Sunday evening
- A pain-in-the-ass business partner

and

- Two ccs of Juvederm in my nasiolabial folds

I dread this. I don't want to hear anyone else's litany of miseries, like one of those late-December double-sized Year In Review magazines—"and then on such-and-such a date I cried until my eyes bled"—so it's only fair the group shouldn't have to daydream through mine. We've all suffered enough.

Andy and I would always set the alarm clock to tone stings. We chose the dit-dit, dit-dit, dit-dit over radio station music, which condemned you to hearing that song in your head for the rest of the day. Now, I wonder: what's so wrong with waking to song, even if it's something awful, like Rod Stewart singing standards? Docking my iPhone in my iHome can at least determine what I face the day to.

I wake to the cast recording of *Ballroom*, Michael Bennett's follow-up to *A Chorus Line*, about Bea, a new widow who takes up ballroom dancing. The song is "Fifty Percent." (I've been on a Dorothy Loudon kick since Marjorie shared some anecdotes of her time as the original Miss Hannigan.) Comes a time, the lyrics of the eleven o'clock number make clear, you gratefully accept whatever you can get, even if it means going halvsies on someone's else's husband. While it's a tour de force, it's an anti-inspirant. I'm not quite ready for it to become my own. But a life measured by percentage, and Shorty's simple desire for a full cup of something new, stays with me.

I tap out my assignment in the Theatricilious office. Six single-spaced pages emerge from the printer. I do a fine edit, print again. Over five pages. I rewrite. Print. Almost five pages. Changing font makes the words too small to read, and it is still four pages. A status light blinks. I need replacement toner. How many times have I printed this? Simplify. I said it so often to customers who would overreach, even if it meant losing a sale. You don't need two of something equally spaced on your mantle. One, off-center, will do. I pare down, combine separate thoughts, and finally strike through entire paragraphs. I rehearse my composition aloud as though bound for the UN, then I make Artie sit while I try it out. Within minutes he acts like he's been tied up and strains to break free from the chair. I skip ahead to the last few sentences.

"Now I feel like this half-glass. Somebody drank when I wasn't looking. They weren't quite quenched by Andy, so they downed my mom, too. Now I'm stuck plodding along with that half-glass of sediment. So know what? I want a full fresh beverage. Don't top it off. Just pour."

Artie stands. "The whole half-full, half-empty glass... really, who cares? Either way, it's mostly backwash. It feels like a more-clichéd-than-usual Dan Savage column."

As it often does, inspiration comes from something innocuous—a grocer ad, the basket of green apples on page three. It's not the price per pound that attracts me, it's how they're mounded. I cut it out. I think about Tome Village, Jarod and his subway art, that heartbroken Valentine's Day tableau of people who sliced off the heads of those they once loved.

I don't have access to all of the normal mementoes I usually would, so I do my best constructing not a collage but more a decoupage. I find the David Edward Byrd *Follies* logo, the lady in the headdress with the cracked face. A photo replication of Mom rocking Daisy. I incorporate pictures of a bowling pin, the southernmost buoy, the original cover artwork for *Valley of the Dolls*. I staple on the tag from Andy's pillow, the one you're not supposed to remove. I center a color screen capture of Oscar that Kinko's took from the DVD. I glue The Little Mermaid in one corner. I fill gaps by layering and overlapping images: dentures, an ad for Compound W, a Mercedes Benz logo, cockatiels, some small seashells, a cartoon of a caterpillar, furniture pictures, Wonder Woman and her cape.

It's probably obvious where I'm going with this.

I apply a coat of lacquer, then flick lavender rhinestones over it all. (These are, surprisingly, the biggest bitch to find. The downtown queens must rip them out of the shipper's hands.) I lacquer it twice more at Theatrilicious.

Now I don't know if they'll even get to me. It's been seventeen minutes. We're still on the first ovarian cyst of Gretl's late girlfriend Patrice. Her heartfelt retelling is compelling in a poignant-swallow way, but one-third of our group has drifted out of the room. Even our moderator, forthcoming with tissue (making a comeback) gives her a wrap-it-up elbow squeeze. By the time Patrice loses her battle, I have my thumbtacks out.

The room converges around my twenty-one inch by thirty-five inch art. I watch them do what New Yorkers do best: overanalyze, to find more than there is yet miss the intended.

A man looks at me like I'm daft. "It reminds me of Monty Python."

A woman mumbles, "I was going to say Dali. It's eloquent. Expressionistic."

A voice behind me I can't identify blurts, "Show-off." Several peer closely.

"Writing would have been less work."

I lift my shoulders. "The sieve of me didn't filter the assignment that way."

"The sieve of me! I'm writing that down," a woman who ought not to be in pigtails bleats. I should tell her I stole it from some Aaron Sorkin dramedy in case she's working on a novel, but I don't.

I feel bad when I see that a little Ghost Bike, no bigger than a coin and peeking out from under a starfish, upsets someone enough he needs consolation.

"It's a mosaic of crap," says someone who's rude.

"That wasn't very friendly," says someone who's polite.

A head tilts. "Is the whole thing an optical illusion?"

"Or like Where's Waldo?" someone excitedly blurts out, as though I brought a game.

When Overalls touches her heart and whispers to me, "Everything represents something. It's like a medley of your greatest hits," I feel like I got cookies and gold stars.

"But the assignment was where you're at," someone says, a little shrill. "I don't even see you."

I thought it would be obvious. "I'm everywhere."

Some slob smacks his lips. "Who's the hottie, upper left?"

That's Andy. I trimmed him from one of last year's birthday photos. Above it all, he dances shirtless and alone. He's been placed on a bit of fabric I took from the tail of the Tommy Bahama shirt, like he's surfing. He is God's go-go boy, presiding over this abstract retrospective of my life.

Chapter Twenty-Four

Marjorie's Reveal

NO WELL-HUNG stud card needs to tell me what day it is.

I get up, put on Andy's Tommy Bahama shirt, scarf down a pretty spectacular breakfast mush of leftover broccoli rabe-and-prosciutto tabbouleh, and head off to work like the rest of New York will.

Floor 14 spelunks his ear with a Q-tip, then plants the swab into a lobby spathiphyllum. I look in it. A picket fence of Q-Tips emerge from floral moss. I take this to mean I should pay careful attention today when addressed.

The owners of the 8th Avenue storefront have been more responsive than I'd predicted. The surplus of commercial estate obviously has them jittery. It's been gutted; I have keys and free reign, so my due diligence can begin on this blank palette. I am hungrier for this than I expected. It is clear to me I will always have the stabbing pangs, that I will keep recreating and populating Tome Village in different guises, environs in which I feel safe, whatever safe is. *That* is my endgame, Raoul. Besides, maybe my best work, if not my best day, lies ahead of me. Alfred Uhry wrote *Driving Miss Daisy* at fifty-one and won a Pulitzer. Here I am, also at the wheel, bossy old bag behind me, but the only thing I covet is an amnesty letter from the state Department of Taxation and Finance for the final two quarters of last year's unpaid sales tax, another detail Marjorie ignored as bothersome.

The building has a huge basement, more a coal mine on the verge of cave-in, damp as a grotto. Exploring it again, I expect to see a 1912 subway car coasting by like the Flying Dutchman. With proper dehumidification, this can be our Download Dungeon, a free collective for emerging cabaret performers, musicians and songwriters. We won't have lighting rigs or fog machines, and no amount of baffling will give the artists impeccable acoustics, but it will be an unplugged showcase and a way for them to immediately sell tracks via download from our dot-com or theirs. Artie was given the charge of manning the dedicated hosting site, to minimize the wait for artists to see compensation. I also gave him directive to develop a store App, which he freelanced to a geek nephew at Stanford who apparently writes code the way Stephen Schwartz writes power ballads.

Most importantly, if we must remain Theatrilicious, I want to *own* the ridiculous name. I tell Artie to animate our website Comedy and Tragedy masks that Marjorie thinks are so doggone novel for a theater-based store.

"What do you suggest they do?"

"You can give them long, pink tongues and they can French kiss, I don't care. I want action and irreverence on the home page." For too long our home page has been this quaint, static portal into un-illustrated lists of what we carry or can procure. We need to step up our media platforms.

Yet growing our digital footprint is equal to my mission of taking two steps back. I am eliminating compact discs unless they're impossible to find or imports. We're going to carry vinyl, filling the gap left by the demise of places like Footlight Records.

"Downloads are invisible," I explain. "Or they're in fileshared pieces until someone requests it. Some things need to be discovered! I don't like Kindle. How do you fall in love with a novel that has no glossy dustcover? Will you take it fondly from the bookcase one sleepless night to rediscover? It's about tactile. I *want* to dog ear, I want to drop it accidentally into the bathtub. Same with albums. I like that they don't fit so great on a shelf, I like the art, the liner notes."

"Give me the imperfect over a gigabyte any day! We'll be the anti-PDA," Soapsuds crows.

I build on her enthusiasm. "We could sell turntables under our own brand.'"

"We can call it KID: The Kinda Inconvenient Device," Karen announces.

"Our customers are collectors and always will be. They won't, they *can't* live on a cloud. They want to handle their shit," I say.

"We should just rename the store Handle Your Shit," Artie decides.

I don't tell them I intend to start my own blog about crazed theatrical collecting. I'm going to call it *Hoardway*. At last I will be able to openly discuss my limited edition Valjean and Javert salt and pepper shakers. Instead, I reveal that Marjorie and I will begin investing in and sharing producing credit on limited-release vinyl cast albums, new shows or studio recreations. I can Notch and Drill for real.

This piece of news kicked off a new round of handles being bandied about the workroom. Artie reminded everyone I will be the unlikely second half of this duo—the one with sense and the windfall—and he named us Cloak and Fagger.

Me, I like Marbarry.

Not even Marjorie knows yet of my intent to take the small space next door. I am considering a browsing library and café stocked with my own theater books, many out of print. I'd rather see someone enjoy them rather than nudge them further and further into a corner in Dee and Potsy's basement. I have time to refine a plan before a ten-year lease would kick in after the New Year.

My infusion of capital and establishing an actual line of credit will allow Marbarry to pursue another idea of mine that has nothing to do with 8th Avenue, and that's pop-up shops in major cities with Broadway touring show schedules, where productions sit down for at least two weeks. We wouldn't sell just that show's merchandise, but the entire season's worth. If Halloween costumes and Girl Scout cookies can do it, why not Theatrilicious? Atlanta, Louisville, and Minneapolis are three markets I'm keen on.

From a wall taken to studs, I wriggle out a 1960s Swedish manual on lovemaking. I laugh at the presilicone tits and unretouched cellulite.

"Why are you laughing?" Marjorie's voice bounces around the cavernous space. "Did the handsy ghosts of peep-show patrons tickle you?" I come down the extension ladder from the unfinished second floor as she further demands, "Why are you here?"

I wipe my hands on my jeans. "What a question."

She has completely neglected to draw on one eyebrow; her other disconcertingly pitches and lifts like a woolly conductor's baton. "Today being what it is. Am I right?"

I rub my relationship band, which I have returned to my finger.

"Yes. The person I loved the most died today. I was also born to someone today. Maybe that makes me born again."

"Reborn sounds better. Doesn't require baptism or a narrow mind." Marjorie extracts While You Were Out notes from an interior cape pocket. "You've had a ton of calls." She reads one aloud. 'I can't believe my grandmother actually felt me up.' From *Sixteen Candles*?"

"Right again." I toss the porn back into a wall.

"Molly Ringwald's a sweet girl," Marjorie recalls. "She was my personal favorite orphan."

"In *Annie*?"

Marjorie is pleased. "Broadway replacement. Someone doesn't know his musicals the way he thinks. Stick with me, kid."

She's full of crap. Molly Ringwald played the tough Pepper in the second, LA-based touring production. Marjorie had better stick with *me*. But I don't argue.

I inspect my other notes. Cards have been coming all week, many from people I never before got a birthday wish from.

"The good news on this really bad day is I'm still forty-five."

"You held over." Marjorie nods approvingly.

"More like I wrote off the last twelve months as a total loss."

"Take it from Big M: no year survived is a loss."

Big M? I wince. She's overheard us.

"What have you survived, Marjorie?"

"Would that it was past tense," she says slowly. "After a quick bite with friends, I'm going for my weekly cortisone shot. I have Adult Scoliosis."

I study her salmon cape of polished cotton.

"Stow that look. My mother had it, too, yet did I also get her emerald eyes? No."

"How long?"

"Too long. The docs hope it doesn't progress into something like Lou Gehrig's Disease. For now, I wear this full spinal brace around my shoulders, up and under my armpits." She explains this TLSO brace, from its mechanical origins to special laundering requirements, things I don't need to know unless I don one in unity. It's the minute detail of someone relieved to unburden herself. "A blazer won't hide it. Sweaters are hot. So there! Marjorie's mysterious affectation, solved."

"Better eccentric than vulnerable." I clap my hands. "Cape closed." Maybe someday she'll also admit she's broke.

The next note gives me pause.

"This one's in your writing and says Jerry Poole. Was it maybe Jarod Pugh?"

"Maybe his voice changed as he said it." She draws in her cheeks. "Young love."

I flinch. I know what she means—the shy freshness, then the schism, of a new relationship—but the words just sound NAMBLA. But I'm touched by Jarod's gesture. He knew what a clusterfuck this day would represent.

"Are you a couple?" Marjorie asks.

"Not really." I unroll architectural blueprints from tubes. "When are we going to talk about the new Theatrilicious?"

She covers her ears. I yank the hem of her tunic.

"Tomorrow!" she promises. "One thing: please deal with Artie. Some theater forum has our store on deathwatch, and he wants to officially respond."

"Rumors are good. They drive business, people looking for markdowns. We'll debut our new location plans at the Flea Market next Sunday." It's an annual event of celebrity-staffed booths, the perfect time to announce.

Adjusting my backpack, I guide Marjorie through the front door. I can now always accurately claim that I got Jeff Stryker off. No one needs to know it was a faded promotional decal on a vestibule window. I feel the brace under her cape. She continues up 8th. How did I not notice her affected walk? If she straddles a subway grate just so and grabs her TLSO straps, she could probably hang glide like a Cirque du Soleil aerialist, remaining airborne on other 8th Avenue crossdrafts all the way to Lincoln Center.

I see Marjorie embrace Mike Nichols, then Diane Sawyer.

I rap on the window of Knock Yourself Out. Walt, karate-chopping pillows on the ratty divans, dashes to the open door.

"Want to see what turned up in lost and found? You'll love it."

Walt rummages beneath the bar. He'd previously shown me the box that holds everything left drunkenly behind and still unclaimed—innocuous stuff like street vendor umbrellas, police panic whistles. He produces an upper denture that is missing a front tooth.

I pound the bar, overcome with laughter. "Isn't that the whole point of false teeth? That they're intact?"

"Who empties their mouth in a bar and then leaves? Maybe it was a dare."

"Everybody's missing something in this town," I decide. "If no one claims them, can I have them?"

He wraps a napkin back around them. "Um, sure."

I'll send them to Kerrick. I just got a great idea about a Mini Me denturelier that has points of light, like a disco ball, made exclusively from dentures missing teeth.

"Am I going to see you later?"

I simulate tipping a martini glass into my mouth. Walt crooks a bicep at me and struts back to what he was doing.

Ahead is a Ghost Bike. Although I usually turn right at the last block for home and can't be completely sure, it's new. The white paint is not yet dulled by city fallout.

I am reminded to look along 8th Avenue for my newsstand girl. Kids change so quickly. How anyone identifies a missing child from a rendering, no matter how technologically advanced, I don't know. A haircut, different glasses, and things in the ceiling can make your own child unknown to you.

I pass orange plastic netting, the yield sign of another drafty walk-up being razed in favor of another towering colossus of luxurious glass and a lot of caulk.

I decide that I need flowers. A corner foodmart with buckets of reasonably fresh cuts I have passed before—the one with the *Free Smells!* window signage, a dubious come-on—is just one block north.

I defiantly walk under and through the shadow of a city's unique breed of attack fowl: the swooping crane. Fall on me, you creaking bastard. Go for it.

Epilogue

Everything Okay.

THE right vessel will keep the daisies from flopping over too much. I can't remember what I brought. I have not had flowers or even a live plant since I moved here.

"It's called a vase!" my mother would have cried out. "You and that highbrow store of yours."

Perhaps I should have gone for the pom-pom mums. They're more a fall flower. Or maybe the orchids. With refreshed water and trimmed stems, they last longer. I could have swept up the lowly alstromeria, who stubbornly cling to life even after their stems have gone yellow and flaccid.

I hear it again.

"You change."

How many songs have been written about changing? The content made complete sense; it was the context I was missing. You have to, you're forced to, everyone else did and you didn't. I could sing one, probably write one, standing here. Friendships change, minds change, cities change, fashions change, months, loyalties, passions, store names, genders and—

"—you change."

My cashier clearly wants to finish the transaction.

This whole "You change" thing isn't much better than the Mongolian grill Mom always favored. She called it Everything OK!, missing an apostrophe, the S, and screwing up the whole contraction thing.

"They named it how they say it," she replied, indignant when I questioned her emphasis and pronunciation. "That's their tableside follow-up. 'Everything okay?'"

"It should be a question mark, not an exclamation."

"Not to the Mongolians!" She thought. "Like I care. It's $6.99."

It became an ongoing routine.

"Where'd you eat?"

"Everything OK!"

"Your dining experience sounds very average."

Proof came one day. Sarajane photographed her under the sign, her finger cocked at Everything triumphantly. No S, no apostrophe, an exclamation mark.

I need to find that picture.

Now Bunwoman is tapping the $18.03 on the register.

"Eighteen dollah, three cent."

Yes, I'm going full-blown with the phonetics.

And then she drops the three quarters, two dimes, and two pennies back into the drawer. Smiling, with fingers oily from weighing poorly sealed containers, she takes three pennies from a counter cup.

"Better change!"

From declarative to direct threat. Downright cheeky, this one is. Better change. *Or else.* That did it. I want to see what that hair looks like down.

She adds another one-dollar bill to the one she still holds. She says it again: "Better change." And she hands me two one-dollar bills back.

It *is* better change.

I didn't see this one coming, even if my life has lately been an O. Henry omnibus.

"Know what?" I slide open the cooler. "I think I'll buy a Coke or something."

She's really quite pretty and probably not the age I'd guess her at. The crinkle of her eyes indicates she's as capable of happiness as she is of acceptance. I'm not the one to determine if there is a difference.

Outside, sunlight hits and warms my face. It dries tears I didn't know were there.

I weave through the many people on this pulsating crosswalk, wishing I had an oversized canvas to struggle with, like Jill Clayburgh at the end of *An Unmarried Woman.*

Of self-awareness, I stand convicted.

Come to think of it, Jill puked too when she discovered, figuratively, that she'd lost her man.

But all I have are the daisies and the Coke. I am going back to the apartment. I will swig my Coke along the way and then I'll walk Hayley before her tupper. It's not as late in the afternoon as I'd thought and it's so bright out.

Acknowledgments

GRATITUDE must be extended to:

Diana, Dee Dee, and Suzy, for their love;

Jill Carroll, Connie Timmons, and Loren Myer, for their encouragement;

Karonavich, FPOYA, Groina, MJP, Pretty, Peffy, and Curly Hoofers, for friendship that has endured life's hiccups;

Those folks in The Treehouse;

Coco and Sunny and their beautiful Moms;

Luann Grosscup, the first to read my manuscript;

Elizabeth North, for plucking me from the Submissions pile; Lynn West and her associates for pointing out inconsistencies with grace while lauding passages they admired; and Anne Cain for her evocative cover art.

RODNEY ROSS lives in Key West, Florida.

He is a former advertising Creative Director, so he's accustomed to making things up.

Past achievements include multiple ADDY Awards and an optioned screenplay and play (both currently unproduced). Other screenplays earned Honorable Mentions or runners-up citations in the Monterey County Film Commission, FADE-IN and the LGBT One-In-Ten Screenwriting Competitions.

Join Rodney at either https://www.facebook.com/RodTRoss or https://www.facebook.com/RodneyTRoss; follow him on Twitter https://twitter.com/#!/RodTRoss; or e-mail him at RodneyTRoss @aol.com.

BUTTERFLY'S CHILD

ALAN CHIN

Also from DREAMSPINNER PRESS

username
7mark8

Beware what you share.
a blogumentary by:
n i c k   h a n s o n

http://www.dreamspinnerpress.com

CPSIA information can be obtained at www.ICGtesting.com
Printed in the USA
BVOW010609130612

292521BV00007B/39/P

9 781613 725047